Praise for *The Moonlight Gardening Club*

'Sweet and heartwarming'
Marian Keyes

'The word "uplifting" was invented for this tender and poignant story. I adored all the characters and the warm, loving community of fascinating people who come together in support of each other. It's a beautifully written debut'
Judy Leigh

'What a delight . . . a gorgeous, emotional read with characters to hold your heart'
Liz Fenwick

'A poignant, heartwarming, uplifting story of the enriching gift of friendship. A terrific debut novel that will enthral readers'
Patricia Scanlan

'Full of warmth and heart, *The Moonlight Gardening Club* is an absolute delight. Ruby and Frankie are characters to really care for and will inspire you to grab your wellies and get out into the garden! Rosie Hannigan is an exciting new voice in Irish fiction. I look forward to reading more from her!'
Hazel Gaynor

Rosie Hannigan is the pen name of Amy Gaffney, who hails from Kildare and is a graduate of UCD's Creative Writing MA. In 2021 she was shortlisted for the Penguin Michael Joseph Christmas Love Story Competition. Her poetry is published in *Poetry Ireland Review* Issue 125, and the *Irish Times Hennessy New Irish Writing*. Amy's short story *Mother May I* was shortlisted for the Irish Book Awards in 2019, in the Short Story of the Year category. She has mentored at University of Limerick's Winter Writing School and has been a panel member at various discussions there, and also hosted the Reading Corner at the Murder One Crime Writing Festival in Dublin in 2019.

THE
MOONLIGHT GARDENING CLUB

Rosie Hannigan

avon.

Published by AVON
A division of HarperCollins*Publishers*
1 London Bridge Street
London SE1 9GF

www.harpercollins.co.uk

HarperCollins*Publishers*
Macken House
39/40 Mayor Street Upper
Dublin 1
D01 C9W8
Ireland

A Paperback Original 2023
1
First published in Great Britain by HarperCollins*Publishers* 2023

ISBN: 978-0-00-859911-9

Typeset in Sabon LT Std by Palimpsest Book Production Limited,
Falkirk, Stirlingshire

Printed and Bound in the UK using 100% Renewable Electricity
at CPI Group (UK) Ltd

MIX
Paper | Supporting
responsible forestry
FSC™ C007454

For David, the most important person in my life.
You always said I could do it – and now I have.
You were right, thank goodness.

1

Ruby

Ruby turned off the ignition as she parked on the wide driveway, out of sight, on the far side of Eyrie Lodge, the six-bedroomed, angular holiday house she would now call home. The electric gate behind her shut automatically with a slow groan. Ruby breathed out, allowing her shoulders to slowly drop from the hunched position she'd driven in all the way from Dublin. She pushed her sunglasses back into her hair, feeling how long it had gotten. She really should have had it coloured; her greys were showing more than she was comfortable with. She closed her eyes, and a tentative smile crept across her face. She opened them again and blinked rapidly.

'I did it,' she whispered. 'James, I did it – I drove here myself. I wish you were here to see it.'

Pressing her lips together, Ruby gripped the steering wheel, tears spilling down her cheeks. Her makeup would be ruined, but she didn't care. She was glad she'd decided to come down a day early to beat the Easter weekend traffic that would have rattled her nerves. The holiday weekend promised to be sunny, and the roads would be crazy on Friday with families taking advantage of the long weekend.

In the eighteen months since James had passed away, she'd been busy sorting and arranging his business affairs and, more recently, selling their Dublin home and moving back to Castletown Cove. She'd made no plans for her early arrival, and hadn't told anyone she was coming down a day early either. Coming back to Castletown Cove was precisely what she'd been craving. Now all she wanted was to enjoy the peace and have a large glass of wine while watching the sea from the balcony.

She grabbed her overnight case and bag and got out of the car. The warm and familiar scent of the sea hit her immediately, and she gulped it in. Like a hug from a best friend, the smells and sounds of her hometown were a balm to her nerves. The sound of crashing waves made her turn to face the view she'd always loved. With her house keys gripped tight in her hand, Ruby's gaze swept from left to right.

The cove before her shone golden in the evening sun. The sea glittered and the gulls swooped low and long over the waves. To her left, the coast road led to the main public beach and the village's two small hotels. Both were busy with tourists and locals enjoying drinks and dipping chunks of buttered Guinness bread into their bowls of chowder. The smaller hotel by the beach, where she'd worked part-time for pocket money during her school summer holidays, was much the same as it always had been, except it was painted cornflower blue now instead of sunflower yellow. The more prominent hotel, a stately former private residence, was still white, although it seemed to glow apricot as the sun set. To her right, the playground across the road was busy, and the tennis courts beside it hosted a doubles couple finishing their game.

Further down the road, the boats in the harbour bobbed, chiming and clinking as the waves rolled beneath them. The spring breeze picked up and Ruby shivered. Her city outfit, chic as it was, didn't cut it here. James had gifted her the Missoni fitted dress for her fifty-fourth birthday two years ago. It was perfect for hot city days, but the lightweight knit was no match for the sharp sea breezes that had a habit of whipping up out of nowhere here.

Ruby loosened her grip on the house keys. Coming back to Castletown Cove had been the right thing to do. She'd grown up here, knew every laneway and landmark, could tell you who owned which field and who was related to who. Although most of her family had now moved away, she still had a small number of Dublin friends who said they'd be lining up to come visit her in her seaside abode – Pamela insisted she'd be the first down, as long as the gin was good and the sand soft. Ruby smiled. Pamela would be in for a treat. The Cove had three beaches to choose from, an art gallery to browse and lunch at, and several exceptionally well-reviewed restaurants nearby. It would be fun hosting her friends, she thought as she gazed out over the sea, but it would be hard without James.

For a start, she'd have to get to grips with the new improvements he'd insisted on doing to Eyrie Lodge without him showing her how to work them. For as long as she could recall he'd taken charge of all that kind of stuff, upgrading alarm systems, installing security cameras, and programming their heating system. The last thing he had done was to install motorised window blinds. They were her favourite of all his crazy upgrades. 'They're fool-proof,' he'd told her. Even *she* could operate them from the app he'd installed on her phone.

Ruby turned away from the ocean view, a heavy weight crushing her heart. Her husband had always loved this place. From the moment he'd first laid eyes on it he'd worked hard to obtain the house from the previous owners. Ruby smiled at the memory. He'd practically courted them until they'd sold him the property, then he'd gutted it and created the spectacular modern cliff-top villa it was today. He'd not only changed the whole house but renamed it too. When Ruby had remarked that as kids they'd always called the original house the Crow's Nest, he'd grimaced and immediately set to work changing it. They'd been in the kitchen mixing their Friday evening gin and tonics when she'd mentioned it.

'Crow's Nest?' James had said. His lips curled. 'Why did you call it that?'

'Well.' Ruby had laughed at his disdain. 'First of all, look at your face – you're such a snob!'

'It's called having standards.' He'd flicked a tea towel at her. 'And it's a good thing one of us has them.'

Ruby had let the remark slide. James hadn't meant anything by it. Instead, she'd pulled a face at him. 'It's overlooking the sea and high up,' she'd said. 'And that odd roof angle over the front door juts out like a crow's nest on a boat.'

'I get it,' he'd said, his brows lowered. 'Crow's Nest . . . well, what's the proper name?'

'Number Three Harbour Road.' Ruby had sliced limes and added them to the gleaming glasses in front of her.

'Ouch,' James had said. 'I don't know which is worse.'

'Doesn't matter.' Ruby had added tonic to his gin. 'It'll always be the Crow's Nest to the locals.'

'You say that now,' he'd said. 'But by the time I'm done with it, they won't remember what that place looked like. All they'll see is beauty and carefully balanced proportions.'

'I have no doubt.' Ruby had smiled at him.

'I like the connection to nature, to birds,' he'd said as she handed him his glass. He'd sipped and smiled. 'Perfect.' He'd raised his glass to her. 'As always.'

They'd gone out into their suntrap of a garden and stayed there until it got cold. It had been a rare Friday night at home, one that Ruby remembered fondly. It was when they were heading to bed that he'd announced the new name.

'Eyrie Lodge,' he'd told Ruby as she'd brushed her teeth. 'That's it. I knew the place reminded me of something . . . when I was a kid we stayed in a house in Maine called Eyrie Lodge for a summer. It had a similar sea view. I always loved it there.'

He'd picked up his toothbrush. Ruby remembered how she'd looked at him and marvelled at childhood holidays in America. It was far from holidays she'd been reared on. They'd gone to her aunt's house in Carlow for a week once. All the kids had slept on camp beds in the back kitchen, where the fries were cooked for the men. A fry-up was a treat, but it didn't match up to Maine lobster rolls. Brushing her teeth, she'd shrugged. It didn't matter to James that changing the name might bother her, and she wasn't sure it did. Sometimes, though, she did think that Eyrie Lodge was far too grand and aloof for Castletown Cove. It wouldn't have been such a bad thing if he'd simply left it as the Crow's Nest – it was what the locals still called it anyway.

They'd planned on retiring to Eyrie Lodge, but James hadn't stopped working, despite his age. At his seventieth birthday dinner party he'd announced to all their guests that he was going to continue working until he was forced to stop. Ruby had laughed along with everyone else while she quelled a ripple of frustration. James was a workaholic; everyone knew it but knowing it didn't help. It would have been nicer if he'd discussed it with her before the party. Instead, all she could do was laugh, nod and pretend to be on the same page. No one was surprised, not one bit. They all said he was a force to be reckoned with, that if you wanted anything done, you should go to him, that he wouldn't know what to do with himself if he actually retired. Ruby wished she'd seen it coming, though. Her face hurt from smiling at everyone.

His death had come as a massive shock to not only Ruby but also to friends and colleagues who relied on his expertise and gravitas in the construction industry. It was a shock that she was still reeling from. Even though some people thought she should have expected it – she was fifteen years younger than him, after all – it was a blow to her stomach every morning that she woke up and he wasn't there. He had been her rock; without him she was left floundering and growing exhausted by her attempts to tread the cold, forbidding water of the rest of her life.

When she'd toyed with the idea of selling Eyrie Lodge, saying to Pamela that it was too painful for her to think of it, Pamela had reminded her of his love for the house.

'Ruby, darling, listen to me.' Pamela had squeezed Ruby's hands and then rubbed them to warm them up. 'If there's anything that you should *not* do, it's sell that house. It's too soon. You're still in shock – I worry about that. You need to give yourself some more time to grieve. There's nothing wrong with taking a bit of time to think things over.'

Ruby remembered glancing away, and taking her hands from Pamela's. She'd wrapped her arms around her body and felt the prominent outline of her ribs under the many layers she had been wearing. It was ironic that after years of dieting and exercising, it was when she least felt like slipping into a slinky dress or bikini that she'd achieved her goal weight. James would have praised her. He'd been so encouraging of her attempts to get slimmer, continually reminding her of what she was aiming for. He'd even spent a fortune on a Victoria Beckham dress in a smaller size to help her to feel motivated. Ruby had swallowed and tuned back in to what Pamela was saying.

'And James loved it.' Pamela had leaned forward and tapped Ruby's knee. 'Remember, he always said that nowhere on earth made him feel so rejuvenated. He used to tell me, "Pam, sweetheart, I never feel better than when I'm by the sea. *Ah! What pleasant visions haunt me as I gaze upon the sea! All the old romantic legends, all my dreams, come back to me.*"'

'Henry Wadsworth Longfellow said that.' Ruby had sniffed. 'It was one of my favourite poems.'

'Henry who?' Pamela's brow had furrowed, then

cleared. 'Oh, I see. I thought it was rather poetic of James. Wasn't it sweet of him to memorise a line from your favourite poem?'

Ruby had smiled.

Pamela had clapped her hands. 'Finally!' she'd said. 'A smile! You should do it more often – it suits you. But seriously, Ruby, you need to give it more time. Don't sell the place yet. Think it over. James would want you to at least spend some time there – as you two had planned.'

That was it, Ruby remembered as she let herself into Eyrie Lodge. That was the moment when she knew she couldn't sell it. Pamela had been right. James, despite his declaration to continue working, had teased her with prom-ises of morning walks along the golden sand followed by brunch and tennis. He'd talked of buying a boat – and she knew he didn't mean a small boat or a fishing trawler. She wondered how they'd have taken to him down at the harbour in his deck shoes and Panama. It was no marina, that was for sure, and the men there were tough and well able to read people. They'd have had the cut of James in an instant. Ruby sighed. If she were very honest with herself, she didn't think he'd have been readily accepted there, but without a doubt, he'd have charmed them all eventually.

She passed straight through the house and upstairs into the kitchen. It was one of the first things James had decided to change, and Ruby was glad he had turned the house upside down. The sea views from the first floor were spectacular. The kitchen was gleaming, Ruby noticed. Sandra, the housekeeper, was a gem. She'd stocked the fridge and pantry with the basics, and a vase of fresh flowers stood on the end of the large white island unit.

Ruby took out the freshly prepared goat's cheese salad Sandra had left for her. She sat at the island and ate absentmindedly while skimming through the post Sandra had left on the counter. One letter was addressed to James. Ruby's hands shook as she set it aside. It was still difficult to see post addressed to Mr Knight arriving, almost as strange as it had been to see her own name change after they'd married. With a groan, she set the letter aside. She'd thought she'd notified everyone of his passing. She made a mental note to contact the sender.

It was only then, when she got to the bottom of the salad bowl that she remembered that she didn't particularly like goat's cheese. It had been James's favourite. They'd always had it on arrival at the holiday house. It was a tradition, and somehow she hadn't thought to tell Sandra that she'd prefer something else.

Pushing her bowl away, Ruby checked the time. It was still light out, and the sky was barely fading to night. The sounds of the sea were silenced by the triple-glazed doors that led to the balcony. The absolute quiet made her shiver. She got up, poured a glass of white wine and walked over to look out of the balcony doors.

Everything had suddenly quietened down. The playground was empty. A single luminous tennis ball sat in the far corner of the court. Even the gulls had fallen silent. She couldn't discern where the sea met the sky anymore as a sea fog rolled in and engulfed everything. She snorted. The fog had sneaked in, fast and silent, and had taken her view and evening away from her, just as James's death had taken her joy and future. The streetlights flickered on, their faint peach glow blending with the fog.

'Typical,' Ruby muttered. 'If I were looking for a sign that I made the right decision, then this is not a good start.' She lifted her wine glass to her lips and was surprised to find it empty. She was about to pour a second glass when she felt James's presence as if he were standing beside her. She could almost see his raised eyebrow and hear him ask, 'Is that wise when you've barely eaten all day?' The bottle of wine felt suddenly heavy. She slipped the stopper into the neck of the bottle and returned the bottle to the fridge. She was already feeling tipsy, whether from the adrenaline crash from making the journey down alone or from the wine, she couldn't tell, but she knew he was right. He knew she hated feeling drunk; being so out of control always upset her.

Ruby raised her empty glass. 'Cheers, James,' she said. 'Thank you for always having my back. I miss you so much.'

2

Frankie

The sea sparkled under the morning sun, making Frankie smile even though they were running late. She stopped hurrying and pulled the soft, warm April air deep into her lungs, relishing the slightly salty tang. The weekend rolling into the Easter break was promising to be glorious. For the first time in months, Frankie was glad it was Friday.

A long weekend, she thought as the sun glinted on the sea. She might even get a lie-in if she was lucky, but first, she needed to get this job out of the way.

She tucked a curl of red hair behind her ear as she hurried towards Number Three Harbour Road, her phone gripped in her hand. Her six-year-old son, Dillon, trailed behind her. His own red curls, in need of a cut, fell over his eyes.

'Dillon, come on,' she called over her shoulder. 'We're going to be late.' She'd promised Sandra she'd do her this favour before dropping Dillon to school for the midterm

Easter camp that she'd scraped together enough money to pay for. Sandra had offered to take him for the week, but Frankie had declined. It had been kind of Sandra to offer, but Frankie had always managed to take care of Dillon without help outside the family. Although it was harder now Aggie was gone.

'I can't.' Dillon paused. 'Look what I found. It's a lady-bird, and it might be a harlequin one. Teacher told me about them; they're invaders.'

Frankie stopped and waited for her son to catch up with her. She bent down to examine the ladybird on the back of his hand.

'I think we're safe,' she said. 'This fella is tiny. Harlequins are bigger, remember?'

Her phone beeped. Another message from Sandra.

I meant to tell you I left washing in
the machine by mistake. Could you
hang it out?

Frankie rolled her eyes. When would she get away from these menial jobs? The tasks were never-ending. With some luck, hotel management would take her application for the receptionist position seriously this time. She didn't need a degree in management or hospitality to do it – she knew the hotel inside out – but it felt as if management ignored her experience. There was a possibility that they'd hold her lack of computer skills against her, even though she covered the desk at least once a week when Irina had to leave early to take her mother to the hospital. In the meantime, she was stuck with the job she had. She texted Sandra back.

No problems. I'll sort it.

Dillon looked up at her, his little face bright. 'I think you're right, Mammy. I didn't remember that bit. How come you can remember stuff so easy?'

Frankie booped his nose and slid her phone into her jeans pocket. 'I don't remember lots of stuff,' she said. 'Once, I forgot that I had to be somewhere important, and by the time I did remember, I had to run all the way there, and I almost missed it.'

'What was it?' Dillon asked.

'I'll tell you another time,' Frankie said. She pulled his fleece closer around his slim shoulders and stood up. 'We're late – remember!'

'Oh, yes.' Dillon nodded. 'We should hurry up.'

Frankie watched his exaggerated wiggly speed walk as they approached the house she'd promised Sandra she'd go over to. *One day,* she thought, *I'll tell you that I was almost late to see your daddy and that the best thing I ever did was to go and tell him that I loved him and that I was sorry.* She closed her eyes briefly, opening them as Dillon turned back to wave at her to come on. Whatever had put that memory into her head, she didn't know, but she sure as hell didn't have time to dwell on it. Sandra had said that the chances were that the owner of Number Three Harbour Road – or Eyrie Lodge as the sign on the gate announced – wouldn't be there until after eleven, as that's when the removal vans were due to arrive.

'Although, I don't know where she'll put anything,' Sandra had said. 'He has that house immaculately laid out. Everything is designer. The sofa came from Harrods,

13

for crying out loud, Harrods! I believe it cost almost twenty thousand euros, not including delivery. Anyways, that's neither here nor there. There's barely any storage, so where is she going to put anything else? And will I get paid more for the extra cleaning I'll have to do?'

Frankie had shrugged. She'd never been in Eyrie Lodge but had always wanted to look around it. From the outside, it seemed serene and ordered, a safe haven in a wild and woolly world. She imagined the interior as she would have decorated it: warm whites, soft greys, and misty blues on the walls and drapes. The furniture would be like the Danish wooden furniture she'd seen on Pinterest, all honey-toned smooth lines and velvety to the touch. If it were hers, she'd paint a wall in the kitchen with chalk paint for Dillon to draw on and for shopping lists and reminders to pay bills, and out in the garden, she'd install one of those fantastic wooden play centres with swings and slides and a playhouse. No need for a sandpit. She smiled as she punched the gate code into the pad – the beach was just down the way.

Taking Dillon's hand, Frankie made her way around the left side of the house to the utility room. Sandra told her she'd leave the alarm off, so she didn't need to worry about that. All she had to do was to put the goat's cheese salad in the bin – apparently, Sandra had made it on autopilot, only later remembering that it would remind the owner of her deceased husband – and make up a fresh chicken Caesar one instead. She slid the key into the lock. Frankie's hazel eyes widened as the door opened to reveal a state-of-the-art utility room.

'Holy moly, Mammy,' Dillon said as he slipped by her. 'This room is bigger than our house.'

'It is,' Frankie said. She ran her hands along a flawless white marble countertop. The room was painted entirely white with a patterned floor tile in shades of grey and white and black that Frankie knew, from her Pinterest trawling, harked back to the Victorian era. Large windows lined the right wall, and at the end of the dazzling white counter sat the largest washing machine and tumble dryer duo she'd ever seen. White baskets were neatly tucked away on shelves above the machines, and a drying rack hung with tea towels and dishcloths stood against the far wall. Frankie spun around. The space opposite the windows was a perfectly finished mud room. There was wall space for coats, a neat bench to make it easier to take mucky boots off, and plenty of shelves for those mucky boots to reside. Only two pairs sat side by side, one black and the other pink. Neither were muddy. They looked barely worn at all. Cupboards reached from floor to ceiling, and Frankie's finger twitched to look inside. She sucked air in through her teeth. Maybe later, after she'd made the salad and hung the washing out, she'd take a peek inside. She peered around again. This was exactly how she'd imagined her dream home; only hers would be less white.

'It makes me squinty,' Dillon whispered as the sun blazed out from behind the April clouds.

Frankie blinked rapidly. 'Yeah,' she said. 'I'd hate to be stuck in here doing the ironing with this sun. Come on, let's get cracking. You can watch telly while I do my work.'

'Telly? Really?' Dillon danced on the spot.

'Yes, really – don't act like you never get to watch telly.' Frankie shook her head and smiled. 'Come on, Sandra

15

said the kitchen is upstairs. Imagine – the kitchen is upstairs!' She opened the door and led Dillon down a wide hall to a broad, carpeted staircase. She took one look at the pale carpet and frowned.

'Oh, buddy, I think we should take our shoes off,' she said and slipped her feet out of her old trainers. Dillon sat down on the bottom step and tugged his off. Frankie prayed that the seat of his trousers was clean and wouldn't leave a mark when he got up. Her socks looked grubby against the cream, and she exhaled as she picked up their trainers and went back to the utility room, where she popped them on the shelf next to the boots. Maybe this wasn't such a good idea after all, but she did owe Sandra a favour, and at least now it would be done.

Frankie tiptoed up the stairs, taking Dillon's hand as she made her way through the open-plan upstairs. Space after space opened up before her, all with spectacular views of the Cove. She stood in front of the balcony window and caught Dillon's hand just as he was about to place it in the middle of the gleaming pane. She blew out a breath. How did Sandra manage to keep this house in such pristine condition? The place was huge, and everything in it was shiny and perfect. She spotted the famous Harrods sofa at the end of the long room. Frankie grimaced. Of course, it was a warm pale white and not something she relished her messy six-year-old son clambering over, not with his penchant for digging up worms and rooting in woodpiles for creepy-crawlies. Lord knows what resided under his nails – she'd almost given up scrubbing them because he was capable of getting mucky within minutes of being washed.

Glancing around, she saw a charcoal check throw neatly positioned on the end of the ottoman, and she snatched it up. Too bad, Sandra would just have to rearrange it perfectly when she got back. With a flick of her wrist, she spread it on the sofa and positioned her son squarely in the middle.

'Don't move from that spot,' she said kissing his head. 'I'll be ten minutes making this salad, and then we'll go back downstairs.'

Dillon froze. His eyes glinted. 'This spot?' he murmured while trying not to move his lips.

'Yes!' Frankie laughed. 'That very spot! I'm terrified that sofa will get Dillon Dirty!'

'I'll be careful, Mammy, I promise.'

'I know, buddy – you're a good boy.' She picked up the remote control and stared at it. How could something so small control a television so large that it almost filled a whole wall? Eventually, she must've pressed the right button because the huge screen flickered on. Pressing another button, she breathed a sigh of relief as the channels appeared on the screen. 'CBeebies?' she asked her son.

Dillon nodded and slowly leaned back against the throw. Frankie looked at him, and her heart double beat. When he did that, he always reminded her of how calm Liam had looked when he'd proposed to her. Liam had leaned back the same way when she'd said yes, before bursting into happy laughter. There'd never been any doubt on her behalf. She was always going to say yes; she'd always been sure of his love for her. She swallowed the lump in her throat and reached for the engagement ring on her left hand, twisting it as if she was making a wish.

'You can go now, Mammy. I won't move.' Dillon's soft voice pulled her back to the present. He was already engrossed and didn't notice her tears. She smiled.

'I see how it is,' she said. 'I'll just be in the kitchen, okay?'

Dillon nodded. Frankie smiled and walked back along the room towards the kitchen. The kitchen took her breath away. It wasn't anything like she'd expected. There was a lot of clear space, and everything was cleverly designed. It took her a few minutes to find the chopping boards as they had their own little slot under the worktop, and another hot minute to realise that the kitchen tap was one of those taps that also gave out boiling water. Shaking her head, she reached into her bag and pulled out an empty lunchbox before going to the fridge to find the goat's cheese salad she was to get rid of. Such a waste, she thought as she rifled through the fridge. It was filled with the freshest produce, and she felt less guilty about considering popping the goat's cheese salad into her own lunchbox instead of wasting it.

'Wilful waste,' Aggie, her granny, always said, 'is woeful want.' Well, it would be if she could find the salad first. Sandra must've gone mad. There was no goat's cheese salad to be seen. Frankie rolled her eyes and pulled out a fresh head of cos lettuce and a slab of parmesan. She placed them on the counter and turned back to the fridge. A pot of Dillon's favourite yoghurt caught her eye, and she picked it up.

Suddenly a man's voice boomed into the kitchen, something about losing his socks at the beach but not to worry because the Octonauts would find them. Slamming the fridge door, Frankie dashed into the living room, where the noisy man blared from the television.

Dillon had his hands over his ears, and his face scrunched up. 'I only wanted to turn it up a little bit,' he yelled. 'But it wouldn't turn down. I didn't mean it.'

'It's okay,' Frankie scrambled around his legs, placing the pot of yoghurt beside him, and grabbed the remote control. She stared at it for a minute. 'What did you press?' she called to Dillon.

'I don't know,' he wailed. 'I'm sorry!'

'It's okay.' Frankie gritted her teeth and tried to keep calm. She turned around to face the television and fumbled with the buttons, frantically pressing each one until the sound turned down. Then turning back to Dillon, she placed the remote control on the ottoman.

'It's loud enough, now, all right? Don't touch the controls again.' She waited for Dillon to nod. His eyes glistened with tears, and her heart sank. She knelt down in front of her son and hugged him. 'Ah, buddy, don't cry. It's fine – it was an accident. I'm not cross—'

'Who are you?' A woman's angry voice cut clear across the room. For a moment, Frankie thought it was coming from the television again. She let go of Dillon and turned around. A woman wearing grey silk pyjamas stepped forward so that she was framed in an open doorway.

'I said, who are you?' the woman barked. 'What are you doing in my house?'

'Oh, you're not supposed to be here,' Frankie blurted. Scrambling to her feet, she knocked against the ottoman and stubbed her toe. 'Jesus! No, sorry, I'm sorry.' She hopped back, then rubbed her toe with her other foot.

'Well?' The woman had her hands on her hips now. Frankie stared at her. She was a slight woman with messy bed hair, yet she reminded Frankie of the teacher she'd hated most. The teacher who'd constantly humiliated her and never let her forget that she didn't have a father. Frankie drew herself up straight. She could face down anyone with bed hair.

'I'm Francesca,' she said, using her full name for impact. 'Sandra asked me to come over to do some chores she forgot about. She said you wouldn't be arriving until later.'

The woman looked her up and down. 'And part of that means that you and your . . . son . . . get to run amok in my home does it?'

'No,' Frankie said. 'Of course not. But what was I supposed to do? Leave him on the doorstep while I made your salad?'

'I wouldn't put it past someone who is so clearly irresponsible,' the woman drawled.

'What is that supposed to mean?' Frankie took a step forward. The hairs on her forearms prickled. The teacher she hated had often referred to Frankie's mother as irresponsible and used the phrase *the apple never falls far from the tree*. What kind of person says that to a ten-year-old?

The woman gestured to the pot of yoghurt on the sofa.

'It's not open.' Frankie grimaced. 'And I wasn't going to give it to him. It was in my hand when the telly blared.'

'Right.' The woman nodded, looking sceptical. Frankie took a breath and sucked in her lip.

'Look, I'm sorry,' she began. 'I was only doing Sandra a favour—'

'You've already said that.' The woman moved towards the ottoman, picked up the remote control and turned off the television.

'Whatever.' Frankie shrugged. 'I'm done with this. Make your own salad. Come on, Dillon, let's get out of this lovely lady's hair. She needs some alone time.'

'Okay, Mammy.' Dillon rolled over and pushed himself up from the sofa, his little hand squashing the yoghurt pot as he did. The pot popped open, and the yoghurt spurted up and out, completely missing the charcoal throw and landing all over the sofa. Flecks of strawberry and a river of pale pink began to sink into the warm white fabric. The woman and Frankie shrieked in unison and dashed to the sofa. Frankie skidded to her knees, the rips in the knees of her jeans tearing even more, and began scooping up the yoghurt with her hands.

'Oh my God,' she cried. 'I'm sorry.'

'For crying out loud, stop – you're making it worse.' The woman's face paled as she watched the strawberry stain spread. 'Leave it – just leave it.'

Frankie stood up. Her hands dripped yoghurt onto the wooden floor.

'I was only trying to help.' The words caught in her throat.

'Well, you're not.' The woman yanked up the sofa cushion and ran to the kitchen with it. Frankie heard the sound of water running. She blinked and looked down at her yoghurt-covered hands. Why did she always do the wrong thing? It was always the same. Would she never learn?

'Mammy.' Dillon's small voice called her back. 'I didn't mean it.'

'I know, buddy. Come on. Let's go.'

With her hands held out in front of her, Frankie slipped silently into the kitchen and hooked the handle of her handbag with the one finger that wasn't covered in strawberry yoghurt. She abandoned the empty lunchbox on the counter, averting her eyes from the woman. Scrubbing sounds and sighs were the last things she heard as she guided Dillon down the stairs.

3

Ruby

Ruby stood at the balcony window and watched the feisty young woman stomp down her driveway and through the gate. Her gaze lingered on the little boy, wondering if he was the woman's son or her little brother. He was cute, she thought grudgingly, although in need of a haircut and a little dishevelled, but then, little boys should be messy and disorganised. It showed his curious nature. The little boy looked up and waved at her as he passed through the gate, and she found her hand returning the wave of its own accord. Biting her lip, Ruby turned away and walked back to the kitchen, where the sink was filled with the cushion cover and dish soap. If she and James had been lucky enough to have had children, they'd surely have had red hair too. His family was littered with auburn tresses; his sister had the most glorious hair, which, even at sixty, had never been dyed. Her children, all six of them, had the same shock of hair. Ruby smiled sadly: with a name like hers, kids with red hair would've been perfect.

Sinking her hands into the suds, she grasped the cushion cover and vigorously rubbed the fabric until the stain lifted. Sweating, she let the water out and squeezed the cover as tightly as she could. James would have flipped if he'd been here, she thought as the rinse water swirled down the plughole: at the yoghurt accident and the fact that she was up to her elbows scrubbing. That sofa was more trouble than it was worth. It had taken ages to have it delivered, and it marked with the slightest of touches. James had surprised her with it after a trip to London, where she'd made a throwaway comment about liking it. It wasn't as if she wanted it all that much, really. She definitely didn't like it enough to justify losing her temper in front of a child like that.

Ruby pressed her lips together. She didn't know what had come over her earlier, but she shouldn't have let that happen. The poor child had flinched as her voice had risen – she had seen him. It was awful to think she'd scared him. She should have controlled herself, she berated herself – should have asked what was going on more politely, and then she wouldn't have flipped out. Wiping a tear from her face, Ruby sighed. She had been wrong, and really should apologise to the young woman, Francesca. Maybe Sandra would have the young woman's number and she could call her to try to explain herself.

Her phone rang, and reluctantly she grabbed a tea towel and dried her hands, hoping that the cushion cover wouldn't shrink while it dried. She picked up the phone. It was Sandra.

'Hello? Frankie called me – let me explain what happened,' Sandra blustered down the phone. Ruby held the phone away from her ear for a moment and then, pinching the bridge of her nose, listened to Sandra's excuse.

'Sandra,' Ruby said when Sandra paused for breath. 'Listen, stop, please. I've got the stain out of the sofa. There's no need for you to call over this afternoon. I wish you'd told me you'd asked someone else to drop in.'

'Well, that doesn't make any sense.' Sandra's voice rose over the phone line. 'You would never have known if you weren't there.'

Ruby's brows knitted together. 'Sandra, this is my house. Home.'

Sandra continued as if she hadn't heard Ruby. 'Frankie is a lovely young woman, she needs the work, and I knew I could depend on her. The way you behaved made her feel like a criminal – shouting at her in front of her son. He's only a child!'

'Well, I didn't mean that to happen,' Ruby said, tears welling up in her eyes. 'I shouldn't have spoken to her like that.'

Sandra lowered her voice and carried on talking. Ruby wiped down the sink with the tea towel and half listened to Sandra's excuses. They were eroding her desire to apologise to the young woman who Sandra was now calling Frankie. Ruby knew she shouldn't let Sandra's blathering affect her, but the longer she went on, the less inclined she was to listen – until Sandra mentioned the washing in the machine. Biting back an instinct to tell Sandra that she still should have told her some stranger was going to be in her house, she ended the call, placed her phone face down on the counter and walked down to the utility room. She began to unload the washing machine, a little insulted that Sandra didn't think that she could hang out a load of washing. It wasn't as if she had never worked – she'd been part of a hardworking housekeeping team once, so she knew what it took to run a laundry room. Sandra should've remembered that; after all, Ruby had worked with Sandra's sister, Valerie. Granted, that was a long time ago – she counted back and recoiled. Well over thirty years ago. Thirty years . . . How did the time go by so fast?

Ruby shivered and rubbed her arms. Wishing she'd worn her warm flannel pyjamas, she ignored the load of washing now dumped in the basket. The house was cold despite the bright day outside. She'd still not mastered the art of *how to turn on the heating*, and wished she had a fireplace. Grumbling, Ruby remembered how she'd suggested putting in an open fireplace the night they'd come down to check the plans on site, years ago when all the work was being done on the house.

James had spread the plans for the renovation out across the table. He'd been entirely engrossed in them until Ruby had leaned over the table to study the plans. There was no fireplace or stove, no range even. She'd squinted and frowned. James had caught her puzzlement as he'd topped up her wine glass.

'What is it? Don't you like it?' he'd asked.

'I do. I love it,' she'd replied quickly. 'Where's the fireplace going to go?'

'Oh, there is no fireplace.' He'd laughed as if she was being silly. 'It's a passive house.'

'And what does that mean when it's at home?' Ruby had initially tried to listen, but she'd found herself zoning

26

out as James launched into what a passive house was, what building it entailed, and how it was the way to go for efficiency. She'd tuned in as he'd finished up.

'It's the way forward, Ruby. This project allows me to fully understand how it'll work.' He'd grinned at her. 'So that's why we can't have an open fireplace.'

Ruby remembered looking at James and wondering how to say that it would be lovely to sit by an open fire in the living room in the winter, enjoying the sight of the waves crashing in the distance. She'd desperately wanted one. An open fire was one of the things she loved most. No matter how bad her day was, settling down by an open fire in the evening always soothed her. She remembered coming home from school – wet, windblown and tired – and warming herself by the fire and eating the warming bowl of soup her mother always had ready for them. It was the only thing to have when you lived by the sea all year round, particularly during the inevitable harsh winters. If they were going to retire here, she'd have to insist on an open fire, she remembered thinking. But it hadn't gone to plan.

To this day, she still regretted not asking him to change his mind. She missed the cosiness of a fire, and now that this was going to be her full-time home, she wished she'd had more input into the whole thing.

Mid-April sun blazed in the utility room windows. The forecast promised an unseasonably warm spring day, much like the day before, although not as calm. But then the wind often switched here along the coast, she remembered. You had to be ready for all manner of weather. Hitching the laundry basket up on her hip, Ruby eschewed the tumble dryer, went out to the washing line and quickly hung the sheets and towels, relishing the crack of the sheets in the strengthening wind. The wind whipped her hair into her eyes, and she reached up to brush it out and looked around.

The garden stretched out before her in shades of green. Clipped hedging edged the boundary and the path that ran straight from the main house to a small summerhouse down the end of the garden. She never used the summerhouse, always thinking it was filled with spiders and earwigs. Shivering, she took in the oval-shaped rose beds set in the middle of the lawn on either side of the pathway. The roses were miserable-looking. They'd been hacked back hard by the gardener. The bare branches jutted skywards in an almost angry and accusatory fashion, but in the summer, they'd fill the space with verdant foliage and huge magenta flowers. Their scent was overpowering, and Ruby hated them with a vengeance. They reminded her of her sister-in-law, who loved roses, but had never embraced Ruby into the family. She was polite in company, but James had told her she'd called Ruby a gold-digger at the engagement party, so it was hard to like her or any roses after that.

After that, Ruby had hated not working and relying on James for everything. It didn't matter that he told her he needed her at home, that she was his rock and his refuge. The words had pierced as they were supposed to, like a thorn through a leather glove. Roses, as far as she was concerned, were as two-faced as her sister-in-law. Blousy and showy, but sharp and cold.

Now she looked over the acre of garden with a critical

eye. It was boring. There was nothing pretty or fun about it. The house in Dublin had a smaller garden, but it had been carefully designed and planted up by some famous, award-winning gardener who'd been so obnoxious that Ruby wouldn't stay in the house when he was around. He'd made her feel simultaneously like a visitor in her own home and like a failing hostess as he wrinkled his nose at the tap water she'd given him to drink. All the same, he had done an amazing job on the garden, she conceded. Everywhere you looked held something interesting. There were secret seating areas and even a cute pond. They'd spent quite a bit of time entertaining their closest friends there. She was undoubtedly going to miss it.

She squared her shoulders. Surely it couldn't be that hard to have the garden she wanted. Making a decision, Ruby stepped over the low box hedge and marched around the lawn. The first thing she'd do would be to pull out the staid roses and add more colour, yes. Lots of colour and more shapes, lots of different forms. A shiver of anticipation ran down her back. There was a garden centre not far from the village; she could go down and pick out a load of plants today. She could have them planted by the evening, and the whole garden would be ablaze with colour come midsummer. It wasn't ideal, but it would be a start, and then she'd plan for the next stage. A quick shower and a bit of breakfast, and she could be on the road in under an hour.

Hurrying back up to the house, she laughed and clapped her hands. A project was just what she needed to start feeling human again. Somehow, in the year and a half since James's death, she'd slowly left every group she'd been part of. The last one to go by the wayside had been her book club, the one that she'd set up. The worst thing was that it hadn't even hurt to let all her hobbies slide. It had been easier to walk away from the familiar faces, some sympathetic, some not at all interested in her sadness or loss. Pamela had been the only friend who'd tried to keep her included in their circle, sometimes begging Ruby to come out to the theatre or a poetry reading, but the others had mostly left her alone. She thought that maybe her grief was too raw, but the truth was that she'd never quite fit in anyway. She was sure they'd only included her because their husbands did business with James. It didn't matter now, she thought; she had a garden to grow. She'd be busy, and her head wouldn't keep straying to memories of her old life.

The shower was the quickest she'd ever taken, and she barely tasted the yoghurt she'd decided on for breakfast. She grabbed her handbag and car keys and ran lightly down the stairs to the front door.

A loud buzzing sound made her jump, and she opened the front door and peered out. A huge navy removal van was parked in the gateway, and a young man stood by the intercom. With a sigh, Ruby dropped her handbag on the hall table and pressed the gate button allowing the van to drive in, nodding to the three men as they parked at the front door. She'd have to wait to start her new gardening adventure.

4

Frankie

'You're kidding me,' Frankie sighed as she looked at her schedule sheet.

'Sorry, kid,' Valerie said. 'They're coming down from Westmeath – I think one of them has cancer and needs to rest, but they're all travelling together, so they'll all arrive together.'

'I'll do my best,' Frankie said.

'I know you will,' Valerie said. 'You're a trouper. Oh, by the way, I've put in a good word for you with management. Told them they didn't know how lucky they were to have you on staff. Fingers crossed they listen this time, eh?'

'Thanks, Val, I'm crossing everything crossable!' Frankie flashed her a grin, then hurried to her first room.

Frankie promptly set the timer on her phone and swept her auburn curls into a ponytail. She had three rooms to clean before two o'clock, Valerie, the executive house-keeper had told her, as the guests had requested an early check-in for a family wedding. *Super early,* Frankie thought uncharitably. The wedding wasn't until the next day!

The first room was a quick one to turn over. The previous guest had barely left a ruffle in the sheets. Frankie opened the windows and set to work, leaving the place gleaming in no time. The last room, however, was a different story. The place stank to high heaven of drink, the bins were overflowing with bottles and cans, and the room service tray had toppled over onto the carpet. There was no way she'd have it done and make it to the school on time to pick up Dillon. Rolling up her sleeves, Frankie stepped over the tray to open the window. Outside the ground-floor room, the April sun shone through the stately oak trees just coming into leaf. A couple of employees were gathered around a fire exit, smoking.

Frankie watched them briefly, smoothing down her tunic. They were laughing and joking, chatting about guests. Some were making arrangements for a drink after work. Frankie didn't smoke, so she wouldn't have been out there with them even if she did have time. Anyway, she was too busy taking care of Dillon to make friends.

Frankie hunkered down, picked up the tray and got to work. She finished the room with minutes to spare and took off down the back road from the hotel at a run. Panting, she arrived at the school just as the teacher was about to head back in with Dillon.

'Sorry,' Frankie panted. 'Got a bad room.'

'No worries.' Maggie, Dillon's teacher, smiled. 'I guessed that you'd be on the way, and anyway, Dillon is no trouble. If I could have a class full of Dillons, then life would be perfect.'

'Thanks.' Frankie smiled back tightly. She ignored the voice in her head telling her that she was only five minutes late, that Maggie really didn't mind. She hated being late collecting Dillon. It wasn't fair on Maggie. Her job was teaching six- and seven-year-olds, not to supply after-school care.

'Anytime,' Maggie called over her shoulder as she made her way back into the school.

Frankie squeezed Dillon's hand. 'Sorry for being late, buddy.'

'It's all right,' Dillon said. 'Miss said not to worry, that she'd keep me forever if she could. I think she likes me.'

'I think she does.' Frankie pulled him close. 'And why wouldn't she? You're adorable.'

Dillon beamed. 'She gave me a loan of a book from the library. It's got lots of new insects in it. Can I read it in bed? I promise not to stay up late with my torch again.'

'You can,' Frankie said. 'We have to pop into the post office on the way home, okay?'

'Okay,' Dillon said, trotting alongside his mum. Frankie looked down at his bouncy curls.

Raising her chin, Frankie marched quicker towards the post office, anxious to get her weekly social welfare payment. She felt her face redden as she walked up to the counter and handed over her card for the familiar woman to swipe. Of all the things in her life – being a child without a father, her absentee mother, her ramshackle home, her second-hand clothes – this was where she felt the most shame. She knew what people said about the likes of her, scroungers wasting the decent taxpayers' hard-earned money, slut . . . but without the weekly social welfare payment she wouldn't be able to get by. Dillon would be seven in two months, though, and then the payments would stop, and she'd have to find a way to make ends meet.

Frankie's breath shallowed as she watched the woman nod and tap on the keyboard. Valerie had said she'd try to give her extra shifts, but she couldn't promise they'd be during school hours. Childcare costs were beyond her budget, and there was only so much she could ask of her friends. None of them had kids – one was planning her wedding and was embroiled in what seemed to be a constant conflict with her mother and mother-in-law to be about the guest list, and the others were more concerned with partying than parenting. Tears prickled. Frankie didn't expect to ever marry. Not now, anyway.

'Can I withdraw the full amount?' Frankie asked as the woman looked up. She blinked back the tears and grate-fully pocketed the money. Dillon skipped beside her as she headed out of the post office and turned to walk along Harbour Road to their house. As they approached Number Three, Frankie drew her shoulders up. That woman was standing on her balcony with a cup in her hands, seemingly watching as a large navy removal van pulled out of the gate. Frankie allowed herself a quick glance and hoped the woman wouldn't notice them. She looked as grumpy as she had this morning, despite her pulled-together look.

Frankie brushed down the front of the Barbour waxed jacket she'd picked up in a charity shop. It was okay, she reasoned, not too shabby. It was holding up well, considering she'd worn it almost every day from October to May for four years. Some patches looked worn and were letting the rain in, but she'd read online that she could get the jacket waxed or buy a pot of the wax and do it herself. She'd meant to order the pot of wax, but somehow it had been relegated to the end of her to-do list. Every day there seemed to be another thing to fix and another bill to pay.

Dillon waved at the woman, but she didn't seem to notice him. His little mouth pressed into a line. He kept his eyes on her until they'd passed the house. Frankie watched his face cloud over.

'What is it, buddy?'

He sighed. 'She's so sad. I want to give her a hug.'

Frankie rolled her eyes. Trust his big heart to warm towards the woman who'd most likely call the guards if she saw them again.

'Maybe she's not sad,' Frankie said as they plodded past the playground. 'Maybe she's just thinking. Sometimes grown-ups have a lot to think about, and it makes them look sad or angry.'

'I know that, Mammy,' Dillon said, sounding slightly exasperated. 'You do it all the time. She's not thinking the same way you think when you're sad.'

Frankie swallowed. 'Oh. And how do you know that?'

'I just do.' Dillon walked on.

Frankie hurried after him. Of course, that woman wasn't thinking the same things that she was. For one, she clearly didn't have money worries, and two, she wasn't worried about how she was going to take care of her child. Her kids were most likely well grown and working big jobs that made them plenty of money.

'I think she's probably just thinking about whatever new piece of furniture has arrived.'

Dillon shrugged, and Frankie shook her head. He was stubborn sometimes, as stubborn as she was. As stubborn as his father was too. What the hell was going on with her today? All her thoughts were morose and intense. The sea breeze whipped up the dust on the side of the road, and Frankie turned her head away from the sharp gust, blinking to keep the grit from her eyes. Shaking her hair, she slowly opened her eyes and focused them on the sea. In the distance, she could make out a ferry, and closer to the cove, some smaller boats bobbing along the coast. The few trawlers that still went out fishing from the harbour were docked, the men gone home to rest. Dillon had already slipped up the laneway to their small roadside cottage.

Set back slightly from the road, the small, low cottage looked lonely against the grey clouds that skittered overhead. The soft coral paint had flaked from years of being battered by winter winds, and the front door needed replacing. The wooden door didn't quite fit the frame. It was as if it had shrunk since it had been fitted almost ten years ago. Frankie slid the key into the lock and pushed the door open for Dillon, who dashed in and disappeared. Frankie stood in the doorway and looked out. The tiny patch of garden at the front of the house was well kept. She'd sneaked cuttings from garden centres and the hedges of gardens she passed by, as well as wild bulbs and flowers from the surrounding countryside, and transplanted them here. The garden was a mass of bluebells, and their subtle scent drifted up to her as she tried to quell the fear building up inside her.

Frankie touched the warm wooden door where Aggie,

her grandmother, used to lean and chat with her friends. She loved her home, but the last six months had been tough. Everyone said the first year after someone died was the hardest, but Frankie knew that wasn't true. It was always going to be hard, forever and ever. Aggie had reared her, had been the mother she'd never had. And now she was gone.

Her real mother had brought her here when she was six months old and left her in Aggie's warm, kind arms. Aggie had taken her in and loved her without reservation, and for a long time, Frankie had almost believed that Aggie was her real mother and that the woman who called in every once in a blue moon was a family friend. But Aggie wouldn't hear of it.

'We'll have none of that nonsense,' she'd say whenever Frankie called her *mammy*. 'I'm your granny and I'm happy to be your granny and I won't have anyone say that I've been hiding you away.'

'What do you mean, hiding me away?' Frankie would ask, but Agnes had always managed to change the subject.

'You call me Nanny Aggie or Granny. That's the end of it, now.' She'd wave her arms and send Frankie out to play. 'Skedaddle with ya. I've a cake of bread to get on with.'

Agnes had been a tough cookie, Frankie thought. It was probably where she'd gotten her own backbone from. She remembered standing in the doorway at Agnes's wake and thinking how absurd it had felt to see her petite coffin in the tiny confines of the sitting room. That day a neighbour had regaled Frankie about the time Agnes had chased Father Cribbin away from the front door.

37

'Agnes never used to miss morning mass before you arrived,' the neighbour had said. 'She was great for keeping the altar flowers fresh too, God bless her. They missed her devotions after Father Cribbin called in and asked if she'd ever thought of giving you up for adoption.'

Frankie had almost dropped the cup of tea she was cradling. 'I never knew about this.'

The neighbour had nodded. 'I was here when he called, and sure you were only a babby, and just landed on her doorstep a day or so earlier. Agnes was in love with you from the moment she saw you. Father Cribbin said the Christian thing to do was to offer the child, you, up to a husband and wife who had no children; he had a lovely family lined up, professional, with money. They'd offered compensation, too.'

Frankie's knees had almost buckled. She remembered looking around the room for her real mother before remembering she hadn't come. Not even to meet Dillon. With great effort, Frankie had tilted her head towards the neighbour, willing her to go on.

'Well, I never saw anything like it,' the woman had said. 'Agnes all but lifted Father Cribbin by the scruff of his collar and threw him out the door. "The Christian thing to do is to forgive and offer solace and a home to one of my own, Father," she said. I tell you, Francesca, I'll never forget that. I'd never thought of it that way before. Agnes only went to church once a week and on feast days after that. Mary McAvoy took over the altar flowers, and sure she's no good. It's as if her hands are weed killer – the flowers don't last a wet week.'

Standing in the doorway now, in the house that no

longer contained her grandmother, a tear slid down Frankie's cheek. 'I don't know what to do, Granny Aggie. I don't know how to keep going,' she whispered to the garden. 'I'm so lonely.' She waited for a minute, straining for anything that might be a sign from Agnes. Nothing happened. Frankie sighed. Why was she surprised? Agnes had had no truck with the supernatural of any kind. 'When we're gone, we're gone,' she'd always said. 'And received into the arms of the Lord, so no, I won't be hanging around sending messages and the likes. Sure, what would I want here on earth that I won't have in heaven?' She hadn't noticed Frankie's face crumple when she said that, nor had she noticed the smile Frankie had plastered on when she said that she would be happiest when she was up there with her Martin, who was waiting for her, God rest his soul.

Frankie went inside. 'I wish I'd an ounce of your practicality,' she said to the chair Agnes had preferred. 'Then maybe I'd . . .' She shook her head and marched into the small kitchen. For a start, Agnes – if she was hanging about somewhere – would be annoyed at her moping around. She'd be telling her to get on with it – there was a little boy in need of his dinner and a story before bed.

The meagre contents of the fridge did little to whet her appetite. In fact, they did quite the opposite. Frankie wasn't in the humour for peeling potatoes and making cottage pie tonight, no matter how cheap the dish was. She'd kill for that goat's cheese salad or anything else in that woman's fridge, come to think of it. She checked the date on the packet of mince, flung it in the freezer, and slammed the door.

'Dillon,' she called as she grabbed her bag from where it hung on the bottom of the stairs. 'Come on, let's go and get a chipper for dinner.'

Shucking her jacket on, she waited for Dillon to come running. He loved chips. He'd usually be down the stairs and out the door before her when she said they were getting chips.

'Dillon,' she called again. 'Chips, let's go!'

She stopped moving, and listened. The cottage sat in silence. The sky had darkened and there was no light from upstairs. Swiftly she ran up, taking the stairs two at a time. The upstairs was cramped, a half-formed space. She bent down to look out the landing window as she passed. There were only two tiny rooms up here; one was hers and the other was Dillon's. She pushed open his bedroom door, peered into the darkness and then snapped on the light. The ceiling sloped down to the shoulder-height wall on each side of the room, and his bed was set in the centre. The room was empty, and his schoolbag was open on his bed, the library book on insects poking out from inside it. Frankie's mouth dried up. This wasn't normal. Dillon wouldn't leave a book like this unopened. Dropping to her knees, she looked under the bed.

'Dillon,' she called, her voice quivering. 'Come on, stop messing with me. Let's go. Chips.'

There wasn't a sound. She stood up and bumped her head on the ceiling and cursed. Then she noticed that his desk was pushed up tight under the room's only window. The window was wide open, and the flat roof of the kitchen below was the perfect escape route.

'Ah, Dillon, no,' she gasped and ran downstairs, regretting having told him about how she'd climbed out the window when she was little.

'Don't have fallen, don't be hurt,' she muttered as she ran back down the stairs. She dashed to the back door and flung it open, sure that he'd be in a jumble on the ground, hoping that he'd just had a fright and no broken bones. But he wasn't there. Only his hat was on the ground. With a cry, Frankie ran around the side of the house and frantically looked up and down the road. Where on earth had her curious little son run off to?

5

Ruby

Ruby rested her hip against the stainless steel balcony rail and watched the sun set over the harbour. The furniture removal men had taken all day to move in her favourite Dublin pieces, stopping for the coffee and tea she'd stupidly offered every hour. She hadn't considered where she'd put the pieces, thinking that she'd just know it instinctively when they arrived – after all, that's what she was good at. Everyone knew she had an eye for design. Her art teacher had begged her to apply to the National College of Art and Design, but Ruby knew her mother wouldn't manage without her, let alone be able to afford to send her. So she'd spent what little she kept of her wages on interior design magazines and her spare time wandering around McNally's Hardware examining paint and wallpaper samples.

Ruby tapped the balcony rail with her fingers, remembering the opportunity she'd missed because she'd left to be with James. Old Mrs Mullally, the hotel owner, had heard her talking about her passion and asked her to design one of the suites. Ruby had almost fainted as the elegant woman walked away from her. She'd rushed home to tell her mother, dreams of a glorious career in design flashing before her eyes. If she could prove herself to Mrs Mullally, then maybe things would be different. Perhaps she'd get other jobs from Mrs Mullally's friends.

Then James had proposed. Ruby cringed recalling how her mother had tried to reason with her; then, when that didn't work, she'd resorted to calling Ruby crazy, telling her that no man James's age was up to anything good proposing to 'a child of barely twenty-two who comes from the wrong kind of background'. Feeling her cheeks redden with shame, Ruby remembered slamming the door and storming to the phone box at the end of the road to call James to come get her. She left her lovingly catalogued stash of interior design magazines behind, and the chance to impress Mrs Mullally and her friends. It had almost broken her heart, but he had been worth the heartache, she'd thought. And he had taken good care of her, as he'd promised to.

But now, here she was, left with a pile of furniture that clashed with the carefully curated house James had created. He'd been so wrapped up in renovating Eyrie Lodge that Ruby felt he'd completely forgotten how much she loved interiors and design. He hadn't asked her opinion on anything. He'd planned it all, right down to the last dot of paint. It had stung a little, but she'd pushed past it, knowing how happy it was making him. It was supposed to be a holiday home, after all. Rubbing her temples, she pushed away thoughts of her career dreams and furniture-filled hallways. Maybe she'd figure it out in good time, but it felt like it might've been better to have sent the Dublin furniture to the auction house or storage, as Pamela had suggested.

Her stomach growled, and she pushed away from the balcony. She shivered and rubbed her arms. The warmth of the day didn't linger at this time of year. She decided to take a hot water bottle to bed to stave off the cool spring night. Wondering what to eat, she half-heartedly peered into the fridge. Salad in bags, fresh fruit, yoghurt. She sighed. What she wanted was egg and chips. Sandra might have put some potatoes in the cupboard, she thought. But they didn't own a fryer. Egg and toast would have to do. But it wouldn't be the same. Surely there was a chip shop nearby. Grabbing her bag, she ran lightly down the stairs.

'I can't believe I'm doing this . . . Keys, where are my keys?' she muttered into the depths of her handbag as she searched for her car keys. James wouldn't approve; he'd remind her of her VB dress still waiting to be worn.

'Well, I've nowhere to wear it,' she said aloud to the empty house. Then she laughed. 'I'm going crazy, talking to no one. Running out to get chips almost in the middle of the night. James, if you're watching me – I'm sure you are – this is a one-off. I just need to . . .' She paused in her second attempt to leave the house that day; then, finding her keys, she brandished them in the air. 'If this isn't a sign to get chips, then I don't know what is.'

'You just need to what?' a small voice said. Ruby jumped. She stared down the dark hallway towards the bedrooms. The darkness loomed closer, the hall light barely reaching the first bedroom door.

44

'I'm over here,' the voice called. Ruby spun around.

'Oh my God,' she screeched. 'What – how did you get into my house?'

The little boy from this morning was standing halfway on her porch, halfway in her hallway. He inched in a little more, the light catching his red hair. Finally, he shrugged and raised his hands.

'The door was open.'

'The door was open?' Ruby muttered faintly, shaking her head.

'Yeah,' the little boy said. 'Just open a teeny bit, enough to let a Clouded Drab in.'

'I'm sorry, a what?' Ruby raised her hands. 'Where's your mother?' She looked past the boy and into the garden.

'Oh.' His face fell. 'She's going to be angry with me. I climbed out the window, like she did when she was little.'

'You climbed out a window?' Ruby said. 'Why did you climb out the window?' She stepped forward and went out onto the porch. There was no sign of the fiery redheaded young woman anywhere.

The little boy followed her. 'I didn't mean to mess your couch up. It was by an accident.'

'By accident.' Ruby automatically corrected, her hands on her hips.

'What?' The little boy wrinkled up his nose.

'It was by accident – you weren't *by* an accident. You didn't see an accident . . .' Ruby tried to explain. 'It's just something that my husband used to say . . .'

'But I kinda was by an accident,' the little boy said. 'The accident was on the couch, and I was beside it. I didn't want you to be sad.'

Ruby let her hands drop. 'You didn't want me to be sad?'

'Yeah, you looked sad.' The boy gave a shrug. 'Like my mammy does sometimes.'

'Oh,' Ruby said, a huge lump suddenly caught in her throat. 'I see. What's your name?'

'Dillon. What's yours?'

'Ruby. Dillon, do your parents know where you are?'

'I don't have a daddy, only a mammy.' Dillon sighed. 'She thinks I'm in my bedroom reading my new library book. I didn't tell her I was coming to see you.'

'Okay, right. Well, listen.' Ruby hunkered down and took Dillon's hands. A wave of love washed through her; his hands fit into hers so well. They were soft and warm, a little grubby. He gripped her tightly and nodded. 'It's not a good idea to go out somewhere and not tell your mammy where you're going. She'll be worried when she knows you're not at home.'

'But I know the road really well,' Dillon said, his eyes widening. 'We go this way nearly every day. So I wasn't going to get lost.'

'I know that, Dillon,' Ruby said. 'But that doesn't change the fact that your mammy will be worried. How old are you? I guess maybe six or seven?'

Dillon frowned, nodded, and then shrugged. Ruby squeezed his hands. 'Listen,' she said. 'I know you're a big boy and well able to walk from your house to mine, but mammies will always worry about you, no matter how big you get. When I was seven, I took art classes at the gallery with my friend. Her daddy used to drive us, and one evening I got bored waiting for them to come get me, so I walked there. It was wintertime, so it was really dark,

46

but I knew the way. I was fine, but the grown-ups were all angry with me. I didn't know then, but it's dangerous for children to walk around on their own, and my mammy was upset with me.'

Dillon's eyebrows rose. Ruby continued. 'I didn't like to see her sad, so I didn't sneak off anywhere else after that. It wasn't worth seeing her sad, you see? You don't want your mammy upset, do you?'

Dillon shook his head. 'I didn't think . . .' he said. Then he smiled at her. 'You can walk me home, can't you – then I won't be on my own.'

'I can – let's go.' What choice did she have?

Ruby stood up. She picked her bag up, and suddenly his arms were around her waist. He whispered, 'Thank you.' Her heart contracted tightly as he squeezed her. He was exactly the little boy she imagined her son would've been. She took a deep, calming breath and broke away from him.

Taking his hand, she started down the driveway. 'What's Clouded Drab?' she asked. 'You said it a few minutes ago – is he a superhero?'

Dillon giggled. 'No, it's a moth. They hatch in the springtime and are really important pollinators.'

'Is that so?' Ruby looked down at Dillon. He smiled back up at her and nodded.

'I know loads about moths,' he said. 'Can I tell you some interesting facts?'

Ruby nodded, smiling as he took a deep breath and began talking. He was still talking ten minutes later when they arrived at the cottage.

'This is my house,' he said and ran in the gate. The

front door was ajar, so he pushed it and ran inside. 'Come on, Ruby, I'll show you my library book.'

Ruby hovered at the end of the path before looking back down the laneway, then back up at the house.

Dillon's cottage was the last of the tiny houses on the road, higher up than the rest as the hill rose away from the sea. It stood apart from the terrace of council cottages where Ruby had grown up.

She could see from where she was standing now the mid-terraced house where her mother had given birth to five children, but only raised two, and she couldn't tear her gaze away. Her heart pounded as she took in the dark windows, the shabby and ripped net curtains. There was an old black rubbish bag in tatters on the front doorstep. Her mother would've been so ashamed. Ruby rubbed her arms and tried to breathe. The house seemed derelict. The low metal gate she used to swing on was pushed back against an overgrown box hedge, and the tree they'd planted one year had grown far too big for the garden.

The last time she'd seen the house was when she'd left to go to James in Dublin. She hadn't even come back to this road when they'd bought Eyrie Lodge, and all the times they'd stayed there since. She swallowed the lump in her throat. Her mother had stood at that gate and called for her to come back, saying that she'd regret leaving this way. Then she'd stopped calling out to her and Ruby knew that she was trying desperately to maintain some dignity. She could almost see the neighbours' shadows behind their gleaming white net curtains.

A shiver ran down Ruby's spine and her face burned as her eyes scanned the terrace for anything familiar. There was nothing else left now to remind her of her childhood. The remaining houses had been modernised, some with jutting windows extending into the postage-stamp-sized front gardens, some with attic conversions. Which one had been Valerie's? She couldn't remember now, and she wouldn't call in, anyway. Ruby scanned the terrace. None of the refurbished houses had net curtains; they were a thing of the past. James would approve of some of the alterations – he always said you never got a second chance to make a first impression.

Some of the gardens had been converted to parking areas, so the road wasn't cluttered with cars, but not Frankie and Dillon's little cottage garden. Ruby squinted at the tiny cottage. Her teenage friend, Nicole, had lived in this house. They'd lost touch after secondary school – Nicole had flitted from job to job in the town before getting a secretarial position in Dublin. She came back for a while, but they'd never picked up their friendship in quite the same way. Nicole had soon moved on again. She seemed never to be able to stay still. Now it was Dillon's home, and the garden that Ruby remembered as barren was now jammed with bluebells, and the framework of a climbing rose was evident against the house. Boisterous grass shimmied in the breeze, and dandelions romped happily with the daffodils.

Ruby stepped over the threshold and held her breath. The minute hallway was the same as she remembered, more or less an inner porch with four doors and a staircase leading off it. The door to her left was open. Calling out hello, she walked through and into a bright sitting room. No one answered her. She called out again and listened. Again, there was no answer. The house seemed to be empty. Ruby frowned and looked around. Who left a seven-year-old child alone like this? She scrutinised the space. A two-seater couch was cramped up close to an old wood-burning stove, a worn armchair sat opposite. The wall lights made the room cosy, as did the wallpaper, which had been painted over with a warm primrose yellow. Photographs sat on the mantelpiece over the stove. Most of them were of Dillon. Ruby smiled and picked up one of him grinning into the camera and pointing to his hand, where a large butterfly sat.

'Cute,' she said and put the photo back. 'Dillon? Where are you?'

'In my room.' His voice floated down to her.

'Well, I'm not going up there,' she called up.

An angry voice answered: 'I should bloody well hope not.'

Ruby spun around to look out into the hallway. Dillon's mother stood there, her hands on her hips, her lips quivering.

'What the hell are you doing in my house – with my son?'

'Frankie?' Ruby stepped forward. She raised a hand shakily. 'Hi, I'm Ruby, from—'

'I know where you're from,' Frankie said. She looked Ruby up and down.

'This isn't the way it looks,' Ruby said, raising her hands and voice. Taking a breath, she forced herself to be still. It wouldn't help either one of them if she took up where she'd left off that morning. It was bad enough regretting that outburst without adding to it. 'Look, Dillon came to my house, and I just brought him back home.'

Ruby moved to the hallway. Frankie didn't move, so Ruby inched back towards the stairs.

Frankie glared at her, then called up to Dillon. He came running out onto the landing and peered down at the two women facing off in the hall.

'Honestly.' Ruby tried again. 'He told me he'd slipped out, and I knew that you must've been out of your mind with worry—'

'Don't presume to know anything about me,' Frankie cut across her. 'Who do you think you are? Oh, I know . . . Mrs Bigtime with your big house, and big-city ways sauntering into my town as if you're better than any of us, wandering into my house telling me how to take care of my son. You know, at least I had a key to your house. You just walked right into mine without an invitation. Now, get out, before I call the guards and have you locked up for trespassing and attempted kidnapping!'

Ruby paled. 'That's not fair,' she said. 'I . . .'

Frankie yanked the door open and swooped into a bow. 'Get. Out. Of. My House. *Now.*'

Ruby slipped past her, her face burning. She turned back and caught sight of Dillon. He was grasping a large book in front of him, his mouth an O-shape as he slowly sat down on the top stair. The door slammed behind her and she stood on the doorstep for a moment before shakily hurrying down the hill.

The salty taste of the sea came in on the breeze as she slipped by her old home place, not daring to look at it as she passed. Pulling up her hood, she hoped no one was watching her scurry away, or worse, that no one had heard Frankie's threat. She burned with indignation. As if she would ever harm a child! Not one person could say that about her. She loved kids. At the end of the road, she abruptly stopped, about-turned, and walked in the opposite direction of the village, all thoughts of a chipper dinner abandoned as her stomach churned.

What a mess this was. She was barely back and she was already causing ructions. She should just stay in her lane, as James used to advise her when she tried to talk to him about some of her ideas surrounding how she spent her time. Since they'd married, time had hung on her hands and she was desperate to do something, but somehow time had slipped by doing all the things James had wanted to do. Now he was gone, and she was stuck alone in that too big, too empty house where the rooms echoed . . . Her thoughts ran to design, as they often did, and she began thinking of how she could make Eyrie Lodge a home.

What the rooms needed were curtains to soften the sound. The windows had blinds that worked on a motor controlled by an app on her phone, but she still hadn't figured out how to use the app properly, so the blinds went up and down randomly, making her think that the house was haunted. The smooth sound of the motor and the swish of the movement in one of the rooms was enough to set her on edge. The only thing awaiting her return was a box of James's stuff that she'd shoved into the office. His personal files could wait. His watch collection and expensive cuff links . . . what was the point in looking at them? There was no one to pass them on to.

Picking up her pace, Ruby walked towards the harbour

and then past it. She wasn't wearing the right shoes, but it didn't matter. What mattered was the feeling of the wind in her hair, of moving forward towards something even if she didn't know what it was or where she was going. Within minutes, the back of her left leg began to ache, and a blister was forming on the ball of her foot. There was a bench outside the entrance to the cliff walk, so she hobbled towards it, hoping that there wouldn't be a blister, that the pain would subside and leave just a tender foot.

Settling on the bench, she slipped her foot out of her shoe and examined the ball of her foot. It was too dark to determine if there'd be a blister, so she slipped her shoe back on and leaned back just as the full moon came out from behind the slow-moving clouds. Tilting her face to the sky, she stared hard at the moon and made a face out of the grey and white moonscape. She resisted the urge to turn her money over in her pocket, as her mother always had done in the hope of doubling her luck in the year to come. Superstitions had been thrown out of her life long ago. James always said that you made your own luck. *It's easy to say that when you come from money and can afford to cut your losses, though.* The thought rambled unbridled into her head, and, red-faced, she immediately banished it. It wasn't James's fault that he was born into money, no more than it was her fault that she hadn't been. Having money had brought them together. He'd been considering buying the larger of the village's hotels – something he'd previously passed on – and she'd been working an extra shift when they'd met.

'If I hadn't changed my mind and come down to check

it out, on a whim,' he'd told her many times, 'and if you hadn't taken that extra shift – we'd never have met.'

'And you'd never have gotten your wallet back,' she'd say fondly.

'That's for sure,' he'd said. 'I was lucky it was you who found it. It was an honest thing you did. Not many people would do that.'

There had been a lot of money in it, Ruby remembered – too much for someone not to be worried about. At the time she'd thought it was someone's wages, or holiday money. Savings for a rainy day. It wasn't until she'd gotten to know James better that she realised he'd always carried a large amount of cash.

'Cash is king,' he'd always said. She still didn't quite understand what that meant, but she'd always smile and nod when he said it. She'd never carried cash on her, until the caterer for his funeral asked to be paid in cash. Then she'd had to figure out how to get it. She had her own bank account, into which James had transferred a modest monthly allowance, but she hadn't had enough to cover the funeral and the catering costs. Pamela had stepped in and helped her out until her inheritance tax and probate were sorted out.

In that moment, it had shocked her to the core that she'd become so dependent on him for everything in her life. Everything. She had no idea how to run their home; she didn't even know what day the bins went out as the housekeeper took care of all that stuff. Moving out and selling the Dublin property was the most stressful thing she'd ever done, and she didn't want to do anything like it again, ever. It was no wonder that she was thinner and haggard these days.

A man and a woman walked by her. The woman carried a bulging bag with both hands, and the man carried what looked like a spade. He smiled at her as he passed. Ruby's mouth dropped open – then she closed it quickly as she thought of James. But still, she couldn't take her eyes off the man. He was gorgeous. His smile felt as if it was just for her. His fleece stretched across his broad shoulders as he pushed a dark curl back from his eyes.

'Looks dodgy, but I promise you it's not,' he called to her, and waved the spade. 'Not burying bodies!'

The woman laughed and nudged him. 'Eoin, stop! Tripadvisor will be full of bad reviews – people will think we're a town of delinquents!'

'Speak for yourself.' Eoin laughed. The woman elbowed him again as they went through the fence towards the cliff walk.

Ruby watched them as they went. There was such camaraderie between them. What was that like? Getting up, she thought about taking the cliff walk too, but they might think she was a creep following them. Her blistered foot let her know that she wouldn't be able for the whole walk either, so she turned towards home, in no hurry to get there. Eoin's hearty laugh drifted back to her, and she smiled. She could listen to that sound all day.

6

Frankie

Frankie looked around at the motley crew gathered for the Moonlight Gardening Club. More had turned out than she thought would have. With it being Easter Sunday, she'd thought most of them would be home stuffed to the gills from the traditional lamb dinner and Easter eggs. But almost everyone had made it out tonight, and the lawn was busy with chatter. The garden was just through the entrance to the cliff walk. Just over a year ago three scraggy and awkwardly shaped acres had been donated to the townspeople. Old Mr Matthews, who owned the castle after which the village was named, had insisted that it was no longer of any use to him. The land was completely separate to the rest of his estate, he'd told them all, and would be better served in the hands of the community.

The community had pondered over how best to use the space, and it was by chance that they came across the notion of a Moonlight Garden. As it turned out, many of the people involved could only work in the garden during evening time and later into the night. That reminded one of the gardeners of an article she'd read about mental health and needing to be able to see the light at the end of the tunnel. Someone else had chimed in with information on how gardening was intrinsically linked to mental health too, and that wouldn't it be a great idea to create a Moonlight Garden – a place where they planted only plants that shone in the dark, scented the night-time air, and lit up dark nights so that those in need of seeing the light had somewhere beautiful to go, and the knowledge that they weren't alone.

Frankie now knew it had been Jürgen who'd made that suggestion, and she was grateful the committee had agreed with him. While there were members who came and gardened during the day, it was the Moonlight Gardeners who got the most out of the project. Daytime was too harsh for people sometimes. It was under the soft moonlight that they tended to come and sit, and work, in the garden, gaining companionship and solace in the calm and centred space. Most of the members were now regulars, and new or part-time gardeners were always welcome. So far it was a roaring success, and Frankie loved it with a passion.

Frankie shuffled on her spot. When Aggie had gotten sick, she'd insisted Frankie do something to get her out of the house and had more or less harangued her into joining the group. 'You'll be getting fresh air, and exercise, and sure you're only down the road if I need you, so don't be worrying about me,' she'd said. 'The club needs new members, and it'll do you the world of good.'

Now, Frankie felt she knew the underlying motive

behind Aggie's insistence she join the gardening group. There was enormous pleasure in seeing your physical and sometimes hard work blossom throughout the year. Things you thought were dead suddenly burst into life. The connection she felt to the earth when she ploughed her hands into the soil zinged through her, bringing her back to herself in ways she hadn't realised she needed. All her frustration and grief could be taken out on the earth.

As well as having lost her grandmother, she had recently been feeling anew the loss of the future she'd planned before Dillon came along. She'd wanted to be a counsellor, but had had to drop out of her degree when she got pregnant. She could apply what she'd learned in her two years in university to her job at the hotel, but apparently management didn't care much for half degrees. They didn't value what she could bring to them, and it seemed there was nothing she could do to change their minds. If she had her way, she'd be back in university finishing her degree and then get a well-paid job and make sure Dillon had his chance in university too. He would be the first in his father's family to not go out to fish, and Frankie was grateful for that.

Frankie picked at her nail as she looked around, her eyes catching on Jürgen. To be honest, the continued success of their club was all down to him. He was the glue that held everyone together. He spent a lot of his time tending the garden, and rallying the club members into action. Frankie tried to remember when he'd arrived in the village, but couldn't. He owned a small shop that they all called the Angel Shop, which sold crystals and essential oils and the like, but he spent most of his time in his own garden or at the Moonlight Garden. It was as if he had always lived there. Not a day went by without someone popping in to see him for a chat or some of his sage-like advice.

Jürgen used to come and work alongside her when she'd first come to the garden. He'd start a chat and they'd work side by side companionably. Once, he'd commented that she seemed to prefer the no-dig method of gardening, as it turned up no unruly wildflower seeds, and she'd known he was no longer talking about gardening, but about her lack of willingness to talk about herself and her problems. Jürgen rarely said something like that without intention, but she hadn't taken the bait. The seeds she'd buried deep in her heart were better left in the dark where the light wouldn't help them to grow. She didn't have the time to think about the should've, would've, could've beens of her life, even if she wanted to. No, somehow life seemed more manageable when memories remained buried.

In general, Frankie didn't mind most of Jürgen's mad feel-better activities. Usually, they did make you feel better. But tonight, spending half an hour doing laughing yoga was not a prospect she was enamoured with. Shaking her hair, she pulled it into a low ponytail and rolled her eyes. There was no point in going home, though. She'd asked Valerie's eldest, Katie, to babysit, and had helped her with her English homework in return, and was really looking forward to the gardening after the group activity. The garden already looked lovely in the dusky sunset, and tonight there was a full moon so it would look truly spectacular. It wouldn't be long before the stars sparkled down on them all and the garden worked its magic. She couldn't wait to breathe in the jasmine and daphnes while the quiet night stilled her mind and restless soul.

A splutter from Josie, one of the owners of The Birds, the local pub, made her turn her head away from the starry sky.

'Oh, crap. It's that laughing yoke tonight. I'd forgotten,' Josie said. 'I'm not able for this, not after all the chocolate . . .' She pushed up the sleeves of her long-sleeved organic cotton top.

'I feel like an Easter egg.' Her partner, May, joined her. She patted her midriff. 'Why did we let Jürgen talk us into this?'

'Just don't fart when you're in downward dog,' Josie instructed.

'Me? I never – it's you we need to be upwind from.' May snorted, her dark eyes flashing with humour. 'And you had cabbage last night.'

'Well don't tell everyone.' Josie glared, then waved Sandra over to them.

'How are ye, ladies?' Sandra smiled. She zipped up her pink fleece, which matched her lovely pink cheeks, and a strand of blonde wavy hair caught in the zip. Tugging it out, she looked around. 'All set?'

'You could say so,' May said. 'Where's Val? She said she'd be here.'

Sandra shuffled closer. 'John is after calling in for a *chat*.' She air-quoted the word.

May shook her head. Frowning, she said, 'Honestly, I don't understand what he was at, playing away and then being so bloody awkward about everything.'

'She told you, then?' Sandra said sadly.

'She did,' Josie said. 'I can't believe it. They were great together and now he's got another woman. It's all wrong.'

'I know,' Sandra said. 'I know she's my sister, and I try my best to help her, but she's not listening to me these days. Keeps telling me that this is a midlife crisis he's going through. Midlife crisis me hole! He's wanting to have his Easter egg and eat it, too.'

'Preach,' Josie said solemnly.

May pulled a face and looked at her. 'I'm sorry, what now?'

'Preach,' Josie said again. 'It's what all the kids say when you're saying something spot on.'

'Oh, for the love of God.' May rolled her eyes and called over to Frankie. 'Is this true?'

Frankie laughed. 'I'm not quite one of the kids,' she said. 'But I think so.'

May shook her head comically. 'I don't know.' She laughed. 'I give up!'

There was a rustling as everyone turned to face Jürgen, who had just walked through the gates. A tall, lithe man with long locks of silky dark blond wavy hair, his youthful air belied his age of sixty. His face was barely lined, and only his eyes gave him away. When he was alone, they seemed sad, as if he was looking into the past and adding up his regrets, Frankie thought, but tonight they sparkled.

The woman next to Frankie immediately fluffed her hair, and the woman on her other side straightened her posture. Frankie's lips twisted into a smile that she tried to hide. In the year since she'd joined the group she'd watched both men and women preen before Jürgen but, in all that time, Jürgen seemed immune to any attempts at flirting. He was passionate about the garden and people's wellbeing, and his intensity when answering the questions they asked, whether about plants or wellbeing, seemed to fan the flames. On more than one occasion he'd completely missed a blatant invitation to go home with someone while somehow managing to make the inviter feel even more special than before.

Jürgen clapped his strong, tanned hands and smiled at the small group.

'Ah lads, it's so good to see so many of you turn up for this wonderful experience. I promise you – you'll go home . . .' he paused and tilted his head towards the group expectantly. A well-trained team, they obliged by finishing his sentence: '. . . feeling better.' He laughed again, a deep belly laugh that made Frankie grin. No one she knew laughed like Jürgen did.

Despite her misgivings, she resolved to try and enjoy the laughing yoga session he'd organised. She hadn't a clue what it entailed, but she'd never gone home feeling worse than when she'd come out to the gardening club, and Jürgen was partly the reason. The other reason was that she could come and create a garden with people who loved the project as much as she did. Someone always knew something about a new plant, or how to prune this, or propagate that. She wished she could participate more with cutting and seedlings, but her back garden was tiny. Every time she'd splashed out on one of those mini green-houses from Lidl, the wind had picked it up and hurled it around the small space as if it was a tornado, scattering compost and seed trays all over the place. That was the joy of living up on a hill by the coast: spectacular sea view, absolute rubbish for her garden.

A small, curvy woman with a huge smile ambled through the gate and stood next to Jürgen. His arm went easily around her shoulders and Frankie laughed quietly as the woman's smile got brighter. Clearly, she was as enamoured with Jürgen as the rest of the women in the club were. The men in the group sighed and sucked in their bellies. Jürgen hugged the woman closer to him.

'You might laugh at this, but laughing yoga isn't about yoga at all.' Jürgen smiled around at everyone. 'Like yoga, it uses breathing and movement, but unlike yoga, that breathing and movement is used to deliberately create intentional laughter. I know you're all dying to know why laughter is so important. Well, it not only makes us feel good but also inhibits cortisol – the stress hormone – and helps our immune system while giving our abdominals a decent workout. So, with that in mind, I know you'll all warmly welcome Grace of Amazing Grace Yoga,' he said as he gave Grace another squeezy hug. 'She's travelled all around the world with her practice. This evening she's going to remind us how important laughter is in our lives and give us tips on how to incorporate more laughter on a day-to-day basis.'

Frankie glanced at the men, who sucked their bellies in even more. The women shuffled and laughed nervously. 'Like anything will sort out this menopausal mess,' one of them muttered. Jürgen smiled and walked over to her. Standing directly in front of her, he placed his hands on her shoulders. Even in the deepening shadows, Frankie could see the woman blush.

'I'll partner up with you, Maura.' He smiled down at her. Lifting his eyes, he called over to Grace. 'I'll leave it in your capable hands, Grace.'

Grace nodded and encouraged everyone to find a partner. Frankie faced Sandra, wishing they'd all hurry up, when the woman who'd brought Dillon home – Ruby, had he said? – came through the gate. The woman stopped in her tracks. Her mouth dropped open as she took in the scene. Frankie frowned. What in the name of all that was holy was she doing here? The woman raised a hand to her face, then tucked a strand of hair behind her ear. She looked tired, as if she hadn't slept in a while, Frankie conceded. And a little nervous too. Her hands were jittery, as if she didn't know quite what to do. She took a step backwards as if to go, but Jürgen was already at her side.

'Hello, I'm Jürgen.' He smiled. 'Welcome to the Moonlight Gardening Club. We're so glad you found us. Come in and we'll get started.'

The woman shook her head and looked like she wanted to sprint away. Jürgen ignored her. 'It's always lovely to have new members of the club; there's plenty of gardening to go around. Many hands make for light work.'

Frankie watched with interest. The woman frowned. She scanned the group, her frown deepening when her eyes met Frankie's. She seemed to shrink under her gaze. Frankie swallowed. Maybe she'd been a little cruel the other night; she'd overreacted out of embarrassment and worry when she hadn't even known what was going on. If Dillon's account was true, then the woman had actually been very nice. And she had brought him back home straight away. Dillon said she'd known a lot about bees, and that she'd always wanted a hive, like her own mother had once.

'She could beeeeee my auntie.' He'd giggled at his joke. Then more seriously he'd said, 'And I don't have an auntie, so I might ask her to be my auntie.'

'You do have an aunt,' Frankie had told him. 'You have Auntie Paula.' She thought of Paula, his aunt on his father's side. They hadn't heard from her since Christmas, but that was Paula. They'd never gotten on, and Frankie had been glad when Paula had finally moved away to her husband's home place after Liam's mother died.

Frankie looked at the woman again. What she should have done was thank her for bringing Dillon home safely. Frankie sucked in her bottom lip. She hated being wrong, but it was hard to accept help, especially from a stranger. Rolling her head back, she stretched her arms up to the sky, groaning as her muscles ached. She'd had a particularly gruelling day. Dillon had woken well before seven, just as the sun was rising, and had been at warp speed since then. Eating two Easter eggs hadn't helped, she thought, but he never got treats so she'd indulged him. Valerie had asked her and Dillon over for dinner, but she'd declined. Easter was like Christmas in Valerie's house, and Frankie knew that money was tight for Valerie after her husband had skedaddled off with another woman. She didn't need to be scrimping to pull together a meal for two extra mouths.

Frankie picked at a hangnail. Valerie had understood when she'd turned down dinner but had still issued the invitation a second and third time. She probably should have gone to Val's but she was fine on her own – she didn't need to rely on anyone else.

When people had asked her if she'd wanted help after Aggie's death, she'd refused. She didn't want help. All she wanted was some time and maybe a small lottery win, and other than that, sure, wasn't she fine? There wasn't a bother on her now. She'd managed to get this far, and she'd manage to keep going – 'just keep swimming,' as Dory the fish said in *Finding Nemo*. *Keep your sunny side out*, she thought as the group quietened when Jürgen began talking again.

Frankie bristled as she watched the woman still hovering uncertainly beside the gate. She was woefully dressed in linen trousers and a shirt with a jumper thrown around her shoulders. Frankie brushed down the dust from the front of her cosy fleece. Ruby, if that was her name, wouldn't last long in that rig-out, she thought as Jürgen glanced in Frankie's direction. Shaking her head slightly, Frankie's frown deepened. She was in no humour for Jürgen and his pushing people out of their comfort zones tonight. With a huge sense of relief, she smiled as Jürgen skipped by her. She turned away from Ruby's pinched face. She certainly didn't need to be dealing with this woman barging into the Moonlight Garden during her downtime. Thank goodness Jürgen seemed to have noticed her reluctance to partner up with Ruby, Frankie thought as she rubbed her arms; at least she wouldn't be forced into small talk with a woman who'd managed to make her feel like a bold child in one swift move.

7

Ruby

Ruby gaped at the collection of people gathered in a semicircle on the lawn of the Moonlight Garden. She'd only come down to the garden out of curiosity, dying to know what exactly the handsome man had been doing with his shovel the other night. Now she was rightly caught out. The garden was filled with people, and they all stared at her as a strange, tall, vaguely familiar-looking man loped over to her, his hands outspread to welcome her – or attack her, she wasn't sure which. Shrinking back from him, Ruby pointed to the gate as if to leave, but he had reached her by then, and taken her hand in his. Without further ado, he pulled her through the gate and led her towards the group, introducing people here and there. He looked around. His gaze landed on Frankie for a moment and Ruby experienced a thrill of dismay at the thought that he might make them be partners, but seeing that Frankie was paired up already he moved on.

Ruby looked around, her breath slightly clouding in front of her as the evening grew a little chilly.

The garden was really quite beautiful. Deep green shrubs grew in mounds and threw shadows across the lawn, but those shadows were lit by warm white flowers. Creamy daffodils danced in the April breeze, and on closer inspection, she saw the shrubs were dotted with tiny, star-like flowers, lifting the darkness. They gave off the most intense fragrance that mingled with the light champagne scent of a large thriving magnolia tree. Ruby touched a waxy magnolia petal, feeling a slight smile bloom on her lips. Magnolias had always been one of her favourite trees, and this one, in full flight, was a joy to behold. Its branches reached right into the sky, its blooms mingled with the stars, and Ruby felt lifted by its very presence. Clusters of daisy-like flowers rambled around the base of the tree, leading her eye to a wide-branched shrub heavily laden with white blooms like diamonds on green velvet. A neat, lichen-covered statue of the Three Graces snuggled in the undergrowth as if it was growing too, so perfectly did it sit amongst the green and white. A glowing border wrapped the lawn, leading Ruby's gaze to a bench where beds had been cleared.

The sky darkened with every minute as the sun set, but the flowers glowed under the bright rising moon. Ruby longed to see what it would be like later, when it was truly night. She almost forgot she was in company, the garden had captured her completely, and she only startled back to reality when Jürgen's voice interrupted her garden-gazing.

'Unfortunately, it looks as if everyone has a partner.'

Jürgen frowned. 'But I'm thinking you could join a couple. Would that work, Grace?'

'Sorry I'm late.' A deep voice boomed as the gate clanged shut. Jürgen's frown disappeared. He clapped his hands as Eoin joined the group.

'Eoin, just in the nick of time,' Jürgen said. 'This is . . . ?' He turned to Ruby with an inquisitive glance.

'Ruby.' Her voice was barely a whisper. A bubble of anxiety burst in her stomach. Eoin was the gorgeous man she'd seen carrying the shovel the other night.

'Ruby, lovely to meet you. This is Eoin. You can partner up with him for the session.'

Someone behind Ruby tutted. 'Oh, for the love of God, can we just get on with this?' The woman huffed and turned her back on the newly formed pair. 'We'll be here all night.'

'Don't mind her,' Eoin said, taking Ruby's hand. 'We're a friendly bunch, I promise.'

Ruby darted a glance at Frankie to see if she'd noticed, but Frankie seemed to be studiously ignoring her. Ruby couldn't blame her. She'd probably do the same if she was in her position. Suddenly, fully aware that Eoin was holding her hand, she felt a heat in her chest. His hand was warm and rough, his touch quietly firm. She swallowed and prayed he wouldn't notice her sweaty palm, but his full attention was focused on Grace as she began to instruct the session. Within seconds, Eoin had dropped her hand as Grace had everyone tapping their bodies up and down, from ankles to stomach, hands to chest. Ruby surreptitiously wiped her palm on her linen trousers, deeply aware of how inappropriately dressed she was. Everyone else was in leggings and fleeces, or, as in Eoin's case, clothing favoured by outdoorsy men. His clothes reminded Ruby of James's hiking gear, only Eoin's khaki multi-pocketed trousers were smeared with mud and were well-worn.

'Start at your hands,' Grace called out cheerily, pulling Ruby's attention away from Eoin and back to the task at hand. 'Work your way up your arms and back down again – that's it, keep going . . . now work across your shoulder, your chest . . . Smile!'

'This feels ridiculous,' Ruby muttered. She looked around the group at everyone as everyone looked around too. 'What's it supposed to do?'

'Dunno.' Eoin panted as he bent over to tap his way up and down his legs.

Ruby whispered. 'It's . . . a little weird.'

'I won't argue with you there.' Eoin shot her a grin. 'But we might as well give it a go.'

Ruby wrinkled her nose, then glanced over at Frankie and Sandra. They were grinning from ear to ear and tapping themselves quicker and quicker. Every now and then Sandra would giggle, and Frankie chuckle as if she couldn't stop herself. Ruby tapped her arms harder, her brows knitting together as she tried to figure out what all this tapping was supposed to do. James would have sneered at this craziness, she thought, and there was no way he'd have allowed himself – or her – to be roped into it in the first place. She wished with all her might she hadn't given in to her curiosity and gone down to the garden. The place was full of lunatics, by the looks of things.

'Swap partners with the pair to your left!' Grace called suddenly.

70

Sandra immediately snaffled Eoin, leaving Frankie and Ruby standing face to face. Frankie's smile dulled. Ruby resisted the urge to roll her eyes, then wondered what on earth was making her feel so sassy. It wasn't like her to be mean, but all the same, it wasn't as if she had kidnapped Dillon; she had literally been returning him! If Frankie couldn't see that then that was her problem.

Ruby set her mouth into a firm line, ignoring Grace's instructions to smile, although it was hard to do so when everyone else was beginning to grin and giggle. A niggle stirred inside her and she found herself speaking before realising it.

'Listen,' she said. 'I'd like to apologise—'

'No,' Frankie said, interrupting her as they swung their arms like windmills. 'I understand your reaction now. It's horrible and frightening to find a complete stranger in your home.' She said the final sentence pointedly, and Ruby sighed. Clearly Frankie was not in the mood to accept her apology.

Ruby nodded, determined to be the bigger person. 'About as horrible and frightening to find that your son has gone missing, I'd say.' The whole conversation was crazy. Here they were, apologising and swinging their arms like children. They must look ridiculous. A slight smile whispered on her face, and she quickly doused it out, but not quickly enough. The corners of Frankie's lips lifted slightly.

'Yeah,' Frankie said. 'That wasn't the best moment.'

'Now laugh!' Grace called out. 'Even if you don't feel like it – do it. Our brains are amazing organs but your mind doesn't know the difference between forced laughter and real laughter. Making yourself laugh is a trick you can pull to cheer yourself up.'

Ruby grimaced. 'I think I've forgotten how to laugh. It's been that long.'

'I've had years of Dillon's terrible home-grown jokes, so I should be an expert at this,' Frankie said, her voice a touch more friendly now. 'I can tell you one if you want any help?'

Ruby smiled. 'He tells jokes?'

'Badly,' Frankie said. 'Here's one: What do you call a fly without wings?'

Ruby shook her head. 'I don't know.'

'A walk!' Frankie started to laugh. 'Told you they were bad, but he thinks they're hilarious. He'd find this hysterical too. If he was here, he'd be right in the thick of it, probably up there with Grace, bellowing laughter.'

Ruby began to smile. She could totally see Dillon in the middle of things, holding his little round belly and laughing. In the short walk from her house to Frankie's cottage, he'd shown himself to be a real live wire, full of chatter and giggles, and finding the weirdest things interesting and funny. Ruby had learned more about moths in those ten minutes than she needed to know, and he'd told her about the game he'd made up one night in his room. Her lips twitched thinking of it.

'He's a dote,' she said to Frankie as they continued swinging their arms in time to Grace's swooshing sounds. 'He told me about his Super Insect Man game. What a fantastic imagination he has.'

Frankie snorted. 'That he does,' she said. 'Did he tell you that he was wearing his underpants on his head too so that his eyes peeped out of the leg holes?'

'No!' Ruby sniggered.

'It gets worse.' Frankie laughed for real. 'He made me do it too, so the pair of us were leaping around the room, screeching as we saved the world, when our neighbour Jimmy knocked on the door with a parcel that had gone to his house by an accident. And I stuck my head out of the window, with the pants on . . .'

Ruby looked at her, a huge grin on her face. So that's where Dillon got his *by an accident* line from.

'I was mortified,' Frankie laughed. 'But sure, what was I to do?'

Ruby began to laugh, shyly at first, then with more gusto as Frankie joined in. Tears rolled down her face and she bent forward to hold her sides. Wiping her face, she caught Eoin from the corner of her eye. He was creased with laughter, and wiping tears from his eyes. He looked so at ease that she smiled, and laughed again, surprised at how natural it was beginning to feel.

'That's too funny,' she gasped. 'I love it!'

When she finally calmed down, she stood up and caught Frankie looking at her with a slight frown.

'Listen,' Frankie began. 'I wouldn't have called the guards.'

'Thanks,' Ruby said as the volume of the group increased around them. 'I appreciate you saying that.'

'Now, well done!' Grace beamed around the group. 'I want you to pretend you're pushing a lawnmower – move around, keep laughing – and when you pass someone you need to pull that cord on that lawnmower engine – rev it up! Go!'

The pairs separated and Ruby watched as Eoin made

his way around the garden. Chuckling, he pushed his imaginary lawnmower over to her, and paused as she passed him to yank the imaginary engine cord. Ruby jumped back and, genuinely amused now, pulled on her imaginary engine cord. Eoin grinned at her, delighted, then moved away to continue on his laughing lawnmower journey. Ruby burst out laughing. He made it look easy! She began scooting around the garden, pulling on her cord as she passed other gardeners. Everyone was red-faced and laughing. Even Sandra, who was a tough one to crack, was glowing with laughter. Grace motored past, yanking her imaginary cord and bearing a huge grin. Then she swivelled into the centre of the lawn.

'You guys are naturals,' she called out as she began to sway from side to side. 'I want you all to come together and create a circle. Lie down, heads to the inside of the circle, and laugh as long as you need to.'

Ruby stood back and watched as the group all shuffled into a circle, then they lay down, quieter now with the occasional chortle or snort of laughter. Frankie lay down, her red curls, now loose from her ponytail, fanned around her. Ruby somehow found herself lying down on Frankie's right side, while Eoin navigated his way to Ruby's other side. A softly laughing Jürgen lay to Frankie's left. The group giggled on and off as the sky above them darkened, with the occasional outburst of laughter that made everyone else laugh too.

Gradually, everyone quietened down, and the mood became peaceful and contented. Beside her, Frankie took a deep breath in and let it out slowly. Ruby stared up at the sky. The constellations were already clear. She could make out Orion and Cassiopeia, but couldn't think of the names of the others that she thought she recognised. With a shuddering breath, Ruby realised she was crying. Warm tears trickled down the side of her face into her hair. Trying to stifle her tears, she turned her head to the side and found Frankie's solemn eyes watching her.

'Are you okay?' Frankie whispered.

Ruby nodded. 'I will be.'

Frankie nodded and turned back to the stars. Ruby turned her eyes to the heavens and placed her hand over her heart. Would she ever not feel lonely? Was there any hope for her now James was gone? The last eighteen months had felt like an eternity. How would she manage to live on without him? Ruby lay there, waiting for her mind to stop asking impossible questions. The scents and sounds of the garden began to push them away. Something was shuffling in the shrubs near her feet, and she pictured a family of hedgehogs.

What could have been minutes or hours later, she heard others around her begin to shift and sit up. Pushing herself up as well, she smoothed back her hair and groaned. The ground beneath her had grown a little chilly, and damp. Slowly members were getting up, creaking and complaining a little about sore knees and hips that needed replacing. Her calf was aching with a stiffness she didn't recognise, and she massaged it absentmindedly. On her other side, Eoin had sprung to his feet as if he was a teenager. He offered his hand to her, and she hesitated for a split second before taking it.

It's just a kind gesture, she told herself as she wiped down her trousers, *a friendly one. It doesn't mean anything*. But still she blushed as he smiled down at her. Her stomach clenched as she glanced behind him for Frankie, but she was already striding towards the sheds. Eoin folded his arms. Ruby took him in. His fleece jacket clung neatly to his shoulders and his midriff, where she was sure there would be no flab to be found. When he pushed up his sleeves she almost gasped aloud. His arms were tanned and muscly and had that dusting of dark hair that she'd always thought was so sexy on a man. Ruby swallowed. He was so handsome, but so much younger than she – he had to be. His dark hair had a few streaks of grey – not enough to make him the same age as she was, she concluded, but enough to show that he wasn't what Pamela would call 'a baby'. She shook herself: what was she doing thinking of another man in this way, flirting with a strange, *younger* man?

'Are you glad you came down to the Moonlight Gardening Club?' he asked, flicking a strand of hair back from his face.

'I didn't know it was a gardening club,' Ruby said. 'I just wondered what was in here, you know, besides the entrance to the cliff walk.'

'Ah.' He smiled. 'And there I was thinking you were one of us.'

'One of us?' Ruby's eyebrows raised.

'A gardener,' he said. 'We're not all professionals, most of us just enjoy it as a hobby. Me, however, I got lucky – I'm a landscape gardener and I get to do this too. Best of both worlds. What about you? Are you a gardener too?'

'Not really,' Ruby said. 'Although I do appreciate landscaped spaces. I just never had the time to get into it.' She shoved her hands into her pockets. That was a lie, she acknowledged. She'd had plenty of time, only it was always filled with other things – things that were approved by James. He'd never liked finding her in the garden, nor sketching. They were pastimes for old fogies as far as he was concerned. Within a few months of their wedding Ruby had packed away her pencil case and had relegated the gardening tools to the shed. James had told her that her spare time was better spent training at the gym, getting fit for the hikes he dragged her on. He'd signed her up for tennis lessons and swimming lessons, embarrassed that she wasn't proficient in both sports already.

'Listen.' Eoin tilted his head. 'Most people hang around here and do some tidying up after a session.'

'Oh,' Ruby murmured. Then she noticed that almost everyone was gardening while softly talking to each other. The shed lights were blazing, and Frankie seemed to be inspecting a pair of shears. 'I didn't know.'

'Well, you're a newbie.' Eoin smiled at her. 'Jürgen looks busy, so would you like me to show you around, tell you a little about the place?'

Ruby clenched her hands in her pockets. The whole evening hadn't gone as she'd expected and she was exhausted by everything. She stifled the yawn that threatened to give her away. She hadn't been sleeping well lately.

'Maybe the next time,' she said, longing for her own space and some quiet. 'I think I'll just head home.'

'I'll walk you,' Eoin said. 'If that's okay? It's on my way anyway.'

'Aren't you staying to help?' Ruby's eyes widened.

77

'Nah.' Eoin grinned. 'I've done my bit this week. Got to leave some work for the others or else they'll give out.'

'Okay, sure,' Ruby said. 'That's kind of you.'

She followed Eoin out of the Moonlight Garden, pausing to look back at the hive of people pottering away pulling weeds or digging soil. Frankie was still in the shed, and Ruby felt a pang of guilt. Though they'd both made steps towards apologising, she wished they could have buried the hatchet completely.

Just then, the moon glided from the clouds and illuminated the garden as it encircled the group, holding the gardeners in a verdant embrace. With a sigh, Ruby slipped away through the gates, wondering if she'd be brave enough to return.

8

Frankie

Without meaning to, Frankie found herself behind Eoin and Ruby on the path. She'd been unable to shake a melancholy that had settled into her after seeing Ruby's distress. She abandoned any notions of gardening, longing instead to be at home with her arms around her little boy. Eoin and Ruby walked stiffly ahead of her, seemingly unaware she was behind them. Ruby took short steps, Frankie noticed, as if she was waiting for Eoin to take the lead. Half wishing she was a fly on the wall to their conversation, Frankie reluctantly turned away and hurried up the laneway to the cottage, her hands clenched tight, her thumb rubbing her engagement ring. There was a deepening chill in the air that she didn't like. It reminded her too much of the night she and Liam had argued. Pushing the memory away, she plastered a smile on her face and slipped in the front door of the cottage just as the first splashes of rain began to fall.

Dillon and Katie were cuddled under a blanket on the

couch, going through the library book Maggie had given Dillon. Katie unfurled herself and stood up. She tucked the blanket around Dillon, and gave Frankie a smile.

'He's been as good as gold,' she said. 'Even taught me the difference between dragonflies and damsels. I didn't even know what a damsel was.'

'As long as it's not a damsel in distress, we should be good,' Frankie said. Katie looked at her blankly, and Frankie shook her head. 'Bad joke – don't worry about it.'

Katie nodded. She picked up her schoolbag and began packing away her books. 'Thanks for the help earlier,' she said. 'And I forgot to tell you this: my teacher said there's a huge improvement in my essays. I didn't tell her you were tutoring me.'

'Ah, I'm so pleased,' said Frankie, beaming.

'Oh, and Mam said to tell you she's doing a stir-fry with the leftover lamb tomorrow if you and Dillon want to come for dinner.'

Frankie bit the inside of her cheek. There wasn't much in the house to eat; she should take Valerie up on the offer, if only for Dillon's sake.

'Thanks, Katie. Tell your mam we'll be down.' Frankie gripped her hands tightly behind her back. Valerie meant well, but it stung Frankie to depend on her so much. But if it wasn't for Valerie she'd never have spotted the mould in Aggie's room until it was too late.

Frankie thought back to the evening when Valerie had called in with a lasagne and a bunch of pink roses, Aggie's favourite, from her garden, brushing aside Frankie's protestations and declarations that she could make herself and

Dillon a decent dinner. Valerie had come straight into the hallway, then wrinkled her freckled nose and said something about a musty smell.

'I don't know what it is,' Frankie had told her. 'It's horrible these last few days. The bins are empty. I bleached them all. The bathroom is scrubbed but the whole bloody place is reeking.'

'It smells like mould,' Valerie had said sagely. 'You'd want to get it sorted sooner rather than later. It won't be pleasant in the winter.'

Frankie had groaned. 'I think I know where it is.'

Together they'd gone into Agnes's room, and sure enough, the wall behind Aggie's bed had been black with mould. Splodges speckled the top corner behind the old wardrobe, blooming like painted fireworks on the wall.

'Looks like it's been here a while,' Valerie had said. 'Didn't Agnes tell you?'

'I didn't know about any of this.' Frankie's eyes had filled with tears. 'She never said a word. She must've been cleaning it all herself in secret. Looking back, I should've noticed something – we got through a bottle of bleach every week.'

'You'll have to get it taken care of as it can be dangerous for your health.'

'Seriously?' Frankie's heart had dropped. She'd taken a step towards the bedroom door.

'Yeah, it can affect your lungs – something to do with mould spores and it getting into you.' Valerie had scrunched up her face. 'Come on, I'll give you a hand to clean this away tonight, but you'll have to get a professional in.'

Frankie had nodded. Valerie was already in the kitchen,

her head under the kitchen sink pulling out the basin and a bottle of bleach. 'Rags,' she'd called out. 'Ones you won't use again because they'll be going straight into the bin.' She'd hunkered down and rubbed her forehead with the back of her hand. 'Agnes wasn't afraid of a bit of work, so we won't be either.'

Now, standing in the sitting room, Frankie smiled at the memory of that day. Valerie had helped Frankie more than she knew, with her good humour and banter they'd washed the walls down with scalding hot bleach water. In no time the whole place had smelled like a hospital, which was preferable to the mouldy dampness of before. Ever since, Frankie had cleaned it once a week.

Watching Katie as she said goodnight to Dillon, Frankie was struck by how lucky she was. Katie was cast from the same die as her mother. Kindness was in her every action, and like Valerie, she saw when people needed help or wanted to be left alone. Accepting the offer of dinner would be good for Valerie, Frankie realised as she closed the front door behind Katie: it would make Valerie feel that she was doing something nice. But after that, she'd have to take no for an answer. There was no way she could ever repay Valerie, so it was better for everyone if she just got back on her feet and tried harder to provide for herself and Dillon alone. That was another Aggie trait she'd inherited, Frankie supposed: her desire to be independent and not ask for anything from anyone. 'There's no such thing as a free lunch' was one of Aggie's favourite sayings, and the longer Frankie managed alone, the more she applied it to her life.

The only thing she could give back to the community

was her time, knowledge and strength in the Moonlight Garden, and it wasn't enough to pay back all the wonderful things the gardening crew had done for her the last few months.

Take Eoin for example, Frankie thought as she washed up the few cups in the kitchen sink. He'd arrived at her door the last weekend in December with a small but beautiful evergreen tree. He'd bundled it through the door and set it up, lights and all, beside the stove, ignoring Frankie's protestations. 'Aggie always kept Christmas,' he'd said as she'd watched him in awe. 'She wouldn't want you two sitting without a tree at this time of year.' Frankie remembered how the warm pine smell had filled the house when he'd gone, and how he'd come back the first week in January to take it away for her just as she had been wondering how she was going to dispose of it. What was she going to do to pay him back for that kindness? Nothing, because she had nothing to give him, she thought miserably. And he really was a good man. He deserved to be paid back. Ruby was lucky to have him as her neighbour.

With a sigh, Frankie pulled herself back to the present, where Dillon was yawning and trying to stay awake on the couch.

'Come on, you.' She tweaked his toes where they peeped out from beneath the blanket. 'Bedtime for little monkeys.'

Following him up the stairs, Frankie decided she'd go to bed herself. That way she wouldn't have to think too much, or sit in the rapidly cooling living room. Hopefully the weather would pick up and she'd be able to stop lighting the fire every evening to try to warm the place up – that would save a bit of money. As if on cue, a roll of thunder crashed outside.

'Did you hear that, Mammy?' Dillon stuck his head out of the bathroom, his mouth foaming with toothpaste. 'It was right over us.' His eyes were wide.

'It sure is right over us,' Frankie said. 'I think I might just come to bed now. What do you think?'

Dillon's eyes gleamed. 'Does that mean I can sleep with you in your bed?'

'Yes, so get a wiggle on!' Frankie laughed as he did a wiggly dance back into the bathroom. Dillon jiggled his toothbrush around his mouth, missing more teeth than he was brushing.

'I can't wait to tell Ava,' he mumbled. 'She never gets to sleep with her mammy.'

'Is that right?' Frankie sat on the edge of the bath and nodded at him to hurry.

'Yup.' Dillon pulled the foamy toothbrush from his mouth. 'And neither does Ben. Poor things.'

Frankie stifled a grin. Ben and Ava were his only friends at school. Maybe they could sleep over one night, she pondered as he rinsed his toothbrush and scrubbed his face dry with a towel. Ruffling his hair, she smiled, glad he was as happy to snuggle down with her as she was with him. Stormy nights always made her sad, and tonight she didn't want to be alone. With some cajoling, she soon managed to get Dillon tucked up in her bed. Then she ran down to the kitchen to fill their hot water bottle. Outside the rain sluiced down the drainpipes, sounding eerie and ghostly. Shivering, Frankie locked up the house and headed up to bed. An early night never did anyone any harm.

9

Ruby

Ruby arrived at the gate to her house with Eoin still by her side. He was soft-mannered and very good at small talk, she thought to herself as they slowed down, but she could hear the questions in his voice and prayed he wouldn't ask them.

'Well, that was kind of you,' Ruby said. 'I hope I didn't put you too much out of your way?'

'Not an inch,' Eoin said. He pointed to the small house next door. 'That's me there.'

Ruby laughed, delighted despite herself to find out that they were neighbours. 'Maybe a few inches out of your way. Thanks anyway, Eoin.'

A splash of rain landed on her cheek and she looked out to sea where a blaze of sheet lightning flashed across the sky, and the stars slowly began to disappear as clouds rolled in. She held out her hand as heavy raindrops began to fall.

'You'd better get in,' Eoin said, sounding reluctant to see her go. 'It looks like it's about to lash.'

Nodding, Ruby punched in the gate code and slipped through the gates.

'Ruby?' Eoin's voice carried over to her.

Her name on his tongue made her stop.

'Don't be afraid to call me if you need anything,' he said as the sky rumbled above them.

The skin on her neck prickled. She could tell this strong, kind man that the love of her life had passed away, leaving her alone and struggling to get through each day. She could tell him that she really did appreciate his kind offer of help, more than he could ever know, but her throat tightened and the words wouldn't come. Eventually, she just called, 'Thanks, I'll keep that in mind.'

The sky lit up again with lightning.

'Goodnight, Eoin. Thanks again for walking me back.' The gravel crunched as she walked towards the house.

Upstairs, she flung her bag onto the kitchen island. She picked at her nail polish while walking through the rooms. Making a loop, she turned on a few lamps, returned to the kitchen, opened the fridge, and poured a large glass of wine.

Sidling up to the balcony windows, Ruby glanced out into the darkness. She took a deep breath in, holding it until her lungs tightened, then she released it in a fast and cathartic whoosh. The dark sea crashed and roiled against the cliffs beyond the beaches. Large, heavy drops of rain splashed down, turning into a downpour. Ruby leaned her forehead against the glass and closed her eyes. Unbidden, she wondered if Eoin had gotten indoors before it started. The rain splattered against the glass, and Ruby jolted back. Taking her wine, she wandered into the sitting room and sat down on the oversized armchair closest to the window. Outside, the wind gathered and across the bay the sea crashed against the cliffs higher than she'd ever seen before.

The Moonlight Garden would take a battering, she thought as the storm strengthened. Lightning flickered, followed by a crash of thunder. The lamplight wavered. James would've loved this. The threat of losing electricity always excited him. Not so Ruby. Lighting a candle just in case, she shivered. He'd have had something to say about Eoin, for sure.

If he'd been there this evening, he'd have made sure to mark her as his with the slightest of movements. A hand on the small of her back, a slightly raised shoulder to the suitor, a squeeze of her shoulder. His attention to her in those moments always made her feel special. She knew how the conversation would go. The last time he'd been her knight in shining armour, as he'd called himself, had been at one of Pamela's charity gigs. One of the sponsors had been explaining to Ruby how their new online business worked when she'd noticed James watching them closely. He'd had that knowing smile on his face that made her skin flush. Once the man had excused himself, James had slid to her side.

'He's a flirt,' he'd whispered to her. 'If he was any closer to you, he'd be in your knickers.'

Ruby had blushed. 'Don't say that!'

'Why not?' James had laughed softly. 'It's true.'

'You make it sound like I'd let that happen.'

'Ah stop.' James had nuzzled her neck. 'That's not what I meant, and you know it. You're gorgeous, and you're all mine . . . lucky me. I get to go home with you and Casanova can only dream of you.'

'Casanova? Ah James, we were only talking.' She'd glanced around to see if anyone had heard what he'd said.

She remembered how he'd smirked. 'You're such a silly billy. Can't you see that he was flirting with you? And you made him think that he was in with a chance.'

'I swear, I wasn't – I didn't mean to . . .'

James had silenced her with a kiss. When he'd pulled away, he'd said, 'Why wouldn't he want to be in your knickers . . . I'd be in there right now if I could.'

Her cheeks had flamed painfully as his fingers ran up her arm to her neckline, but her eyes were on those around her, hoping they hadn't noticed his behaviour.

'It turns me on,' he'd continued. 'Seeing other men want you.' Then he'd raised his whiskey to his lips and she remembered how his eyes flitted around the room, like a panther watching its prey. It wasn't the first time she'd felt uneasy by his side, but it was the first time she remembered thinking that maybe she, too, was his prey.

They'd gone home shortly afterwards and had passionate, energetic sex in the kitchen. How persistent James had been, how he'd made sure the other man knew she was going home with him, and, blushing even now, she remembered how he'd flashed a smile at the man as they'd left, as if to rub it in that she belonged to someone else.

Ruby shivered remembering that night. Yes, it was good that he hadn't been there to see Eoin talking to her.

Setting the candle down on the coffee table she took a sip of wine. The house was still, only replying to the storm with echoes when it thundered. Ruby leaned forward towards the window as if to invite the weather in. After all, it was the only thing keeping her company. The urge to go out onto the balcony washed over her. She imagined how the rain would feel on her skin. It would sting, sharp and cold, maybe even bruise. The wind would cut her to the bone, lift her from the ground and force her to move, force her to choose to go with it or fight against it. Thunder would swallow her screams, and the lightning would only serve to briefly illuminate the lonely world she lived in. She wouldn't go out there, she knew, but she could imagine it.

Pressing her hands against the glass, Ruby savoured every raindrop as it travelled down, tilting her head as it hammered on the window. A flash of lightning seared her eyes, and the whip of the wind in the trees competed with the waves as they erupted over the rocks and sprayed high into the air.

Then suddenly, darkness. The power had gone out, plunging the whole house and the street into darkness. Somewhere out at sea a light bobbed wildly. Ruby squinted as her eyes adjusted to the candlelight – she was pleased she'd thought to light one. There was a boat out there, she was sure. It couldn't be a buoy, but who'd be crazy enough to go out in such a storm? A knot of fear in her stomach made her sit back down in the chair. She trained her eyes on the tiny light moving across the horizon. It disappeared a few times only to reappear further to the right of where it'd been.

Ruby pulled her legs beneath her and sipped on her wine, praying for the little boat. The storm moved quickly out to sea and within minutes the rain had softened to a drizzle, the wind seemed to have blown itself out, and the waves lapped over the rocks as if exhausted. Ruby leaned back. Wiping her face, she was surprised to find she'd been crying, and she couldn't find an adequate explanation for those rogue tears. James would've handed her a tissue and told her she was too sensitive, but James wasn't there, and it was getting harder to picture him in her head. Sometimes she had a clear image of him, how he'd stand, how his keys would jangle from his fingers as he waited for her to come downstairs, but lately the only reminder of him was coming in moments when she was sure he'd be annoyed by something. For some reason, it was easier to see him in that way.

Shaking, Ruby put the wine glass down. She hadn't really eaten much again that day, and with a heave she pushed up from the chair. Taking the candle, she wandered into the kitchen. The fridge was dark as she poked around inside. The cooked chicken Sandra had left smelt delicious, so she took it out. The idea of a roast chicken sandwich with a good dollop of coleslaw and salt and pepper made her mouth water, and within minutes she was devouring it, delighted that her missing appetite seemed to have resurfaced. She ate with relish, knowing that she'd be back on her diet in the morning. She still had that VB dress to wear.

She thought back over the last few days. Returning to Castletown Cove wasn't going as smoothly as she'd thought it would. Between arguing with a single mother, somehow winding up at a crazy yoga garden, and allowing herself to be walked home by a handsome stranger, she didn't recognise herself. Normally she was the one introducing herself and making people feel at home; but here, she seemed to be well beyond her comfort zone.

With the power still out, Ruby left the plates in the sink and went to bed. She lay in bed and waited for sleep to come, but, like most nights, it eluded her. Shuffling around, she finally dozed off for a few hours.

*

She woke feeling exhausted and delicate. Her bedside clock flashed, telling her that the power was back, but she couldn't remember how to set it, so she unplugged it.

The electric blinds slowly pulled back to reveal the last remains of the night. The sun was a huge shimmering disc on the horizon, throwing a sprinkle of gold onto the calm, indigo waves as it slowly rose against a lavender sky.

Ruby slid from the bed and headed to the kitchen to make a coffee. It was a brand-new day; she'd try harder to settle in. She'd go for a walk and reacquaint herself with the town she grew up in. She'd find Frankie and apologise properly. And somehow, she'd work up the courage to talk to Eoin – even if it was just about the Moonlight Garden.

10

Frankie

It was just after seven on the Saturday morning of the May Bank Holiday weekend, but Frankie had been up since half six as Dillon had come in and bounced on her bed until she'd gone downstairs with him. It wasn't something Frankie relished, and this weekend she'd be busy. The May Bank Holiday always was. All the holiday homes were fully booked out, as was the hotel. Dillon had no school, so she'd have to bring him with her to clean the five houses she took care of on a Monday evening when the holiday people left. Lord knows how she'd manage the hotel, though. It was times like these that she missed Agnes even more. She'd always insisted Frankie get out to work, no matter what, and had made no fuss of taking care of Dillon during the busiest season of the year.

On the end of the couch, scrunched under a blanket, Frankie shifted position. Her right foot had pins and needles. CBeebies jingled on the telly. Dillon sprawled across the couch, completely engrossed as Steve Backshall tracked down some of the world's deadliest animals and insects. With a mug of steaming coffee beside her, Frankie flicked through the pages of the gardening book on her knees until she found the plant she was searching for and read the page over three times to memorise the details. Then tapping the page, she smiled. She was right. That plant was in the wrong place. She had thought it was and now she was sure. It was a fortnight since the laughing yoga session. Afterwards, Jürgen had loaded her arms with books before she'd left and told her to read up on some of the plants he was hoping to get over the May Bank Holiday weekend. He'd pushed a crumpled piece of paper into her hand with the plant list written in his sloping block capitals.

'Senecio "Angel Wings",' she read the list aloud. '*Euonymus japonicus* "White Spire". Astelia "Silver Spear". Elaeagnus . . .'

'That's like Granny Aggie's name,' Dillon piped up. 'Agnes. Can we have something to eat now?'

Frankie put the book down and pulled the blanket over his little toes. She tucked it in around his legs. 'Warmer? Good. Now, do you want chocolate sprinkles or jam on your porridge?'

'Both!' Dillon laughed.

Frankie shook her head. 'You cheeky maggot! Hmmmm. Well, okay, just this once, and you'd better eat it all up!'

After breakfast, with Dillon washed, dressed, wrapped up warm and sent outside to find new insects in the garden, Frankie stood in the hall at Agnes's bedroom door, a bucket of hot soapy water in one hand, a basin of rags and bleach in the other ready to clean down the mould again. Agnes had passed six months ago almost to the day. Until she'd discovered the mould Frankie had gone into Aggie's room only when she absolutely had to. Since the discovery she had had to clean the room weekly, yet the musty smell was getting worse. She could smell it from the front door when she entered the house. She was in work at eleven and if Instagram was telling the truth, then her fellow cleaner Chloe had gone to a house party last night and from the state of her posts, she wouldn't turn up for work. Frankie sucked air in through her teeth and rolled her eyes at the thought of her flaky colleague. It was typical of Chloe. She'd no responsibilities. She lived with her parents, who'd given her a Mini for her twenty-first birthday and who still paid for the insurance on it too.

Dillon had taken his first steps on Frankie's twenty-first birthday, which had been exciting and also terrifying. She remembered thinking that he'd be into everything and anything and wondering how on earth she'd manage alone. Without Liam, everything loomed larger and seemed more terrifying. Closing her eyes, she tried to see Liam in her mind, but his image had faded a little more. At least Dillon had his eyes, and his smile, she thought as she peeked out the front door to check on her son. He was fine and happy, singing away to himself while he used his magnifying glass to look at some insect. Turning back to the bucket and rags, Frankie grumbled. Chloe hadn't the first notion of what it was like to be responsible for someone – she could barely take care of herself. She was pushing her luck at work, but her rooms would be added to Frankie's list, which was fine – the extra money was dearly welcome.

Pulling a scarf around her mouth, Frankie went into Agnes's room and opened the curtains and windows as far as they would go.

Agnes's bed was pulled out from the wall, and made up as if she was coming home. Her favourite quilt was spread across the end, her pillows plumped and crease-free. Tears pricked the backs of Frankie's eyes. Quite apart from missing her grandmother fiercely, it was hard managing the house without Agnes. She'd been fit and hearty almost up to the last minute, still able to make her bed and spend time with Dillon talking about bugs and the 'divilment' she'd gotten up to as a child.

Frankie resigned herself to scrubbing the room down. Usually, she tried to do it when Dillon wasn't around but she'd taken on all the extra shifts she could during the last week and hadn't been able to do it while he was at school.

Within forty minutes the walls were washed and wiped dry, and Frankie was sweating. Wiping the back of her hand across her brow, she sat down on Agnes's bed. Her feet knocked against something under the bed, and she reached down to see what it was. Tugging out a large plastic storage box from under the bed, she wondered how she'd not come across it before.

With a glance over her shoulder to make sure Dillon hadn't come in, Frankie opened the box. Her hands flew to her mouth. It was filled with mementoes of her child-hood. There was a homemade file filled with birthday cards and Christmas cards. All of her report cards were carefully stored in date order. There was a photo of her mother sitting beside the stove, a Christmas tree in the background – the one Christmas she'd come home for. Frankie shoved the photo back into the file, her lips pressed together. Her mother, ever absent, ever on her mind, hadn't even sent a mass card on the passing of her own mother's life.

Frankie had had trouble tracking her down ahead of the funeral, wasting precious time searching and calling people instead of being with Dillon, who had worryingly gone completely silent. When she'd finally made contact, it was via text message. Her mother told her that she was sad to hear of Agnes's passing, and that she couldn't make it back for the funeral because she hadn't the money to make the trip, but that she was sure Frankie would give the old lady a decent send-off. Frankie felt a dart of fury at the memory.

She slammed the lid back on the box, then grabbed the bucket of manky water and the foul rags. Emptying the water down the drain out the back, she snarled, 'A decent send-off, hadn't got the money. The bloody cheek of her.' She flung the black rags into the bin and slammed the lid shut. If only she could forget about that woman, never need to think of her again. What did her mother know of not having money, anyway? Frankie looked around the little kitchen with its faded lino and painted cupboards. The microwave had yellowed over time; one of the rings on the hob didn't work. Agnes had been too proud to go with her hand out, as she called it. She'd refused to apply to the council for a grant for a new kitchen. Until now, Frankie had agreed with her. Now, as she surveyed her home, Frankie realised that the whole place looked like something from the 1950s. Decrepit and grimy. She considered going to the council, but her stomach churned, thinking of what Agnes would say if she was around.

Frankie put the bucket down in the corner, and then moved it beside the back door. No matter where it went, it was in the way. She ran her hands through her hair. Everything was so close to her, she could touch the wall and the sink with both hands and still tip the back door shut with her toe. The pantry cupboard seemed to loom over her, and the hot press doors wouldn't stay closed. Frankie closed her eyes tightly and sucked in a breath.

With a growl she opened her eyes and dashed to the hall, grabbing her rain jacket as she passed through.

'Dillon,' she called. 'Come on – we're going to the Moonlight Garden.'

She marched quickly down the road, her steps short and sharp. Work could wait. The rooms weren't her responsibility and maybe if they realised how much they relied on her to be available she'd get a raise, or even a promotion. It was so insulting to still be a chambermaid, as if she'd no ambition just because she had a child. No one ever thought of her as ambitious; no one even asked her what she wanted. She snorted and walked faster. Maybe the hotel manager would quit idolising Chloe if they had to properly deal with the consequences of her bad work ethic. They might actually reprimand her for her lackadaisical attitude, although chance would be a fine thing.

Dillon ran to catch up and she took his warm mucky hand in hers, her frustration and anger mellowing slightly. She slowed her pace. He said nothing but gave her hand three quick squeezes. Frankie swallowed down the lump in her throat, and she squeezed his hand back four times.

'I love you, too,' she whispered. More clearly, she said, 'You're the love of my life – you know that?'

Dillon nodded sagely. 'I know. I'm the fruit of your lions.'

Frankie blinked. 'The fruit of my what?' She looked at Dillon. He looked straight ahead, quietly serious as he was prone to being when she was 'down in her dumps', as he called it.

'Fruit of your lions,' he said again. 'I read it in a book in the library. It's kinda weird though. I don't know what it means.'

Frankie stifled a laugh. 'You don't need to know,' she said. She shook her head as he slipped from her towards the Moonlight Garden and through the gates. She heard Jürgen call out a hello to Dillon as she gathered her gardening gloves and tools, planning on dividing some of the agapanthuses. Casting a glance at the garden, she saw Jürgen rambling around the shrubbery. He was whistling softly and making notes. An old robin followed him, flitting from branch to branch, its bright eyes watching everything Jürgen did. Jürgen called Dillon over and showed him the ants' nest he'd found.

Frankie headed across the garden and cut around the first clump of agapanthus. Grunting, she hefted the plant out and stood back. The garden was quiet. Dillon and Jürgen had moved down the far end and were busy turning over the compost. They'd be there for a while; it was one of Dillon's favourite things to watch. He'd find a load of creepy-crawlies there.

Then, out of the corner of her eye, over on one of the benches tucked behind the evergreen oaks, Frankie saw

Ruby. She was sitting still, staring straight out to sea, seemingly unaware that Frankie was standing a short distance away from her. Ruby's hands were gripped tightly in her lap. A lump formed in Frankie's throat as she watched Ruby's thumb moving over the back of her hand as if she was rubbing a worry stone. Frankie knew that gesture well. She'd spent a lot of time sitting looking out to sea in the same manner after Liam had gone. Ruby didn't look like someone who was in a good place, she thought. In fact, she looked like someone who was on the verge of giving up on everything. Twisting her hair around her finger, Frankie wished she knew what to do. Part of her still rankled at the way Ruby had treated her and Dillon, despite their slight thawing at the Moonlight Gardening Club, but another part wanted to sit with Ruby and tell her that everything would be fine.

With a sigh, Frankie pushed the forks deep into the soil. Ruby would be fine; all she needed was time, she thought as she wriggled the forks back and forth, but something made her stop digging and turn around. Ruby hadn't moved. She'd even stopped rubbing her hand. Frankie's heart pounded. Maybe time wasn't enough for Ruby. Perhaps she needed someone to talk to. If something happened – God forbid – she'd never forgive herself for not talking to her. Frankie pushed her sleeves up, then walked towards Ruby. She cleared her throat, and Ruby looked up.

'It's only me,' Frankie said. 'Don't get up.'

Ruby half-smiled, and settled back on the bench. 'The view is so beautiful,' she said haltingly. 'I was mesmerised by it.'

'Yeah,' Frankie agreed. She settled on the bench beside

Ruby. 'It's something else. I sometimes sit here and look out, too.'

Ruby looked sideways at her, and there was a moment when Frankie felt that she could talk to her, and that Ruby would understand everything she'd been through. She looked out to sea and suddenly realised she was rubbing the back of her hand in the same way Ruby had been moments earlier. With a shake, she slipped her hands under her thighs and sat on them to keep them still. Ruby didn't seem to notice, but two pink spots bloomed on her cheeks as she swivelled around to face Frankie.

'Frankie, I want to apologise for how I treated you that morning—'

'No,' Frankie said. She pulled her hands up. Laying one hand on her chest she continued. 'I'm the one who needs to apologise. I was out of line and rude.'

Ruby smiled. 'That's exactly what I was going to say.'

'Great minds, eh,' Frankie said.

'I wouldn't usually be so rude.' Ruby looked down at her hands. 'It was very unlike me.'

Frankie shrugged. 'It's fine, honestly. I've had worse.'

Ruby laughed. 'Really?'

'Oh, yeah.' Frankie snorted. 'I work in hospitality and some of the guests at the hotel are so obnoxious.'

'I can imagine,' Ruby said.

'One even offered to pay me for extra services,' Frankie said with distaste. 'And then threw a wobbly when I told him to go do it himself.'

'What?' Ruby's eyebrows shot up.

'Yup,' Frankie said. 'So please, don't feel bad. I'm well able for—'

'—for contrary old women raving at you in their PJs.' Ruby's lips broadened into a wide smile.

With a slight giggle Frankie pulled a face, then grinned.

'Thought so!' Ruby said. She nodded towards the two forks standing in the ground beside the uprooted agapanthus. 'What's going on over there?'

Frankie got up. 'I'm trying to divide this monster of an agapanthus. Come on, I'll show you.'

She pulled the forks from the ground and pushed one fork into the clump of roots. She felt Ruby's eyes on her as she slid the second fork in, so the two forks were back to back. Frankie pushed against both handles trying to separate them, but nothing happened.

'That's a tough one,' Ruby said. 'Want a hand?'

Frankie nodded. The women tugged the fork handles, which inched slightly apart, only to spring back together as Frankie eased off pushing.

'Ouch!' Frankie jumped back and shook her hand. 'Oh, blast.'

'What happened?' Ruby's eyebrows shot up. 'Are you okay?'

'Just a pinch,' Frankie said, pulling the gardening glove off. There was a red welt on the pad of her hand. 'I thought the fork was going to snap, so I stopped pulling and it pinched my hand. It'll be all right in a bit.' She shook it again. Ruby reached over and took Frankie's hand gently.

'Let me see. Oh, that looks sore – you're lucky it didn't break the skin.' She gently touched Frankie's hand, and Frankie's mouth went dry. No one had ever touched her in such a tender way, not even Agnes. It was just how she imagined a mother would hold her child's hand. Her eyes filled with tears as Ruby rummaged in her bag.

'Here, put some of this on it. It'll help with the bruising.' She held out a small tub. 'It's arnica. You can hold on to this. I've got another one.'

'Thank you.' Frankie's voice was husky. The tin was warm in her hands. She blinked and hot tears fell from her stinging eyes.

'Oh, Frankie.' Ruby reached for her. 'Is it that bad? Show me again.'

'It's fine.' Frankie pulled her hand away. 'I'll be fine.'

Ruby dropped her hands. 'Okay.'

Wiping her nose on the back of her good hand, Frankie clamped her mouth closed, but the tears kept falling. She thought back to the time her mother had returned for a visit. She'd hurt her knee climbing up the old apple tree. Other kids in school always ran to their mother when they were hurt, she knew, and now her mother was home, she'd surely help her feel better. Frankie had hobbled to the front door, where Nicole sat on the step nursing a mug of tea. Limping over, Frankie had held up her skirt and showed her bloodied knee and waited for the hug she knew should follow. But Nicole had grimaced and shrank back. 'Go away, will ya?' She'd clambered to her feet. 'Blood makes me feel sick.' Leaving Frankie on the step, Nicole had shuffled inside, calling for Agnes to deal with it.

Back in the present, Frankie trembled. What was going on today with all the memories and reminders of tough times? She looked up at Ruby, then without a word she shook her head, spun on her heel and ran across the garden to the shed.

'Frankie,' Ruby called, hurrying after her. 'Wait. I'm sorry.'

'It's not your fault,' Frankie sniffed. She pulled a length of blue tissue from the dispenser above the sink and wiped her eyes. 'It was me.'

Ruby frowned. 'What do you mean?'

Frankie gasped. 'Nothing.' She rubbed her hand briskly. 'Nothing at all.'

'Frankie,' Ruby began but was interrupted by Dillon, who dashed into the shed, his hands cupped gently. In the soft yellow light, he held up his treasure for Frankie to see. She gave what she could feel was a strained smile, oohing over the cluster of woodlice in the palm of his hand.

'Jürgen says these are good for the compost,' he said, but then his face crumpled as he caught sight of his mother's red eyes. 'Mammy, why are you crying?'

'Hurt my hand.' Frankie held out her hand for his inspection. 'But I'm all right now. Don't worry, buddy. It's just a pinch.'

11

Ruby

Ruby watched Frankie hunker down to look at the woodlice. She clearly didn't want to talk about what was upsetting her. It couldn't just be her sore hand – it didn't look that bad. Ruby noticed that she kept her face averted as if she needed a minute to herself. Casting her eyes around the shed, Ruby saw an old hacksaw hanging on the back wall.

'This should do the trick,' she said with forced brightness. 'I'll do it. You rest that hand. Dillon? Would you like to come with me – we can finish the job your mother started while she looks after her hand? If that's okay with you, Frankie?'

Frankie nodded. 'Thanks, Ruby.'

'No problem.' Ruby jerked her head towards the garden. 'Come down to us when you're ready.'

Dillon followed Ruby down to the agapanthus. Ruby could see that he was worried. His little face was tight, and his brow was low over his dark eyes. His step had lost its bounce. He wasn't holding the woodlice any longer.

'Tell me about woodlice,' Ruby said as she wielded the hacksaw above the large mound of roots they had left on the lawn. 'Why are they so good for the compost?'

Dillon brightened up a little and skipped to catch up with her.

'I think they do the same thing as worms do,' he said. 'I'm not quite sure. Jürgen was telling me, but I got distracted by a wolf spider.'

'Oh, no,' Ruby said seriously. 'I'm not a fan of spiders. I found one in my bed once and it was huge.'

'Spiders aren't that bad,' Dillon said. 'They're really good for the environment too.'

'I know,' sighed Ruby. 'But they've got far too many legs.'

Dillon laughed. 'That's what Granny Aggie says.' His hand flew to his mouth. 'I mean used to say.'

'Who's Granny Aggie?' Ruby asked.

'She's Mammy's granny,' Dillon said looking over his shoulder. 'She died at Halloween time. I miss her.'

'I'm sorry,' Ruby said, her heart aching for the little boy. 'It's tough missing someone like that.'

'She made the nicest bacon cabbage dinner in the world.' Dillon sighed.

'Do you like cabbage?' Ruby smiled at the turn in the conversation. 'I hated cabbage when I was your age.'

'I like it when Granny Aggie makes it.' Dillon's nose wrinkled. 'When Mammy makes it, it's not as good. Mammy doesn't make the best dinners. She's better at hot chocolate.'

'Oh,' Ruby said. 'I like hot chocolate. I haven't had one in a long time.'

'You should come to our house,' Dillon said. 'I'm sure Mammy will make you some. She puts cream on top, but not all the time because cream is expensive. Why are you holding that saw like that?'

Ruby glanced down at the saw in her hand. She'd been so engrossed by Dillon's chatter, she'd forgotten what they were supposed to be doing. The blade was rusty, the teeth were bent and some were missing.

'I'm going to cut this agapanthus in half,' she said. 'I just hope the blade is up to it. Let's give it a go.'

Dillon immediately hunkered down on a small rock nearby, his eyes on her. Ruby stretched her arms out in front of her and laid the blade on the mound of roots. With a deep breath in, she began sawing. The blade juddered across the earth and roots, sending vibrations up along her arm. Minutes later, she was sweating and red-faced and hadn't made much difference. The thing was still solid. She sat back on her heels and dropped the hacksaw. Her hand felt cramped from her tight grip on the metal handle, and she massaged it with her thumb. Dillon rubbed his nose, watching Ruby closely.

'Why are you cutting it in half?' He shifted closer and knelt to look at the root ball.

'Sometimes,' Ruby said, 'things grow better when they are separated or divided. When they're close together, they can be too close, overcrowded. There's no room to grow.'

Dillon nodded. 'Oh, I get it. Granny Aggie used to say that about Nicole. She had to leave because there wasn't room for her to grow here. Well, at least, I think that's what she meant. She used to say there wasn't enough room for all of us.'

Tilting her head, Ruby looked at Dillon. Was it possible that he was Nicole's grandson? If so, then Frankie must be Nicole's daughter. Nicole had never said anything about a baby, but then again, Nicole wasn't one to tell you too much. She never had been. Still, it wasn't as if they were in touch. They'd lost contact for a while, and anyhow, Nicole didn't stay in one place for too long. The way Dillon didn't seem bothered about Nicole made Ruby think that maybe he didn't know her – which must be hard for Frankie. Ruby had barely kept in touch with her mother after she'd married James . . . she knew what it was like to miss your own mother. Best not to mention that she had known Nicole, she thought. It probably wouldn't go down too well. And besides, it was so long ago.

Picking up the hacksaw, Ruby thought back to their Debs ball. Nicole had somehow come up with the most sophisticated dress Ruby had ever seen. While everyone else had looked like an extra from the movie *Pretty in Pink*, Nicole had arrived in a one-shoulder black sheath dress, her auburn curls piled elegantly on top of her head. She'd worn red lipstick and black mascara. Ruby remembered looking at her and feeling childish in her lavender satin dress with its wide underskirt. There was no way she could wear red lipstick. Her mother wouldn't allow it, so she'd worn a peach shimmer and hoped Sean Redmond would like it. It appeared he preferred red lipstick, as he'd hovered around Nicole for most of the night.

Ruby bristled at the memory. Nicole paid no heed to Sean Redmond, though, choosing instead to dance with

Ruby all night. Ruby wondered what Nicole was up to now; how come she wasn't here in Castletown Cove with her daughter and grandson. It sounded as if Nicole wasn't around, which wasn't much of a surprise. She'd always said she wanted to leave Castletown Cove, that the world was waiting for her and that she didn't want to be anchored down like a fishing boat constantly working the same dreary routine day in, day out, that she didn't want anything to tie her to one spot. But if Dillon was her grandson, she didn't know what she was missing.

Dillon started humming. Ruby peered at him as he poked around in the dirt. He did look like Nicole from a certain angle. And there was something else about him too, which she just couldn't put her finger on. Dillon smiled up at her, blithely unaware of how cute he was. There was a gap in his teeth where a new tooth peeked through, and his red hair curled over his forehead. Ruby longed to hold him in her arms, and imagined him as a baby full of smiles and joy, and as optimistic then as now.

Ruby began sawing once more, hard and fast. Dillon, blithely unaware of Ruby's memory, began rifling through the shrubs. He took his magnifying glass from his pocket and began to peer through it in earnest. After another minute, she stopped sawing again, stood up and rubbed the small of her back. The hacksaw was useless. It had barely made any progress – it was possibly more difficult than using the forks. She flung the hacksaw on the ground by her feet.

'Did I catch you at a bad time?' Jürgen said, appearing as though from nowhere.

'No,' Ruby puffed. 'This is far more difficult than I thought it would be.'

'Hmmm,' Jürgen said. 'Isn't that always the way? It's hard work, gardening, digging and sorting through what we can let go of, and questioning what we should learn from it.'

'I suppose.' Ruby's forehead wrinkled. Was he talking about gardening or . . . ? She rubbed her sore back again. Jürgen picked up the hacksaw and turned it over a few times.

'This old thing,' he said. 'It's seen me through thick and thin. I bought this with my first paycheque. I'd almost forgotten about it. It's in good shape but I think I should replace the blade. It should make things easier, don't you think?'

Ruby looked at him, again wondering if he was still talking about gardening. A warm smile crept across his face.

'It's really good to see you here,' Jürgen said. 'I was hoping you'd come down, and that you might like to join our gardening club . . .'

Rocking on her feet, Ruby wrapped her arms around her thin frame. She raised her hand to her hair and tucked it behind her ear.

'The garden is an essential part of the community.' Jürgen gestured. 'It's a place of sanctuary for those in need, where people can come and feel a sense of calm and of belonging, and maybe even help them through their darkest days. This is why we only plant flowers and shrubs and so on that shine bright in the dark. Everything here has been specifically chosen. Everything is either white or silver in tone. Of course, we have shades of green – you need the darkness to appreciate the light, just as you need the light to guide you from the darkness.'

She hadn't really noticed it, but now that he'd told her she saw that what daffodils remained were white. Under the trees, small anemones lit up the shade. Tulips, still tightly in bud, stood tall under the graceful arches of mock oranges. She could tell that they were all white too.

'An all-white garden?' Ruby looked around. 'That's amazing.'

'It really is.' Jürgen smiled. 'I'm so proud of the community that's grown alongside this garden. The whole town has been wonderful – even those who won't call themselves gardeners.' His gaze fell on Dillon. 'It's been a marvellous space for the kids too, although not all of them are as into it as this little fellow.'

'I can imagine,' Ruby said. 'He's quite extraordinary – from the little I've seen, that is.'

'Gets a bit of stick in school.' Jürgen lowered his voice. 'He's not into football or anything like that. The other kids seem to have trouble with that, especially as he's into creepy-crawlies and the environment.'

'Kids can be so cruel at his age,' Ruby mused. 'I think we forget that younger kids can be quite mean and judgemental. If you were to believe the internet, they're all angels who sprout only the most prosaic, amusing things.'

'You have kids?' Jürgen raised his eyebrows.

Ruby swallowed. 'No, unfortunately.'

Jürgen's lips twisted into a half-hearted smile. 'I'm sorry. It was the same for me.'

Ruby's head jerked up. His eyes were soft, as if he was

thinking of the children he'd never had. He blinked and sighed. Shrugging, he slipped his hands into his pockets.

'Maybe it was for the best,' he said quietly, almost to himself.

'I tell myself that all the time,' she said. 'I'm not sure I've managed to convince myself yet.'

'It's not easy to get over, is it?' Jürgen squared his shoulders.

'No. It's not.' Ruby rubbed the skin between her thumb and index finger.

'It's okay,' Jürgen said. 'Maybe one day we'll talk about it. But in the meantime, use the garden as your therapy – it's what I do.'

'Therapy?' Ruby squinted at him.

'Ah, you don't really want me to talk about my therapy theory.' Jürgen laughed. 'I'd bore you to tears. In a nutshell, though, I believe that a person's health and wellbeing are intrinsically linked and benefit from active participation in their community and in nature. Gardening, in my view, is the perfect combination of community and nature – and this space here, well, it offers the whole town the opportunity to heal and connect. Not to mention the fact that we should all be connecting with the earth in some way. We need to feel rooted and safe. Even if someone has a nomadic personality they need somewhere to call home . . .' He stopped and laughed. 'Sorry, I feel very passionately about it – I've seen first-hand the effect gardening has on my clients.'

'Yeah, that comes across,' Ruby said. Behind him, she caught sight of Eoin talking to Frankie in the shed. He was holding Frankie's outstretched hand tenderly and looking down at the bruised skin. Ruby couldn't take her eyes away from them, and found herself wishing that it was her hand he was examining.

Eoin looked up. His eyes locked with hers and a slow smile spread across his face. A rush of blood flushed Ruby's cheeks. He looked as if he knew what she'd been thinking. She pushed a strand of hair back from her face, crossed her arms, and focused on Jürgen, but he'd turned around to see what had grabbed her attention.

'I'll leave you to it,' Jürgen said, smiling slightly as Eoin waved at them. He held up a piece of paper and a pen. 'I'm making a list of plants to fill the east border – if you think of anything to add to it, let me know.'

'And checking it twice, I hope,' Eoin said as he reached them.

'Of course.' Jürgen shook the list before he strolled away.

Eoin turned to Ruby with a smile. 'You came back.'

Ruby nodded. 'I did. This garden . . . I don't know how to explain it, but there's something about it.'

'So it wasn't the laughing yoga that convinced you then?' Eoin grinned.

'Hah! It was an experience all right. I've never been a lawnmower before.' Ruby laughed.

'We've a Yoga by Moonlight night coming up for the June Bank Holiday.' Eoin's eyes twinkled. 'Real yoga, this time, if you're interested. There'll be lots of plants in flower. You'd get to see the garden at its best.'

Ruby tilted her head. 'We'll see.'

'I hope so,' Eoin said softly. 'I promise you if you come here regularly, and do a bit in the garden each time, by the end of this month you'll be feeling much better – and sleeping better too.'

She stared at him, wide-eyed. 'How do you know I'm having trouble sleeping?'

'I live next door to you,' Eoin said. 'I see your light on most nights. It's not as stalkery as it sounds – I don't sleep much either. I never have, it's the way I am – but I think this is a new thing for you. Am I right?'

'I haven't slept properly since my husband died. It's been well over a year now.' Ruby's throat tightened. 'I can't seem to do anything to be honest. It's just . . .'

'I'm so sorry,' Eoin said. Ruby looked up at him, and saw his face was tight with sincerity, his mouth a thin line. 'Grief is . . . it's got claws,' he continued. 'It gets into everything, even parts of your life that you thought were safe spaces. But we can tame the beast, and I'm around if you ever need to talk.'

'Thank you,' she said softly, then cast around for a change of subject. 'So . . .' She faked a bright smile.

'So,' Eoin echoed. 'Well, I'd better get cracking.'

'Oh, actually,' Ruby blurted as he turned to go. 'I'm, um, well I'm thinking of doing up my back garden, but I need someone to help me plan it out and I thought I'd ask . . . you!'

'Is that so?' Eoin beamed at Ruby, who blushed hard. 'It's good that your next-door neighbour is a landscape gardener then, isn't it?' She nodded. Dillon was still rooting around in the soil. He looked up at Ruby and then at Frankie who was making her way towards them, then at Eoin, who was still smiling, finally bringing his eyes to rest on Ruby's face.

113

'You've gone all red,' he said, with all the mortifying candour of childhood.

Ruby's hands flew to her cheeks again. Her eyes met Eoin's. 'I, eh, yes. I don't want to put you on the spot like this, that's all.'

'Not at all,' Eoin said. 'I'd love to get on board – if you'll have me.'

'Yes, of course, I'd love to have you – I mean, yes, that would be great,' Ruby said.

Eoin extended his hand, his eyes twinkling. 'Let's make a deal: we'll work on the back garden early in the morning, to make use of those hours neither of us is using for sleep.'

Ruby looked at Eoin with curiosity. He was a good-looking man, lean and tanned. Although it was quite chilly, he wore cargo shorts, and a well-worn Guns N' Roses T-shirt that looked as if he'd picked it up at a concert way back in the early Nineties. A band she used to listen to. His outstretched hand, which was tanned and strong, was waiting for her to take it.

Over his shoulder she saw a huge smile on Frankie's face. She nodded at Ruby and gave her the thumbs up, mouthing, 'Do it!'

Ruby's breath caught under her ribs. Hell, what had she to lose? She wasn't committing any crime. She was just getting some help with the garden – that's all. She reached out and slid her hand into his firm grip.

'It's a deal,' she said, looking up at him and wondering what on earth she'd got herself into.

114

12

Frankie

It was the busiest May the village had ever had – and the hottest, too. Since the bank holiday two weeks ago tourists had arrived daily, either to check in for a few days or just passing through. It was as if everyone had decided that taking the kids out of school for a few days was worth the trouble they'd get into, with the weather being so good. They almost always stopped and had some food at the hotel or at the smaller tea rooms that lined the sun-kissed roads.

Frankie had never seen the tiny beach so packed. Beach towels and rugs were laid out as close to their neighbours as was decently possible. Children squealed as waves tickled their toes and filled their buckets. Sun cream was the top note of the air, so much so that the brininess of the sea became the heart note that would only be noticed later after showers and baths had washed the sand away.

Stopping for a moment at the wall that looked down onto the smallest beach, Frankie watched some teenagers on paddleboards laughing and flirting with each other. Over by the rocks, a group of slightly younger teens were jumping into the deep pools, too self-conscious to flirt, but just aware enough to smooth their hair back quickly after each dive. Chatter and laughter drifted up to her.

The wall was cold, but she forced her hands to relax. Seeing families on the beach made her heart tighten. Everyone looked normal – pale and stressed for the first day or two, then more relaxed and golden as their holiday progressed. She could never imagine having time like that with Dillon, never see him wearing one of those cute all-in-one swimsuits that kept the cold out – not now his father was gone.

The church bells chimed midday, and Frankie tore herself away from both the sea wall and her wistful thoughts. Chloe had resigned from the hotel and was now serving food at the Pirate's Rest, which she said was a lot nicer than changing dirty sheets and scrubbing bathrooms. Frankie sighed, thinking about the extra work Chloe's departure made for her. But extra shifts meant extra money, and if she was careful she might earn enough to sort out the mould problem at the cottage.

She turned into the Moonlight Garden just as Eoin arrived in his truck. He waved and parked up, the back of the truck heaving with plants.

'Thought I'd never get here,' he called. 'There's so much traffic. Give us a hand, will ya?'

His face lit up as he craned his neck to look behind her. Frankie squinted at him, then heard Jürgen and Ruby's voices coming from the garden behind her.

'It's crazy,' she said as she took a tray of bedding plants from the truck's flatbed. 'I haven't a minute to think straight. What has you here midday? I thought you'd be flat out landscaping the new housing estate.'

'The site is finished.' He lifted another tray of plants. 'The last house was signed over during the week. What has you so busy?'

'Chloe's gone, and I got her rooms,' Frankie followed Eoin into the garden where they left the trays down by the shed. 'But I can't clean them that fast. Then there are the rentals. They're not so bad but the last one was horrible. They left food in the bin and bluebottles got in – it was full of maggots by the time I got to it.'

'I'm guessing Dillon was thrilled?' Eoin said as they went back out to the truck.

'My skin was crawling, and he was enthralled,' Frankie said. 'Bet he'll be a forensic police officer when he grows up. He's got a lead-lined stomach. Nothing turns it. But the money from the extra work is welcome. I've a mould problem that needs looking at. Or I could just save the money and take Dillon to Disneyland.'

'Definitely Disneyland.' Eoin passed her some shrubs. 'Unless the mould is really bad?'

'The whole place is falling apart,' Frankie said, hearing the worry creep into her voice.

'You never had to think about it before,' Eoin said. 'Aggie did it all.'

Frankie frowned. 'How did she manage it, Eoin?'

'I dunno,' Eoin said. 'The women of that generation were a different breed altogether.'

'Don't you start that crack,' Frankie grumbled. 'It makes

me feel useless and disregards the hardship those women endured.'

'All right.' Eoin raised his hands. 'I'm only messing.'

'Of course, you are.' Frankie smiled at him. 'Don't do it again.'

They lugged the rest of the plants into the garden and stood back to admire their good work. Jürgen wandered over, a thoughtful look on his face. He clapped Eoin on the shoulder.

'Good man,' he said. 'But there looks to be more here than I'd ordered.'

'Finbarr said he couldn't sell these ones. They're too leggy,' Eoin said. 'He thought you'd be able to save them, so passed them on to us.'

Jürgen clasped his hands in front of him. 'Oh, my, what kindness there is in the world. Ruby! Come and see.'

Ruby, wearing a dirty T-shirt and old jeans, came over. Her hands flew to tidy her ponytail the moment she saw Eoin. Frankie watched as they smiled shyly at each other. Jürgen pointed out the extra plants and wondered aloud if they'd manage to get them all down before the week was up.

'I can do that,' Eoin piped up. 'I've this week free before my next job starts. Just show me which beds you want clearing first.'

Jürgen clapped his hands. Frankie saw that he was smiling so wide, she thought his face would split. 'Frankie, come with me and I'll get the plans for Eoin. Maybe Ruby would show him the beds we've been working on while we make some tea.' Frankie hid a smile behind her hand: Jürgen's attempts at matchmaking were so obvious.

'That would be great.' Eoin flashed a smile at Ruby, who looked star-struck in the glow of his attention. 'Would you do that?'

'Sure,' she said. 'Of course, yes.'

'Great.' He shrugged one shoulder. 'Fancy a coffee before we get started?'

Ruby nodded. 'Sure.'

'I'll be right back,' he called over his shoulder as he strode towards the shed.

'He fancies you,' Frankie said as soon as he was out of earshot.

'He does not!' Ruby grunted as she lugged the plants into the wheelbarrow and wheeled them over to the prepared flower bed.

'He does.' Frankie set the plants out in their possible plant positions. She stood back, hands on her hips, surveying their work. 'And you're into him, too.'

'He's too young for me,' Ruby said, but her blush gave her away.

Frankie pointed her hand trowel at Ruby. 'Come on, I can just see ye together and you've thought about it, you must admit.'

'Maybe for a moment,' Ruby said. She dug a hole with the spade. 'But like I said, he's too young. Should we put the agapanthus here?'

'No, stick to Jürgen's plan or there'll be war,' Frankie said. 'For a chilled-out dude, he's really uptight about putting "the right plant in the right place".' She air-quoted the last part, rolling her eyes affectionately. 'And can I point out that Eoin is doing your garden – not a euphemism – and that not only is he an absolute ride, as I've heard some of the other women say, but he's won awards too.'

'Awards for what?' Ruby asked, her interest piqued.

'He's into rewilding, and wild meadows and conservation,' Frankie said. 'He was even interviewed by the BBC.'

Ruby stopped digging. 'He never said anything about that.'

'That's just Eoin,' Frankie said, rolling her eyes. 'He just gets on with things, doesn't ask for rewards or praise. Which is why we all get so excited when he wins things.'

Ruby bit her lip. Frankie caught the slight movement and laughed.

'I see that twinkle in your eye,' she said. 'You're more interested in him now.'

'Okay, so he's intriguing,' Ruby said. 'And what about . . . you know . . . ?'

'Single for a while now,' Frankie murmured. She glanced over at Eoin. 'There was someone a few years ago – Claudia. I think it was serious, at least Jürgen said it was. He mentioned once that Claudia was an actor. She was offered a job touring with a big musical and she took it, he said, but Eoin didn't go with her.'

'Oh,' Ruby said. 'I suppose he must've been heartbroken.'

Frankie tilted her head. 'I don't know if he was. I mean, he was down for a while, but he never said.'

'Sometimes people don't say,' Ruby said quietly.

Frankie nodded. 'That's true. I didn't think of that.'

Looking over at Eoin, Frankie realised how self-absorbed she'd been. Since Aggie had passed away, he'd been super kind to her and Dillon. When Dillon came to the

Moonlight Garden, Eoin always took him for a walk around the garden to show him new bugs and asked him about school. It was as if he knew Frankie could do with a break from Dillon's chatter and boundless energy. Reddening, Frankie realised she'd never ever asked Eoin how he was, or how his day had gone. She hadn't learned much about him, had taken him for granted. She'd assumed he was happy, but now that she'd seen how he reacted around Ruby, she knew he hadn't been as happy as she'd thought. With a slight smile she turned to Ruby.

'So . . . you're interested in Eoin?'

'I'm interested in his gardening skills,' Ruby blustered. 'I've been interested in the environment for years only I wasn't taken seriously . . .'

'Yeah,' Frankie said. 'There's a lot of fools out there who only jump on the environment bandwagon when there's something in it for them. But not Eoin. He's genuine about trying to fix it. And he likes you, a lot – I've known him years so I can tell. I think it's that you're so calm and sophisticated – not like the rest of us here!'

Ruby looked up from dragging a large shrub over to the hole she'd dug. 'You think I'm sophisticated?'

'You are,' Frankie said. She waved her hands at Ruby. 'You're calm and together, and you always look ready for tea with royalty. Even now in jeans and a T-shirt covered in dust, you look as if all you need to do is to wash your hands and boom! You're good to go. There's just something about you.' Looking up at Ruby, Frankie smiled, but Ruby didn't smile back. Her lips pressed shut. One hand was on her hip, and the other pressed to her chest.

'I'm sorry,' Frankie said. 'Did I say something wrong?

I didn't mean to.' Her mouth filled with a bitter taste. She could've kicked herself. Although they hadn't had the best of starts, in the few weeks since they met, she'd realised what a lovely person Ruby was. She was great with Dillon, always finding time to poke around in the muck with him and printing things about insects and bugs off the internet for him. Last week she'd confessed to Frankie that she'd never bothered with the internet before, and now, because of Dillon, she was learning so much. Dillon had even started calling her Auntie Ruby, although he hadn't said it directly to her yet. Frankie wondered if she should mention it now, but it didn't feel like the right time.

Ruby was lovely, a good listener, and an easy person to be around, and now she'd said something to upset her – the last thing Frankie wanted to do was to hurt her. Twice Ruby opened her mouth to say something, but nothing came out. After a few seconds' silence, Frankie stood up and reached to touch Ruby's arm.

'Ruby, I'm sorry. I meant it as a compliment.'

With a quick smile Ruby shook her head. 'It's okay – I know. It's just that I don't feel very sophisticated. I never have.' She tilted her head at Frankie. 'I grew up only doors down from your house. This is my village, my home place.'

Frankie's mouth dropped open. Ruby laughed.

'But it's never felt less like home,' she said. Her laughter drained away.

'I'd never have guessed,' Frankie said, amazed. 'Wow, so we could've been neighbours – if you'd stuck around. What made you leave?'

'A man – my husband.' Ruby's hands twisted the bottom of her T-shirt. She smiled. 'James. He was called James.'

'Was?' Frankie asked, then rapidly raised her hands. 'Sorry, you don't need to tell me anything.'

'I don't mind.' Ruby looked away briefly. 'I was working in the hotel, not Castletown House where you work – Seafront Sands, and he was a regular guest. He didn't notice me, and I suppose I didn't notice him. He was quite a bit older than me and wasn't on my radar. I was into the sous chef at the time.'

'Always a mistake.' Frankie laughed. 'The ones at the hotel are either exhausted or temperamental, and they have such egos.'

'Well, yes, that's it, and this guy was the full package, which was instant trouble. But he was gorgeous, a ringer for Patrick Swayze.' Ruby grinned. 'Of course, I was mad for him.'

'I get it – who wouldn't be?' Frankie nodded. 'There's something about Patrick Swayze, but . . .' She wrinkled her nose and twisted her lips.

'Exactly, there's always a "but".' Ruby shifted. 'And his was drink and drugs – and listen, I was no angel, but I couldn't keep up with his drama and demands.'

'Sounds about right.' Frankie sighed. 'Is it because timing is important in cooking?'

'Couldn't just be that. That's too simple.' Ruby pondered for a moment. 'I don't know . . . he'd ask me to take things from rooms, and to keep things from the lost and found.' Ruby paused. Her face flamed. 'I did it a couple of times. I didn't know how to say no, and, well, that's how I met James. He left his wallet behind, and I found it . . . and instead of handing it over to Rick, I gave it back to James.' She flicked some hair from her face. 'He saw something in me and took me away from here and from doing nothing with my life – he took me all over the world.'

'At the risk of repeating myself, wow!' Frankie smiled. 'That's my dream: to see more of the world.' Her smile slipped. 'I doubt it'll happen, though. I've my hands full with Dillon – not that I'd have it any other way. I follow some Instagram accounts where they travel the world with their kids – a real nomadic lifestyle, you know? – and it looks idyllic but how do they make money? Not only that, but I think it's important that Dillon knows his roots, you know? So, thank God for Google Earth. I'll get to see most of the world someday if only through the internet.' She pulled her smile back on.

'Roots . . . yes. I thought that coming back here would give me some sense of belonging.'

'It hasn't?'

'Not really. I don't know the village like I used to.' Ruby nodded towards Jürgen. 'He knows more about the place than I do, and he's not even from here.'

'Don't you have family here?' Frankie asked.

'Not anymore. My father died when I was very small,' Ruby said. 'My mother never remarried. There is only my sister, and she lives in New York. We used to be close, but she never liked James so we drifted apart. I miss her, and her kids.'

'I'm so sorry,' Frankie said. 'I know how you feel. Sort of. I'm an only child, and now that Granny's died there's only me and Dillon left.'

'It's strange how life works out, isn't it? We never seem to get what we want,' Ruby said quietly. 'Although I never really knew what I wanted. I never had any aspirations to travel. Those were James's dreams, although of course I did enjoy them. Kids were the only thing I thought was a given, but they didn't arrive, so . . .' She paused, and Frankie got the impression she was taking a moment to collect herself. 'Anyhow, you sound like you had plans once. Where would you go, or what would you do if money was no object?'

Frankie didn't need even a second to think about it. 'Everywhere and anywhere – starting with Italy, for the food and the landscape. Then Japan, for the same reasons.'

The sound of Jürgen singing drifted over to them from the far side of the garden.

'He's been to Japan.' Frankie jerked her head. 'He said the best time to go is in late April when the cherry blossoms are all out.'

'He's really into his gardening,' Ruby said. 'I thought he was a therapist.'

'His wife was.' Frankie lifted a tray of bedding plants from the wheelbarrow. 'But he doesn't talk about her, so I don't ask. I have to run. School's out in a few minutes.'

Ruby nodded and picked up a trowel. Frankie watched her scoop the earth out. Ruby's thin shoulders and slight movements reminded her of a much younger Aggie, and for a second she almost said so. Instead, she found herself rooted to the spot as a strange warmth rippled through her.

'Hey, Ruby.' Frankie shuffled closer. 'We might see you later, if you're up for some company?'

Ruby sat back on her heels. Her eyes shone. 'Sure, that would be lovely. Why don't you come by for tea? I'd love to see Dillon.'

'Great,' Frankie said, feeling warm and fuzzy inside. She set the tray of plants down. 'It's a date – or at least it will be when Eoin asks you out.' With that, she skipped from the garden, smiling at the bemused expression on Ruby's face.

Dashing down the road, Frankie took the shortcut that brought her to the seafront and along the pier. Beside what once was the old harbourmaster's cottage stood the large monument commemorating the lives of those lost at sea. This time, instead of looking away as she usually did, Frankie paused and found the name that she was looking for: Liam. His name stood out in heavy black inscription, as if it had only been yesterday that he'd gone. It was followed by his age, and the date the sea had taken him, his father, his brother, and his uncle. A whole family wiped out in minutes, and there wasn't anything anyone could have done to save them. Frankie rubbed the tip of her nose and walked down the steps to the monument. She touched his name with her fingertips.

'I miss you,' she whispered. 'I wish you could see him now.'

The school bell sounded and echoed off the rocks, startling her. Frankie rubbed her eyes and hurried away.

Most of the villagers raved about the wall of names, said that it was a fitting and elegant remembrance, that it was only right that there was something to mark their time on earth. Frankie looked back. There was a cluster of tourists standing there now, pointing and shaking their heads as they realised that so many lost souls shared surnames and the same date of passing. It was too much, and Frankie marched away, feeling as raw and bruised as

126

she had the day he'd died. There should be a grave with his body in it, with a neat headstone engraved with his name, tucked away in the far corner of the graveyard where she could mourn and visit him in private. This public monument was well and good, and it did its job serving as a reminder to all who stopped at it that the sea was not to be trusted. But it wasn't the same, this public display of tragedy. It didn't give any sense of peace, like they'd said it would. His name was there, with so many others. No, there was no peace in this monument. Just a reminder that he was gone, and that she was alone.

13

Ruby

The hallway was becoming more and more cluttered. First thing on Monday morning the furniture guys came back with another load and stacked it Tetris-style into the hall. James would have been furious at this mess. Ruby staggered against a large drinks cabinet, grimacing as she banged her shin. Now it was Wednesday, and she'd only moved a few pieces to their new positions in the house. Somehow, they still looked out of place. They were too different from the rest of the furniture James had selected. Some colour on the walls would make them work, she thought, and if she moved the blander pieces out then the place might feel more like home.

Her mind was buzzing as she mentally flicked through colour combinations and fabrics she might choose. The best place to start, she decided, would be the guest rooms. That way she'd be able to flex her long-relaxed design muscles and if she made a mistake, well, it was only a guest room. She wouldn't see it every day. After half an hour of analysing the carnage, Ruby left the house with a spring in her step.

There was no point in staying indoors again – the weather was glorious and the furniture wasn't going anywhere, quite literally. A short walk garden gazing, as she'd started to call it, and she might get some ideas about what to do with the house. Being out in nature always inspired her.

Ignoring the hollow ping of tennis balls, she walked on. She hadn't played at all since James had died. The tennis courts were busy every day, but she really didn't miss it all that much. She'd only played to keep James company. Laughter drifted up to her and she smiled. The playground was all go. Kids were running around with sunhats and sandals on, their parents relaxing on the benches chatting. A small boy was busy climbing backwards up the slide, much to his friend's consternation. A smiley woman over at the coffee cart called over to a group of parents and one of the men got up. Ruby did a double take – he was gorgeous. He had a tanned, ruddy face and the kind of white teeth you only saw on the silver screen. His hair was brushed back from his forehead, tousled and sun-kissed. He jogged over to the woman and took a tray of coffees from her, his smile genuine and warm. The muscles on his tanned forearms flexed and Ruby swallowed, her eyes wide.

She looked away from him, back to the group. Their accents were local but Ruby couldn't place them.

There was an animated burst of laughter from the group as the man carrying the coffees said something. One of the women looked over at Ruby only for a split second, but that was all it took for her to think they'd been laughing at her. She scolded herself for being paranoid. It meant nothing. She just happened to be in the woman's line of vision. She rushed away, her heart pounding.

How had it come to this – ogling strange men in the street? Getting all 'hot and bothered', as James would say. 'I see you,' he'd say, a hint of steel underlying his jokey voice. 'Getting all hot and bothered over Mr Handsome over there.' She pushed his voice away. Strangely, she was hot and bothered by this man. He reminded her a little of Eoin, only Eoin's hair was darker. If James was here he'd have something to say, something that would make her feel bad. He'd been so insecure about their age difference.

'You're going to get bored of me one day,' he'd say. 'And run off with a newer model, some hot young buck who'll keep you satisfied.'

'I won't,' Ruby always said. 'What would I want with a younger model when I have you?'

'When you *have* me?' James would smirk. 'Explain that one to me.'

'You know what I mean,' Ruby used to say with a coquettish smile.

'Tell me,' he'd demand. 'Tell me in detail how you'd *have* me.'

She'd always blush. It always came back to sex with James, always. He'd been insatiable, and Ruby had often felt that she wasn't enough for him, and couldn't figure out why he was ever worried about her not being satisfied. But every time, she'd swallow her pride and tell him.

'You've a filthy mind,' he'd whisper hoarsely. 'Look

what you've done to me.' He'd guide her hand down to touch him as his hands would roam down her body. 'It's such a turn-on hearing you tell me what you want. You're a vixen. You don't realise how much power you have.'

She'd always said yes. There was no other answer. How else was she to show him that she wouldn't run away with 'some hot young buck'? How else was she to explain those words and those actions she always said to him?

Laughter from the group in the playground drew her away from her memories. Standing outside the playground, Ruby swallowed. She missed being intimate with someone, missed being desired, missed being appreciated and lusted over, even if sometimes she had needed 'a little more warming up' before getting on with it. She walked on fast, her feet pounding the pavement, the gardens going by without notice. He'd called her his vixen, sometimes when out with friends, showing her off and fawning over her. She'd loved it at the start, but after a while it became embarrassing. His friends' wives, all so much older than her, had taken a while to warm up to her, and it was only when Pamela took a shine to her that she really began to be taken seriously by them. She missed Pamela. She'd promised to come down this weekend, but that felt ages away.

With one glance back at Coffee Man, Ruby shook herself. Whatever was up with her lately, it wouldn't be cured by lusting after a strange man who was simply taking care of his children at the playground. Moving on, she forced her eyes onto the gardens across the road. Her favourite, at first, was filled with colour and looked like a tropical oasis, but she kept thinking of the Moonlight

Garden and its calmness and serenity. She could just go there and soak up the serenity. What could be more wonderful than that? With a determined smile and a nod, she made her way to the garden. Her phone buzzed just as she passed through the gates. It was Eoin.

> Hi, I've a free day – would you like to
> plan this garden of yours?

A tingle ran down her back. She sent a text back, trying to sound calm and together.

> Yes, that's a great idea. What time
> suits you?

She waited for his reply, a huge smile on her face. It came in almost immediately.

> I'm in Moonlight now. I could be over
> in five minutes?

Ruby's head shot up, her cheeks burning as she looked around for him. Pulling at the hem of her shirt, she rounded a corner and spotted him sitting on the bench over by the evergreen oaks, his phone in his hand, waiting for her reply. Ruby grinned and ducked back a bit. She fired off a text and peeked from behind a tall shrub to see his reaction.

> It's well you're looking.

Eoin's face broke into a grin. He looked around and then back down to the phone.

Where are you?

Ruby stifled a giggle and came out from her hiding spot. She waved over at him.

'Great minds,' he called and patted the bench. 'Sit down and tell me, what has you here?'

'I came out for inspiration.' Ruby perched on the edge of the bench. 'I like to look in gardens along the road – I call it garden gazing.'

'Garden gazing.' He mulled over the term. 'I like it. So, what's tickled your fancy then?'

Ruby's eyebrows shot up. Choosing not to rise to the possible double meaning she gestured to the garden around her. 'Well, this garden is gorgeous, but it's very . . . safe.'

'The Moonlight Garden?' Eoin looked around. 'Yes, I suppose it is. That's the intention.'

'And I think I'd like the complete opposite,' Ruby said. She suddenly knew that she wanted a garden far removed from the constraints of her old life. A garden that was wild, free and a little crazy, and not at all what James would approve of. Her eyes flashed as she said, 'I need a riot of colour – oranges, yellows, blazing reds and dark greens – you know what I mean? Something to stir the senses instead of calming them down.'

Eoin sat forward. His face lit up. 'Tropical?'

Ruby nodded. 'Yes, I think so. We're on the coast, so I was thinking of those trees that look like palms.'

'I know exactly the ones,' Eoin said.

133

Ruby sat back, relishing the firmness of the warm bench. 'It feels like what I need right now.'

Eoin nodded. 'Sounds like a great plan. Fancy a bit of breakfast?'

Right on cue, her tummy rumbled and she blushed. 'Um, yes. Yes please.'

'The Birds do the best,' Eoin said. 'Come on.'

*

An hour later, Ruby's tummy was groaning instead of grumbling. Wiping her lips with her napkin, she sat back in her chair.

'I didn't realise they did breakfast in here.' She looked around the bright and cosy pub. The walls were painted bright teal, and velvet curtains in the same shade but trimmed with gold hung in the wide windows. She absolutely adored the colour combination and stored the idea away for her largest guest room. Light streamed in and shone on the brass fittings and lights. Old books lined up on a shelf that ran around the top of the walls, and a small stage was tucked by the fireplace. Above the stage hung a hand-painted sign declaring the space was 'Booked in Advance on Wednesdays and Weekends for Musicians and Other Chancers'. The whole place was spotless, despite the clutter of memorabilia, and not one table empty. The chatter was warm and lively. The woman behind the bar caught Ruby's eye, waved over and called, 'Be with you in a minute.' Ruby waved back and smiled.

'Best breakfast menu in town,' Eoin said. 'I don't know what we did before Josie and May took this place over.'

'Ate boring porridge at home,' Josie said as she slipped into the chair beside Eoin. Smiling widely, she held out a hand to Ruby. 'I'm Josie. You were at the laughing yoga that night, weren't you?'

'Ruby,' Ruby said, shaking Josie's hand. 'Yes, I was taken aback by it, to be honest. I wasn't expecting that at all.'

'No one ever knows what to expect from Jürgen.' Josie laughed. 'He's a treasure.'

'And not from here, either,' Eoin added taking a bite of his toast. 'Just like us.'

Josie raised her mug. 'Cheers to that. We're a bunch of blow-ins, and the more the merrier!'

Ruby grimaced. 'I'm not quite a blow-in, more of a returner.'

'Oh really? Tell me more,' Josie said, leaning her elbows on the table.

'I left thirty-four years ago,' Ruby said. She wrinkled her nose. 'God, now I feel old.'

'Old! You look like a young one!' Josie laughed. 'And after that long being away you may as well be a blow-in. I bet everything has changed. What made you leave?'

'My first love – I was so young.' Ruby blushed. 'He swept me off my feet.' She stared down at her plate. The remnants of her pancakes and fruit sat in a pool of maple syrup.

'Sounds romantic.' Josie sighed. 'My first love was a complete disaster – played for seven football teams and was getting up to all sorts with all sorts . . . and yes, I married him. But that was before. I know better now. I left him and everything behind and started again. Then I met May and my whole life . . . well, my whole life made sense.'

'Now that's romantic,' Eoin said.

'You big softie.' Josie nudged Eoin before turning back to Ruby. 'You own that big house on Harbour Road, don't you? I love that house.'

Ruby smiled. 'Thanks. Why don't you pop in?' she surprised herself by asking.

Josie beamed. 'Really?'

'Sure, anytime.' Then another idea struck her, and she said it before she could talk herself out of it. 'Why don't I have you all over for supper sometime – all of us blow-ins?'

'Oh, that would be fantastic,' Josie said. 'Just give us a bit of notice and we can get Jimmy to run the bar, so we both could come.'

Ruby nodded. 'Of course. Hey, listen – I have a friend coming over this weekend. Would Saturday night suit you?'

'I'll make it suit me,' Josie said. She got up and began clearing the table, a huge smile on her face. 'Thanks, I'm looking forward to the weekend now, but I'd better get back to work before May cracks the whip.' She swooped away, her hands full of plates and cutlery. Ruby turned to Eoin and cleared her throat.

'The invitation extends to you, you know,' she said.

'I hope so,' he said. 'Me being a blow-in and all. We should ask Jürgen too.'

'We should,' Ruby said, smiling at his use of 'we'. '*We* will have to come up with a menu.'

Eoin laughed. 'Sorry! It's your gig – I'm overstepping the mark.'

'Not at all,' Ruby said. 'You're grand. I'd love to ask Jürgen.'

Eoin tilted his head at Ruby, his eyes twinkling. 'So, what have you in mind for the menu?'

'Oh,' Ruby gasped. 'I don't know! Any ideas?'

Eoin picked up his mug and took a long sip of tea. 'Something simple,' he said eventually. 'So we can chat and not worry too much about our manners.'

Ruby thought for a moment. 'I've just the thing,' she said. 'Leave it with me – no airs or graces required!'

Ruby watched his face relax. He lifted his bright blue eyes to hers.

'I can help with the prep, if you like. I'm a dab hand in the kitchen.' He smiled broadly and raised an eyebrow at her. 'In my youth I spent a bit of time as a sous chef, you know?'

'That's good to know.' She laughed. 'I'll definitely take you up on that. And, eh, how old are you, Eoin?'

'Forty-seven, according to my birth certificate.' Eoin frowned. Then he grinned. 'But emotionally and mentally I'm seventeen at most.'

Ruby spluttered into her tea, much to his surprise. 'Seventeen! That old?'

He laughed and shrugged one shoulder. 'What can I say? I'm young at heart?'

'I'll raise a mug to that,' Ruby said. She clinked her mug against Eoin's.

With a smile, Eoin finished his tea. He held her gaze for a minute then spoke as a blush crept across his cheeks. 'This was lovely. I haven't had such a tasty breakfast in a long time.'

Touching her hair, Ruby sucked the inside of her cheek. It looked like Frankie had been right: he was into her. A warmth flooded through her, causing the back of her neck to tingle. What would it be like to go out with him? Would he want to kiss her? It had been so long since she'd been kissed, she'd forgotten the feel of someone's skin against her own. Her hand flew to her mouth, her fingertips touched her bottom lip. Ruby's cheeks turned pink. She dropped her hand to the table. What if he expected sex? He was young, a good nine years younger than she was. How could she compete with women in his age group?

In the warm May sunlight he looked gorgeous, utterly different to James, but then again, James had always looked different to everyone else. It was the way he carried himself. Eoin looked as confident as James, but it was a different kind of confidence. James had always been more watchful and concerned with taking stock of everything around him. Eoin's confidence was quieter, and less brash. Ruby shivered. It was strange to think of James as brash, but against Eoin's gentle firmness that's how he seemed. And James had never looked at her quite as delightedly as Eoin was looking at her now, as if she was a rare blossom that he'd waited years to see bloom. He leaned his elbows on the table, his hand wrapped around his mug. The muscles of his forearm stretched and relaxed as he took a sip. Ruby swallowed.

'It was a delicious breakfast, but . . .' she started, but trailed off, not knowing quite what she had intended to say. She twitched her nose at him, and stood up. 'Come on, sous chef, if you're seventeen at heart, I've a few jobs for you!'

'Ten-four!' Eoin laughed. He hopped up and saluted.

14

Frankie

On her knees in the middle of an empty flower bed, Frankie dug up a stubborn dandelion. She'd nothing against dandelions in particular, only they were bright yellow and there was no room for yellow in a moonlight garden. Beside her, Maggie – Dillon's teacher – weeded around the base of a magnolia.

'He gets on great with older kids,' Frankie said. 'Take Katie, for example. He loves when I come here and she gets to mind him. I don't know why kids his age pick on him for liking bugs. You'd think they'd all be into bugs at their age.' Frankie jammed the trowel into the earth. 'So I don't want them knowing we can't afford the school tour.'

'I'm working on those kids,' Maggie said. 'We're doing an across-the-school programme about empathy next week and we'll be touching on respecting other people's hobbies and differences. I've got my eye on Dillon. I promise you I won't let it get out of hand.'

'Thanks, Maggie,' Frankie said. 'I know you won't. You're a super teacher.'

'Frankie,' Maggie said. 'About the cost of the school tour . . . it's not charity. It's a subsidy.'

'And does everyone get this subsidy?' Frankie asked, then looked up at Maggie. 'Pass over those nemesia.'

'Nem . . . ?' Maggie frowned. Frankie pointed at a tray of white flowers. Maggie nodded.

'Well, no.' Maggie hunkered down next to Frankie. 'It's just that you know how excited Dillon is. The money was raised by the parents' association and given to the school specifically for students who come from disadvantaged backgrounds.'

'Whoa!' Frankie knelt up. 'Disadvantaged?' Her nostrils flared.

Maggie raised her hands. 'Oh God, no. I mean . . . that's just what it's called in the department. It doesn't mean anything other than they don't have the same opportunities as other kids because of a lack of financial means. It doesn't mean you're a bad parent, Frankie. Come on . . . you know I'd never let that be said about you.'

Frankie stuck her trowel into the earth. 'I know, I'm sorry. I'm a little sensitive about it all.'

'Yes, and you're worried,' Maggie said. 'I get it. But it would be such a shame for him to miss out. Look, have a think about it. I'll hold a place for him, of course. Let me know when you're ready.'

'Thanks, Maggie,' Frankie said. 'I appreciate that.'

'No bother,' Maggie said. Eoin was carting some bales of compost across the garden, his T-shirt clinging to his

140

chest and shoulders. Maggie fluffed her hair and straightened her T-shirt. 'Now tell me, what did you call this flower again?'

Frankie laughed. 'Nemesia. It can be an annual or a perennial.'

'I've no idea what gobbledygook you just said,' Maggie said. 'But it's gorgeous and looks like it needs some of that stuff Eoin has.'

'Oh, dear God.' Frankie laughed. 'I think he's got his sights set elsewhere, but you'd make an impression if you actually planted that one instead of ogling him.'

Maggie pulled a face and stuck out her tongue. 'I'm here, aren't I?'

Knowing that Dillon was happy with Katie watching him, Frankie settled into planting the bedding. The garden was soothing her worries, as it always did. The smell of freshly turned earth almost had a personality of its own: one full of gusto and optimism. Burying her hands in it, she inhaled deeply, scrunching up her hands as she exhaled. With renewed vigour, she worked until dusk. As the sun kissed the petals and branches goodnight a deep sense of calm came over Frankie. She brushed back her hair, leaving a streak of mud on her brow just as Jürgen arrived to call everyone together for the usual winding-down chat.

'Come on,' Maggie groaned as she got up from her knees. 'Let's get this over with.'

Frankie smiled. Jürgen encouraged everyone in the garden to come closer and form a circle. Her heart sank when she realised it was a sharing circle. Tonight wasn't the night for sharing what was weighing her down. Nevertheless, she joined the circle, standing just a little further back than the others. Jürgen waved her in closer so she took an extra step and smiled tightly at him, the familiar constricting band of a headache wrapped around her forehead. Taking a deep breath, Frankie closed her eyes on Jürgen's instructions and followed them, breathing in when he said so, and out. When she opened her eyes, she saw that he was watching her with a gentle expression, as if he knew not to go too far with her this night. He held her gaze for a moment, then opened his arms to the group.

'It's so lovely to see you all, and to see the inroads that you're all making in the garden this year. It's a balm to see such camaraderie and hard work. I know it's not easy for everyone to commit, so tonight we come together under the full moon to share and release our emotions and those toxic thoughts that drag us down. The full moon is the completion of a cycle – we made it through another twenty-eight days!' Jürgen looked around the circle, his warm eyes pausing every now and then on someone. He clapped his hands. 'Tonight's sharing circle is about gratitude,' he said. 'Let's take a moment to remind ourselves that this is a safe and caring environment, a non-judgemental space where we are free to talk about our lives. We all have different lives and different experiences of life – one person's worry or gratitude may not be the same as yours, or you may struggle to comprehend theirs. You may feel they have more or less than you, and that's normal. Remember to be respectful and kind, and to take some time to try to sympathise or empathise with others. Let's begin by tuning in to the natural world that surrounds us.'

Under Jürgen's instruction, Frankie closed her eyes and

allowed her shoulders to drop. The air was warm, she realised, even now as the sun sank lower, and it was perfumed and soft. The daytime hum of insects had quietened to a low *hmmmm*, and the salt of the sea tickled her nose. Her headache slipped away as she listened to the others share their thoughts, and by the time it was her turn knew exactly what to say. Her concerns over Dillon at school, her fears that they'd soon be broke were still there, but she had Maggie and Valerie and, surprisingly, Ruby too. She knew they wouldn't let her down.

Opening her eyes she focused on the glowing viburnum that was flowering profusely as if it hadn't a care in the world. Jürgen smiled at her, and she took a deep breath. 'I'm lucky to have friends who support me and look out for me and Dillon, and friends who care enough to have the awkward conversations and ask me if I'm doing all right.' Her gaze went around the small group, as smiles and nods came her way. Valerie was sucking in her lips and nodding, as if she was trying not to cry. Maggie was beaming at her, and mouthed, *Well done*. A weight lifted from Frankie's shoulders. It was good to be able to say it aloud, and even better that those who needed to hear how grateful she was for them had heard her say it too. Frankie blinked away tears that threatened to fall and tuned back in to the group.

It was Ruby's turn to talk. She twisted her hands together, her forehead creased. She opened her mouth twice before speaking. Frankie smiled gently at her, knowing the awful churning-stomach feeling she must have. The first time she'd shared she'd felt sick for hours afterwards, wondering if she'd said too much or too little, not quite understanding that that didn't matter. What mattered was that she'd said something, and that something was for her and no one else. Ruby looked at her and Frankie nodded and mouthed, *It's okay.*

'I . . . grateful for . . . I'm . . . I can't.' She shook her head. 'I'm sorry.'

Jürgen walked forward and taking Ruby's hands stood in front of her. 'It's all right.' Ruby looked up at him and nodded. She didn't let go of his hands, and kept looking into his face. Frankie looked around. Everyone was watching them, barely a breath between them. They looked serene and connected, the tall lithe tanned man and the slim genteel woman, the perfect couple, yet to Frankie they simply looked like two people lost in grief, each acknowledging the other. Frankie looked away. Maggie was a mess. Tears rolled down her face, which didn't surprise Frankie.

'It should have been our wedding anniversary today,' Ruby said hoarsely. 'Thirty-three years . . .' Her shoulders shook as silent tears flowed down her cheeks. Jürgen stepped forward and held her until her sobs finally found a voice. Frankie's throat choked up and there wasn't one dry eye; even Eoin was suspiciously bright-eyed, and looked like he wanted to take Jürgen's place comforting her. Eventually, Ruby's cries quietened, and the group shuffled closer. Frankie glanced to her left and saw Eoin shift backwards a little. He wiped his eye and looked up at her. Frankie held out her hand to him and he took it gratefully, squeezing her hand tightly as the circle tightened and people shared what they were grateful for.

As the final person finished speaking, Frankie quietly slipped away to sit alone on the bench. Her jumbled thoughts battled for her attention. Yes, she was grateful to have such considerate friends, but at the end of the day, she was alone, and probably always would be. She'd never be able to stand in a circle and say she'd been married for thirty-three years. Frankie's lips twisted. Liam would've gotten a good laugh out of this, but he'd also have come with her for the experience. They'd have had a great night and probably would've stayed up late talking about it. But now that would never happen. Now she was relegated to doing laughing yoga on her own, and with a shiver she realised she'd become used to doing everything on her own.

She supposed it was because she'd been brought up by an independent, strong woman. Aggie had been widowed early in her marriage, and had never entertained looking for love again. She'd done everything herself, depending on no one else right to the very end. Frankie shifted uncomfortably, the bench hard against the backs of her thighs. Aggie had been happy, she thought as Valerie beckoned her. Aggie had been fine, and so was she.

Walking home with Valerie, Frankie was quiet. Valerie kept the chat going, though, filling her in on the holiday she'd booked in Spain.

'I can't bloody wait,' Valerie was saying. 'I just hope it's still hot in September. The last time we went in October and we were frozen – you'd want a jumper on ya in the evenings. I want to be baked like a cake, sizzled like a sausage, fried like an egg.'

Valerie's excitement finally won Frankie's attention. She laughed. 'Just use sunscreen, will you?'

'In my day, we slathered ourselves in baby or cooking oil and sat out for hours,' Valerie said.

145

'That's disgusting.' Frankie wrinkled her nose. 'What were ye thinking?'

'Sure we didn't know any better,' Valerie said. 'We thought we were the bee's knees, tanned and fantastic. It was the thing. Nowadays, it's all out of a bottle.'

'For good reason,' Frankie said.

'Yeah, I suppose that's true,' Valerie said. 'I'll walk up with you to yours, and say goodnight to Dillon. Got to get my steps in.'

'You mean, check that Katie is doing her study.' Frankie winked. Valerie was on the go all day long. It was unlikely she'd need to reach her steps goal.

'You bet,' Valerie said. 'She's a right messer; says she wants to be a lawyer but hasn't done a tap since Christmas. Her mock exam results were grand, but she'll need to do a lot more if she wants to get a place at university.'

Frankie shoved her hands in her coat pockets. Valerie kept talking about college places and how much it was going to cost them, how she'd cope if Katie got a place in Dublin. Frankie nodded and smiled at the right times and tried not to think about the college course she'd had to give up when she discovered she was pregnant with Dillon. There'd been no other choice. It was bad enough that Aggie had been forced to bring up her granddaughter as if she was her own child, let alone bring up her great-grandchild too. There was no way she was going to do that to her. She'd made the same mistake as her mother by getting pregnant out of wedlock, but she wasn't going to foist her responsibilities on someone else and run away. She'd be the mother Nicole never was.

'Well, I hope she gets what she wants,' Frankie said as

they walked by Valerie's house towards her cottage. 'It'll be the making of her. I hope Dillon wants to go to university.'

'Ah, he will,' Valerie said. 'Anyone can see he's got brains to burn, and he's got an interest that will probably take him all over the world.'

'As a what? An insectologist?' Frankie giggled. 'Is that even a thing?'

'Couldn't tell you,' Valerie said. 'But there must be a course that includes insects – sure, the critters are everywhere. Ah, here, what's this now?'

Frankie looked up. Both Katie and Dillon were sitting outside on the step of the cottage, looking forlorn and cold. Dillon's hat was pulled down over his eyes and he held his chin in his hands. Frankie could hear him singing softly to himself.

'Katie,' she said. 'Is everything okay?'

Katie jumped up. 'Oh, thank God, I tried calling you but the call went straight to voicemail.'

Frankie winced. Her phone was almost out of credit so she'd switched it off. 'Sorry. What's going on?'

'There's water flowing down the wall in the sitting room.' Katie pointed inside the house. 'I didn't know what to do. I was going to go down to our house but Dillon didn't want to go. So we just sat here.'

'What!' Frankie ran inside, banging the door off the wall. Flinging the sitting room door open she stared in horror at the stream of water that flowed down the wall between the sitting room and the kitchen. It took a wide berth and dripped from the light switch on the far wall as it trickled down and over the doorframe. She ran over

147

to the wall and touched the water, jumping back as the chill seeped into her.

'No!' She ran her hands through her hair and spun around. The carpet beneath her feet squelched. Looking down, Frankie saw the whole thing was sodden. She rubbed her face and held her hands over her mouth. Valerie stood in the doorway, her phone in her hand.

'I'm calling Eoin,' she said. 'Hold tight – he'll know what to do.'

Frankie paced the room. Katie and Dillon hovered outside the sitting room door.

'Mammy.' Dillon's eyes were wide. 'What're we going to do?'

'I don't know, buddy,' Frankie said. She stopped pacing and stood beside him. 'I don't know.'

Valerie nodded and hung up the phone. 'Eoin's on the way. He said we're to try to turn off the water mains. It's usually under the kitchen sink – I think. John used to do all that, so I'm not sure. Go in and give it a go. I'm going to take these two down to my house to get them warm – I'll be back shortly.'

Within ten minutes, Eoin arrived. After leaping from his van, he hurried into the house. Frankie jumped up from where she was sitting on the bottom of the stairs. She grabbed hold of his arm.

'Eoin, thank you,' she said. With chattering teeth, she led him into the kitchen where water cascaded down the wall. 'I can't find how to turn off the water. There's a small valve under there but it's stuck. I couldn't twist it.'

'No worries,' Eoin said soothingly. 'We'll get it sorted, okay?'

He disappeared under the sink but after a minute or two stood up and groaned.

'Looks like it's good and jammed.' He rubbed his jaw. 'There must be another valve – maybe outside.'

Frankie followed him out the front door. 'Where's the water coming from?'

'The tank in the attic is my guess,' Eoin said. 'That's usually the case.'

'God, I feel so stupid.' Frankie slumped down on the step.

Eoin lifted a manhole and reached in.

'That should stop it,' he said, turning the water off. 'Now, let's take a look in the attic.'

Upstairs, Frankie opened the small hatch that led from Dillon's room into the tiny attic space above. She let down the ladder and Eoin crawled in. Frankie looked around Dillon's room. Water was pouring from the centre light right onto Dillon's bed. It was soaked through. The floor was sopping and the ceiling had a huge bulge in it. She could hear Eoin slowly crawling along, and his curse as he found the tank.

His voice floated down to her. 'It's the tank.' Frankie hugged her body tightly. 'It's completely burst.'

Frankie swallowed hard and rubbed her face. Eoin appeared at the hatch and he lowered himself down the steps.

'It's one of those old galvanised tanks,' he said. 'Bound to go at some stage. I'm sorry, Frankie.'

Frankie nodded mutely. Eoin looked around the room and sucked in a breath as he saw the bulge in the ceiling.

'It must have been leaking for ages,' he said. 'You never noticed anything?'

'No,' Frankie said quietly. 'I didn't. It wasn't a problem until now.' She stared into the attic space. The ceiling groaned.

'She's going to go,' Eoin said. 'I could feel it when I was up there.'

'Bug!' Frankie rushed forward and grabbed Dillon's favourite tatty soft toy, a long, multi-coloured caterpillar, from the bed. She dashed back to the door just as the ceiling collapsed onto the bed with a low tumble and a loud bang. Frankie shrieked. Water poured down into the room as the dust settled.

'Oh my God!' Frankie's hand flew to her mouth. Eoin took Bug from her other hand and she steadied herself against the doorframe. 'Dillon could've been in bed.' Her hands shook as she pushed her hair back and held her head. She turned to Eoin. 'What am I going to do?'

'You'll stay tonight with me,' Valerie came up the stairs. She stared into the destroyed bedroom. 'See if you can get him some clean dry clothes – we'll figure the rest out tomorrow.'

15

Ruby

Pamela was a star. She'd arrived that morning unusually early for Pamela on a Saturday, with a selection of wine from her cellar for the dinner party that night. In the kitchen, Ruby held a bottle in her hand and read the label.

'Are you sure you want to open this?' She waved the bottle. 'It's probably not going to be appreciated by us country bumpkins.'

'Darling,' Pamela said. 'You're doing me a favour. Russell bought a dozen cases on his golf trip that I need to make room for. Pop it in the cooler and we'll open it as soon as we're changed for dinner.'

'I hope they like it.' Ruby fussed over the napkins. Pamela popped a hip and laid her hand on the kitchen island.

'They will,' she said. 'Why wouldn't they?'

'I don't know.' Ruby polished a fork. 'It just feels . . . like a test of sorts.'

'A test? If tonight's dinner is anything like your previous

dinners then you've already passed with flying colours, darling.' Pamela tapped her fingers on the counter. 'By the way, I like what you've done here. I didn't think the Dublin furniture would work but the place has a personality now.'

'I don't know,' Ruby said. 'It feels like it's messing around with James's vision for this place. He was so pernickety about things . . .'

'Well,' Pamela said. 'I don't mean to speak ill of the dead, but sometimes he got it wrong. You've made everything work. The house is far more homely now. If he'd any sense he'd have let you loose on the Dublin house and saved a fortune on those designers who made it feel like a hotel lobby.'

'The Dublin house did feel a little generic, didn't it?' Ruby said. She leaned against the table. 'But this place is so big. It echoes. Listen . . .'

The house echoed back at them.

'Ah, the sound of silence.' Pamela half-smiled. She ran a finger over the island worktop. 'You do know that half the women in this country would kill for a minute of this solitude. Maybe you should open it up as a day sanctuary for frazzled mothers.'

Ruby tucked her hands behind her back to stop them from cradling her stomach and thinking of the children she'd almost had. Pamela didn't mean it; she didn't realise what she was saying. What the house needed wasn't frazzled mothers looking for peace and quiet. It needed, as it always had, the joyful noise and chatter of children. She squeezed her hands together harder, her arms growing cold as pins and needles tingled. She looked up from her toes.

'You look different,' Pamela said. Tilting her head, she waved her hand. 'It's the clothes. I've never seen you so casual, not even on holidays. Jeans and a shirt . . . and are those Birkenstocks? I know they're all the rage, but I never thought I'd see the day you'd wear Birks. As I recall, you said you'd rather die than be caught in flats.'

'Unless they were Chanel ballet flats,' Ruby said, remembering her comment. 'It's just that it's more relaxed down here. Half the time I don't even wear makeup.' She rubbed the front of her foot against the back of her calf, feeling the swelling from a bump she was sure she'd gotten from moving the furniture around during the week.

Pamela gasped. 'Please tell me you're still moisturising and wearing sunscreen!'

'Of course,' Ruby said with an affectionate smile. She crossed her fingers behind her back, wincing slightly as a twinge acted up. She should have been more careful moving that last heavy set of drawers. The top of her left leg hurt. She'd looked it up and was sure it was sciatica. She'd get it checked out when she was back in Dublin. 'Always. Listen, let's go for a walk – I need to pick up a few last-minute things and to tell you about tonight's guests.'

Grabbing her bag, Pamela slipped on a pair of sunglasses. 'Lead the way, darling.'

*

Settling into her chair, Ruby sat back and looked around the table. In the candlelight, everyone looked younger and happy. She smiled softly. This was the first dinner party she'd given since James had passed away, and – she took a breath before allowing herself to think the thought – was probably the nicest and most relaxed one she'd ever been at. Everyone was in high spirits, and stuffed to the gills. Her homemade paella had gone down a treat and now there was a stack of empty dessert plates in the centre of the table. She smiled. She'd always been a dab hand at profiteroles.

Pamela had risen unsteadily to her feet and was tapping her glass with her knife. 'I'd like to propose a toast to Ruby, and to you fine people. I've never had more fun at a dinner party.' She raised her glass high and beamed at Ruby as everyone cheered. Pamela continued with a magnanimous smile and a wicked wink. 'So tell me, which of you is the owner of the huge yacht in the marina? And who is the film director? I heard this place has been used in a few movies, you know.'

Josie and May laughed simultaneously, then laughed at their simultaneous laughter. 'We're not quite as glamorous as all that,' Josie said.

Pamela pursed her pink lips. 'Ooooh, I don't know about that. You seem glam as anything to me, and far more fun than anyone I've met.'

'You charmer,' Ruby called across the table to her friend. 'Josie and May own The Birds pub and I'll take you there next time you're down. Their food is out of this world.'

'I'll hold you to that,' Pamela said and turned back to chat with Josie and May, who were clearly enchanted by Pamela.

In a matter of minutes, Pamela had turned to talk with Eoin. Ruby watched his fine, strong hands. He was gesticulating enthusiastically, and she wished she was in the conversation too. Jürgen leaned across the table to listen to them. Pamela turned to him.

'Jürgen, isn't it?' She sparkled at him. Then she squinted, taking in every inch of him. 'Isn't that Swedish for George?'

'Possibly.' Jürgen shrugged her question off and nodded towards Eoin. 'Did Eoin mention his plans for a wildlife garden at the Moonlight Garden? No? Well, we're thrilled about it – he's an award-winning landscaper, you know?'

'And Jürgen knows more about plants than anyone in the whole world,' Eoin interrupted Jürgen. His cheeks reddened. 'Seriously, he knows every plant. Ask him.'

Jürgen grinned and sat back. 'Well, I do have quite an encyclopaedic knowledge . . .'

'Shut up!' Sandra called up-table good-naturedly. 'We know!'

Ruby giggled and stood to top up people's glasses. Without a word, Eoin was by her side, taking the bottle from her with a gentle smile. His fingers brushed against her skin, sending shivers along her arm.

'I've got this,' he said gently. 'Sit down and enjoy your guests.'

'You're my guest too.' Ruby smiled shyly at him. 'I should be taking care of you, not the other way around.'

'I like helping,' he said, his eyes on hers. 'I feel awkward if I don't.'

'Well, okay then,' Ruby said. 'I'll allow you to help.'

Eoin smiled, and Ruby's skin tingled all over as if she'd fallen into a bath of champagne. When she looked up, she caught Pamela watching the exchange and knew there'd be questions later. Pamela stood up and swapped chairs. Now she sat in Ruby's seat with Valerie to her right. With a smile she turned to Valerie.

'Valerie – you're the head housekeeper at the hotel, aren't you?' Pamela said. 'Tell me, how do you deal with obnoxious guests like myself?'

'Hah.' Valerie swirled the wine in her glass. 'I see your trick question and raise one of my own: why are you people so obnoxious in the first place?'

Pamela lowered her chin and chortled. 'Well . . . possibly inbreeding?'

Valerie snorted and the two women creased into laughter. Ruby slipped into a seat at the end of the table next to Frankie. Things were going great, she thought, although Frankie was most definitely off form. Ruby looked up and caught Frankie's eyes flickering over Pamela in her finery.

Wincing, Ruby saw Frankie take it all in and for the first time saw her friend through different eyes. Pamela was laughing loudly. She'd pushed back her chair and her crossed legs, the gems on her fingers flashed in the candle-light. Frankie seemed to shrink before them. Ruby sat back. There were dark circles under Frankie's eyes and her clothes were crumpled, which was unusual. Even when digging and pulling weeds down at the Moonlight Garden, Frankie had always managed to look more put together.

'Frankie, is everything all right?' Ruby asked, her voice low.

Frankie started wiping down the table in front of her. 'All good,' she said. 'Dinner was lovely. Dillon's begged me to bring him home some dessert, if that's okay?'

'Of course it is. I've kept a plate for him. It's in the

back of the fridge.' Ruby touched Frankie's arm. 'Are you sure you're okay?' She caught Frankie's eyes flicker to Pamela and back. 'Pamela is one of my best friends. Her bark is worse than her bite, I promise.'

When Frankie didn't say anything, Ruby squeezed her arm. 'Frankie. Tell me what's wrong.'

Frankie's face reddened. 'She's nice, your friend.'

'She is, but you're avoiding the question,' Ruby said. 'I can't help you if you don't talk.'

'You can't help me anyway,' Frankie said. 'No one can. It's a huge mess and it's pointless.'

'What is?'

'My life.' Frankie pinched the bridge of her nose. 'I'm a mess – the cottage is a mess, and I've nowhere to go.'

'Whoa,' Ruby said. She leaned forward. 'Things can't be that bad.'

'Yeah, I suppose the rest of the cottage could've caved in on us, then we'd really be in trouble.' Frankie sniffed.

'Hey,' Ruby said. She tapped the table. 'What's happened?'

Frankie stared at her, her lips pressed tightly together. Her eyes scanned Ruby's face, filling with tears as Ruby reached forward to brush a hair from her face.

'I'm sorry, Ruby. I didn't mean to snap.' She wiped away the tears that rolled down her cheeks, turning her face so the other guests wouldn't notice. 'Basically, me and Dillon are homeless. We're sleeping on the couch in Valerie's living room because the cottage is destroyed. The water tank burst, the ceiling came down on Dillon's bed. The insurance is up on it next month so I had an assessor out and he told me the place was uninhabitable and that they probably won't offer me a renewal on the policy. He said there's damp and mould on one side of the house because the brick is old and crumbling. And they won't cover the repairs.'

Ruby's eyebrows shot up. 'When did this happen?'

'A few nights ago,' Frankie said. 'If it wasn't for Valerie I don't know what I'd do. But I can't stay with her forever. I went to the council and they're no help. They put me on the housing list, but what good is that to me? There are hundreds of people waiting for houses and they're all on that list before me.'

'I'm sorry.' Ruby's hand flew to her chest as the old tightening sensation she used to get when the money lender would call to her mother's door came rushing back. 'Oh, poor Dillon.'

'He's not doing too badly,' Frankie said quietly, as if all the fight had gone out of her. 'No one at school knows yet, so he's not getting picked on any more than usual.'

Ruby blinked back tears. 'He's a great kid,' she said hoarsely.

Frankie nodded. 'We've gone back to the house to collect what we can, but much of his stuff is no good now. He was mostly upset about the library book he borrowed from school.'

Ruby shook her head. 'This is horrible. I wish I could . . .' She sat up and leaned forward, thinking hard while Frankie scrubbed away her tears. 'Frankie, I have a proposition for you.'

Frankie's forehead creased.

'Eoin is helping to do my garden, and well . . . who other than Eoin is the best gardener in town?'

'Jürgen,' Frankie said without hesitation.

'After Jürgen,' Ruby said.

Frankie shook her head. The crease between her eyes deepened. 'Ruby, what do you want?'

'Frankie, I want you to come and live with me and be Eoin's sous-gardener.' Ruby rapidly tapped the table.

'A sous-gardener?' Frankie blinked.

'I know there's no such thing,' Ruby said. 'But couldn't you and Dillon come and live with me? My house is huge – there's lots of room. You'd be welcome and . . .'

'Are you serious?' Frankie stared at Ruby.

'Of course she is,' Pamela said as she slipped into the chair next to Frankie. 'As long as I've known Ruby, she always follows through.'

'Oh my God,' Frankie said. 'Ruby. Dillon . . . he'll be delighted. But we can't just land in on you like that.'

'You can, and you should. In fact, Dillon would be really helpful as well, with all his knowledge about insects and wildlife.' Ruby reached across the table and grasped Frankie's hand. Squeezing it, she smiled at Frankie. 'Say yes, please.'

'Um, yes? I suppose.' Frankie shook her head. 'But we need to put some ground rules in place, and we need to . . .'

'We'll talk it through, it'll be fine. I promise,' Ruby said.

'Okay,' Frankie said. Her face had lost the pinched look she'd had earlier, and Ruby's heart swelled as she realised how much this meant to Frankie. 'I can't believe this is happening. Dillon will go crazy. Cross my heart, we won't be any trouble.'

'I know,' Ruby said. 'Come over as soon as you can and we'll talk it over.'

'I'm free tomorrow evening after work.' Frankie got up from the table. 'I'll be back in a minute . . . I just need to . . .' She turned and hurried away towards the bathroom.

Pamela took a sip of her drink and watched Frankie walk away. 'Are you sure about this?' she asked turning to Ruby. 'You could be getting a lot more than you're bargaining for.'

'I'm sure,' Ruby said. She shifted in her seat, her leg still aching from earlier. 'I've this warm feeling right here in the very centre of me, like I'm glowing inside. This is the right thing to do, and I'd never forgive myself if I didn't do it. Honestly, Pamela, I've never been more sure of anything in my life.'

16

Frankie

The next day flew by. Frankie and Dillon moved into Ruby's home without any hiccups or mishaps. It was as if they were just coming home. After a quick bath, Dillon went to bed without any fuss. Now, kissing Dillon's curls, Frankie tucked him in then slipped from the room. He'd been unusually quiet all evening as they'd moved their belongings into Ruby's house. Despite Ruby preparing two bedrooms for them, Frankie decided she'd sleep with Dillon that night. It might help him feel better about all the recent changes in his life.

Leaning against the wall outside the bedroom, she felt tired. It had been a long, rough day. Not only had she worked all day at the hotel, but she'd traipsed up and back to the cottage by foot until Eoin had caught wind of what she was at and had insisted on helping her. It was humiliating to be moving like this, and she refused to let Ruby help her. Moving into Eyrie Lodge, in all its pristine glory, had shown her how poor and dilapidated her home was and there was no way she was letting Ruby in to see the squalor.

Ruby had been waiting for her after each trip, and had taken boxes and bags into her home without questions. Instead, she'd made sure everyone had tea, toasted sandwiches, and she offered plenty of hugs for Dillon. She seemed genuinely thrilled to have them there. Frankie sighed. She'd been glad Pamela had left that morning and wasn't there to see her shabby belongings. It was hard to see Ruby with a friend like Pamela. She thought Ruby seemed far more down to earth. A whisper caught her attention and she edged closer to the half-open bedroom door.

Dillon was talking quietly to Bug. Frankie held her breath and leaned closer.

'I know, Bug.' She heard his soft voice whisper in the lamplight. 'It's scary, but I think Auntie Ruby likes us, so we have to be good. That way, she'll want to keep us.'

Frankie's heart pounded as she listened to him assure Bug things would be okay. She didn't need to have done two years of a psychology degree to know that really, the gentle assurances he was giving to Bug were meant for himself.

She ran through their lives together, trying to understand what was weighing on his mind. She'd always done everything to make sure he knew he was wanted, loved and treasured, having had a fine example in Agnes. Her own upbringing had been slightly different to his – no father on the scene, no mother either, just Aggie – but she'd always felt safe. When she was at home.

It was when she was at school that she'd come up against the rumours and gossip. Maybe that's where he was struggling. Someone at school must've said something to him. She'd ask Maggie if she'd noticed anything going on.

The room was quiet now, and Frankie peeked around the doorframe. Dillon had finally fallen asleep. He was starfished out across the bed, as always. Frankie climbed the stairs slowly, wandering into the kitchen as her tummy rumbled loudly. Ruby was sitting on the balcony, a glass of wine in front of her. Eoin sat next to her. Frankie was once again struck by how right they seemed to fit together, only she had a sense that Ruby wasn't allowing herself to feel it. Her tummy rumbled again and without thinking she opened the fridge. She took in the mountains of food inside and suddenly realised with horror that she was rooting around in someone else's fridge. Her mouth watered. Trays of leftovers from the dinner last night were in neatly stacked glass lunchboxes. She'd love more of the delicious quinoa and paprika chicken salad Ruby had served as a starter at the party last night. Glancing back at Ruby and Eoin, Frankie's hand hovered over the containers. Then she closed the fridge and tiptoed over to the open balcony door.

Ruby was pointing to the garden designs she'd created, and Eoin was leaning in to get a better look. They were entirely engrossed in their conversation and didn't hear Frankie.

'Sorry to interrupt,' she said quietly. 'But, um, would it be okay if I had some leftovers from last night?'

Ruby looked up. 'Oh, yes! Of course. You don't need

to ask, Frankie. This is your home now. Let me get that for you.' She made to stand up but Frankie raised her hand.

'No! Stay there. I can look after myself,' Frankie said. 'Don't mind me.' She scuttled back to the fridge and took some food.

'Come out here,' Eoin called as she settled at the island unit. 'Join us, and bring a glass.'

Frankie looked around, feeling that she couldn't say no. She picked up a small glass from the cupboard and took her plate to the balcony. Eoin poured her some wine.

'This is lovely,' Ruby said, looking from one to the other. 'It's just how it should be. People in the house and everyone happy.'

Frankie nodded, her mouth full of chicken. She watched Ruby and Eoin discuss the plans Ruby had sketched for her back garden, smiling at how they argued gently about the colour scheme and the riotous feeling Ruby wanted for the place. More often than not, Eoin gave in to Ruby. Frankie had never seen him so enraptured by someone. Finishing her food, she bade them goodnight and left them to it. Heading downstairs to the room she was sharing with Dillon she hoped he'd have a good day on his school tour on Wednesday. Ruby was as excited as he was and had promised to walk him to school to wave him off.

*

On Wednesday, the two women stood side by side, waving as Dillon boarded the minibus that was taking his class on their annual school tour.

'See you later, Mammy,' he called from the step. 'Bye, Auntie Ruby, love you!'

Frankie heard Ruby's intake of breath, and reached for her hand to squeeze it. They watched Dillon sit next to his best friend Ben, while Ava slipped into the seat in front of him. Their little faces peered out the windows as they waved to Frankie and Ruby. Frankie breathed out heavily. They were going to a wildlife park and it had a butterfly farm. She was glad she'd swallowed her pride and taken the place Maggie and the school had so generously offered him. She stood back as the bus pulled away, smiling and waving until the bus turned at the end of the road and disappeared out of sight.

'I hope you don't mind him calling you Auntie Ruby,' she said to Ruby.

'I love it!' Ruby enthused. 'I'm sure I'll get used to it in no time.'

Frankie frowned. They walked back down the road towards the seafront. 'Surely your sister's kids call you that.'

'I'm just Ruby in Ireland to them. And my sister-in-law doesn't see me as truly part of their family, so while I adore her children I'm just Ruby there too.'

Frankie linked Ruby's arm and squeezed. 'Well, you'll always be Auntie Ruby to us.'

'Thanks, Frankie.' Ruby smiled. She paused for a moment. Then said, 'You know, I was almost a mother, once. We'd been trying for a baby for five years and nothing was happening. Then we'd the chance to adopt a baby.'

'Oh, Ruby,' Frankie said. 'What happened?'

165

'I'm not sure,' Ruby said softly. 'I think the birth mother changed her mind.'

'Oh,' Frankie said quietly. Liam's sister, Paula, had tried to convince her to give Dillon up for adoption when she was pregnant. At the time she'd been angry, but now, faced with Ruby's evident desire and love for a child, she felt a little sad.

'Well, that was then. This is now. So, will we kick the bucket?' Ruby asked as they picked up the pace. Frankie laughed. She'd introduced the phrase to Ruby in the week since they'd moved into Eyrie Lodge. The village was spread out along the coast, with roads winding around and back on themselves. The bucket, as Frankie called it, was a walk that started on Harbour Road and went down past the harbour and up by old Paddy Whack's place. The original was long gone now, but his son had inherited his land, his bad temper, and his nickname. If they turned left at Paddy Whack's and walked along the boreen, they joined the cliff walk about halfway into it, and then left again brought them back to the Moonlight Garden. Going straight at Paddy's just added another couple of miles to the walk as it joined up with the end of the cliff walk out by Jimmy Moo's dairy. They'd gotten into the habit of 'kicking the bucket' most evenings before heading to the Moonlight Garden.

'I'm in work in half an hour, so I'll have to skip it,' Frankie said.

'They don't know how lucky they are to have you,' Ruby said.

Frankie said nothing. She bit the inside of her cheek, thinking of the position she'd applied for back in April.

Valerie had pushed the hotel manager on the matter, telling him he was looking for trouble if he didn't take Frankie more seriously, but it hadn't stopped them from hiring someone else. Someone with a college education.

'And I'm flat-out busy sorting the cottage this week, so maybe we can kick the bucket next week?' Frankie said.

Ruby grinned. 'I'm holding you to that. Go on, or you'll be late. I'll pop into the Moonlight Garden instead.'

Frankie nodded. 'See ya.'

She watched Ruby walk away towards the Moonlight Garden, noticing that she seemed to be walking with a bit of a limp, feeling just a tad jealous that she couldn't spend the day doing exactly as she pleased. Shaking off the ungenerous thought, she began to plan how to fix the cottage. It was a shambles. Dillon's room was uninhabitable. The tank had drained into his room and caused colossal damage to the kitchen and sitting room below. The assessor had been out in a flash, making Frankie wonder if the insurance company had assessors sitting around waiting for jobs like hers. With a grumble, she hurried into work and took her list of duties from the board. There was no money to make the repairs, so the best she could do was concentrate on her work and make as much money as possible.

Working quickly through her assigned rooms, Frankie hoped Dillon was having a good day at the wildlife park, but fantasies of a new, improved and stylish cottage kept springing into her mind. The things she'd do if she had money . . . She'd put in new windows – that was for sure. She wiped down the bathroom mirror and blew out a deep breath. It fogged up the mirror and she vigorously

167

polished the steam away. Daydreams were well and good, but it was hard work that would get her places, and the hard work was only just beginning. After her shift she was going to the cottage for an hour to salvage what she could before collecting Dillon. Maggie had said they might be a little late home, and that she'd text the class group chat if that was the case. Frankie crossed her fingers and hoped that they would be; that way she'd have some extra time to sort things out. She wanted to wash and dry Dillon's favourite blanket and put it on the bed in Ruby's house, and get Bug washed, too.

Frankie double-checked the room she'd just cleaned. It was pristine, crisp and fresh – perfect for the weekend. She'd read reports about the housing crisis, and watched the programmes about families living in cramped and unsuitable hotel rooms, and couldn't imagine how they coped. And that was after they'd spent months in homeless hostels and shelters. She could be in the same situation if it wasn't for Ruby insisting they move in with her. A shiver ran down Frankie's back. She had to do something to help Dillon feel more secure. After Aggie had passed away, he hadn't talked to anyone for over a month. She didn't want a repeat of that. It had been terrifying. But Dillon adored Ruby, and more than once Frankie had come back to find them snuggled up on the wretched Harrods sofa watching BBC *Springwatch*, which Ruby had recorded for him, or reading some book on creepy-crawlies, so maybe things would be okay.

Frankie moved on to the next room. She scanned the room, as usual. The previous occupants had left some pamphlets and brochures on the table. They must have picked them up thinking they were *Things to Do in Castletown Cove* brochures. Frankie picked up the top one and flicked through it. The brochure advertised higher diploma courses and night classes. It was a private institute and the costs were eye-wateringly high. The next brochure was for the night classes in the local secondary school. Sitting down, Frankie read through it, skipping past the flower arranging, dance and art classes to the certificate courses for universities. Eagerly, she read the description of the psychology course. It wasn't the same as the degree course she'd had to give up when she'd discovered she was pregnant, but it was a step in the right direction. Even so it was a pipedream and far beyond her means.

On the opposite page a mindfulness and positive psychology course caught her eye. It was a fraction of the cost but the description didn't appeal to her. It sounded like something Jürgen would do, all breathing practices and guided meditations. That was all very well for the Moonlight Garden, but she didn't see herself making it her whole life. Slipping the brochure into her overall pocket, she surveyed the room again and returned to work.

Later, Frankie let herself into the cottage just as it began to lash rain. The cottage was cold, already smelling damper than before, and abandoned. Putting on the radio, Frankie steeled herself, refusing to let the tears flow.

Pull yourself together, she thought. *You're no good to Dillon if you're whinging and moaning all the time. Get on with it.* She swept through the living room, gathering photos from the mantelpiece and the tattered filing case that Aggie had meticulously kept up to date. All their essential documents had miraculously survived, even though the case had been leaning against the wall the water had flowed down. Leaving the box of bits and bobs by the front door, she ran upstairs and filled her backpack with some of her clothes. Moving piecemeal was proving to be a painful option, but it was what it was. The bag only held a few days' worth of clothes, all of which seemed shabby and cheap. Frankie pushed the shame away and threw the backpack on.

*

Letting herself into the utility room at Eyrie Lodge ten minutes later, Frankie was struck anew by how large and modern the place was. She emptied her backpack into the washing machine and turned it on a quick wash. It should be done by the time she got back from collecting Dillon, and she could hang it out and have it dry by bedtime. She dashed down the hallway to the room she shared with Dillon and dumped the box from the cottage on the huge bed, then took the stairs two at a time up to the kitchen. He was always starving when he came out of school, and would be specially so after all the excitement of the wild-life park, so she grabbed a banana from the fruit bowl and turned to head up to the school.

The whole house was quiet. She was at the top of the stairs when she looked back, thinking of getting a banana for herself, when she caught sight of Ruby lying on the sofa. Frankie tiptoed into the room. Ruby was pale and in a deep sleep. She didn't stir as Frankie reached for the throw to lay over her. Frankie smiled softly, then hurried away to get Dillon.

17

Ruby

After dinner that evening Ruby bent over to put a plate in the dishwasher. 'I had some job reassuring Sandra that you weren't taking her place here as housekeeper,' she said to Frankie. Frankie stopped wiping down the counter.

'Are you serious?' She dropped the cloth into the sink and rinsed it out. 'I wondered why she was so short with me in the village earlier.'

'Really?' Ruby frowned, thinking back to her conversation with Sandra. 'I told her you were a guest. And that she shouldn't feel threatened by you.'

'You didn't!' Frankie's eyes widened. 'Now she's going to think I've gotten above myself.'

Ruby straightened up. She shook her head. 'I don't understand – what's wrong now?'

'You called me a guest, which to Sandra means she has to clean up after me and Dillon. She won't like that one bit.'

Ruby sighed and rubbed her forehead.

'Look, come down to the garden later and we'll chat

with Sandra.' Frankie wrung out the dishcloth. 'I'm sure she'll understand. I don't mind too much about her knowing about why I'm here.'

'Are you sure?' Ruby leaned against the counter. She watched Frankie wipe the already clean counter a second time. 'I don't want you to feel like you need to justify anything to anyone.'

Yeah,' Frankie said. 'Sure, she's Valerie's sister so she probably already knows.'

'Right,' Ruby said. 'We'll do that. It's probably the best way to deal with it. Any idea what Jürgen has lined up for us this evening? I'm a little tired and not up for Zumba or anything energetic.'

'Zumba is at the end of the month,' Frankie said. She narrowed her eyes. 'You're tired?'

'I didn't sleep last night,' Ruby said, frowning. 'I think I've restless legs or something. I couldn't settle down 'til about five.'

Frankie looked at her for a moment, then shrugged. 'I think Jürgen has some musician lined up for tonight. Should be an easy one.'

Dillon wandered into the kitchen, holding a small bug hotel. 'Can we put this outside before my bath?' His brown eyes sparkled.

'Where did you get that?' Frankie dropped to her knees and took the bug hotel from him. She turned it over in her hands.

'The man at the wildlife farm gave me a prize cos I knew all about centipedes and wasn't afraid of them.' Dillon stuck his hands in his pockets. 'Then Mya made fun of me and called me Bug Boy until Teacher made her stop.'

'Well, I'd rather be a Bug Boy than a spoilt brat.' Frankie's brows knitted together. Her knuckles went white. 'Who is this Mya? Does her mother collect her after school?'

Sensing Frankie's anger, Ruby stepped forward and ruffled Dillon's hair. 'Come on, Dillon, let's find a spot in the garden for this fine hotel. You coming, Frankie?'

'Be there in a minute.' Frankie had her phone in her hand. 'Just sending a WhatsApp to Maggie.'

'Stay cool,' Ruby advised with a stern look. 'Don't get too angry. It won't help.'

Frankie nodded. Her shoulders dropped. 'I won't. Promise. Go on, I'll be down in a few minutes.'

Ruby held out her hand and Dillon slipped his warm one into hers. The rain had passed and the cloudless evening sky was punctuated by swooping swallows. Higher up, aeroplanes left trails of lace behind them. Ruby watched as Dillon marched around the back garden, scrutinising different areas for their suitability.

'Here might work well,' Ruby suggested. 'Near the apple tree should be a good spot.'

Dillon scratched his nose. 'The man said it has to be up high and out of the wind.'

'Maybe this isn't the spot then, it gets windy here,' Ruby said. She peered around again.

Frankie came down the garden path.

'What about on the side of the summerhouse?' she asked putting her phone into her back pocket.

'Good idea, Mammy,' Dillon said. 'So the man said we need a drill for the screws . . .' Dillon looked at the two women expectantly.

'Um, I don't think I have one.' Ruby reddened.

'Crap,' Frankie said. 'We only used an old hammer to hang things up, and that's buried under the sink in the cottage. Well . . .' She winked at Ruby. 'You'll have to ask Eoin to bring his screwdriver next time he comes around.'

Studying the side of the summerhouse as if it was the ceiling of the Sistine Chapel, Ruby tried, unsuccessfully, to hide the smile that seemed to come to her face every time she thought of Eoin. He'd been wonderful with Dillon these last few days, and had quietly and with great sensitivity helped Frankie move most of her things up from the cottage. Not to mention how encouraging he was about Ruby's garden plans. He was a good man. She smiled as she remembered that that was exactly how Pamela had described him after her dinner party last week.

Touching the weather-roughened timber, she recalled Pamela had flirted shamelessly with Jürgen on the doorstep as he left after the dinner party. However, he hadn't cottoned on to what she was doing, and had continued singing Eoin's praises, much to Pamela's chagrin.

'If it wasn't for Eoin, the garden would only be half complete. Who else around here has the skills and the know-how to build a pergola in a weekend?' Jürgen had said to Pamela as the two women said goodnight to him on the front door step. 'We've a lot to be thankful for.'

'It sure looks that way,' Pamela had trilled. 'Goodnight now, Jürgen. Don't get lost on your way home!'

Jürgen had ambled out the gate. The last thing the two women heard was him singing softly as he wandered down the road towards home.

'He's a good man,' Pamela had said to Ruby.

'He is, isn't he?' Ruby had closed the door.

'You realise I'm talking about Eoin?' Pamela had said. 'Don't let him pass you by, Ruby. I think he'd be good for you.' She'd kissed Ruby goodnight and sashayed down the hall to her room. Ruby could hear the sound of water running coming from the kitchen upstairs. With a pounding heart that she was sure everyone in the village could hear, she'd made her way up to the kitchen where Eoin was at the sink, a tea towel slung over his broad shoulder. He'd stayed until every glass was washed and put away, seemingly unfazed by how she hadn't been able to take her eyes off him. He'd even laughed when she'd said she'd never seen a man do as much in a kitchen before.

Now, back in the garden, with her hand still touching the side of the summerhouse, the thought occurred to Ruby that James would've instantly spotted her attraction to Eoin. Ruby shook herself. James's opinions on Eoin weren't wanted, and she refused to let them in.

'Ahem,' Frankie called. 'Earth to Ruby! Penny for those thoughts – they looked filthy!'

'All clean, I promise,' Ruby said, blushing.

'Yeah, I don't believe that,' Frankie said. 'One mention of Lover Boy and you go all gooey.'

'Lover Boy?'

'Oh, come on!' Frankie giggled. Eoin waved from his patio, calling Dillon to come to see the wasp nest he'd found. The women watched as Eoin lifted Dillon over the wall and the two rambled away, muttering about pollination. 'You never finished telling me about what happened after the dinner party,' Frankie continued. 'You got as far as telling me that Eoin stayed and helped clear up . . .' She raised an eyebrow at Ruby.

'He did,' Ruby said. 'But nothing happened.'

'Something *should* happen,' Frankie said. 'Look, as men go, he's one of the kindest and loveliest men I've ever known. You couldn't do better.'

'It's just he's . . .' Ruby started, '. . . he's really so different from James.'

'Well, that's a good thing,' Frankie said. 'I'd be more worried if you liked him because he was a carbon copy of your husband. That'd be twisted. Also, he's well within your range – the rules say half your age plus seven.'

'There's a rule?' Ruby asked.

'Yup, or else you'd be a cougar.' Frankie waved over to Eoin and Dillon, and called Dillon home for his bath. Eoin lifted Dillon over the fence and waved to Ruby as Frankie and Dillon disappeared indoors. Ruby waved back, her eyes on him as he turned away to take a phone call.

She made her way up the garden, stopping to listen to Dillon's laughter coming from the bathroom next to the utility room. With tired arms she began to take in the washing from the rotary washing line, enjoying the freshness of the sheet and towels that had spent all day in the sun. She had a theory that the laundry soaked up all the happiness of the sunshine and gradually released it into the house later, but she'd never told James that. He'd hated the idea of a washing line, but she'd insisted they put one in.

'I don't want my laundry on display,' he'd said as they'd watched the landscaper install the rotary line. 'And none of your lingerie, either.'

'For goodness' sake,' Ruby had said. 'Everyone wears

176

underwear. Relax, James. It's the Cove, and no one is looking at anyone else's washing. They're too busy taking care of their own.'

'I don't care,' he'd grumbled. 'I'm not just anyone else and I don't want my laundry on that line.'

'Well, that's fine,' Ruby had harrumphed. 'But we're not using the dryer for every wash. That's irresponsible.'

'What are you on about now?' James had strode away leaving the question hanging in the air. Ruby had followed him.

'We have to think of the environment,' Ruby had said as she'd caught up with him. 'We must do our bit. The dryer eats electricity.'

'The environment.' James had stopped. He'd tilted his head back at the rotary line. 'And this is going to counteract all the damages being done around the world, is it?'

Even now Ruby could feel how her cheeks had reddened. He'd made her feel so silly. 'Well, of course not. But it's a start.' She'd put her hands on her hips, annoyed at his blasé attitude. 'Come to think of it, your company could do with an overhaul when it comes to how seriously it takes climate change.'

'Hmmm.' James had looked at her, then past her as if he was reading something over her shoulder. She'd resisted the urge to turn and see what it was he was focused on, knowing that this was his way of thinking. He'd smiled then. 'You might be right. In fact, I think that's something we should get on top of. I can see where some investigation and reports on waste and resources could possibly save us some money.'

177

'Save you money?' Ruby had frowned. 'What about the environment?'

'We're building a passive house for ourselves, aren't we?' He'd rolled his eyes at her mutinous expression. 'One step at a time, Rubes. We're in the middle of a recession. The rest of the world isn't ready for passive houses.'

'It should be,' Ruby remembered saying hotly. 'It should've been years ago.'

'One weekend in the country and you've turned all hippie on me.' James had laughed. 'We'll agree to disagree on this one, okay.'

It wasn't a question. It never was. He'd turned and gone back to the house and into the room he used as his office. Ruby hadn't seen him for the rest of the day.

It was weird, she found herself thinking as she dropped pegs into the basket, that in all the years they'd owned Eyrie Lodge, in all the time they'd come to the Cove for a short break, she'd never noticed Eoin before. James probably had, she thought. He always noticed other men who might be a challenge to him. He'd never mentioned their neighbour, though, which was strange. Ruby sucked in her bottom lip. James definitely had noticed Eoin, she decided as she glanced over the washing line now and trained her eyes on Eoin as he paced back and forth on his deck – how could he not have? With a shake of her head, Ruby imagined James scrutinising Eoin, and deciding not to mention him to Ruby. She didn't realise she was still staring at Eoin until he waved at her. Blushing hard, she waved back.

He ended his call then he called over. 'Have you got a minute? I've been thinking about what you said about the garden.'

178

'Sure.' Ruby dropped the towel she'd been folding into the laundry basket. She stood back as he hopped over the wall. A warmth washed over her – he looked so good, healthy and glowing with divilment.

'What?' he asked as she grinned at him. 'What'd I do?'

'Nothing,' she said. 'I'm just thinking of Dillon and his bug hotel.'

'Right,' Eoin said turning to the upper end of her garden. 'I was thinking of what you said about the tropical feeling you wanted to create here. I think we can do it. I've made a list of plants that you might like. Can I walk you around to show you where they'd go?'

Ruby nodded. She followed him around the garden as he, enthused about her plan, got more and more animated as they went.

'I completely love this idea of creating a series of rooms within the garden,' he said to Ruby when they'd made a circuit of the garden. 'You're really very good at this. I have some books you might like to read, if you'd like them. They're about garden design – I think you'd enjoy them.'

'That would be great,' Ruby said. She could barely stop smiling. 'Eoin, thank you.'

'For what?' He raised his eyebrows.

'For believing in this.' Ruby gestured to her garden plan that he held so carefully in his hands. It was covered in her scribbles and rough notes. James would've laughed at her. He'd have called her an amateur and tossed her plans aside.

'No problem.' His eyebrows relaxed and he smiled. 'Like I said, it's brilliant. But listen, I've got to go. I told

Jürgen I'd get those plants down at Moonlight this evening. Why don't you come with me?' He seemed almost as surprised as Ruby at his suggestion.

Ruby sucked in a deep breath. It was now or never. She should take Frankie's advice and make something happen. As her old friend Nicole used to say: 'What's the worst that could happen? They say no, and so what? At least you know you tried.'

'Sure,' she said. 'Let me change my shoes.' Grabbing the laundry basket, she hurried inside and dumped the basket on the counter in the utility room. She glanced down at the loose jeans and Breton top she was wearing and shrugged. Unlike James, Eoin never commented on what she wore, only sometimes said she might be cold, but he would definitely have something to say about her footwear. She shucked off her deck shoes while rummaging in the ironing basket for a pair of socks, then grabbed her pink wellies and pulled them on.

'I'm heading on up to the garden,' she called in the general direction of the bathroom. 'See you up there.'

'Cool beans!' Frankie's disembodied voice came from the bathroom, followed by Dillon's sweet voice.

'Mind the wasps, Auntie Ruby. They're out and about!'

'I will!' Ruby was out the door and crunching across the gravel in no time to the gate where Eoin was waiting for her. She rubbed her calf as the gate groaned open. The bump on the back of her leg was bothering her, stinging a little where it rubbed against the top of her welly as she matched Eoin's pace. It didn't seem to be getting any smaller, but at least it wasn't too sore at the moment.

Once in the garden, Eoin got straight to work. Ruby

was struck by how alive and vibrant he was. His face took on a stern expression as he loaded a wheelbarrow with bark mulch, but he smiled the moment she caught his eye. She loved how his forearms were tanned up to where his T-shirt sleeve finished; she'd heard Frankie tease him about his farmer's tan, but it made him all the more attractive in Ruby's eyes. She watched him heave the arms of the wheelbarrow up, and shimmy the mulch out onto the flower bed, his T-shirt riding up as he did. Then just as quickly he lowered the barrow and stood back to wipe his brow with his forearm. Ruby felt a shiver at catching him off guard. Pamela was right. He was a lovely man. He turned around and caught her watching him, a smile blooming on his face as he strode towards her. He didn't take his eyes off her, not once.

'You're an asset to this place,' she said, feeling warm under his admiring gaze.

'So they say.' Eoin grinned. A butterfly fluttered between them, landing on Eoin's arm. Ruby wished she'd the nerve to just touch his arm right where the butterfly sat. Eoin stood still, glancing at Ruby, his eyes shining.

'It's a common blue,' he whispered. 'Dillon taught me that.'

Ruby's heart melted a little at the thoughts of Eoin and Dillon chatting about butterflies.

'Do you fancy a cuppa?' Eoin asked as the butterfly fluttered and took flight. 'Head over to our bench while I make it and take a look at what I was working on yesterday.'

'Our bench,' Ruby whispered, as he strode away towards the sheds. He looked back at her and smiled.

181

'No milk, half a sugar, isn't it?' he called, grinning as she nodded, then turned back to the shed, whistling as he went.

Crossing the garden, Ruby stood by *their* bench. She shook her head in amazement. Gone were the straggly hydrangeas that Jürgen said had never settled in; gone was the overabundance of groundsel and crane's bill that flourished in the warmer weather. Catching the gold of the setting sun was a swaying wave of tall grasses; their silvery swathes were dotted with white yarrow. Clusters of spiky grey eryngiums were under-planted with drifts of sea campion, all promising white blooms in the next week or so. Nestled in amongst the back of the grasses, close to the dark evergreen oaks, almost invisible amongst the soft blue-green *Salix alba* was an old weatherworn wooden figurehead from a ship. The curves of a woman clad in a Grecian dress were greying and cracked. Moss grew on one side, and the lacy leaves of a white jasmine clambered up over an arbour that hadn't existed yesterday. Ruby gasped as she took in the transformation. In the soft sunset the figurehead took on an almost lifelike glow, peach and pink, her smile soft and sensuous.

'She reminded me of you.' Eoin appeared beside her.

'Old, grey, cracked,' Ruby offered, only half-joking. She took the mug of tea he handed her.

'You could say that,' Eoin agreed much to her surprise. He sipped his tea. His voice deepened. 'You could also say timeless, elegant, graceful.' He took a step closer to her. If she reached out she could touch his face, feel his stubble catch the pads of her fingertips.

'Oh?' Ruby whispered.

182

Eoin took her tea. He placed the two mugs on the arm of the bench.

'So . . .' he said as he turned back to her. Brushing a strand of hair from her face, he pulled her close to him until her hips leaned against his. She shivered as his hands found a home in the belt loops of her jeans, and he leaned his forehead against hers. 'Can I kiss you?'

Something should happen. That's what Frankie had said.

'Yes.' Ruby nodded, and before he stopped smiling she was on her toes, pressing her lips to his, relishing the softness of his mouth and the warmth of his breath. She felt his hands pull her hips closer, then run up her back to cradle her head. He moaned softly and pulled away to look at her. His kiss had not been at all what she'd expected. His tenderness made her heart ache with want, but behind the desire, a lead weight lodged in her chest as his hands gently held her face and he gazed into her eyes. James had never held her that way.

'You've no idea how long I've wanted to do that,' he said, a little breathlessly. 'Ruby . . .'

'I think I do,' Ruby shifted her hips away from his, a deep blush spreading from her neck up to her forehead at his arousal. Eoin buried his head against her shoulder.

'Say you'll walk me home later?' Ruby surprised herself with her boldness. 'And stay for coffee.'

'I can do that.' Eoin raised his face with a bashful smile. 'Coffee it is.'

18

Frankie

Frankie rolled over in bed and opened her eyes. She just as quickly closed them as she realised what day it was. There was no escaping it, there never would be. The June Bank Holiday would always be a reminder of what could've been and what was lost. Seven years since Liam had gone to sea and never returned. The villagers who remembered his family would visit the memorial and lay flowers today, and the ones who remembered Dillon was his son would cast a pitying side-eye at her. Those who knew her better would check in with her, gently asking how she was feeling and was there anything they could do.

She pulled the duvet over her face. They meant well but it never helped, all their sad eyes and kind offers. There wasn't anything they could do. She wasn't their responsibility, and neither was Dillon. They couldn't give her a home, or a job, or help her to do better. As far as they were concerned, she was doing fine, because that's how it looked. There was no way she'd tell them about the nightmares she'd had after Liam's death, how the doctor said the depression she'd fallen into likely caused early labour. Nor would she ever mention how she worried about Dillon and how sad he was sometimes. They didn't need anyone feeling sorry for them. They'd always managed alone.

But now, she remembered, they had Ruby. Slowly, Frankie lowered the duvet from her face. Beside her, Dillon slept on, blissfully unaware of the importance of dates. He snuggled down and turned over, taking a fair share of the duvet with him. Frankie picked up her phone and checked her bank account. Her wages had gone in, thankfully. Sometimes the bank holiday messed up her payments. She frowned. Ruby had refused any rent or money, saying she was more than earning their keep with her work in the garden, but living there rent-free bothered her. There was no way Ruby was as flush as she said she was: the house was huge, surely she'd a mortgage and bills to pay – and she didn't work. If only Ruby would agree to take something from her, then she'd feel better. Frankie twisted her lips. Opening the banking app on her phone again, she transferred a meagre amount to the savings account she'd set up to cover the cost of the repairs to her cottage. At the moment it was all she could manage to put by, but God knows when she'd ever have saved enough to get the work done. She put her phone down, sighing.

Money. It always came back to money. There was never enough of it, and when you did have it, it didn't last. It was what had caused the biggest row she and Liam had ever had. Well, it had kicked it off. Frankie closed her eyes, thinking back to the boy she'd lost. Liam had been a risk taker, and fun. He'd always pushed against boundaries but was respectful and had a moral compass that she'd never seen before or since. It was one of the things Frankie loved about him the most. Finding out they were expecting a baby had shaken him, but after the initial shock had melted away he'd been happy – he'd even suggested they run away and come back married. His impulsivity had scared Frankie a little, but she'd laughed and said she'd rather wait. It wouldn't be fair to take the joy of a wedding away from Aggie when Frankie was all she had. He'd nodded and placed a ring on her finger, saying that one day he'd exchange it for a proper engagement ring, one with a diamond.

When he'd said he was going to sea with his father and brother and uncle that bank holiday weekend and asked her to postpone their night away, she'd thrown all her toys out of the pram.

'Don't you dare!' she had yelled as he'd cast his eyes downward. 'No, Liam, that's not fair. I'm seven months gone, and we've been planning this night away for ages. If we cancel the B&B we lose our money.'

'I'll make three times the cost of the B&B on this trawl,' he'd said earnestly. 'It makes sense.'

'Oh, so money is more important than spending time with me, the mother of your soon-to-be-born child.' Frankie remembered the hot tears she'd cried that night as he'd tried to explain his plans.

'You know that's not true,' Liam had said quietly. 'I just worry about after the baby comes. What if we don't have the money—'

'We'll never have money!' Frankie had raised her hands and dropped them. 'Don't you get that? We're not the kind of people who get rich. You're a fisherman, and I've had to give up university. All I'll ever be is a mother and a wife who sits around worrying and waiting for her husband to either come back from sea or to come down to earth.'

'Jesus, Frankie, that's cruel.' Liam had paled. Even now, she could recall how he'd run his hands through his dark hair, how he'd looked at her anxiously. 'Why are you always so negative lately? You used to think anything was possible.'

Frankie had opened her mouth, then closed it. Pursing her lips, she'd shaken her head. He hadn't heard the women at the bus stop talking about her – they sure as hell didn't talk about him other than to comment that wasn't he a great lad to stick around and support her. What the hell else should he be doing, she'd wanted to know, when he was about to become a father? She'd sucked on her teeth and swallowed down all the things she knew would really be cruel to say, like how she'd slowly but surely become isolated and trapped. Home had become a prison now instead of a haven. People she'd thought were friends had gradually disappeared, left for uni or just were too busy to spend time with her. The heat that summer had been excruciating. With a groan she remembered how she'd spent most of her time lying down with her feet up against the wall to try to keep them from swelling, while he'd been out and about, popping in to see her before he went for one pint, which invariably wound up being four. A wave of dizziness had forced her to sit down on her bed.

She'd been so angry that she wouldn't let him help her. Pushing him away as he'd fussed around her. With a grunt she'd hoisted her legs up onto the bed and up against the wall. Liam had sat there in silence beside her, his hand almost

187

touching hers on the quilted bedspread. She remembered how his energy radiated from him, his whole being poised to do whatever she needed, except stay home from the fishing trawl. He didn't have to say it. She just knew it from the way he looked at her. His dark eyes beseeched her, but she'd said nothing, just stared up at the ceiling until he finally got up. The memory of him standing in the doorway still made her heart beat fast. He'd stopped and looked back at her.

'You know I love you, don't you?' he'd asked her quietly.

Frankie choked up as she wished with all her might she'd spoken then. But instead, she'd just blinked and nodded mutely. He'd looked at her for a moment longer, then left. She'd heard his footsteps on the stairs, then the soft click of the front door – he hadn't even stopped to say *see ya* to Aggie – and then there'd been silence.

'I just don't want you to go,' she'd said to the empty room.

She'd been so angry. He'd left without them coming to an agreement, left with anger between them, something they'd made a promise to each other not to do. Aggie called her down for dinner, and she ate in silence. She'd watched television with Aggie, barely noticing what was going on in their favourite soap, before wearily going to bed. Sleep hadn't come easy, and when it did it was a replay of the conversation they'd had. She remembered waking up that night with a start. Her digital bedside clock had shone at her, half past one. She remembered sitting up, sweat beading her top lip as her breath caught in her throat. Something was going to happen. She knew it. In an instant she was out of bed and hauling on her leggings and T-shirt. She'd smoothed it down over her bump and pushed her feet into her sandals. As quietly as she could she'd made her way downstairs and let herself out of the house.

It had taken her longer than she'd expected to get to the harbour, but she made it in time. The men were just about ready to go. She'd stepped out of the darkness and crossed the concrete, carefully stepping over ropes and chains, towards the trawler. Liam had been in the thick of it. He'd looked so strong, and healthy, smiling and laughing as he worked. One of the men had caught sight of her and called to Liam. He'd immediately seen her, and left what he was doing.

'Frankie.' Liam had taken her hands and led her over to a box to sit her down. 'What are you doing here?'

'You left and we were fighting and we never do that.' Frankie had picked at her nail. Her breath had slowed and her nose had fizzed the way it always did when she was about to cry. 'It felt all wrong.'

'Come here to me.' Liam had pulled her to him. She'd held him close for a moment before pushing him away. His overalls stank.

'I can't,' she'd said. 'The smell!'

He'd laughed. 'Sorry, I forgot how sensitive your nose is now.' With a more serious face he'd squeezed her hands. 'Thank you for coming down.'

'I had no choice,' she'd told him. 'I love you.'

'I love you, too.' Frankie closed her eyes and remembered how he'd tilted her face to his and kissed her deeply. 'I'll be back soon, I promise, and we'll have enough made to go buy the baby's buggy *and* go away for a night.'

She'd nodded silently, but her stomach had tightened and the back of her neck had prickled. The hairs on her arms had risen. Something was wrong.

'I feel like something bad is going to happen,' she'd said quietly, her eyes on the trawler where Liam's dad and brother waited patiently. Liam had taken her face in his hands.

'Like what?' he'd asked gently.

'I don't know, but something isn't right.'

'It'll be all right – don't worry.' He'd looked over his shoulder at the waiting men. 'Look, I have to go . . . I'll see ya soon.' He'd kissed her again and gently touched her belly. 'Look after the two of ye.'

She'd climbed the stairs to the top of the harbour wall and watched as the trawler made its way out of the harbour until it disappeared in the darkness. The top of the wall had been cold, and stones came away easily in her hand. The wind had picked up and she'd shivered in her T-shirt, only deciding to leave when the first heavy drops of rain began. She'd been soaked through by the time she'd gotten home. Shivering and blue, she'd peeled her clothes off and draped them over the radiator under her window. Wrapped up in her dressing gown, she'd pulled the duvet and pillows from the bed to set up camp by the low bedroom window. The rain had already stopped, and she could just make out the sea; it had been dark and squally. The waves rose and broke into foam as the sun began to rise, but nothing to be worried about. Cradling her bump, she'd smiled as the baby moved and began to kick.

'He'll be home soon,' she'd crooned softly. 'And then we're going to look for a flat so we can be a proper family. It's going to be great fun. We can come up here to see Granny Aggie and make sandcastles up on North Beach. Daddy will show you how to catch crabs and how to swim. He's a great swimmer you know. He even managed to teach me.'

She'd watched the sunrise, mesmerised as it had crested over the waves and sent sparkles and glitter over the sea. Yawning, Frankie had lain down on her nest of blankets and within minutes had fallen asleep. It was after eleven when she'd woken. The house had been quiet; nothing stirred. Sitting up she'd peered out of the window again. There had been a strange sound, a kind of chatter, as if there was a fair or market going on. Heaving herself up from the floor she'd dressed and gone downstairs. Aggie hadn't been there. A bag of potatoes had lain open on the counter in the kitchen, Aggie's peeling knife beside it. The sink had been filled with water. The same dread she'd felt the night before had crept over Frankie. Her stomach had churned as her hands absentmindedly stroked her bump.

Outside the sky had darkened. The bright morning had been rapidly swallowed up by fast-moving rain clouds. Frankie had gone outside anyway, and had made her way towards the seafront. People had been hurrying home, heads down against the spitting rain, sand buckets bouncing against knees and legs. The strange chattering sound had grown louder as she'd turned towards the harbour. No matter how many times she replayed the memory in her mind, Frankie would never forget the moment she saw Aggie walking towards her, nor could she forget the way her shoulders had drooped. She remembered standing still and watching Aggie's slow progression, and how – when Aggie had finally looked up – there were tears on her face.

Frankie remembered, as if it had happened in slow motion, cradling her bump and shaking her head as she tried to move, desperate to get away from Aggie before she could say what she knew was true.

'No, no, no. No,' she'd moaned as Aggie had pulled her into her arms. Aggie – warm, soft, and tiny – had held Frankie tightly to keep her from falling to her knees.

'They don't know anything yet,' Aggie had said. 'They're searching. Come on, we'll light a candle.'

'I don't want to light a candle.' Frankie hadn't been able to move.

'What harm can it do?' Aggie had said. 'Come on now, I won't have you standing here with them all watching you. Raise that chin up and come with me now. I'm not listening to no.'

Frankie had stared at the tiny woman in front of her. She remembered Aggie wiping away her tears and then staring just as determinedly back at her.

'All they know is that there was a distress call,' she'd said. 'The boats are gone out. There's every reason to hope.'

Frankie had followed Aggie to the church, knowing with all her heart that no amount of candle lighting would bring them back. The sea, the beautiful, treacherous sea, had done exactly what it had been doing for as long as it had existed: taken as it pleased and moved on without a whisper of regret. She'd sat in the pew beside Aggie and listened to the old woman mutter prayer after prayer until she was almost in a trance. Unblinking, she'd stared at the rows of candles, the bright flames flickering and dancing as more and more people came in to add their own light to the dozens of others. The murmuring had grown louder as the pews in front of the statue of Mary, Star of the Sea, filled up with villagers.

It hadn't been long before the priest had come out to

sit among the women whose heads were bent in supplication. Frankie remembered the kind words he'd offered and how he'd joined them for a while, his weather-beaten face lacking its usual animation. That's when she knew it was real. Father Cribbin was a steadfast and devout priest. He'd been new to the parish back then, but he knew how to read people, unlike Father Long, who was all for calling you a sinner, even as you confessed.

She remembered thinking that night had surely come as the church darkened until the glow from the candles was the only source of light. Rain had pelted the solid stone structure, pounding at the stained glass so hard that Frankie had been sure it would shatter. Everyone inside had been quiet. They'd passed knowing looks and then someone had started a decade of the Rosary. She'd listened to the rise and fall of subdued voices and had leaned back into the pew. They'd seen this all before. The outcome wasn't going to be good. Black dots had swarmed her vision, her breath sharpening and catching in her ribcage.

Pushing against the faint she'd staggered to her feet and run outside and stood in the pouring rain, staring out to sea. Someone had thrown their coat around her and tried to bring her back inside, but she'd pushed them away. Only Aggie had been able to convince her to come in as the Coast Guard helicopter flew overhead. The search and rescue had rapidly turned into a search and recovery operation as the news filtered back that the trawler had sunk. Liam's uncle had been found in the water, his brother too. They'd both drowned. His father had been airlifted to the hospital but pronounced dead on arrival. They'd never found Liam's body.

There was an inquiry into the sinking of his family's trawler, but nothing untoward had been found and the investigation was dropped as quickly as the storm had begun that day. The burial of the three men had happened so quickly that Frankie couldn't remember if she'd gone or not. She had vague memories of being in the church, a notion that Liam's mother had hugged her and asked her to sit with them in the first pew. She remembered thinking she should have run away and married him when she had the chance.

God knows what happened after the church. Her memory drew a blank. What she did remember was that the days seemed to last forever and the nights were twice as long as the days. Everything had been muted or black. Sounds had come from underwater and she'd imagined that was all Liam saw and heard now. Sometimes she'd walk for hours only to find herself back at the harbour where she'd seen him last. Sometimes she'd find that she was standing on the edge of the pier, staring down into the dark water and thinking that maybe it was where she should be, down there with him.

It had been Liam's mother who persuaded her to see the doctor, right before she'd moved away, back to her home place, hours away in Donegal, leaving Frankie and Dillon behind. The doctor had suggested she go to therapy to help deal with her grief, but Frankie had gone inwards and didn't want to take his advice. Instead she'd taken to walking late at night when she couldn't sleep. That was when she'd met Jürgen for the first time. She'd gone out very late as an unusual fit of energy had come over her, but had struggled to walk far. She'd made it as far as

Jürgen's Angel Shop before she'd doubled over as a contraction seized her. That's where Jürgen had found her. She'd been almost incoherent with fear and confusion. The baby wasn't due, she remembered babbling as Jürgen had taken her to the hospital, but Dillon had been insistent and had come into the dark world she inhabited early.

Tossing her memories aside, Frankie pushed the duvet from her legs. There was no point in remembering the bad times, she thought as she padded down the hallway and up the stairs to make a coffee. She should just think of the good times. She paused and listened. Ruby was, for once, still sound asleep. In fact, she'd been sleeping more since she and Eoin had become something of an item. Frankie took her coffee to the balcony and stared out at the sea. Dillon had never gotten to meet Liam, but she'd made sure that he had a photo of him and that he knew Liam loved him.

Sipping her coffee, Frankie sighed and closed her eyes. She'd never asked either Nicole or Aggie about her father. He was never referred to, nor mentioned. Aggie acted as if he didn't exist, like Nicole had gotten pregnant in some contemporary immaculate conception. Maybe it was time she knew who he was, now that she had no one else in the world but Dillon. Well, her mother existed, but what exactly she'd be willing to say about the man who'd gotten her pregnant was anyone's guess. Frankie rolled her eyes. If the past was anything to go on, Nicole would say nothing. The place to start looking would be among Aggie's files and records. Surely there was some clue there.

19

Ruby

'Thanks.' Ruby took the steaming mug from Eoin and sipped. He made the best coffee she'd ever tasted, and had yet to tell her his secret. Sitting on the deck outside his house, she gazed out at the sea. Eoin draped a throw over her knees and settled in the chair beside her.

'I was surprised to see you up early this morning,' he said, his eyes crinkling. 'I've missed our dawn chats this last week. Something's been keeping you in bed.'

'I'm a little more tired lately.' Ruby stifled a yawn. 'So I'm trying to rest. I read an article that said that if you can't sleep, then rest. Apparently, it's almost as good as a full eight hours of shut-eye.'

'Ah.' Eoin winked. 'So you're not fast asleep dreaming of me, then?'

Ruby stuck her tongue out at him and he grinned. She'd grown used to Eoin's easy-going manner and forward ways. Since the May Bank Holiday, she'd been joining him on his deck for a very early morning coffee. He'd noticed her up and about, as early as he was, watching the sunrise and the sea shifting. They were fellow light sleepers, although Ruby remembered that she wasn't always like that. Before James, she'd easily sleep a whole night without stirring, and she only ever woke up early when she was a teenager and doing school exams. Since James's passing, she'd been sleeping when she needed to – which wasn't a lot, apparently.

There'd been so many new obstacles to overcome; every day brought her a new learning curve. Everything was exhausting – the grief, the loneliness, the not knowing what to do, what to cook, where to go, what to wear. She'd started opening up to Eoin during their early morning coffees. He listened deeply, and when he asked questions, it always felt that he cared, and wasn't just probing for information on how much money she had, or which charity she was supporting this year. Leaning forward, she tugged the throw closer to her and twisted her lips.

'I don't know,' she teased. 'Maybe I am. But . . . I feel guilty, sometimes.' She frowned. 'James . . . there never was anyone other than him, and now look at me: I'm here with you and it's lovely, so please don't take this the wrong way, but it feels like I'm cheating, you know?'

Eoin said nothing. He sipped his coffee, and looked out to sea. Ruby, following his gaze, stared out to sea too.

Eoin cleared his throat. 'You don't wear your wedding ring,' he said finally. 'When did you stop doing that?'

Fidgeting with her mug, Ruby felt the heat rise in her face. 'Only recently, and it's only sometimes I don't wear it,' she admitted. 'It didn't feel right wearing it. It connects me to James – and I'm not sure he'd like some of the things I'm thinking, or doing, these days.'

'But he's not here,' Eoin said gently.

'No, he's not.' Ruby twisted the mug in her hands.

'So, why is he in your head, then?' Eoin asked. 'What's he telling you?'

'Oh, God.' Ruby shifted and put the mug down on the tree stump that served as a makeshift coffee table. 'What's he telling me? That I'm too old for you, and that he knew I'd be out of control without him to rein me in.'

'Out of control? You?' Eoin's eyebrows shot up. 'You're not someone I'd ever say was "out of control".'

'Oh, I used to be,' Ruby said. 'When I met James I wasn't steady. I'd party all weekend, and was . . . well, I thought I was just being friendly, but James told me men saw me as a flirt, a tease, and I didn't like that.'

'You didn't like what he said?' Eoin asked.

'No, I didn't like being perceived as a tease,' Ruby said. 'He was right to point it out.'

'But you were young when you met him, right? Barely out of your teens. Ruby, I have to ask,' Eoin said. 'Did anyone else say you were a tease?'

'I was twenty-one,' Ruby said. She rubbed her arm briskly and avoided answering him. A line formed between her eyes. 'I was grown-up enough to know better than to flirt with men like that.'

'Men like what?' Eoin asked.

'James's friends, his work colleagues, and, you know . . .' Ruby stopped rubbing her arm.

'Older men who should also know better than to take advantage of a young woman from outside their social circle.' Eoin took another sip of his coffee. He looked into his mug. 'Think about that for a minute, will you? I'll make us some fresh coffee.' Unfurling his long limbs, he got up from the chair and went into the kitchen, leaving Ruby alone on the deck.

Ruby pulled a face at his back, feeling a flash of irritation. He hadn't a clue, she thought, about her and James's relationship. What was he trying to do – make James into the bad guy? He wasn't like that – controlling and scheming. He wasn't what Eoin was suggesting. Bristling, Ruby crossed her legs and arms, and waited for him to come back.

'Here you are.' He handed her the mug and sat down.

Ruby stared at him. Wrapping her hands around the mug, she bit her top lip before speaking. 'James wasn't a bad man, Eoin.' Her voice shook. 'You manage to make him sound like he was mean, a bully or something.'

Eoin simply nodded and sipped his drink.

Ruby groaned and leaned forward. 'Don't just sit there and ignore me!'

'I'm not ignoring you,' Eoin said. 'I'm thinking about what you're saying and what you've told me about James already.'

'And?' Ruby snorted. 'And what? What are you thinking?'

'Honestly? I'm thinking that he was a manipulative person. He moulded you, from a young and impressionable age, to be what he wanted you to be . . . whatever his reason was – I don't know. He's in your head every minute of every day, and yes, that's normal after a loss, but the way he's in your head is unhealthy. His presence in your head disrupts your choices. It makes you question everything you do. I've watched you dither over a menu for far too long, eventually choosing the salad and no dessert. Fine, if that's genuinely your choice, but I don't think it is.' Eoin paused. Ruby paled and sat back in her chair, shaken by his astute insights into her. She wrapped her hands around her mug. The fresh coffee steamed the air between them.

Eoin scratched his chin before continuing. His blue eyes trained on Ruby's face, taking in every twitch and sigh she made. And when he continued, his voice was softer than she'd ever heard it. 'I'm thinking that you're not ready to hear what I'm saying, because you've defended him so ardently. It's almost as if you're fighting with yourself. I think you know what you want, but you're not used to doing that. You're used to pleasing someone else all the time. You've been trained to consider what James wants, what he thinks is right, and to do it.'

Ruby pursed her lips. She looked stonily at him. 'My husband of over thirty years loved me. He took care of me, and gave me opportunities the likes of which I'd never even dreamed of.' She leaned forward again, her elbows on her knees.

Eoin nodded. 'He did. He gave you the opportunities he wanted you to have.'

Ruby stared at him, stunned. 'What?'

'Did he give you any of the opportunities that *you* dreamed of?' Eoin asked gently.

'Opportunities that I dreamed of?' She sat back. 'I . . . I don't understand what you're saying.'

'You met him when you were young. You must've had

dreams and desires – things you wanted to do, places you wanted to go. Did you want to travel, or have a career?'

'I suppose I did,' Ruby said. 'Didn't everyone?'

'I know I did,' Eoin said. 'I wanted to be an astronaut when I was six. Then I thought I'd be a fireman for a while. I discovered how much I loved the outdoors when I was fourteen, and decided to be a gardener. But it was a trip to the Eden Project that changed my whole life. Before I just wanted to create beautiful spaces. After that trip, I wanted to create environmental spaces that were ecologically sound while also uplifting. So, here I am now. What about you?'

'I.' Ruby stammered. 'I, I don't know. I can't really remember what my dreams were back then. I suppose, I wanted to . . . I would've liked to have . . . I don't know. I think I wanted to decorate and design things.'

'What kind of things?' Eoin leaned forward.

'I don't know.' Ruby shrugged. 'Interiors, I wanted to create beautiful spaces, too. But inside, rather than outside.'

'Oh? That sounds interesting.' Eoin smiled. 'What made you want to do that?'

'It started after the time I was put in charge of props at the drama group,' Ruby said. Her face relaxed into a smile. 'We put on awful productions but we'd great support. The best part for me was setting a scene to create a feeling so I'd scavenge the charity shops, and beg or borrow what we needed, and I was pretty good at it.'

She picked up her coffee and took a deep mouthful. Some of her happiest moments had been backstage, racing around making sure the stagehands were doing their job properly. James had found it amusing at first, but gradually, he'd become sneering about it. Eventually, his scathing remarks had hit their target. She'd stopped going, and the group had fallen apart not long after. He'd brought her to shows in London instead, and made comments like: 'See, this is how the theatre should be.' When she said the Castletown Cove Players were only amateurs, he'd laughed and said, 'Barely even that.' She'd laughed, at the time, thinking of how diva-esque some of the players became during show week.

'There was one time, I think I was twenty-two,' she said to Eoin, half laughing. 'We were putting on *Dancing at Lughnasa*, and Valerie was the leading lady. She gave an amazing performance, but it all went to her head. After the show, we went down to The Birds – but it was called McCarthy's Bar back then – just like we always did, and Valerie was showing off. When it was James's round she ordered a double brandy, laughing that she deserved it, seeing as she'd found out she was nominated for an award. He got her the brandy and told her how much he'd enjoyed the performance, when she lit into him. I'd announced I wouldn't be back next year, and she didn't like it.' Ruby smiled tightly. 'James said to not mind her, that I'd soon be flexing my skills and interior designing my own house and didn't need her jealousy.'

She picked at a piece of fluff on the throw. She'd never had a say in decorating the Dublin house, not really. James had somehow managed to get someone to 'help develop her little ideas'. It had never been the same as what she'd imagined she'd be doing, though. She'd never had the freedom to do exactly what she'd envisioned.

'You've definitely got skills,' Eoin said. 'And they're

transferrable. Take the garden plans you've come up with – they're superb. They've a freshness that I've rarely seen.'

Ruby kept her eyes trained on the fluff she was picking at, afraid to look into his eyes and see his honesty. Her garden plans *were* good, she felt it in her bones, but it had been a long time since she'd listened to her gut instinct. She wished she could feel as confident about them as Eoin seemed to be.

She felt Eoin's eyes on her, and her cheeks flamed. As if sensing her discomfort he turned his gaze away and nodded over to Ruby's house, where Frankie had appeared on the balcony. She was staring straight out to sea, and hadn't noticed them. 'How're you all getting on?'

'Great,' Ruby said, glad to have moved on away from the subject of James and forgotten dreams. 'They're not a bother, at all. Frankie is great with Dillon, and he's a fantastic kid. The house is as it should be, now that they're in it. I wouldn't change things for the world.'

'That's lovely.' Eoin watched Frankie. 'Ruby, don't downplay what you're doing for them. Because of you, they have a decent roof over their heads, and I know you're not taking any rent from Frankie—'

'How'd you know that?' Ruby sat up straight. 'Did she tell you?'

'No, she didn't. It's just the kind of person you are.' Eoin turned to her with a smile. 'I hope that Frankie will remember her dreams and try to pursue them.'

'She never talks about anything much, apart from Dillon, and the garden,' Ruby admitted.

'Ah, she still has dreams.' Eoin sighed. 'You should try to remind her.'

Ruby nodded. Her shoulders relaxed and she uncrossed her legs. 'I worry about her, Eoin, as if she's my own daughter. It's weird, isn't it?'

'Not weird, at all.' Eoin put his now empty mug down. 'You two have a great friendship. Why wouldn't you care? You only feel it's strange because of the age difference between you, but age isn't a big deal when it comes to friendships.'

'What about romantic friendships?' Ruby blushed.

'Ah, we're back around full circle, now, aren't we?' Eoin said. 'Let me gently remind you that James was a generation older than you, and you had no problem with that, did you?'

Ruby shook her head. 'No, but . . .' Unsaid words hung between them. She knew he meant that she should give him a proper chance and forget about the age difference between them. But somehow it felt different when the woman was older.

Shrugging as if he'd said enough, Eoin picked up their empty mugs. 'Well, I don't know about you, but I've work to do.'

Ruby got up. She waved at Frankie, but Frankie didn't see her.

'Oh, be extra nice to Frankie today.' Eoin came and stood by her side. 'It's the anniversary of Dillon's father's death. Seven years now.'

'I didn't know.' Ruby turned away from him and back to watching Frankie, now recognising the blank expression on the young woman's face. 'What happened?'

'Lost at sea,' Eoin said quietly. 'He was called Liam. His name is on the memorial down by the harbour, alongside his brother's, father's and uncle's names. She's still hurting.'

'I can tell,' Ruby said. 'When does the hurting stop?'

'I don't know,' Eoin said. 'I just don't know. What I do know is that having a focus helps.'

Ruby squeezed his arm, then turned back to Frankie, wondering what Frankie would focus on if she had the chance. Ruby raked through their conversations and realised that Frankie had never once spoken about what she'd like to do if she wasn't a mother and working at the hotel. Dropping her gaze, Ruby swallowed. She'd been so caught up in her own life that she'd assumed Frankie was exactly where she wanted to be. She had everything that Ruby had always thought would be hers one day: a child and a home place where everyone welcomed her. Rubbing the back of her neck, Ruby realised she'd made an awful assumption when it came to Frankie's life. Frankie's reluctance to talk about anything other than Dillon was more likely because she was stuck in a rut.

Seven years was a long time to be in the same place, mentally and physically. Frankie's daily routine was the same day after day, with some variation when extra shifts at work came about, but other than that, there were no excursions, no holidays, and nothing to lift the spirits. She brought home iced buns every Thursday, but that was it; that was the highlight of the week for Frankie and Dillon. Ruby could've kicked herself. How had she not noticed the monotony of their lives? She'd been so wrapped up in her own existence, torturing herself over silly decisions like furniture placement, and whether or not James would have liked something or some colour.

She should've been more attentive to Frankie and Dillon. After all, they'd lost their home and their anchor, Aggie, all within a year. Now that she thought about it, she recognised Frankie's tentativeness in the house, how careful she was with things, how mindful she was of noise. She was clearly wary of taking advantage of Ruby. She never overstepped the mark and was more considerate than anyone Ruby had ever met.

Ruby watched Frankie, as she stood on the balcony. Frankie's face was still, her lips downturned, her eyes focused on nothing. She needed a focus; they both did . . . maybe finding something together would be the place to start.

20

Frankie

Frankie twisted her engagement ring around her finger. It was Thursday now, and this was the third afternoon Ruby had been acting strangely. She was pacing like a cat on a hot tin roof, moving things about the kitchen and emptying bins that were barely full. She had twice asked her if she'd like a takeaway for dinner – Ruby was becoming fond of takeaways; this would be her second this week. But surely worrying over what to have for dinner wasn't causing such angst – maybe she'd changed her mind about them living with her. Maybe they were too much, taking up time and space in Ruby's life, or she didn't like them enough to want them to stay. Whatever it was, the sooner she said it the better. Frankie gulped down the last of her coffee. Twisting her lips, she put her mug down on the counter a little sharper than she intended.

'Ruby, for the love of God would you sit down!' she blurted. 'That's the third time you've wiped that spot.'

Ruby stopped wiping the counter and looked up startled. She shook her head and threw the cloth into the sink. 'Sorry, sorry! I'm lost in my head,' she said.

'I can see that,' Frankie said. 'What's going on?' A shiver ran down her spine. Now that she'd asked, she didn't want to hear Ruby's reply.

'A couple of things,' Ruby said. 'I don't want to bother you.'

'No, it's fine,' Frankie said, cringing inside. 'I've half an hour before I go collect Dillon from school. You can talk to me.'

Ruby opened the drawer and took out some papers. She slid them across the counter. Frankie reddened painfully as she recognised the night class brochures she'd taken from work. Ruby looked equally embarrassed.

'You left these out, and I was going through them,' she said. 'There's a gardening course. I'm half considering doing it.'

'Really?' Frankie breathed out. Thank God! It wasn't them. It was a night class that was making Ruby act all weird. 'That's a great idea – you absolutely should do it.'

Ruby looked relieved. 'I should – that's what Eoin said. I'll book it by the weekend.' She nodded firmly.

'Well, that didn't take much convincing.' Frankie laughed. 'I didn't have you pegged for a student!'

Ruby touched the side of her nose and winked. 'Ah, see – there's lots about me you don't know. Anyhow, that's me sorted. What'll it take to convince you to do one, as well?'

Frankie blanched. Ruby flicked through the brochure. Frankie watched her find the dog-eared page she'd flicked to over and over. The course ringed with red pen.

'I didn't know you were interested in psychology,' Ruby

said. 'This one here, you've underlined *and* circled it. Certificate in Psychology. I feel bad for not knowing this.'

'Sure, how could you know?' Frankie shrugged, and walked towards the stairs as if to go.

'I should know,' Ruby said quietly. 'We're friends, aren't we? I've told you loads about Eoin, and the garden, and—'

'Don't feel bad,' Frankie interrupted. 'It's just the way the conversations went. And we're only new friends.'

'I suppose,' Ruby said. She looked down. 'All the same, I can't explain this feeling I have – but I have this feeling like I've known you for, well, forever. I'm not a crazy lady – I promise!' She raised her hands and gave a half-hearted laugh.

A warmth flashed through Frankie, starting at her toes and flooding her entire body. She grinned and stopped trying to make an escape. She hovered on the top step, her hand gripping the banister. Turning around she blinked back tears.

'I do, too. Sometimes, it feels like you're my big sister, or something.' She shrugged. 'I can't explain it either.'

'I knew your mother,' Ruby said, suddenly, as though blurting out a confession. 'We were in school together. We were quite good friends, for a while, actually.'

Frankie froze. She swallowed; her hand tightened on the banister. 'Why didn't you say?'

Ruby looked abashed. 'I don't know, really. It never seemed to . . . come up.'

Frankie snorted. 'You probably know her better than I do, then. I haven't seen her in years. She's never been a part of my life, really.'

'I'm sorry,' Ruby said.

'It's not your fault,' Frankie said. 'I don't know whose fault it is, but I try my best not to feel like it's mine.'

'I think she's a fool,' Ruby said angrily. 'But Nicole always had to be different. She couldn't just live her life, had to be out running around the world, living it up, pretending to be something. If she'd given you and Dillon any time at all she'd know what life is really all about – family, and kids, and caring for each other. She doesn't know how lucky she is.' Ruby stopped abruptly, seeming to come back to herself. She snatched up the dishcloth from the sink, and began rubbing at the spotless counter again.

Frankie gasped. Ruby had never spoken as heatedly about anything before. Tears pricked the backs of her eyes. Family. Ruby thought family was important, and she was proud of her. Swiping away a rogue tear, she sniffed and moved back into the kitchen.

'For what it's worth, I think you'd have made a wonderful mother.' Frankie took the cloth from Ruby and took hold of her hand. 'I've never met anyone like you. You're beyond generous, with everyone. I've noticed the little things you do, and you think no one does. You make sure Sandra feels important here, always asking her advice. You bring extra lunch to the garden to share with Father Cribbin. He told me he looks forward to seeing you, that you're more considerate than most of his parishioners. Yes, he really did say that – as well as that he wished you'd come to mass.'

Ruby shook her head, grinned reluctantly and looked away. 'Well, he mostly has a miserable ham sandwich, so I just couldn't help sharing my lunch.'

210

'And,' Frankie continued, 'you laugh at all of Dessie's jokes – even though they are always pathetic, slightly racist, and definitely sexist – while subtly telling him off at the same time. You know he's become more tolerant of others because of you. Now, if that's not the sign of a saint, I don't know what is. You help all these people in the kindest, most inclusive ways . . . You, Ruby, are a good person.'

Ruby studied her toes. 'The person I'd like to help the most, is you.' She looked up at Frankie.

'You do more than enough for me, and for Dillon.' Frankie stepped back. She looked around the kitchen. 'You've given us a home.'

Ruby sighed. 'Frankie, anyone would do that.'

'Not everyone,' Frankie said. Her grip on the handrail tightened again. 'I love you, and Dillon loves you. Thank you.'

'Come here!' Ruby hurried to Frankie. She pulled her into her arms and squeezed her tightly.

Frankie tentatively put her arms around Ruby. Ruby was thinner than she looked – her ribs were sharp beneath her jumper. She'd certainly lost weight recently. She hugged Ruby tightly, allowing her head to rest on her shoulder, and breathed in the soft perfume Ruby liked to wear. It was soft, almost like talc, with a warm note to it. It smelt like coming home on a rainy day, warm, comforting and caring. The last proper, grown-up hug she'd had, had been from Aggie, just hours before she'd said goodbye to her. She shuddered and began to cry as Ruby rubbed her back and shushed her.

'Oh, I'm sorry, I don't know . . .' Pulling away, Frankie

wiped her nose with her sleeve and looked away, to try to hide her eyes from Ruby.

'It's okay,' Ruby said. 'You don't need to apologise.'

'It's just . . . one of those days.' Frankie wiped her eyes.

'I know.' Ruby offered her a tissue. 'We all have those kinds of days. Frankie, listen, I'm deadly serious when I say I'll do a course if you will. I'm not as determined as you are. If I go into this alone, I'll quit. I know I will. But if you were studying too – not the same course, naturally – I'd feel like I have a partner in crime, so to speak.'

'I don't know.' Frankie blew her nose. Moving away from Ruby, she lowered her eyes. There was no way she could afford the course she wanted, even with the payment plan the university offered. There was no point in doing any other course. Flower arranging, photography, accounting . . . none of it was appealing.

'I'll watch Dillon when you're in class,' Ruby continued. 'And I can add you to my car insurance so you can drive there – you can drive, can't you?'

Frankie shook her head. There'd never been a need for her to drive anywhere, and Aggie hadn't had a car. Instead, they took the bus whenever they needed anything in the city. The realisation of how small her world was crashed down on her. There was barely a day when she'd gone further afield than the hotel, or the school.

The course was in the next town. There was a bus there, but getting home would be a problem as the last bus home left half an hour after the class started. But it didn't matter. It was too expensive, and what would happen when the course was over? The qualification didn't mean anything if a full course at the university wasn't the next step.

Ruby was still talking. 'Never mind, I'll teach you. Well, I can teach you the basics. You'll pick it up in no time. Now, I was thinking about the course you're looking at – I thought that, well, I'd pay for it and when you're ready, whenever that is, you can pay me back. That way we both get to do something – we can't sit here all winter and stagnate.'

Frankie widened her eyes. Was Ruby for real? There was no way she could take that amount of money from Ruby, let alone pay it back 'whenever'. Who in their right mind would, or even could, offer to pay over a thousand euros for a night course? Frankie rubbed her forehead. What with the money she was going to have to spend on the cottage, she might be able to pay Ruby back in about ten years . . .

Ruby was on a roll, back at the island unit excitedly poring over the booklet, babbling away about signing them both up as soon as possible. Frankie pulled at the neck of her T-shirt. She needed some air and some time to think.

'Um, Ruby, I've got to go. Dillon . . .' Frankie pointed to the stairs.

'Oh, of course, yes. Go on,' Ruby said. 'Don't mind me. I'm so thrilled! I've never done a class in anything. This is going to be great, Frankie. We'll be on top of the world! Go get Dillon – we'll finish talking about it later.'

The walk to the school went by in a flash, Frankie replaying what had just happened over and over in her mind. Frankie kicked a stone and watched it skitter away. Liam would tell her to go for it. 'Take it – what have you got to lose?' was his motto. He'd said it often enough, but he wasn't here, living in someone else's home, depending on their charity. Scratching her arm, Frankie turned the corner and saw the school. There were cars parked everywhere, up on footpaths and blocking driveways. Frankie squeezed past an SUV, her top catching on the hedge a homeowner had put up to deter errant car parking. The woman in the car didn't raise her eyes from her phone screen, even when it was clear another parent with a toddler in a stroller had to go out into the traffic to pass her.

Frankie recognised the woman in the car. Keeva Smyth-O'Byrne was on the parents' association, and was extremely vocal about the opportunities she insisted the primary school provide her child. Frankie glanced in at the woman, but Keeva kept her eyes down. More than once they'd come to loggerheads over a class Keeva wanted to be included in the children's extracurricular options.

The last time, Keeva had made a pointed remark that some parents just weren't giving enough time or energy to the parents' association's events, resulting in the fact that their children were missing out on, in Keeva's words, 'formative chances to explore their individualities and to expand their strengths'. Frankie's blood had boiled as she'd listened to the woman demand that parents carve out time to create and attend money raisers. Eventually, Frankie had raised her hand, and when she'd been ignored by Keeva long enough, she'd stood up, and quietly, yet clearly, had told Keeva to shut her trap.

'We're all busy,' Frankie had said. 'Working to pay for the extras you've already managed to somehow get passed.' The room had gone deathly quiet before a ripple of muted laughter made Keeva redden. She'd quickly regained her composure and raked her gaze up and down Frankie.

'Ah yes, *working* at the hotel . . .' Keeva had let her words hang in the air. Frankie had gritted her jaw as the woman next to her gasped. 'We can excuse you, I suppose. You're doing your best as a long and loyal staff member. I'm sure everyone will agree with me on that.'

Now, Frankie turned her back on Keeva in her big white SUV. She'd been humiliated. Keeva had also more or less said that Frankie would never amount to anything – she'd been in the same job for so long. Agreeing to do the night classes with Ruby would take her one step away from the likes of Keeva Smyth-O'Byrne. Who knows – her poor darling daughter might end up in therapy, and she might be her therapist! Frankie grinned. She'd go for it, as Liam would say – she'd tell Ruby she'd do the course, but only if they could work out a repayment plan. A twinge niggled in the back of her mind. She had savings she could use, but she'd been saving to repair the cottage, not take a night class. Maybe if she spoke to management again they'd give her a chance to prove herself on reception, or at the very least they'd give her more hours. No one was going to say that she'd risen up by climbing on someone else's back.

Leaning against the wall, Frankie watched as young children rambled out of the school doors. Dillon would be one of the last kids out; he didn't like the boisterous exit most of the boys in his class made, and always hung back. Behind her, Frankie heard Keeva get out of her car and open the door for her daughter to clamber in. They didn't even say hello to each other. Maggie waved from the classroom window, and Frankie waved back. She could just about make out Dillon as he pulled his backpack on. Wait until he heard she was going to go back to school! He'd be so excited for her. Frankie did a little dance, her face one huge smile as he ambled through the gate and towards her. He had yet another book about bugs tucked under his arm.

'Come here to me, buddy!' Frankie called and opened her arms to him. 'I've missed your face today.'

'I missed all of you.' Dillon giggled and squealed as Frankie tickled him with a kiss under his chin.

'I've got some great news,' Frankie said. 'I'm going to go back to school.'

Dillon's eyes grew round. 'Back to school? Here – with me?'

'No, to a special school for adults,' Frankie said. She took his backpack from him and flung it over her shoulder. 'Me and Ruby are going to go together, at night-time.'

'Oh, Mammy,' Dillon said. His eyes shone. He jumped up and down before throwing his arms around her. 'You're going to have so much fun.'

Frankie laughed and ruffled his hair, as Keeva drove past with a face like a wet week. 'I am absolutely going to have the best of fun – what have I got to lose!'

21

Ruby

Eoin chose the yoga mat next to Ruby's, and Ruby found her shoulders relaxing as he did. She'd been worried he'd be upset with her after their last conversation, but he seemed fine, stretching and smiling as she watched him. She smiled back at him, loving how his nose wrinkled when he reached over his head to stretch further.

Jürgen clapped his hands and they all looked over at him.

'Hello, everyone. It's so lovely to see so many of you here tonight, especially as we have the honour of being guided in our yoga session by Heidi Swan, who comes all the way from New Mexico and is touring Ireland this summer. Heidi assures me that yoga is for everyone, movement is the medicine for a lot of our ailments and that this session will suit all levels – from absolute beginners to those who've a bit more experience, as Heidi will personally assist each and every one of you. As always we will wind up our meeting with a sharing circle so don't rush away afterwards.'

Ruby turned to Eoin. 'Are you a beginner or experienced?' she asked with a twinkle in her eye.

'Oh, I've had a little practice.' He winked at her. 'I'm a little rusty, but able and willing to give it a go.'

'I'll keep that in mind.' Ruby grinned.

They were standing on yoga mats beside their bench. She'd shucked off her wellies and shoved them under the bench. They now leaned up against his work boots as if they were meant to be that way. Bending down, she rubbed the back of her calf, feeling the lump that was becoming more and more prominent. Her smile faded. Hopefully no one would notice it, although her leggings didn't hide much. At first she'd thought it was a varicose vein and was embarrassed, but there was no discolouration, and it didn't look like one either. It was slightly smaller than a golf ball and thankfully, it didn't hurt that much. It was just not going away. Straightening up she caught Frankie looking at her with concern, and Ruby gave her a swift smile.

'Are you ready for this?' She gestured to the mats.

'Nope,' Frankie said. 'Hey, is your leg all right? I've seen you rub it a few times now.'

'It's grand,' Ruby said briskly. 'Just a thing – a small swelling. It came up after I bumped my leg on the furniture when we moved it out of your room. It seems to be getting bigger, though.'

'That's not good.' Frankie's forehead creased. She moved closer to Ruby and lowered her voice. 'You should get it checked out; go to the doctor and get it looked at. What if it's a haematoma and you need medicine? Or an anti-inflammatory or whatever they use to fix bruises?'

A shiver ran down Ruby's spine. She didn't rush to tell Frankie that it wasn't a swollen bruise, and that it hadn't been their recent furniture rearranging that was the fault. The lump had been there about three months now. Instead, she shook her head and smiled. 'I will. I'll go this week, as soon as I can get an appointment.'

'Good,' Frankie said. She touched Ruby's arm and rubbed it gently. 'Don't forget, okay?' Then she moved back to her mat, a worried expression on her face, waiting until Ruby nodded before she looked away.

Gentle music filled the garden, and Ruby recognised the piece and immediately closed her eyes. The solo violin was as sweet and hypnotic as the first time she'd heard it. As she moved through the instructed positions, her body felt weightless and calm. Her arms and legs moved elegantly, and her breathing slowed. A warm shiver ran up her back, sending tendrils of pleasure along her scalp as if someone was playing with her hair, and her mind drifted.

The first time she'd heard that music was at the National Concert Hall. James had taken her as soon as he'd discovered she'd never been to a live orchestral performance. He'd held her hand tightly as the violinist finished, and grinned as she shook her head in awe, then he'd insisted she listened to nothing but classical music for a month until she learned to appreciate it properly. She'd been so proud at the end of the month. She'd learned so much and she loved the music, loved how it could match or change her mood, lift her spirits, or even her libido.

In great anticipation she'd dressed for the opera, only to find that it was entirely different from what she'd been expecting. While everyone around her seemed to know what was going on, James included, she'd felt naked and stupid, and a little stung by a remark James had made to his colleague about her education not being up to par. Afterwards he'd brushed away her comments when she'd asked him not to say those kinds of things to his friends.

'What kinds of things?' He'd stopped in the lobby and turned to face her. Glamorous people had milled around them, putting on coats and chatting. 'All I said was your music education wasn't as good as it could have been. And it's not, is it?'

'No, but . . .' Ruby had twisted her hands together. 'That's not how it sounded.'

'How did it sound?' James's eyes had been hard. 'Tell me, tell me how it sounded.' His voice had grown slightly louder. Ruby had reddened under the makeup she'd had professionally applied so she'd look like she fit in.

'Keep your voice down,' she'd whispered. 'People are looking.'

'People are looking?' James's eyebrows had risen. 'And whose fault is that?' He'd waited for her to answer. When she didn't he'd continued. 'I didn't start this conversation, Ruby. You did. All I did was explain to Roche that you don't know anything about opera, so he shouldn't waste his time trying to talk to you about it. He's a big opera fan, and I did him a favour. But you chose to take it as an insult, when it wasn't. Grow up, Ruby, and for once, stop making me out to be the bad guy.'

Ruby slowly opened her eyes as the class wound up, surprised to find the sun setting and the garden bathed in an apricot glow. Lavender-tinged clouds skimmed the sea,

220

and the scent of jasmine wafted from the arbour Eoin had constructed. The warm tingle she'd felt at the start of the session faded away as the memory took hold, even as the evening breeze still carried the heat of the day. Shaking her head, she pushed down the confusion that rose like hot bile in her throat. She'd loved James, without a doubt. And he'd loved her. She was sure of that. Everything he'd done, all the advice he'd given her, the guidance and chastisements, had been for her own good, hadn't they? Without him, she'd have floundered in company, worn or said the wrong things. It was hard to pinpoint when the *training*, as she'd come to think of it, had begun, she reflected as everyone gathered for the sharing circle. Hard to say when he'd stopped finding her mistakes endearing and quirky. Hard to determine when exactly it was that he'd started finding fault with her, trying to fix her . . .

Ruby tried to tune in to the sharing circle, feeling bad for being distracted. Josie was recalling the last time she'd tried something new and how it had made her feel.

'We all know I'm not a baker.' Josie grimaced. 'I wanted to make a special meal to mark the anniversary of the day May and I met. So I thought I'd come up with the perfect menu – exactly what we ate that first night. I'm a better cook than baker, so I made the soup and baked bread with no bother. The ostrich was hard to source so I substituted steak but all the trimmings were the same.'

'Ostrich?' Maggie asked.

Josie nodded. 'Yeah, we met at the height of the boom. Anyway. Steak it was. I was grand about cooking steak – I'd done it a million times before – but the kicker was the dessert. May had brandy snaps that night, and I had chocolate mousse.' Josie looked down at her feet. Ruby held her breath.

'I left it to the last minute to try to make them. May was out at Cut'n'Dye so I googled easy recipes and found relatively simple ones and got cracking.' Josie's voice lowered. 'Making desserts stresses me out. There's too much measuring . . .'

'It's a science,' May said softly and took Josie's hand. 'That's why they call it domestic science in school.'

'Not anymore,' Maggie said. 'I think it's called home economics now.'

May shrugged. Lifting her head, Josie looked around the group. 'Well, I was a little excited too. I wanted the meal to be a success, but I used allspice mix in the brandy snaps instead of ginger, and Ovaltine in the chocolate mousse. The mousse wouldn't set and the snaps were just a mess.' Her pink cheeks glowed in the gloaming.

Ruby's hands started to cramp and she realised they were balled into tight fists. She knew what James would've said if she'd made such a mistake. There was no room for mistakes as far as he was concerned. She leaned forward, willing Josie to finish her story.

'What happened?' Ruby blurted. 'I mean, how did it go in the end?'

'It was fine,' Josie said. 'The dinner was good, and we laughed about the desserts. Sure, what else could we do – it wasn't like it was a big deal or anything. No one got hurt, ya know.'

'I ate the mousse,' May piped up. 'And it was . . . ummmm, but the dinner was five-star.'

Josie grinned. 'That's the last new thing I tried, and maybe I'll try baking again. Who knows?'

The whole circle laughed softly, talking about their own domestic disasters until Jürgen clapped his hands. 'Thank you for sharing that with us, Josie. Can you tell us what you got from that experience?'

Josie squinted. 'Well, it was close to diarrhoea . . . ah no, I'm messing. I suppose you could say I learned to try something new, on my own. I made up my mind to do it and yeah, I made a mess but I had fun. I enjoyed planning the night. I couldn't wait to see May's face – to see her happy was my goal. The dessert made her laugh so I think despite it all, I succeeded.'

Jürgen nodded. 'That's lovely, Josie. I admire your courage and your candour.' He steepled his fingers and bowed his head for a moment before continuing. Raising his head, he connected with everyone in the circle. 'Mistakes are part of the learning process. They don't mean you failed. All it means is that you took a chance, probably put yourself outside of your comfort zone, and you learned what worked and what didn't work for you.'

The group murmured. Good-naturedly, Eoin called over to Josie. 'Just remind me to ask who made the dessert next time I'm in the pub – if I order the mousse, change it to apple crumble!' Josie pulled a face and smiled. Ruby tried to unfurl her hands. Her nails were cutting into her palms. Her mouth dried up. All of those passive-aggressive judgements that James had passed off as constructive criticism were simply barbed jibes that had undermined her, she realised. It was so cruel. Sweat beaded on her forehead, and the breeze made her shiver. Eoin looked at her. He stopped laughing and grew serious. Taking her arm he gently shook her.

'Ruby?'

His voice seemed to come from far away. Ruby looked at his handsome tanned face. It creased into concern. It swung away from her. The ground beneath her feet felt as soft as sand, and slipped away from her. She stumbled forward, her arms out, her face pale. He caught her and lowered her to the grass. Everything went black.

When she opened her eyes, everyone was around her. Frankie was holding her hand, her face blotchy and strained.

'She's awake,' Frankie said, quietly at first, then again more loudly. 'Ruby, can you hear me? Are you okay?'

Ruby fought to keep her eyes open. 'I'm fine,' she mumbled. 'Fine, just forgot to eat. Dehydrated.'

Clambering to a seated position she pushed her hair from her face and looked around.

'You gave us a right fright there,' Sandra said. 'Are you sure you're okay?'

Ruby nodded and got to her feet, mortified at all the fuss. 'I'm okay. I'll just sit down for a while over here. You guys go on and finish the circle.' Eoin's arms were around her in an instant. He sat her gently on their bench before tilting her face to look up into his.

'Sit back. Try to remember to breathe.' His thumb caressed her cheek. 'I'll be back in a minute with a cuppa.'

Nodding, Ruby sat back and breathed out. The others were back in the circle, talking and sharing. She could see Frankie's profile, and every so often the younger woman would look over and check on her. Ruby raised her hand and smiled weakly at her. Then she turned away from the soft chatter and the banter.

It was alien to her. All the simple talk that meant everything and nothing at the same time. These people she'd surrounded herself with were all filled with doubts and fears, and yet stronger than anyone she'd ever met. In a typically Irish way, they could tell you their saddest story in the sharing circle, but be down the pub afterwards making a joke about it, only to check on you minutes later with genuine concern about what you'd shared. What was shared was simultaneously forgotten and remembered.

Ruby leaned back against the warm wooden bench. Looking back on it from this distance, there were times when James made it hard to love him. Times when she wanted to call him out for being mean, or simply too black and white. After over thirty years of venerating the man, this was somewhat of a revelation, and she felt shaken by it. Perhaps that was why she'd had her funny turn?

Back in the circle, Valerie was telling the group how she'd worked up the nerve to look at lingerie and *the likes* online, that she never would have done that when she was married.

'He wouldn't have liked it,' she snorted. 'Liked it? It wasn't about him liking it! It was about me, but that wasn't allowed. So now I've made it all about me and lads, I don't know why I waited – but I'm certainly making up for lost time – and I can tell ya, I like it a lot!'

The whole group burst out laughing. Ruby half-smiled. Valerie was so brave, telling everyone those things about her ex. She watched Eoin closely as he made her tea in the shed. He was the only one she'd ever spoken to so openly about James, and that last conversation they'd had

225

unnerved her. But he'd been right. Her finger picked at a splinter on the wooden armrest. How was she supposed to think of James now? Had their whole marriage been a sham?

Eoin's hand on her shoulder made her jump, and she took the mug of tea from him, grateful to be able to turn her thoughts away from her past and onto her present instead.

22

Frankie

Frankie sat on the floor beside the bed where Dillon was sleeping, and stared at her birth certificate. There was a blank space where her father's name should have been. She'd always known that, and it had never really bothered her, but now she'd decided she wanted to know more, and it had started to irritate her. What did it mean? Did Nicole not know who the father of her child was – was there a choice of men, like in *Mamma Mia*? Somehow, she didn't think it was going to be as much fun trying to find out who he was as it seemed in her favourite musical. Certainly, there would be no Greek sunshine and she wouldn't suddenly find a sexy fiancé, let alone a trio of well-off father figures vying to take care of her.

Frankie shuffled the paper back into the file, then rubbed her eyes. It was close to midnight, and it had been a long day. She'd kill to go to bed, but the urge to try to find some clue as to who her father was kept her searching methodically through Aggie's files. There had to be something. If not, then the only option was to contact Nicole, and of all things she didn't want to have to do, that was top of the list. What was the point? Nicole was in Italy, living it up, eating pizza and drinking Prosecco, flirting with Italian men. The less she knew about Frankie's life, the better. She deserved nothing more than to be left in the ignorance she'd left them.

The next file was stuffed with old letters, Christmas cards, and postcards. Frankie flicked through them, reading the odd one here and there. Aggie had had a cousin who was a nun in Boston who'd sent her a card every Christmas. Frankie read the cards now with a soft smile. The nun was lovely and generous in her writing, always asking first and foremost how the family was. She always finished by saying that she lit a candle every day for them all, and hoped to get home for a visit soon. Her penmanship was a beautiful script, all flourishes and neat, even letters. She never had gotten home, as far as Frankie knew.

She picked up the last card. There was another letter in the envelope. It was closed and addressed to Nicole. Frankie could just about make out the postmark of November 1995. She would have been almost two weeks old, maybe. Frankie held the stiff, cream envelope in her hand. There was an official-looking logo on the bottom left, one she didn't recognise. The envelope had been opened, but had self-sealed again over time. Frankie peeled the flap back, then stopped. She took a gulp of water and bit her top lip. She'd never come across anything addressed to Nicole before.

Scooching her bum back against the wall Frankie glanced up as Dillon murmured something and rolled over.

He was such a busy sleeper, always mumbling and star-fishing all over the bed, but bright and bouncy the next day as if he'd not moved a muscle. He settled back down, and Frankie looked down at her lap. The letter weighed heavily on her thighs, the thick ink handwriting on the envelope seemed dashed off, with Nicole's name underlined twice. Should she feel bad about opening it? Putting the water glass down beside her, Frankie picked up the envelope and determinedly pulled the letter from inside and unfolded it.

The letter was brief, and began halfway down the page. It was just a few sentences really, the name of a hotel, and a date and time, and instructions on what to bring and how to dress. Frankie's fingers turned to ice. *Wear black, look discreet, no heels, nothing that lets anyone know who you are. Look like a secretary.* Her eyes scanned over the scrawl. *Put the baby's things in a sports bag. Don't make a scene, Nicole. This is the best thing for us all. Think of the baby and the future I can give her.*

Frankie's heart was thumping painfully. There was no signature on the bottom of the letter, just an initial, but the thick cream paper had company details printed along the bottom with an address in Dublin. Picking up her phone, Frankie googled the name. Their website was the first on the list, and she clicked the link. Knight & White Construction Ltd. flashed across the screen alongside the logo that was on the envelope. Frankie read on.

They claimed to be an international construction company with an eye to the future while respecting the past. They promised to build better and more sustainable environments for clients and communities. With a dry mouth, and shaking hands, Frankie clicked through the tabs until she found a page listing the board of directors. At the top of the page was a photo of a silver-haired man. His shoulders were straight, his jaw firm and defined, unlike the photos of the other men on the page. He looked older, but fitter than the other board members; his smile had a slight smirk, as if he knew he'd outshine anyone else in the room. His name was J. Knight, founder and chief executive.

Frankie dropped the phone to the floor beside her. Twisting a strand of hair around her finger, she stared down at the letter. *Put the baby's things in a sports bag. Don't make a scene, Nicole. This is the best thing for us all.* Was she the baby? She had to be. What other baby could Nicole possibly have had access to at the time? Pulling her knees up to her chest, Frankie wrapped her arms around her legs and tried to remember what Aggie had said about Nicole leaving them. She leaned her head back and closed her eyes.

She remembered the only time Aggie had ever spoken about it. 'You were only a wee babby,' Aggie had told her. 'A tiny little thing, you were the smallest babby I'd ever seen. Only barely five pounds weight, and with a tuft of red hair I'd never seen the likes of before. She never told me who he was, but I assume he had red hair. Your father. Anyway, she went off on the early bus one day and the next thing you know I get a letter in that very morning's post telling me she was gone to London for a while. I worried for her, you know – she was still bleeding after the birth – and I wondered if she had the baby blues. But she was gone and I'd no way to find her.'

Opening her eyes, Frankie focused on a spot on the ceiling where the painter had missed the second coat. Nicole had left to go see him, but she hadn't brought her baby with her. She'd run away instead. She'd foisted the responsibility of motherhood onto her own mother, abandoned her child and run away from a man who . . . who what? What about him – who was he and what did he want? The baby. He wanted the baby. Frankie swallowed. She was definitely the baby. Was he her father, or some random man who wanted a baby? The latter seemed too preposterous. It had to be the former, but then, what kind of relationship did he have with Nicole, this man – was it a one-off fling? Or had it been a more complicated matter? Lowering her head to her knees, Frankie felt a rush of blood go to her head. Had she been the product of a deal Nicole had made with this man? Was it possible Nicole was a surrogate and had abandoned the agreement at the last minute, leaving the baby to be brought up by Aggie?

There were too many questions and not enough answers. Frankie pushed to her feet. Pulling at the neck of her T-shirt, she tiptoed from the room and up the stairs to the kitchen. She poured a glass of water, and trembled. Her life could have been so different. If she'd been brought up by that man, who knows what opportunities she might have had. University and ski holidays, friends in the right places, and probably a proper career by now. Horse-riding lessons, music too. She'd probably know at least two more languages. Shopping without looking at the price of things. Her own car.

Frankie drained the glass and refilled it. She wouldn't

be a charity case living in someone else's home, ashamed of her tatty clothes and lack of education. Nicole had taken that all from her the minute she'd decided to run – but she'd given her Aggie, thought Frankie, her heart softening. She'd left her in Castletown Cove, where she'd loved Liam. And there was Dillon – all that love couldn't be measured. Everything else dulled beside the love she'd experienced. She'd never, ever, change the circumstances that gave Aggie and Dillon to her. Besides, there was no point in speculating about a life that hadn't happened. That would only drive her insane. It was hard enough living the life she had, and striving to get somewhere, to be someone.

But the question kept coming back to her: was that man her father?

He's the one clue I have, she thought. She reached for her phone, but she'd left it downstairs on the bedroom floor. Rolling her eyes, she pushed away from the counter, then remembered Ruby said she could use the office computer anytime she liked, insisting that she didn't need to ask. Well, now was as good a time as ever to take her up on that. With a determined nod, Frankie slipped into the office.

She closed the door gently behind her and sat down at the desk. The password was on a Post-it note stuck to the side of the screen. Frankie sat in the darkness, illuminated only by the soft moonlight. She typed in the password and immediately opened Google and input the company name. Dozens of articles appeared, newspaper reports, planning permission applications, gala nights, golf tournaments, all documenting the privileged events sponsored by Knight & White Construction Ltd. Frankie leaned forward, her elbows on the desk. It was exactly as she'd imagined. All glitz and glamour. All high life and good times. She clicked on the image tab, then clicked on the first image of J. Knight that came up.

The photo of the older man was accompanied by an editorial piece on Knight & White Construction Ltd. He was tanned and smiling, and she could tell he was tall even though he was leaning against a dark wood desk. His suit was impeccable. Frankie's head spun as she began clicking through the images. She clicked faster, bored with the business ones, longing to find out more about his personal life, when a familiar face flashed past. Stopping, Frankie went backwards to the photo. She peered at the screen, then sat back. It couldn't be – but it was. Standing in an evening gown, diamonds at her throat, her hair, blonde, swept up and off her face in a glamorous up-do, was Ruby. She was standing close to him, leaning against him. They were both smiling into the camera. Ruby clicked on the photo. The caption said: *James Knight and his wife, Ruby, attended the wedding reception at the Powerscourt Hotel.*

Frantically, Frankie read the rest of the article. James Knight – his name ricocheted inside her head. How had she not seen this coming? Ruby had mentioned her late husband a handful of times, but each time she had called him by his name: James. Frankie's breath caught under her ribs and she doubled over. Why hadn't Ruby said something? With a quick glance behind her to be sure she was still alone, Frankie googled Ruby Knight. Ruby's face appeared, almost always alongside James. So many charity

233

events, days at the races, always at events Frankie hadn't even known existed. She looked polished and thin, dressed in the kind of clothes Frankie had never seen her in, all smooth and tailored. Her smile was tight, as if fixed for the photograph; James was always touching her, his arm around her waist, or holding firmly on to her hand.

'Oh, God.' Frankie leaned back in the chair, her hand over her mouth. Her thoughts raced through her head. Covering her face, Frankie started to cry. Leaning forward, she laid her forearms on the desk and sobbed.

They couldn't stay here now, could they? She'd have to leave, and what about Dillon? He loved his Auntie Ruby. His heart would be broken if she told him they had to go. She should've left well enough alone, not gone looking for her father. She'd been fine living in blissful ignorance. Now look at the mess she was unravelling – if James was her father . . .

Sniffing, Frankie pushed her hair from her face and wiped her eyes with the hem of her T-shirt. Holding her head in her hands, she stared at the computer until the screen went blank. Pressing the off button on the computer, she stood up. Nothing felt right anymore. The room around her felt like a stage; the whole house felt like a film prop. Fake and flimsy. The warmth of the place evaporated as she walked back into the kitchen and took the stairs down to her room. The iciness that had started in her fingers spread to her whole body. Her cold feet didn't feel the tile floor; goose bumps covered her bare arms. She tried to stop her teeth from chattering as she passed Ruby's door, convinced that she'd hear and wake up, but they wouldn't stop.

She slipped into bed beside her son, curling around him as her body shook. He was warm and soft, a small smile on his lips. Dillon snuggled into her, throwing his arm above his head and sighing. Frankie gently tucked his arm back in and kissed his sleep-damp head.

'I love you, buddy,' she whispered, and kissed him again. 'I'll make sure we're all right.'

A pounding headache formed in her temples and across her forehead, and she closed her eyes tight, willing the questioning and thousands of thoughts that were whirring around her mind to go away. Aggie had always said, 'If you can't do anything about it right this instant, then cop on and go to sleep – it'll still be there in the morning and you can work on it then.' Frankie clamped her eyes even more tightly shut, but James and Ruby's faces kept appearing. Finally, she gave up and lay on her back, staring up at the ceiling, letting her thoughts run loud and free, but coming up with no answers or even possibilities of what might have happened.

'It might all be a mix-up,' she whispered to the ceiling. 'A complete and utter case of crossed wires. I might have nothing to do with *that* man at all.' But her gut churned and twisted. Deep down, she felt that James Knight was her father. She could feel it in her DNA – but a gut feeling wasn't going to prove anything. Dozing off near dawn, she dreamt of strange men, and confessionals, and babies being carried in backpacks, eventually waking up just before her alarm went off, her mouth dry and her eyes wet.

23

Ruby

The sun was scorching and it was just gone eight in the morning. Ruby flicked through the news app on her phone as a pot of tea brewed. It was the last week in June, and the weather forecast was for more sunshine. They were saying it was the hottest June on record, and were predicting that July would be the same. The news was full of articles on how to reduce your water consumption. Ruby made a mental note to talk to Eoin about installing water butts around the house, and wondered if there was an incentive that might encourage others to install some. It was something they should look at down at the Moonlight Garden. She smiled. Eoin probably was way ahead of her on this.

Taking her mug out onto the balcony, Ruby sat at the bistro set. Sipping her tea, she kept an ear out for Dillon and Frankie, but the house was filled with silence. Normally Dillon would be up and chatting as he ate his porridge. She was amazed he liked porridge, and he'd told

236

her that was what he always had for breakfast. They must've gone out early.

Ruby was hoping to get a chance to talk to Frankie about how they'd manage things in September. They were both enrolled in their respective classes and she couldn't wait to get started. All she needed was to get some jotters and pens for note-taking. She'd make a list and run into the city later to get her supplies. She must ask Frankie what she needed so she could pick them up for her.

Frankie had been quiet the last few days, and when Ruby had suggested maybe getting some chocolate cereal for Dillon as a treat, she'd merely shrugged and muttered something noncommittal. It wasn't like Frankie to be so quiet. She was eerily like James when he had a bee in his bonnet about something. Ruby took another sip of tea and shook her head to clear her thoughts. There was no point in thinking of James right now, not when Eoin was on the way over to walk with her down to the Moonlight Garden. The last thing she wanted was James in her head, telling her she couldn't do anything in a garden. It was bad enough knowing he'd have berated her for not going to the doctor sooner. But in that case, he might have been right.

Frankie had made the appointment in the end and had marched Ruby to the surgery. When she'd shown the doctor, the doctor hadn't seemed worried, but to keep Frankie happy she'd arranged an MRI and a biopsy with a prominent specialist in Dublin tomorrow. Ruby sighed. That's what private health insurance got you: immediate treatment for something that was nothing. She didn't want to go to Dublin. Going to Dublin meant staying the night, and if she didn't call in to see Pamela there'd be hell to pay. Sighing, Ruby hurriedly typed a message and sent it to Pamela.

In town tomorrow for the night.
Staying in The Westbury. I've an
appointment in the morning, but
afterwards I'll be doing a bit of retail
therapy. Fancy joining me?

She crossed her fingers and hoped Pamela wouldn't pick up on the word *appointment*. Why did she have to use that word? She should have said meeting. Then Pamela might assume it was business. The message was sent, though, and there was nothing she could do now. She finished her tea and left her mug in the sink. Then she made her way down to the garden, pausing to grab her pink wellies. Eoin would arrive any minute.

Out on the lawn, Ruby sat at the patio table. She pulled on her wellies and looked around. Was it really a good idea to change her back garden? It was going to be a lot of work, and costly too. The maintenance would eat into her time. Would it be easier to leave it as it was, and cut the grass once a week? A lawn would give Dillon somewhere to play football, although she'd yet to see him ever play football. Eoin waved from his deck, disappearing for a moment, then reappearing as he came around the back of the house. He made his way over to the small patio set Ruby picked up from the garden centre.

'I didn't hear the gate opening,' Ruby said, fixing her hair as she walked towards him.

'I greased it the last time I was here,' Eoin said. 'It's as quiet as a mouse now. You said that it was grating on your nerves.'

'I did say that,' Ruby said, touched by his thoughtfulness. 'Thanks. Tea?'

'Nah, I'm grand.' Eoin nodded towards the gate. 'Are you good to go? I've got the truck ready.'

'I am.' Ruby smiled. 'I'm excited to get these new plants in.' She stumbled as they walked through the gates. Eoin caught her before she fell.

'What happened there?' he asked, his forehead creasing in concern.

'Nothing, just a stumble,' Ruby said, ignoring the new stinging sensation from the back of her leg as the top of her welly rubbed against the lump. She straightened up then hopped into the truck with a strained smile. Eoin leaned into the truck and slid his sketchpad onto the dashboard.

Ruby inhaled his clean scent. Her heart beat faster as his arm brushed against her, and a longing to feel his lips on hers again took her by surprise. Each day they spent together she found herself longing to be touched by him. Crossing her ankles, she felt a stab of guilt. She'd never felt such desire before, not even for James. Lowering her chin to her chest, she looked down at her hands. They were tanned, and her nails were short and free from nail polish for the first time in what felt like forever. Her leggings were the same ones she'd worn yesterday, with muck still on them. Sometimes it felt that with each passing day she stripped away the gilding James had painted on her, and as each layer of gild disappeared she felt more and more authentic.

239

Ruby watched Eoin walk around the truck. He hopped in beside her. The truck radio switched on as he turned the key in the ignition. Andrea Bocelli's dulcet tones filled the cab. Ruby started to laugh.

'All I listen to these days is Andrea.' Eoin smiled at her. 'You gave that to me!'

'And I've been listening to the Chili Peppers,' Ruby admitted. She giggled. 'I haven't listened to them since before I got married.'

'I like it a lot,' Eoin said as he drove towards the Moonlight Garden. 'I think we need to spend more time together teaching each other different things. How about you?'

'Fine. I'll pencil you in.' Ruby tried to hide her smile, but Eoin saw her grinning. His laughter made her warm inside.

The past few days had been lovely. He had coffee ready every morning for her, and he often sent her texts throughout the day, jokes or links to things he thought she might like to read. They'd been to The Birds a few times for food, and once they'd gone to the cinema. He'd held her hand and she'd grinned the whole way through the movie, reminded of being sixteen all over again. But despite all that, they hadn't shared a kiss since that first time, other than a peck goodnight, and it had started to bother her.

Maybe he wasn't ready to get into a relationship, she thought as they drove the short distance to the Moonlight Garden. Her legs felt leaden as she followed him in. She hadn't realised how strongly she was starting to feel about him. Ruby thought back to the chat she'd had with him about James that morning on the deck. It felt somewhat unfinished. Ruby plucked a leaf from a shrub and twirled it between her finger and thumb.

As always, the garden lifted her spirits the moment she passed through the gate. There was no need for a calendar to tell you it was the height of the summer. Verdant greenery billowed from every border. Star-like flowers with the most intense perfume filled the air. Blowsy hydrangeas blossomed amid an undulating sea of silver grasses. The tension behind Ruby's eyes drained away, and her shoulders relaxed as a gentle smile played on her lips. How had she never gardened before? she wondered as she pulled on her gardening gloves and picked up a bucket, intent on doing a bit of weeding. Eoin had gone to their bench. He waved her over and a fizz of happiness displaced the lead in her legs. She hurried over to his side.

Eoin smiled. He stood back and pointed. 'Over there, that's where the wild garden will be. And beside it will be the stargazing garden. It'll be filled with daphnes and Mexican orange blossoms – I can't wait for you to smell them. They're so beautiful. And the ground will have mounds, perfect for leaning back against to look at the heavens. Maybe catch a shooting star and make a wish or two.'

Ruby gasped. She could see it perfectly. The breeze blew a tendril of hair across her face. Tucking her hair behind her ear, Ruby sighed. The hairs on her arms stood up. He'd planned the garden with her in mind. No one had ever done anything as extraordinary for her.

'You mentioned something about stargazing once,' Eoin said bashfully, stuffing his hands in his pockets. He looked sideways at Ruby with a happy smile.

'James never understood how I could sit out night after night all summer long, just looking at the stars,' she said softly, almost to herself. 'He'd never have thought to do something like this.' A ripple of unease emanated from her stomach. It was happening more often when she thought about James.

Eoin blew his fringe from his eyes, then rubbed his neck and sat down on their bench. His usually smiling face was still; his eyes darkened as he ran his fingers through his hair, leaving it standing on end. He needed a haircut, but probably wouldn't bother. Ruby groaned inwardly. How stupid she was to have brought up James when Eoin was sharing his plans with her. She sank down next to Eoin. Picking at her nails, she looked at him for a moment before speaking.

'I'm sorry,' she said. 'I shouldn't have brought James up. It's just that . . .' She felt her chest pound. Quietly, she continued. 'He wasn't the easiest man to live with, as you know. He was moody, I suppose. I never knew what humour he'd come home in.'

Eoin's eyebrows rose. He leaned forward, resting his elbows on his knees. 'Jesus. Ruby.' He touched Ruby's knee. She jumped, and he grimaced and held his hands up. 'I'm sorry.'

'No,' Ruby said quickly. 'It wasn't like that – he never laid a finger on me. He was just . . . I don't know how to explain it – he had standards and these ideals, I suppose. He'd never think of a garden as a worthwhile thing unless it was to do with his work. His mind moved so fast, I could never keep up. It drove him up the wall the way I didn't catch on to things quickly enough. Trying to pre-empt him and what he thought should happen . . . well, it was impossible.'

Taking a breath, she fought against the barrage of memories that rose like weeds sprouting up on a warm spring day. Memories of James rolling his eyes at her, tutting his dismissal of her suggestions, of him cajoling her into going to a party only to arrive home and ask her why she was all dressed up, irritated because he'd told her the party had been cancelled when she knew he hadn't. When she argued against him, he'd walk away with a wave of his hand, muttering about how bad her memory was. Pushing the recollections away, she twisted her fingers together. Ruby sat back, her tongue stuck to the roof of her mouth. She tried to speak, but the words wouldn't come. Her breath caught under her ribs. Choking, her hands clawed at the neckline of her T-shirt. Tears blurred her vision. Eoin was on his knees, in front of her in a heartbeat.

'Ruby.' He took her hands and gently held them. 'Breathe, Ruby. In, out, breathe with me; come on – in . . . and out. That's it. You're doing great.' Letting her go, Eoin took her face gently in his hands. 'Look at me, Ruby, look at me.'

Ruby opened her eyes and stared into his face. His eyes searched hers; his hair fell forward onto his forehead. The crease between his eyes deepened as she stayed still and quiet. Slowly she placed her hands on his and leaned forward so their foreheads touched.

'I'm sorry.' She breathed out as her ribs tightened. 'I . . .'

'Please, no apologies.' Eoin caressed the side of her face, his fingers stroking her skin so softly that she wondered

243

if she imagined it. 'You don't apologise for his behaviour, or for your reactions to the trauma you went through.'

'Trauma?' Ruby blinked.

'Yes,' Eoin said. 'I've had panic attacks too.'

'Panic attacks?' Ruby shook her head. 'What? I didn't have a panic attack; I was just upset. It's all still like it happened yesterday. Like he's here and then I find him lying on his office floor and he's blue and gasping like a fish. I just need time to process it.' Her voice grew shrill.

Eoin sat back on his heels, his hands loose on her knees. Saying nothing, he got up and sat beside her. Ruby clasped her hands together to stop them from shaking, while overhead gulls squawked and swooped. There was nothing wrong with her. She was fine . . .

Eoin finally said something, but she missed it. Swallowing and concentrating, she forced her hands to stay still.

'I missed that. What did you say?'

'I said I think we should start here and dig in the compost,' Eoin said quietly. 'We can plant the shrubs tomorrow or whenever you're feeling up to it.' He gestured to the garden.

Ruby nodded, glad to have the subject changed. Then she remembered her specialist appointment. 'I'm not around tomorrow, or the day after,' she said. 'I'm in Dublin for a few days, but I'll be home on Friday for Dillon's birthday party.'

Turning to her, Eoin pressed his lips together. Frowning he asked, 'Is everything okay?'

'All good.' Ruby forced her smile to reach her eyes. 'Just some business and seeing Pamela.'

'Tell her I was asking after her,' Eoin said. He took

Ruby's hand and kissed it. 'You'd tell me if you were in trouble, wouldn't you?'

'Yes,' Ruby muttered. The back of her hand tingled where he'd kissed it. 'Of course I would. What makes you think there's something wrong?'

'I don't know,' he admitted. 'You look worried and you're quiet.'

'I'm fine, honestly,' Ruby said. Her face hurt from smiling. 'Just thinking a lot lately.'

'I hear ya,' Eoin said. 'Just don't forget to talk, too.'

'I won't,' Ruby whispered.

'Good.' Eoin leaned back on the bench. His hand rested easily between them, and Ruby wished he'd hold her hand again.

A flash of red caught her eye. Frankie was coming up the road. She looked tired. Ruby took a few deep breaths and straightened her shoulders. They were going to plan Dillon's birthday later after he'd gone to bed. A smile crept across Ruby's face; she could hardly believe she was planning a child's birthday party – it was like a dream come true. He'd love a bug-themed party, she thought, with ladybird balloons and a caterpillar cake, and maybe a . . .

Ruby looked at Frankie as she came closer to the Moonlight Garden. Frankie was proud, and while she was willing to let Dillon call her Auntie Ruby, she mightn't take too kindly to her taking over his party, and Frankie didn't take too kindly to charity either. No, better to take more of a back seat and let Frankie make the plan. That was the best way to approach it.

24

Frankie

Two days later, Frankie was balancing on a chair attempting to stick a *Happy Birthday, You're Seven* banner over the television. She prayed the Sellotape wouldn't peel the paint off when she took it down. The tape she was using was the kind that said it peeled off easily, but she didn't believe it. Once bitten, twice shy and all that. Hopping down from the chair, she stood back and grinned. Dillon would love it! He'd never had a proper birthday party before. His birthday wasn't until next week, but today was the last day of June, and the last day of school before the summer break. Frankie thought it wise to have the party before Ben and Ava went away on their family holidays.

Once the word had gotten out that Dillon was having a party, several kids had decided to become his friend. Frankie's jaw had dropped when she'd heard Dillon say that he wanted to invite his whole class. It was only with Ruby's help that she'd managed to whittle down his guest list to ten. Ten kids who actually didn't make fun of him much these days was a massive leap from where they'd been at the start of the year, she thought, and she hoped they'd still be his friends in September.

Checking the time, Frankie smiled. It was all coming together nicely. Ruby had arranged for some helium balloons to be delivered later, in the shape of butterflies, ladybirds, bees and flowers – they'd look great in the corners of the room. She said she'd be home that afternoon in time for the party.

Rolling up her sleeves again, Frankie groaned, and set to pushing the Harrods sofa back against the far wall, then she covered it with a super-king sheet, and hoped it would survive ten hyper seven-year-olds. Ruby hadn't seemed concerned at all when she'd phoned first thing that morning to wish Dillon a happy birthday before he left for school.

'It's only a couch,' she'd said. 'Let the kids have their fun.'

She'd sounded tired, Frankie realised. Pamela must have her run ragged, shopping and dining out and whatever else rich people did on their time off. The open balcony doors let a warm breeze in, which ruffled the banner. Frankie smoothed it back down. Ruby was clearly missing life in the big smoke – she'd sounded busy on the phone.

Frankie chewed on her fingernail. The discovery that her father had been Ruby's husband kept her awake at night, and she knew that she needed to talk to Ruby about it. As Aggie used to say, it would all come out in the wash, so she'd better address it sooner rather than later. Now she wished it had been sooner, but she hadn't been able to before Ruby had left for Dublin. Between extra shifts and Ruby being busy in the Moonlight Garden, they hadn't had a moment long enough for Frankie to bring it up. Besides, what if Ruby knew already and was content to keep it from her? Frowning, she rubbed her forehead. What if she didn't know and Frankie ruined everything by talking to Ruby about it? What would Ruby do then? Would she want to move back to Dublin? She might sell Eyrie Lodge, and then what? Dillon would miss her so much. And where would she and Dillon go?

Frankie sat down on the coffee table with a grunt. It wasn't as if she didn't know they couldn't stay here forever; it was just difficult to think past this September and starting the course because then what? It was time to get real and focus on getting the cottage back together and not depending on Ruby so much . . . but then, how would she find out what happened between Nicole and James?

The office door was wide open. Frankie stared at it. No one would know if she looked around in there. Ruby barely ever went in, unless she had to find something important. Sandra had just dusted and hoovered the space. Now she'd gone out to collect the last few bits for the party. Frankie slipped across the room and stood in the bright and airy space. The wall behind the desk hosted custom-made, built-in cabinets. Sleek, dark wood shelves were filled with photos, and beneath was a bank of drawers. A filing cabinet and safe were also neatly hidden away.

Frankie began at the desk, opening the drawers methodically. There was not much to find except for a bundle of empty envelopes, the same kind that the letter to her mother had come in, a cluster of pens – one a fountain pen in a wooden case. A half-used book of stamps was shoved to the back of the drawer under a diary. Dates of meetings, phone numbers, scrawled golf plans and social events filled the cream pages. Frankie touched the hand-writing – it was loud and confident and took more space than it needed. She wasn't sure she liked it. Putting the diary back, she turned her attention to the shelves and drawers behind her. The filing cabinet was almost empty; only the basics of a household were there: passports, a few old electricity bills from before e-bills were standard, and the planning permission notice for Eyrie Lodge. Ruby's birth certificate was there too, and James's death certificate.

With shaking hands, Frankie read the entire document, word for word. Her fingers grew cold as she slipped it back into the file. Not only had she never known him, now she never would. Closing the filing cabinet, she leaned against it. Creeping around and snooping in Ruby's things felt wrong. She could just ask Ruby. After all, Ruby had admitted to knowing her mother, so maybe she knew more about the whole situation. Frankie closed her eyes. Maybe Ruby had taken her and Dillon in because she felt guilty and wanted to make amends for how her husband, Frankie's father, had abandoned her. Frankie's stomach clenched. She groaned and closed her eyes. If that was the case, well, she didn't know what to do. Being here because of Ruby's generosity was one thing, being here because someone pitied you was another.

No, it was better not to ask Ruby. That way nothing had to change, and they were safe until they had another place to live.

The safe. Frankie opened her eyes. The safe might tell her something. Sinking to the floor, Frankie stared at the small box. It was like the ones they had at the hotel, slim and neat. The keypad looked barely used, unlike the ones at the hotel. Frankie wondered if James had changed the master code. She pressed the digits she knew were the standard master code for most safes, holding her breath in anticipation as she pressed 'enter', but nothing happened. She tried again using the other standard set of master code digits. Again, nothing. She staggered to her feet. She was on the verge of giving up when she had a brainwave. Pulling open the filing cabinet, she took out James and Ruby's passports and tried their dates of birth. Neither worked. Huffing, she shoved the passports back into the file.

Then she gasped. Dropping to the floor in front of the safe again, she input her own date of birth. It was a wild card, but the safe clicked and opened without the ceremony she was expecting to feel. Rubbing her sweaty palms on her T-shirt, Frankie stared at the half-opened safe door. Shakily, she tucked her hair behind her ear. It had to be true. She swallowed. It had to mean something. The chances of him randomly choosing her date of birth as his safe code had to be a million to one, at the very least. Frankie's lips quivered. *He must have loved her,* she thought. But if he did, why didn't he come find her? She was just around the corner, a mere ten-minute walk away from his front door. All these years he'd known who she was but had chosen to be a stranger to her.

Sniffing back a sob, Frankie scooched closer to the safe. She glanced quickly over her shoulder, before fully opening the door.

Inside the safe, there was an old watch, a signet ring in a small box, a batch of letters tied up with a black ribbon, and a notebook. Frankie held her breath and flicked through the notebook. Most pages were blank, but the first couple were written like a diary. Settling down to read, she stretched her legs out in front of her, but as she read the first line, a sound came from downstairs. It sounded like a key slipping into the front door.

Scrambling to her feet, Frankie pushed the documents back into the safe, pushed the door shut, and snuck quietly and quickly from the room, not noticing that the safe door didn't quite close.

Running out into the kitchen, she called down the stairs. Her heart pounded in her ears. 'Hello?'

Ruby's voice floated back up to her. 'Hi, just running to the loo. Be up in a few.'

'Hi! See you in a minute,' Frankie called down. She rubbed her face, then went to take out some mugs for tea. She cursed as she dropped the box of teabags, and tried to calm her breathing.

Ruby came up the stairs slowly. Frankie's breath caught in her throat. Ruby was pale and hollow-eyed. *Had she found out?*

'Ruby – what's the matter?' Frankie stepped forward. 'You look . . .'

Ruby raised her hands and shook her head. 'I know. I look desperate. I hate driving from Dublin. I should've taken the train.'

'The train would've taken you ages,' Frankie said quietly. She glanced at the office door. Ruby followed her gaze.

'Oh, you've made a start on the decorations.' She smiled wearily. 'He's going to love it. Have the balloons arrived yet?'

251

Frankie shook her head and handed Ruby a mug of tea. Then she followed Ruby out onto the balcony. Ruby sat down and nodded towards the other chair.

'Sit down,' she said. 'I have something I need to talk to you about.'

Frankie hesitated, then sat on the edge of the other chair. Fiddling with her mug, she looked down and held her breath.

'I, eh, I haven't been quite honest with you,' Ruby began. 'And I'm sorry, so sorry about that.'

Frankie sat up straight and raised her eyes to Ruby's and was shocked to see Ruby looking strong and level back at her. She'd expected her to be emotional about telling her who her father was. That she'd maybe even be a little ashamed of how things had played out, but Ruby's chin was raised. She didn't look one bit ashamed. Yet something about the way she held the mug of tea gave her away. Her fingers were twitching, almost tapping against the mug. When Frankie said nothing, she continued.

'There's no point in beating around the bush,' she said. 'I'm not well.' Ruby put the mug on the table. 'That lump on my leg . . .'

Frankie's stomach churned. The tea she'd just drunk sloshed around her stomach like rancid fat. 'What do you mean – not well?' Her voice a rasping whisper. She put her mug on the table too.

'It's early days, but I've had scans and biopsies, and I'll know more next week.' Ruby pressed her hands together. 'They think it might be some kind of cancer.'

Frankie's hands flew to her mouth. Scrunching her face up, she shook her head and blinked back the tears that threatened to fall.

'Cancer.' It was more of a statement than a question. 'Are you sure?'

Ruby nodded. 'They said they'll know more as soon as the results are in. I'm lucky enough to get private treatment, so things are moving along quite fast.'

'Is it . . . is it curable?' Frankie said quietly. Under the table, out of Ruby's sight, she twisted her fingers together. She squeezed her legs tightly, pressing them down into the chair as if to ground herself.

'They think so.' Ruby's chin quivered. 'But if it is what they think it is, I might lose my leg. But hopefully we got it soon enough for that not to happen.'

'Soon enough!' Frankie blurted. 'How long have you had this lump?'

Ruby gasped, then looked down at the table. She toyed with the handle on her mug. 'A few months.'

Frankie's mouth set into a grim line. 'Why didn't you get it looked at straight away? You said yourself, you're able to get private treatment – so why the hell didn't you get it looked at straight away?!'

Ruby's face went white. She searched Frankie's angry face for a moment before speaking.

'Because I was afraid.' She held Frankie's hot gaze. 'I was terrified. It's a lump, Frankie. The first thing I did was think, oh God – it's cancer. Then I talked myself out of it. I thought, sure, wait and see if it goes away – and for a while it seemed to have gotten smaller. I thought it was just a cyst, or something like that. I mean, I've never even heard of leg cancer. I convinced myself that I was fine, and I tried not to think about it.'

Tears slid down Frankie's face. She swiped at them and

pushed her hands back under the table. 'What made you get it looked at then?' she asked more gently, her anger fading in the face of Ruby's fearful expression.

'You did.' Ruby sniffed. 'And Dillon. I . . . you two are like family to me.'

Frankie snorted. 'Family?'

Ruby started to talk but Sandra bustled into the kitchen, laden down with bags and goodies for the party.

'Look at you two,' she called out to them. 'Living it up, sunning yourselves out there like you're in the South of France and there's no party to get ready! Sure, look it, I'll grab a cuppa and join ye.'

Frankie looked away from Ruby, who was gingerly wiping under her eyes; she stared out over the sea towards the hazy horizon. What was the point of loving and caring for anyone? Everyone went away. You were only left hurt and alone. First Nicole had abandoned her, and not only that – she'd also managed to take her father out of the equation – and what about him? He'd guessed enough to come back to Castletown Cove, where he knew Nicole had lived, but he'd made no effort to find her. It wasn't as if she'd have been hard to find either. Everyone knew Nicole Farrell; everyone knew Aggie was minding Frankie. It didn't take a P.I. to make that discovery. He could have easily talked to her. Yet he had used her birthday as the code to his safe . . .

Frankie stood up and leaned her arms on the balcony rail. The stainless steel bit into her skin, and she welcomed the cold as it spread along her forearms. Everyone left in the end. Maybe this time, she should be the one to leave first. But how could she leave now when Ruby was going to need help. She didn't have anyone else in the world who would help. A tightness wrapped around Frankie's chest. She knew how to take care of her – hadn't she taken care of Aggie all the way through her treatment? For all the good it had done. Aggie was gone – what if she failed Ruby, too?

Sandra bustled out with a tray holding three mugs and a fresh pot of tea slid onto the small table.

'Here ye are,' she chirped. 'Thought I'd spoil ye.' She looked at Ruby's pale face, and at Frankie's pinched one, and her bright expression faltered. 'What's going on here?' she asked.

Ruby looked down at her hands. Sandra planted her hands on her hips.

'What's going on?' she demanded.

'Ruby . . . Ruby has . . . cancer,' Frankie said quietly. 'And we don't know how bad it is. Yet.'

Sandra turned to Ruby, her normally round and jolly face paled and softened. 'Ruby? What stage?'

Ruby nodded. 'I'll know more next week.'

Sandra sat down beside Ruby, quiet and still. Her incessant chatter had run out of steam. Frankie hunkered down beside Ruby and took her hands.

'It'll be okay, Ruby. We're going to take good care of you. We'll beat this thing. You don't need to worry,' Frankie babbled.

Sandra shuffled her chair closer to Ruby's. With shaky hands she poured the tea.

Frankie looked closely at Ruby and knew she was saying all the right things, even if they were just words, because Ruby's shoulders relaxed, and her face lost that strained

255

look she'd had. Taking the tea from Sandra, Frankie added two sugars to it and stirred in some milk. She handed the mug to Ruby before she realised that she'd made the tea the way Aggie had liked it, and not for Ruby, but Ruby didn't seem to notice and drank the tea without comment.

With trembling lips, she sipped her own tea. Ruby wasn't Aggie, she reminded herself, and they had different cancers. Ruby's might be curable, if they'd caught it soon enough. Frankie blinked rapidly. She crossed her fingers and made a wish, the closest thing to a prayer she was capable of. *It wouldn't hurt to light a candle.* The thought surprised her, but sure, what harm could it do? She'd light one later, when everyone had gone to bed, and maybe one for Aggie too.

25

Ruby

That night, unable to sleep, Ruby let herself out of the house as quietly as possible. She noticed that Frankie had left her bedroom window open, but even though it was warm, Ruby pulled her fleece closer around her. She climbed over the wall, instead of opening the gate, and made her way down the road to the Moonlight Garden. The old gate creaked loudly as she pushed it open. Scrunching up her nose, she left it ajar and padded across to the bench.

The air was still, and the night sky held the remnants of daytime despite the late hour. Perching on the bench, Ruby looked around, her eyes adjusting to the darkness as she slowly leaned back against the silvery wood. The bench groaned companionably, and she stroked the still-warm wood. The sweet, musky scent of jasmine surrounded her, making her think of Eoin. She was getting used to having him around the place. He'd taken Dillon under his wing, even bringing him a tiny toolbox and some child-sized tools. Frankie had hovered over them as Eoin taught Dillon how to hammer a nail into timber, and how to use the small handsaw, but now she just smiled when she saw Dillon shadow Eoin as he went about his jobs at Ruby's or the Moonlight Garden. He really was a good man, almost perfect.

With a shiver, she thought of the term 'emotional terrorist'. On the drive home earlier she'd heard a young woman on the radio say it about her abusive husband as she told the tale of how she'd escaped his control and was now living a life she'd never dreamed of. She'd urged women to plan carefully, if they were going to leave their manipulative partner: 'Save any cash you can, in a secret place. And have a place to go,' she'd advised. 'The thing that saved me was having some clothes packed away, ready for the moment he left. That way I didn't waste time packing on the day.'

Ruby frowned. Her relationship with James had been that bad, hadn't it? Staring up at the blue-velvet sky Ruby let the tears flow. There was no denying it, really, not now. Eoin had shown her how different things could be. God, she wished he was with her. Brushing away the tears she sniffed. The stars were all out, twinkling and sparkling, and she could make out some of the simpler constellations, even though the moon was almost full, and hung low over the navy waves. The church bells chimed midnight.

'Pinch, punch, first of the month,' she whispered hoarsely into the salty night air. Then, 'White rabbit, white rabbit, white rabbit.' Why she'd been compelled to mutter them, she wasn't sure, but any luck would be gladly accepted at this point.

A warm gust of wind sent shivers through the garden and tousled her hair. It had grown so long since she'd arrived back in Castletown Cove. Would she still have hair at Christmas? She touched her head and sat up. As soon as she'd heard the word *cancer*, her first thought had been about her hair. Then they said *amputate* and suddenly her hair didn't seem so important.

Amputation is the surgical removal of part of the body, such as an arm or a leg, is what the NHS website said. It was stated cleanly. The rest of the webpage had been long and filled with lots of advice. She'd scrolled through it quickly on her phone while sitting in the car outside the hospital. She'd been fine, even when she'd read the part that said some amputation took place under an epidural, until she'd gotten to the word: stump. Then familiar black spots had formed in front of her eyes. It had been years since she'd fainted, but the sensation of her head growing heavy and spinning came back all too easy. Stump. She'd managed to get the car seat to recline and lie back before the spots joined together. A few deep breaths and she'd managed to feel almost normal, except for the cold sweat across her back and brow.

They said something about surgery, but that she'd need chemotherapy and maybe radiation, too. They'd have to assess the results first. They made it all sound so simple, possible and even cheerful.

But it wasn't. None of it was. And she was alone, sitting in a Moonlight Garden at midnight worrying and thinking about what she'd do when she was housebound. It didn't bear thinking about, being stuck at home. She'd already spent so long at home waiting. Always waiting, and always depending on James to decide what they were going to do for dinner, where they'd holiday, and whose wedding they'd attend. It had taken her over a year to get back to Castletown Cove, and, even now, although she had Sandra helping her, it was kind of nice to be the one making the decisions without worrying about his input or how his face would fold into dissatisfaction at one of her 'madcap ideas'.

Tossing her head, she focused on the flowers next to her. Tiny, fragrant nemesias neatly filled the spaces between shrubs. She smiled. She could name almost all the flowers and shrubs now; she even knew some of their Latin names. That wouldn't have happened a year ago. No, a year ago she'd only read books on gardening, and watched *Gardener's World* on the odd Friday when James was away. She touched the long, strappy leaves of the blue-green grass that sprang up behind the nemesia. Tucked between them, a spray of white cosmos lifted daisy-like faces from lime-green fronds. They swayed gently in the warm breeze. The past few days had been gorgeous, with radio presenters remarking that Ireland was hotter than the Algarve. Jürgen was positive the plants in the Moonlight Garden would be fine. They were all chosen to survive, he'd said to the Moonlight Gardeners when they'd gathered earlier that evening. The plants were tougher than they looked, he'd said. She needn't worry. For some reason she'd yet to figure out, he'd made a beeline towards her afterwards, but she'd hurried away, taking the cliff walk all the way out to Paddy Whack's place. She'd walked briskly at first, until her leg began to twinge, then slowly, bitterly thinking that she should enjoy every minute of it while she still could walk it.

There was something niggling in the back of her mind. Jürgen reminded her so much of someone. It was in the way he moved sometimes, breaking from his usual calm and languid manner into something more manic, more frantic. She rattled her brain and suddenly she had it. George! Pamela had mentioned the name ages ago, but it only just clicked. Grinning, Ruby congratulated herself for figuring it out. It was crazy. She should have recognised him straight away, but it had been over fifteen years since he'd designed and landscaped her back garden in Dublin. She really could be forgiven for not seeing who he was. It had been his easy-going nature that had thrown her off.

The Jürgen/George she knew had been wired to the moon, and never without a coffee or energy drink in his hand. Not one of his crew looked like they enjoyed working with him. George had been haggard and drawn, which was odd for someone who spent all their time outdoors, but Jürgen was tanned and smiling. His face was relaxed, his hair long. His posture was that of someone who knew their body and mind well, not the slouched, curved shoulders of the George who'd argued with her over topiary shapes all those years ago. Sitting on the bench in the garden, Ruby began to wonder what had happened to George to change his life for the better.

The sound of the gate creaking made her jump. Someone was walking across the garden as if they knew it well. Ruby strained to see who it was, relaxing when she caught sight of Valerie in her familiar red fleece.

'Oh.' Valerie stopped. 'I wasn't expecting to find anyone here.'

'I could say the same.' Ruby smiled. 'What has you here?'

'Insomnia.' Valerie sighed. She sat down next to Ruby. 'Been like this since John left. No use in me sitting in an empty bed, so I come down here some nights and just relax.'

'It's a good idea,' Ruby said. 'I'm sorry it's so hard.'

'Ah, look.' Valerie gave a deep sigh. 'I should've seen it coming. He'd withdrawn from me, and I thought he was stressed from work, and his father was ill too. So, I gave him space, tried to be understanding, you know?'

Ruby nodded. Her shoulders tightened.

Valerie continued, 'I thought I was being supportive, but it turns out it wouldn't have mattered how I'd behaved because he was seeing someone else and she was, in his words, his saviour.'

Ruby snorted. 'His what?'

'His saviour.' Valerie laughed. 'Can you credit that? Anyway, more luck to them. I hope they drive each other up the bloody walls, saving each other and all that malarkey. But what about you – are you . . . are you doing all right?'

Ruby shrugged. It made sense that Valerie knew. Sandra would have told her. Still, it stung a little, especially when she was barely coming to terms with the news. Then again, everyone would know sooner or later; it wasn't something that was easily hidden.

'I'm not, I think.' She surprised herself by saying. 'I'm terrified.'

Valerie grabbed her hand and squeezed it tightly. 'I don't want to say it'll be all right,' she said. 'I don't know if it will – but I want you to know I'm here for you. You can come to me and rant and cry or scream, or just eat cake, anytime. And I mean that, Ruby, anytime.'

'Thanks, Val, I appreciate that.' Ruby sniffed. She pulled at the cuff of her fleece jacket. 'I'll definitely keep it in mind.'

The two women sat in silence for a while before Valerie spoke. 'Frankie's been a bit off the last few days. Have you noticed?'

'I have,' Ruby said. 'She's gone out more, and Dillon goes with her. I don't know. I'm probably reading too much into it all.' Ruby stopped talking. Chatting to Valerie about her diagnosis was one thing but discussing Frankie like this felt a little like gossiping.

'She's always taken Dillon with her when she's cleaning the houses in the summertime. Sometimes the hotel too when the manager is in a good mood,' Valerie said. 'And we're extremely busy this summer – with the holiday homes as well as the hotel. Everyone's coming to Castletown Cove this year – I blame TikTok and that influencer who went viral with her post about how romantic the place is.'

'Viral?' Ruby laughed. 'Castletown Cove went viral? That's quite funny.'

'You'd think,' Valerie said. 'But the phone is hopping with people begging for accommodation – every single one of them seems to have an anniversary or special birthday, too.'

Ruby laughed. 'That old trick!'

'The very one,' Valerie said. 'Right, come on, get up.'

'What?' Ruby watched Valerie haul herself to her feet.

'We may as well do something while we're here,' Valerie called over her shoulder as she headed back towards the sheds. 'Get moving!'

Ruby got up and laughed. Valerie was a tonic, and she was sorry she hadn't gotten to know her better over the years. Following her across the garden, Ruby watched Valerie take the key from under a pot and open the shed. The light flickered on, and a soft glow shone on the grass.

'Ahem.' A voice made her turn around. Jürgen stood there, a flask in his hand and a basket of mugs and biscuits.

'I saw you heading out,' he said. 'And I thought I'd come down with refreshments. I hope you don't mind.' He waved at Valerie as she appeared with hand trowels and kneeling pads.

'Tea? We have tea here,' Valerie said.

'Whiskey.' Jürgen raised the flask. 'I figured something a little stronger would be welcomed.' He looked at Ruby, his eyebrows raised and his face almost as serious as she remembered from his Dublin days.

Ruby smiled. 'What are we waiting for? Why the flask?'

Jürgen's face relaxed and he grinned. 'Can't be caught drinking in public – it's frowned upon.'

'Clever,' Valerie said. 'Come on! Don't be shy – pour us a drop!'

'And me!' Sandra piped up from behind Jürgen. 'I thought you'd be here, Val, so I came down to check.'

'I should've brought more whiskey.' Jürgen laughed, and handed Ruby a mug.

Sitting on the step of the shed, Ruby listened to Jürgen, Sandra and Valerie chat. Jürgen smiled more when Valerie spoke, and Valerie touched her hair whenever he looked at her. Ruby watched them and tried to hide her smile. Something was brewing and she wanted to be around when it happened. Forgetting her diagnosis for a moment, Ruby leaned forward and touched Jürgen's arm.

'I didn't recognise you at first,' she said quietly as the others chatted away. His face stilled, and she rubbed his arm. 'It's okay. I'm sure you have your reasons.'

Jürgen leaned his arms on his knees. Cradling his mug, he looked down. 'I thought you'd figure it out, and I was going to tell you. But the days just went by and each one was another day when I was just Jürgen, and not George.' He lowered his voice. 'I needed a fresh start to heal. As for changing my name . . .'

He glanced up at Valerie and Sandra. They'd picked up on his downturn in mood. Sandra swivelled around. Jürgen pressed his lips together.

'You changed your name?' Sandra asked. 'Why?'

Ruby glanced at Valerie, who was looking at Jürgen curiously, yet tenderly. Jürgen looked directly at Valerie, and spoke softly, as if only to her and no one else.

'I didn't mean for it to become a real thing, I suppose,' he said. 'When I came here, someone called me Jürgen for some reason that I still don't know. Then someone else did. And because I'd come here to get away from my life, it made sense to me to just use it. After a while, I felt like it suited me better. No one was googling George McGrath and Jürgen McGrath didn't pop up anywhere. It made it easier to start again.'

'What were you running from?' Valerie asked.

'Memories,' Jürgen said. 'And a broken heart.'

Throwing her arm around him, Ruby squeezed his shoulders.

'We weren't good together for a long time,' he said. 'She left me around the time I took on your project, and I completely threw myself into it.'

'I noticed,' Ruby said. She squeezed him again. 'I'm so sorry.'

'It's okay now. Back then it was a way to ignore the pain I was in, and the parts of me that needed to be explored. She said she'd come back one day, but . . .' Jürgen shrugged. Then he gave a short laugh. 'The funny thing is that she was a therapist – and the whole gardening as therapy idea I employed here, came from her. She'd actually like me like this, but . . . well, I've moved on, I suppose.'

'There's a lesson there,' Valerie said quietly. 'Don't refuse to grow and learn, especially when it's being pointed out to you – and ask for help, too.'

'I'll drink to that.' Jürgen raised his mug.

Ruby touched her mug off the others. She caught Sandra's eye as she took a sip.

26

Frankie

Just after eleven on Saturday morning, Frankie and Dillon walked from the hotel towards the holiday homes at the top of the hill. Frankie slowed down to allow Dillon to catch up with her. He was dragging his heels and grumbling.

'Why can't I stay with Auntie Ruby?' He kicked a stone in front of him. 'And have some of my birthday cake?'

Frankie swapped the bucket of cleaning products from one hand to the other. He looked mutinous and stopped walking.

'I'm not going.' He put his hands on his hips. 'You can't make me.'

'Ah, buddy,' Frankie said. 'Come on, don't do this. You know how much work I have to get through.'

'It's boring in the houses.' Dillon glared up at her. 'There's nothing to do and I'm not allowed to touch anything. You're just being mean!'

Frankie clenched her jaw. 'Dillon, that's not fair.'

'I'm going back to Auntie Ruby.' Dillon about-turned and began to march away.

Frankie watched him for a moment, sure that he'd turn around and wait for her, but he kept going, his little legs marching determinedly away from her. Dropping her cleaning bucket, Frankie ran down the road to catch up with him.

'Dillon, hold on.' She panted. 'What's going on? This isn't like you, buddy. What's upset you?'

'Nothing.' Dillon pouted.

'Right.' Frankie hunkered down beside him and did a quick mental calculation. 'I see. Listen, buddy, I know it's boring for you and I'm sorry. It's the same thing every day. How about, after I get these last few houses cleaned, I talk to Val and sort out a few days off? And then how about we go on a little holiday?'

Dillon's face lit up. 'Really?'

Frankie nodded. He threw his arms around her and squeezed her tight.

'We'll be like normal people,' he said as he planted a big kiss on her cheek.

Frankie blinked back tears. Is that what they'd been reduced to? Having to try being normal? Was their life so different to everyone else's? At this rate, there'd be no money saved up to have the cottage fixed. Between birthday parties and holidays, they'd be back to square one in no time. Dillon skipped up the road and picked up the cleaning bucket.

'Come on, Mammy,' he called. 'Let's get it done quickly.'

Frankie ran up to him and ruffled his hair. Taking the bucket from him, she took his hand and squeezed it.

Frankie gripped the bucket handle tighter. Now that she knew who her father was, she wanted to get the cottage fixed up more than ever. She was uneasy staying with Ruby now she knew.

It still wasn't clear if Ruby knew who she was, Frankie realised as she plonked the bucket down on the kitchen counter in the first holiday home. There was never any mention of James in their conversations, ever. It was as if Ruby didn't even think of him, which was strange. How could you not think about the man you were married to for so long? Frankie had found some of his belongings stashed away in the wardrobe of the other spare room. There hadn't been much. A box of expensive watches, a pile of clothes and some books. For a man who had it all, it seemed he hadn't much at the end of the day. There was one photo album, half-filled, documenting holidays and family gatherings. One photo stood out. A family gathering at Christmas, with a bunch of red-haired kids clustered at the foot of a Christmas tree, and every one of them looked like Dillon.

Frankie scoured the bath with unnecessary vigour. How did Ruby not see it? And if she did, then she should say something. Dillon singing to himself in the sitting room made her stop scrubbing. It wasn't fair on him. He should be part of that family, be under the Christmas tree with his relations. He should be included, somehow. How could she bring it up with Ruby, though, if Ruby didn't know that her husband had a baby with someone else, and that technically, she and Dillon were related to the Knight family? Wiping her arm across her forehead, Frankie groaned. She couldn't break it to Ruby, not when she was sick.

What if something happened to Ruby . . . Frankie picked up the toilet brush and attacked the toilet bowl. Cancer. Soft-tissue sarcoma, that's what she'd said it was. Seemingly treatable, but it was still cancer, and only treatable if Ruby had caught it on time – which they still didn't know if they had. Valerie and Sandra had been over to visit non-stop, with leaflets and supplements. They dragged Ruby out when she didn't want to go anywhere; last night they'd taken her to see the drama society's latest production. Ruby had come home bubbling and laughing. She'd even opened a bottle of wine, one of the expensive ones. Val and Sandra stayed late but Frankie had slipped away, unable to sit with them all giggling as if nothing had happened. As if Ruby didn't need her rest. As if she didn't have cancer.

Frankie had sat on the bottom step of the stairs and listened to them for a while. Valerie's upcoming holiday to Spain was a hot topic, and Ruby had lots of advice and places for Valerie to go see while she was there. Sandra pondered if it was too late to book tickets to go with her. It was all sounding so good. There was no mention of the night classes Ruby and Frankie had signed up for, though; no excitement at starting that in September. As the conversation lulled and then turned to the Moonlight Garden and Jürgen, Frankie had slipped away to bed. It had taken her ages to get to sleep every night, and she was super tired every morning. It was making the cleaning harder, and everything took so much more effort than usual.

Satisfied that the bathroom was spotless, Frankie moved on to the en suite, determined to get the tougher jobs out of the way first. An hour later, the holiday home was cleaned and ready for the guests arriving that afternoon.

Making her way back along the coast road, Frankie pondered what she'd do for the evening. She stopped at the seafront and contemplated the families making sandcastles and playing in the sea. The warm breeze lifted her hair away from her face and brought a tinge of pink to her cheeks. The gulls were out far at sea, and the water was calm and clear. Frankie squinted and followed a sailing boat until it went around the cliffs and out of sight. Maybe she'd apply for her theory test and driving licence just in case she ever needed to drive anywhere. Ruby had to go to Dublin next week. She was meeting with her specialist to discuss how they'd approach her treatment. She was planning on driving, but how long would she be able to do that? And who'd bring her when she couldn't anymore? Eoin, maybe. Maybe not. He'd only called to the house once in the last week and hadn't stayed for coffee when Ruby offered it. There was something going on there, but Frankie couldn't figure it out.

'Mammy.' Dillon pulled on her hand, dragging her from her thoughts. 'Can we get an ice cream? I'm as hot as a fried grasshopper.'

'A fried what?' Frankie looked down at Dillon.

'Grasshoppers,' he said. 'Didn't you know you can eat them?'

'No, I did not know that.' Frankie pulled a face. 'And no, I do not want to try them, ever.'

Dillon giggled. 'Imagine grasshopper flavour ice cream.' His face creased into a smile. 'Or cricket flavour.'

'Urgh!' Frankie grimaced. 'No thank you, nope. Not a chance.' She straightened her face. 'Would you think they're crunchy? Like honeycomb.'

'Probably,' Dillon said, tilting his head. 'I'd say that would be the best part.'

'Well, I think I'll stick with my current favourite, thank you,' Frankie said. 'Mint chocolate chip has more than enough crunch for me.'

'I'd give it a go,' Dillon said, slipping his hand into hers as they joined the queue outside Sundae Every-day. 'Just to see, you know.'

'I know,' Frankie said. He was growing more and more like Liam every day.

They sat on the low wall outside the ice cream parlour and ate their treat, as more people joined the queue. Across the road, almost opposite them, was Jürgen's shop. A gaggle of teenagers huddled together, looking in the window at the crystals and salt lamps on display. The sign on the door said 'closed' and the disgruntled teenagers loudly complained about it. Frankie couldn't take her eyes off them. They were so tanned and polished. One had the most glamorous mane of hair she'd ever seen. It hung sleekly down the girl's back, almost to her waist, and was the colour of seal skin. The girls all wore versions of the same dress, body con and tie-dyed. They had anklets and beach bags and were full of life as they discussed what they were going to do now the shop was closed.

Frankie finished her ice cream and got up from the wall. It had been a long time since she'd had the freedom of having a day to just live, a day free from responsibilities. Going away with Dillon for a day or two would be a good thing. They'd go to the cinema and eat out afterwards. Urging Dillon to follow her, she walked home, back to Eyrie Lodge. She calculated how many extra shifts she could take on in September when Dillon was back in school and wondered if she should get quotes to get the tank and ceiling repaired, too.

But the holiday was all Dillon could talk about. Frankie listened with a heavy heart as he described the holidays his friends were going on.

'Ava is going to France,' Dillon declared as they walked around the house to the utility door. 'On the ferry. She said they'll be on the ferry for lots of days. She's bringing her granny. Isn't that nice?'

'Uh, yeah,' Frankie mumbled, desperately hoping he'd be happy with the kind of holiday she had in mind. 'Come on, wash your hands; they're sticky from the ice cream.'

Dipping his hands in and out of the water at the utility room sink, Dillon smiled. 'We should bring Auntie Ruby, Mammy. I think she'd like that.'

'Maybe,' Frankie said. His friendship with Ruby was growing. How would he cope when he found out she was sick? He'd already been through so much with Aggie. 'Maybe she won't want to come.'

'Don't be silly, Mammy,' Dillon said. 'Of course, she'll want to come. We should ask her. Right now.'

He grabbed a hand towel and ran from the utility room. Frankie heard the soft thud of his shoes come off, and the dash of his steps as he scampered up the stairs to the kitchen calling for Ruby.

Slowly, Frankie washed her hands, and dried them on a fresh towel. She walked to the bottom of the stairs and peered up. Dillon had dropped the hand towel on the ground, and she stooped to pick it up. When she looked up, Ruby was at the top of the stairs, staring down at her.

'We need to talk,' Ruby said quietly. She spun around and disappeared.

'Crap.' Frankie hurried up the stairs. Had there been some news from the specialist?

Ruby was waiting for her in the hallway. The sound of the television came from the sitting room.

'He's occupied.' Ruby's voice was flat and hard. Her eyes were red and puffy. Frankie swallowed. The news must be bad, because if it was good news, she'd just say it, wouldn't she? She'd be jumping for joy and wanting to celebrate, not crying and low like this. Frankie cleared her throat and straightened her shoulders. What would she say to Dillon? How would he take it? Ruby was staring at her, hard. Frankie looked back and waited. She held Ruby's gaze for a minute, but Ruby said nothing.

Frankie looked down. Ruby had something in her hand. A bunch of envelopes, and a black ribbon hung from her other hand. Her mouth dropped open as her eyes flew to Ruby's face.

'So, you've seen these before, then,' Ruby stated. 'Your expression gives you away.'

'I . . .' Frankie shook her head. She twisted her fingers together. She wished she'd told Ruby sooner, but how could she have? When was the right time to tell your friend that her husband had been having an affair that had resulted in a baby? And besides, Frankie hadn't been sure Ruby didn't already know.

Frankie took a deep, calming breath. 'I can explain.'

'Explain what, exactly?' Ruby snapped. 'That you broke

274

into my safe, or that you're . . . you're . . .' Her voice broke. Ruby shook her head as Frankie made to comfort her.

'No.' She raised her hand. 'Stay where you are. Don't come near me.'

'Ruby,' Frankie pleaded. 'I didn't know.'

'You didn't know!' Ruby choked on her words, as tears coursed down her face. Shaking, she wiped them away with the back of her hand. 'I'm supposed to believe that, am I? Well, I don't believe you. How could I when you were clearly snooping around my house – trying to find what – his will? Looking for your share, are you?'

Frankie glanced towards the sitting room hoping that Dillon couldn't hear them. Her stomach clenched tightly, the ice cream curdling inside her in the face of Ruby's anger.

'I didn't know,' she said again. 'I didn't know until I . . . Oh, Ruby, I'm sorry. I wanted to tell you . . . but . . . I shouldn't have looked. I wish I hadn't. I found a letter from him in my grandmother's things. I can show it to you if you want.' Wiping her nose on the back of her hand, Frankie sniffed. Ruby's eyes were fiery, but her face was pale, her lips compressed into a tight line. She shook her head again and wrapped her arms around her body. Frankie couldn't move. Her legs felt as if the soles of her feet had been stitched to the very spot she was standing on, stitched so tightly that it felt as if she was being pulled through the floor.

'What did the letter say?' Ruby asked in a flat voice.

'Oh God, Ruby,' Frankie cried. 'I'll get it for you.'

'No. Just tell me.' Ruby stared at her. 'Tell me. Now.'

Frankie closed her eyes for a moment. She opened them slowly and focused on Ruby.

'The letter was to my mother from someone who signed off as "J",' she said. 'J wanted her to meet him in a hotel in Dublin, and to bring the baby with her. He said she'd better not make a scene, that the baby would be looked after . . . It was dated about two weeks after I was born.'

Frankie watched Ruby closely. Ruby didn't move. Her arms were wrapped tightly around her body, as if she needed to physically hold herself together. Frankie continued.

'That letter, it made me curious.' Her cheeks grew red. 'And you would be curious too if it was about you, so please try to understand. I looked – of course I looked. What else could I do? I wanted to know more so I googled the company name that was on the letterhead and found him . . . and you.'

'How long have you known?' Ruby asked in a deathly quiet voice. 'Before I took you in? Was the leak in the cottage part of your plan to get in here?'

'Oh, Ruby,' Frankie cried. 'No! It wasn't part of my plan – you weren't part of my plan at all. I didn't – *don't* even have a plan. How could you think that?'

'How?' Ruby finally looked angry. 'Because now you know how much James was worth! That's how.'

'That's disgusting.' It was Frankie's turn to go quiet. 'I can't believe you'd say that, Ruby.'

Ruby's mouth twisted. 'I don't care what you believe. I just want you gone.'

'Gone?' Frankie's head jerked up. 'What do you mean?'

'I want you out of my house,' Ruby said. She raised

her chin and let her hands drop to her sides. 'Out. By tomorrow evening.'

'Ruby.' Frankie's voice cracked. 'You can't mean that – where will we go?'

'I don't care where you go,' Ruby said. Her chin trembled, and she swallowed hard.

'What about Dillon – he adores you.' Frankie started to cry. Fat, hot tears streamed down her face. 'Don't break his heart like this.'

Ruby turned her face away from Frankie.

'Out, like I said. Dillon will be fine. He'll soon forget about me.' She walked away leaving Frankie shivering and crying in the hallway.

'No, he won't,' Frankie said to Ruby's back. 'We'll never forget you.'

27

Ruby

Ruby made it to her bedroom just in time and slammed the door behind her. She leaned back against the bedroom door, rammed her fist up against her mouth and tried to choke back her cries, but her body betrayed her, and she slid to the floor. The tight band that had formed around her head from the moment she'd come across the open safe intensified. Her head felt as if it was going to split open. Frankie's horrified face swam in front of her eyes. Had she really told them to get out, to leave? But there was no other option. They couldn't stay. Not while things were so raw and muddled. How could she face them every day and not be reminded of what James had done?

James . . . her heart lurched in her chest and bile rose in her throat. Staggering to her feet, she raced to the bathroom and vomited into the toilet. Dear God. He'd slept with Nicole. No! He'd had a baby with Nicole. Her stomach twisted and she vomited again. Shivering, she pulled herself to her feet and lunged towards the hand basin. She poured a glass of water and rinsed her mouth. Casting her eyes down, she avoided her reflection in the mirror. She couldn't bear to see what James must've seen every time he looked at her: a barren, pathetic excuse for a woman. Ruby grabbed the facecloth and ran it under the cold tap. Pressing the cold cloth to her eyes, she tried to loosen the chokehold that wrapped around her throat. The absolute cheek of him!

She'd never guessed. Never, not in all their years together – not once had she suspected he'd been unfaithful. He made a big deal of their wedding anniversary every single year, reminding Ruby how fortunate she was to have found him, to have cast her spell on him. Gritting her teeth, Ruby forced her head up. Her knuckles went white as she gripped the basin. How could she not have known?

Casting her mind back, she remembered the time they'd discussed their fertility problem. Now that she remembered it, it was more that she had talked about it; he'd said nothing productive whatsoever. Ruby felt her skin tighten on her forehead. He'd been so dismissive now that she thought of it.

'We should go to the doctor,' she'd said to him. They had gone to Morocco, and were lounging by the pool with cocktails, celebrating their second wedding anniversary. 'Just to get checked out.'

'Christ, Ruby,' James had snarled. 'Is this because I'm forty this year?'

'No,' Ruby had said, taken aback. 'Of course not.'

'Good.' He'd pushed his sunglasses up his nose. 'Because there's no need. We're barely married, Rubes. Give it time. Good things come to those who wait.'

Ruby remembered how she'd lowered her voice so no one else overheard her. 'James, we're two years married, and we've been having unprotected sex since we met – that's over four years now. We've never had a pregnancy scare . . . I think that's more than fate.'

'I'd call it luck,' he'd said, barely looking up from his book.

'I'd call it infertility,' she'd said quietly.

She remembered how he'd closed his book with an angry snap. He'd swung his legs around to her.

'Infertility?' His voice had been tight. 'And whose fault is it, in your opinion?'

Ruby had pulled her knees up to her chest. With his sunglasses on, she couldn't tell if he was looking at her or somewhere else. 'No one's. You still want a family, don't you?' she'd asked.

'Of course. Why else do I work so hard?'

Thinking back now, Ruby remembered how she'd held her tongue. It wouldn't have helped to reply that he'd more or less revealed to her over the years all the reasons why he worked so hard: status, power, control, money, to be better than everyone else but specifically his sister . . . having his own family didn't rate a mention, strangely enough. He'd simply sat there and waited for her to reply.

'I think it's me,' she'd said eventually. 'I think I can't have a baby.'

'Right,' he'd said. 'So how about you go and get yourself checked out. If it's not you, then I'll think about it.'

The memory made her shiver, just as she'd shivered back then. It hadn't been the response she'd expected. Instead of hugging her, saying that she was right, and they both should go to the doctor because they were in this together, he'd immediately cast the responsibility onto her shoulders.

He'd picked up his book and settled back onto his lounger. Ruby had sat still for a few minutes before she'd gotten up. She remembered feeling so claustrophobic, and diving into the pool to try to wash the feelings away. She'd relished the cold water on her hot skin, how she could control her breath and pace herself. Coming up at the far end of the pool, she'd gasped and swiped the water from her face. Smiling, she'd tipped her head to the sun. If there was one thing she was good at, it was swimming. She was even better than James, for all his childhood lessons and foreign holidays. He'd yet to beat her, but always claimed to have let her win.

Now, sitting on the bathroom floor, wiping her face on a cool, damp cloth, she remembered how she'd stared at him that day. The thought that had crossed her mind was that he didn't look like a man who'd just argued with his wife. He showed no signs of distress whatsoever. Ruby had turned away from him, leaned on the edge of the pool and let her body float up behind her.

At dinner that night, she'd watched him closely. He had been, as always, impeccably groomed. His shirt was crisp, his watch expensive. Ruby recalled how he'd looked around the room, taking in who was there and what they were doing. That time he hadn't been snide about the other guests, as he usually would've been. Instead, he'd turned his attention to her.

'I've been thinking,' he'd said, speaking low and soft. 'I wasn't as supportive as I should've been earlier. You came to me with a concern, and I blew it off. I apologise,

Ruby. I felt measured, like I'd failed you. I went on the defensive when I should have assured you that I love you and that things will be all right.'

'I love you, too.' Ruby had looked down. She'd balled the napkin into a million creases on her lap.

'I am head over heels for you,' he'd continued. 'Children are obviously important to you, and your dreams are important to me. We'll do what we have to do to make your dreams come true. I promise.'

Ruby had almost cried as she'd reached for his hand. 'Oh, James.'

'We'll work it out.'

'If . . . if the worse comes to the worse, we can always adopt.' Ruby had squeezed his hand. He'd instantly stopped smiling.

'No, Rubes, adoption's not an option for me. I don't think I could love someone else's child as if they were my flesh and blood.'

Ruby remembered how she'd blinked back tears. 'But we could go to counselling, or something. Lots of people adopt and cope.'

'I said no, Rubes,' he'd said, his voice hardening. She never forgot how his voice had hardened. 'It's you and me and if that's all it'll ever be, well then, that's perfect too. Who says what a family is or isn't?'

'Your sister?' Ruby had mumbled. There was no point in continuing the adoption conversation. He had his mind made up.

'What about her?' James had said. His grip on her hand had tightened. 'I don't care about her. Six kids is just greedy, by the way.'

Ruby had half-smiled. 'Six kids *is* greedy. I agree.'

James had raised his glass. 'To us. To our kind of family. Happy anniversary, my love.'

Ruby remembered how she'd clinked her glass against his, and how she'd ignored the gnawing sensation in her stomach telling her that something was off. He raised his glass again.

Now she knew her fears that day had been right. She should have listened to her gut. She had been the problem and he'd found a way to solve it. He'd found Nicole. They'd made a baby together and then he'd planned to try to pass that baby off on her.

The last time they'd spoken about children was in 1995 when, out of the blue, he'd suggested adopting a baby. Now she knew why he had changed his mind: the baby *was* his flesh and blood. But back then, he'd worked hard to convince her everything was fine.

'I know, it sounds dodgy, but it's legitimate,' he'd said, sitting her down on the living room sofa. 'This young woman is Irish, and she's willing to give up her baby to us. She's not in a good position to take care of it.'

'It sounds all wrong.' Ruby had frowned. 'It sounds illegal.'

'No!' He'd gripped her shoulders and held her tight. 'It's all above board. You'd hardly think I'd do something illegal, do you?' Then he'd dropped his hands from her shoulders. 'I was thinking only of you, Ruby. You're miserable all the time, and that affects me, you know.'

She remembered how her heart had pounded so loud she had been sure he could hear it. A baby . . . She remembered almost cradling her arms as if she was already holding it.

'This young woman . . . how did you find her?' she'd finally asked.

'She works for one of my colleagues. No one else knows she's pregnant, not even her boss.'

'Which colleague?' Ruby had frowned. 'It's not Joe, is it?'

'No, it's not Joe.' James had huffed. 'Look, Ruby, it doesn't matter who she works for. Time is of the essence here. There's another interested party . . . we have to make a decision on this, fast.'

'I thought you said no one else knows.' Ruby had looked at him.

'I meant, no one in her family knows.' James had sighed. 'Sorry for not making myself one hundred per cent clear.'

Ruby remembered how she'd held back the million questions she'd wanted to ask. He'd always been good at making her feel bad for asking questions.

'When's the baby due?' she'd asked. A fluttering in her stomach made her smile. James had held her hands in his.

'Very soon. November. And it's a girl.' He'd kissed her hands as if the deal was done.

'A baby girl,' Ruby had whispered.

Now, with a pounding head, she realised that baby girl was Frankie. She'd always thought James would've held out for a son, but he'd brushed off her concerns.

'A boy? Ruby, I don't care about all of that.' He'd taken her face in his hands. They had been warm and gentle on her skin. 'I want you to have this baby.'

'I want this baby,' Ruby had whispered. 'James, oh God, how I want this baby.'

Back in the present Ruby clambered up from the bathroom floor. Her stomach heaved again as she remembered how he'd pulled her to him and kissed her, kissed her eyes, her lips, her tears, buried his face in her neck. His muffled voice had almost broken her heart.

'Thank you,' he'd said. 'I thought you'd say no.'

They'd made love then, on the sitting room floor, in the middle of a Wednesday afternoon with the curtains wide open. For the first time in months, it had felt right, as if the stresses and strains of the past few months hadn't happened. It was as if they were new lovers all over again. Afterwards, they'd eaten lunch out before he'd gone back to work, leaving Ruby in town to window-shop for baby baths and cots. It had been the best day of her life. It was the one time James had handed her his credit card and told her to get whatever she needed. She'd gone a little over the top, buying two Moses baskets, one for upstairs and one for downstairs. She'd even searched for a Baby's First Christmas decoration even though it had only been coming up to Hallowe'en, convinced that they'd need it and that she'd be too busy in a few weeks to be out shopping.

She'd hurried home and called their interior decorator, happily marking the appointment in her calendar. Then she'd waited, and waited. The baby's room had been finished, the cot and changing table assembled and the curtains hung, but there had been no sign of the baby arriving. Ruby remembered how she'd walked on eggshells around James. He'd taken to working later and later, and she felt as if he'd been avoiding her. Once she'd asked when the baby's due date was, but he'd really and truly lost his temper then. He'd stormed out and hadn't come home for two days. She hadn't dared to ask after that.

It had been when December rolled around that she'd finally realised that it wasn't going to happen. There wasn't going to be a baby. James had been gruff, although a little calmer. His explanation was simple: the mother had changed her mind – she'd decided to risk being an unmarried mother and keep her baby. She was a fool.

Ruby had cried for almost a week afterwards. She'd slept in the baby's room, on the tiny single bed and mourned the baby she'd never have.

Now, opening the bathroom door, Ruby felt like an idiot. He'd pulled a fast one on her, and he'd almost gotten away with it. The letters told the whole story. Nicole was terrified of having the baby, but also terrified of handing the baby over to James. Her letters to James grew shrill and demanding as her pregnancy progressed. She'd needed things, clothes that fit, new shoes, scans and private appointments. Ruby sat on her bed and opened the letters again. She forced her eyes to slow down as she read each sheet carefully, searching for some hint as to how they'd met, why he'd cheated, and mostly, what role Nicole had played in the whole thing.

But the letters were only about the pregnancy. Not once did Nicole or James refer to their time before Nicole got pregnant. James had sent her money. Cash, by post. How risky of him. Ruby dropped one letter and tore open the next. He'd even met her at a private hospital for her appointments. Ruby's stomach heaved. He could've bumped into one of their friends there. Anyone could've seen him sitting there playing happy families with that woman! Ruby trembled as she read the letters. Nicole knew damn well whose husband she was fooling around with, and she still went ahead knowing full well Ruby would be devastated if she ever found out.

The letters piled up beside Ruby on the bed. The urge to shred them to pieces raged in her, but what good would it do? She needed them. Someday, when she was feeling less sorry for herself, she'd need to reread them so they'd fan the embers of the anger that tore through her.

Flinging the last letter on the floor, Ruby got up from the bed. Her hands shook as she grasped the door handle. He'd almost managed to get his true blood child into his home. He'd tricked her into believing he was doing it for her when it was for himself all along. What kind of a man was he? Ruby pushed down on the handle and stormed into the spare room where his things were stored. Methodically, she pulled every article of clothing from the boxes, and searched through pockets and wallets. His shoes were upended, and their insoles torn out.

Panting, she took his wedding ring from its box and weighed it her hand before flinging it across the room. The ring bounced against the far wall, breaking the silence that enveloped the house as it clattered to the floor. The silence returned. There was no chatter from Dillon's play-room, no music from the kitchen as Frankie danced to the radio. Ruby's lip curled up into a snarl. They were gone. Good riddance.

28

Frankie

They'd only been two days in the holiday home Valerie had sneaked them into and already Frankie was exhausted trying to keep it clean and tidy while working and searching for somewhere to live. They'd only another day or two at the house as it was booked up for the rest of the summer. The thought of it was making her head spin. She got up from the table where she and Valerie had been chatting, wrapped the leftover chips in newspaper and shoved the greasy parcel into a refuse bag before tying it tightly.

Valerie hadn't seemed to notice how Dillon was wandering around the house, but Frankie was worried. He hadn't spoken a word since they'd left Eyrie Lodge two days ago. At first, she thought he was exploring the space, but he kept on doing it even though she'd taken out his favourite insect book and put Bug on the bed. Taking the rubbish outside to the bin, she peered through the window into the room he was walking around in. He ran his fingertips along the wall for as long as he could touch it, then took a breath and started again. Frankie rubbed her forehead and ran her hand down her face. He was worse than he'd been after Aggie had died.

Going back inside to Valerie, Frankie picked up a cloth and wiped down the counters and the table until they gleamed.

'I'd let you stay with me,' Valerie said. 'But John is kicking up a fuss. He's talking about putting our house up for sale, and when he heard you stayed there the last time, he went mental. You'd swear I'd taken you on as a tenant, the way he was whinging.'

'It's okay, Val. I get it.' Frankie plumped a cushion and placed it on the sofa. 'You've enough going on without adding me to the mix.'

Valerie sat at the dining table. 'You really didn't know?'

Frankie flicked her hair back. 'No, Val, I didn't. Do you think I'd have moved in if I did?'

'Sorry,' Valerie said. 'It's . . .'

'It's messed up – that's what it is,' Frankie said. 'But I'm not a gold-digger, Val. If I'd known the truth, I'd have given Ruby a wide berth.'

'She must be devastated.' Valerie pushed an errant crumb with her fingernail. 'Finding out your husband not only had an affair but that there was a baby too.'

'Eh, hello!' Frankie said. 'I'm right here – the baby you're talking about.'

'Sorry!' Valerie flushed. 'I didn't mean it like that – obviously it's not your fault.'

'Obviously,' Frankie said. She sat down next to Valerie. 'But I'm the one paying the price for my mother's behaviour, and so is Dillon.'

'He's not taking it well?' Valerie asked.

'No.' Frankie tapped her fingers on the table. 'You wouldn't be either if you were made homeless.'

'What about Nicole?' Valerie shifted in her chair. 'Have you spoken to her about this?'

'No.' Frankie rolled her eyes. 'And I won't, either.'

'Do you even know where she is?' Valerie smiled at Dillon who had walked into the room and was tracing the room's circumference with his fingertips.

'I think she's in Italy,' Frankie said. 'And she can stay there, too. I want nothing to do with her.'

Valerie lowered her voice as Dillon rounded the room in her direction. She nodded her head in his direction. 'It might help . . .'

Frankie shook her head. It looked like Valerie had noticed his odd behaviour. 'It won't. So, anyway, how is she?'

'Ruby?' Valerie sighed and waited for Dillon to move on to the hall. 'She's not doing too well. I called in this morning and she's very down in herself. I tried to get her to come for a walk, but she fobbed me off, saying Eoin was calling in to talk about the garden. I bumped into Eoin at the Moonlight Garden, and he didn't have a clue what I was on about when I told him Ruby was expecting him.'

'Oh, crap.' Frankie's shoulders dropped. 'That's not good.'

'No, it's not,' Valerie agreed. 'Not only that, Eoin told me he'd been trying to give her some space. I told him to cop on to himself and stop acting like a teenager. Ruby needs him now more than ever, I told him. He said he's been talking to her, but she's clearly unhappy. He doesn't know how to help her. Says she's only telling him the bare minimum about what the doctors are saying. She told me she doesn't want to burden him, that it's not his place to take care of her.'

Frankie leaned on the table. 'Oh, Val, that's so horrible. Poor Ruby. Her whole world has turned upside down. First the cancer, then me. I'm just one of the jigsaw pieces of her life that she's discovered was in the wrong place all this time. I'm so sad for her.'

'Yes, I hear what you're saying, but . . .' Valerie tapped the table. 'This whole thing would be a lot easier if she wasn't trying to be so independent, you know? We all need a helping hand every now and then.'

'I suppose.' Frankie frowned.

Valerie nodded. 'You too, by the way.'

'I took Ruby's helping hand, and look where that's got me – homeless.' Frankie got up from the table. 'Right, come on. I'll stretch my legs and walk you as far as the gardens.'

'You're not coming in?' Valerie asked. 'We miss having you around.'

'No, I'll give Ruby some space. I know she loves it there.'

'But she's hardly been down either.' Valerie frowned.

'She needs it more than me,' Frankie said. 'You'll work your magic and get her back there – I'm sure of it.'

Sandra was ahead of them on the path as they walked towards the Moonlight Garden. She glanced back over her shoulder and slowed down when she saw Frankie. Frankie faltered. She hadn't spoken to Sandra since Ruby had asked them to leave. Even though she'd kicked them out, Frankie still felt loyal to Ruby. Ruby wouldn't want to hear anyone talking about her business and her heartache. After all, Frankie didn't want anyone talking about them either.

Passing Eyrie Lodge, Frankie looked up at the balcony, hoping to catch sight of Ruby, but the doors were tightly shut, and the house was in darkness. Dillon stopped walking and pulled on her arm. He pointed to the house.

'We can't go in, buddy.' Frankie hunkered down beside him. 'Not until Ruby asks us to come see her, okay? She just needs some time and space.'

Dillon's face darkened. He stuck his tongue out at Frankie and jerked his hand out of hers, then stomped away from her towards the garden. Frankie stood up.

'It'll work itself out,' Sandra said. 'Time . . .'

'Yeah, time and all that.' Frankie watched Dillon walk slowly on, his fingertips touching the wall. His hands would be filthy by the time they got back to the holiday home; she'd have to make sure he washed them well before he returned to his tracing his way around the house. Valerie and Sandra strolled on, catching up with Dillon. Valerie tried asking him questions about the butterflies she had in her garden, but he stubbornly kept his mouth tightly closed. They were almost at the Moonlight Garden, so Frankie hurried to catch up with the trio. She forced a cheerful tone in her voice.

'Hey, buddy, I'm thinking we should go get an ice cream. What do you think?'

Dillon shrugged.

'That's a great idea.' Valerie ruffled his hair. Taking out

her purse, she pulled out some money and tucked it into Dillon's hand. 'There you go. You get yourself the biggest ice cream in the shop.'

Horrified, Frankie reached out and took the money out of his hand. 'You don't need to do that.' She handed the money back to Valerie. 'We're not beggars.'

'I know you're not,' Valerie said. 'I was just being nice.'

'I'm sorry. We can't take it.' Frankie held the note out.

Valerie looked at it for a moment, then took the money back.

'See you around, Frankie,' she said sadly. 'See you, Dillon.'

Frankie watched the two sisters round the corner and go through the gate into the Moonlight Garden. A mumble of voices came over the hedge, and she was about to turn away when she heard her name being mentioned. Shuffling Dillon along the wall, Frankie leaned closer. Sandra was speaking.

'No, Val. You tell Frankie. Frankie will make her see sense. I'll only cry if I try telling her.'

'Do you think Ruby will listen to her?' Valerie's voice was tight.

'Honestly, I don't know but it's worth a shot,' Sandra said. 'She won't listen to any of us, and she loves Frankie, even if she won't admit it.'

'I don't know.' Valerie sounded upset. 'Ruby is so angry . . . Frankie would try, though. I know she would. She talks about Ruby every time we meet.'

'Talk to Frankie,' Sandra said. 'Please, Val. Tell her that Ruby is refusing to even consider the amputation. Otherwise she'll . . . Well, it doesn't look good, does it?'

'Stop!' Valerie raised her voice. 'I'll try to figure it out. Just stop. I can't bear to think of Ruby . . .'

'I know.' Sandra sniffed. 'But I don't know how we can change her mind.'

Frankie's eyes widened. Ruby was going against the amputation? Why? What was going on? Frankie gripped her T-shirt hem and twisted it. Ruby knew the outcome if she refused the amputation – was she not thinking straight? Frankie glanced down at Dillon, hoping he hadn't grasped the gist of Valerie and Sandra's conversation. He was aimlessly poking a twig into a crack in the wall, and seemed oblivious to all around him.

Frankie hurried away from the wall, annoyed that she now knew. Nothing good ever came from eavesdropping. But now she did know, and the best thing to do would be to talk to Ruby. Even if she didn't want to see her, at least she'd know she still cared for her. She couldn't just give up like that.

Marching back along the road, with Dillon trailing behind her, Frankie caught sight of Ruby as she slipped down the side track towards the harbour. She was carrying a large red shoulder bag and wearing a white sun dress. She looked like a tourist, still, with her hair pulled up into a messy bun and huge sunglasses on. She didn't look sick at all. Frankie brushed down the old band T-shirt she was wearing and shoved her hands into the pockets of her denim shorts.

'Come on, buddy,' she called back to Dillon. He was squatting and examining a bright butterfly where it fed on a dandelion. 'Hurry up, let's catch up with Ruby.'

His eyes lit up and he jumped up, scaring the butterfly

into flight. Skipping up to Frankie, he smiled for the first time in days. Frankie beamed at him, feeling her heartbeat ticking in her neck. Ruby would surely talk to him; she wasn't cruel enough to take out her anger on a child. They hurried down the road and slipped down the side track after Ruby. She was already walking briskly across the harbour road, and onto the path that led to the marina where the fishing boats were lined up, empty and washed down. Frankie's mouth dried up. Slowing down, she pretended to tie her lace, all the while watching Ruby carefully.

Eoin emerged from the Harbour Master's office. He gestured to the sailing club, and Ruby nodded. Frankie breathed out. She turned around to tell Dillon they'd call in on Ruby later as she was busy, but he wasn't around. Turning back, she saw him running across the wide road, waving at Ruby and Eoin. They hadn't seen him, and were walking towards the club, slightly apart from one another.

'Dillon!' Frankie called. She began to run after him, checking the road for fork trucks and lorries. 'Dillon, come back!'

Dillon ran on, his eyes firmly on Ruby's back.

'Ruby!' he called out, his arms waving frantically. Ruby spun around; her face lit up.

Frankie's mouth dropped open. She ran faster, catching up with Dillon as he reached Ruby and Eoin. Panting, she took his arm and started to lead him away.

'Sorry,' she said, keeping her eyes down. 'We didn't mean to interrupt.'

'You're not interrupting,' Eoin said. 'We're delighted to see you both, aren't we?' He glanced at Ruby, whose face was rigid.

'Ruby,' Dillon said again. 'I miss you.'

Frankie swallowed and stepped backwards. The first words he'd spoken in days were for Ruby. Eoin looked back and forth, taking in each woman's defensive posture.

'Listen, we're going down to the club for a cold drink. Why don't you come with us?' he said.

Ruby shifted from one foot to the other. She stayed quiet, kept her eyes averted from Frankie, and crossed her arms.

'Thanks, but we're heading up to get ice cream,' Frankie said. She slid her hand down Dillon's arm and took his hand. 'Come on, Dillon, we'll see Ruby soon.'

'No!' Dillon shrieked. He wrenched his hand from Frankie's and ran towards Ruby. Throwing his arms around her waist, he buried his head in her and started to cry.

Ruby paled. She put her arms around Dillon and hugged him close.

'I thought you were dead.' Dillon looked up at her. 'Like Granny Aggie.'

Frankie covered her mouth as Ruby glanced over at her.

'No, I'm very much alive,' Ruby said, kneeling beside Dillon. 'What made you think that?'

'Mammy said we couldn't see you anymore,' Dillon said.

'It wasn't like that,' Frankie groaned. 'I didn't know how to tell him . . .'

'It's okay.' Ruby looked at her. 'I understand.'

She hugged Dillon tightly, then kissed his head and stood up.

'Dillon, I have to go now. I've plans with Eoin. But I promise you, I'll come see you soon.' She took his hands from her waist.

Dillon stood back as Ruby walked away. He looked up at Eoin, who shrugged and hurried after Ruby. Rushing to Dillon's side, Frankie watched Ruby stride towards the sailing club. Eoin followed her, stopping to look back at Frankie and Dillon. Frankie shook her head and waved him on and watched as he followed Ruby.

'I love her so much,' Dillon said quietly.

'Me, too, buddy,' Frankie said. 'How about that ice cream now?'

Dillon shook his head and slipped his hand into Frankie's. 'Let's go, Mammy.'

Frankie nodded. 'Okay, let's go.'

29

Ruby

'Ruby!' Eoin called. 'Ruby, stop. What are you doing?'

'I'm going for a drink,' Ruby called over her shoulder. 'That's what you called me for, isn't it?'

'Ruby.' Eoin stopped walking after her. 'How could you do that?'

'Do what?' She turned around, hands on her hips.

'Walk away from them like that: they're family.' Eoin walked towards her.

'They're not.' Ruby pushed her sunglasses up her nose. 'Don't get that wrong.'

'They may as well be,' Eoin said. 'And you've just treated them like something you've stepped in.'

'What do you want me to do?' Ruby raised her voice. She swung her arms and looked around, but the marina was empty. 'Well? Embrace the evidence that my husband cheated on me, had a baby that he tried to adopt and pass on to me? Well! Tell me, what am I supposed to do?'

She stopped shouting and spun away. There was a

tightness in her chest that came every time she thought of James and what he'd done, and it came back twice as hard, making her double over. Clenching her fists, Ruby waited for Eoin to reply. His face told her everything. He was horrified. He was looking at her as if she was a monster.

'Stop it,' she said, eventually. 'Stop judging me. I did nothing wrong. Nothing.'

'Jesus, Ruby,' he said. 'I'm not judging you. I'm sorry for you.'

'Sorry?'

'Yes, sorry. I can't imagine what you're going through.' He stood before her. 'You must be heartbroken.'

She nodded; her throat clamped tight over the scream that wanted to tear from her mouth.

'I'm angry,' she said. 'I feel so . . . used.'

Eoin nodded. 'It's not your fault, like you said.'

'I couldn't have children,' Ruby said. 'He said he didn't care about it, but he must have. I mean, not only did he manage to have a child with someone else, but he bought a house right here, right where she lives. I try to understand his motives, Eoin, I do. But it's hard, you know. Why didn't he talk to me about how he felt?'

'Ruby.' Eoin led her to a bench. 'Stop beating yourself up over this. You know that you're never going to find the answers to those questions, don't you?'

'That's not helping me, Eoin.' Ruby wiped her nose. 'It doesn't change the fact that the man I loved, for more than half my life, was a liar and a cheat, and at the same time wonderful and lovely and . . .'

Eoin pressed his lips together. He stared out across the

marina and folded his hands on his knee. Pulling a tissue from her bag, Ruby wiped her eyes and nose. Eoin's profile didn't change. His jaw twitched, but other than that, he was still. Then he shook his head.

'I don't know, Ruby.' He kept his eyes on the gulls bobbing on the waves. 'From what I've seen, you love Frankie and Dillon. You won't want to hear this, and I'm sorry to say it, but you're punishing them for what James did.'

'I'm sorry.' Ruby blinked. 'What did you just say?'

'Whatever James did, Ruby, is on James.' Eoin's fingers twitched and he scratched his chin. Turning to her he looked her straight in the eyes. 'Frankie and Dillon don't deserve to be treated the way you're treating them. It's not their fault.'

'Are you kidding me?' Ruby said. 'Oh, I see. You want me to live with the proof of my husband's philandering right under my nose – is that right?'

Eoin remained maddeningly calm. 'No, it's not.'

Ruby stood up. 'Go to hell, Eoin.'

'That's it, walk away, Ruby. Walk away from the people who love you. I get it. You're afraid of me, afraid of who you are now he's not around.' Eoin stood up and faced her. 'Aren't you? You're afraid of being hurt if you accept Frankie and Dillon as your family. You love them, Ruby. I know you do. Stop running away.'

'Shut up!' Ruby hissed. 'Stop talking like that. It's not that easy.'

'Do you really believe that?' Eoin asked. 'Because it really is. We're all here for you. You're not alone, Ruby.'

'Eoin,' Ruby said, rubbing her hand across her forehead.

She sank back down onto the bench. 'I'm worn out. Nothing makes sense anymore. And now this has to be dealt with too. I'm not able for it. I don't know what to do.' She pointed to her leg.

'You are able for it,' Eoin said. 'We're all rooting for you. Don't give up, please.'

He ran his hands through his hair. Ruby glanced at the sliver of skin that was revealed when his T-shirt rose. Suddenly, James's voice was in her head. It seemed he never rested from demanding she justify her choices and motives for every decision. From beyond the grave he was still ruling her life.

That's it, James's voice said. *Get a good eyeful, why don't you? I knew you were mad for him the minute I saw him.*

Ruby tore her eyes away from Eoin's toned midriff.

'It's not like that,' she said, pushing James's voice away.

Eoin looked at her. A crease deepened between his eyes. 'Ruby?'

Ruby looked at him. 'It's not like that,' she said louder, unsure if she was speaking to James or Eoin, suddenly knowing that she had to choose one or the other. If she wanted to, she could change her world. All she had to do was silence James's voice, his unsolicited comments; turn her back on his watchful gaze, his knowing smile; ignore the brush of his hand on the small of her back whenever she was talking to someone he felt threatened by.

'I need you, Eoin.' Ruby spoke softly. 'I need all of you. I can't do this on my own.'

Eoin dipped his head. His shoulders drooped. When he looked back up at her, she saw he was smiling tentatively. His eyes searched her face until she smiled back.

'How about that drink?' He held his hand out to her. 'We can finish the rest of this conversation another time.'

'I can do that,' Ruby said. 'I want to do that.'

Eoin held his hand out to her. With an intake of breath, Ruby took it. His hand was warm and rough. His thumb moved back and forth over her skin, soft and rhythmic. His grasp was light yet firm. Goose bumps ran up her arm, and she shivered.

'Let's get you inside,' Eoin said, his face crinkling into a gentle smile.

'Eoin, how about we go to The Birds,' Ruby suggested. 'I haven't eaten yet.'

*

Josie cleared the plates and laid a dessert menu on the table between Ruby and Eoin. She touched Ruby's arm.

'I couldn't talk earlier,' she said. 'Chloe let us down, and it was busier than usual.' Josie turned to Ruby. 'But anyway, how are you feeling?'

'I'm grand,' Ruby said. 'Honestly, Josie. There's not a bother on me.'

'When will you have the results?' Josie lowered her voice.

'I've to go up to the specialist next week,' Ruby said. 'I'll know more then.'

'Well, keep me in the loop, won't you?' Josie tried to smile. 'And come in more often. We love your company.'

Ruby nodded. She tapped the dessert menu. 'What would you recommend tonight?'

'Oh.' Josie came back to herself. 'The gin and tonic

cheesecake is my favourite. Light enough for a hot evening yet brimming with flavour.'

'I'll take your word,' Ruby said. 'What about you, Eoin?'

'I thought we'd share?' He grinned.

'Not a chance.' Ruby laughed. 'Get your own dessert!' Ruby flapped her hand in front of her face.

'It's warm in here, all right,' Josie said. 'Tell you what, there's a clean table in the beer garden. I can bring your food out there if you'd prefer. There's a lovely breeze and a few throws if you start feeling cold.'

'That's a lovely idea,' Ruby said. 'Thanks, Josie.'

Ruby gathered her bag and napkin as Josie moved away. 'I hate that I never came in here before this year,' she said to Eoin. 'In all the years, we drove right by it and out the road to that posh place on the cliff, which is lovely and all, but it's not the same as here.'

Eoin said nothing. He opened the door and carried their drinks to an empty table.

Settling at a table under a parasol, Ruby sighed. She picked at the beer mat, thinking about the full dessert she'd ordered. She hadn't done that since before James. He'd controlled everything. She'd never had the right to choose her own way, from a simple coffee, to where they lived, to how she lived. Shortly after they'd married, she'd suggested she study and maybe take a position in his company, even as a secretary, but James had laughed the idea off. 'No one will take you seriously, Rubes, you – the boss's wife – they'll say you're only playing the role of secretary, that it's nepotism. Besides that, wives don't work. I need you at home, fresh to entertain and keep me company.'

She hadn't wanted to buy Eyrie Lodge, but he'd insisted. At the time she'd thought he was snubbing her mother, showing her how rich he was, how fantastically her daughter lived, but now she knew it had never been about her, or her mother. It had always been about him. He'd suited himself in buying the house – to be closer to Nicole, maybe, or maybe to keep an eye on Frankie. She'd never know now.

And now it looked as if she was still being controlled, but this time by her cancer, just as she was finally beginning to understand that she had choices. She knew the specialist would advocate for the amputation, but she didn't want it. To lose her leg would be to lose everything. Her whole world would be turned upside down. The house would need alterations. It was vain, but what about her clothes – what would she be able to wear when she had only one leg and a stump?

There was that word again: stump. Panic rose in her chest. A stump. It would be a physical reminder of her whole life – she'd always been going nowhere, and now she never would. The doctors gave her websites to look at, and brochures to read. Nurses told her stories of how her life wouldn't change that much. They all said that once she got used to it, she'd be able to do anything she wanted to do. The first two months would be hardest, physically, while the wound healed. If it healed well, she could then look at getting fitted for a prosthetic limb, but she couldn't use it every day. There would be days when she'd need to use crutches or a wheelchair. Look at the Olympics, they said. Look at what people can achieve when they set their minds to it.

None of their words lifted her spirits. In fact, they were pretty infuriating. The nurse who'd visited yesterday to check in with her had been lovely. Yet the thought had still flashed through Ruby's mind that the nurse would still have two legs at the end of the day. She wouldn't need help learning how to take a shower with one leg, or learning how to balance all over again. When she got up in the night, she'd just go to the bathroom – she wouldn't need to turn on a light, and squint as she searched for her crutches. In the winter, she'd be fine on icy paths, and in the summer she'd manage to walk on the sand without help. So, for all her lovely, kind advice, Ruby felt that the nurse didn't seem to understand what was really being lost.

Ruby squirmed on the chair. Every minute she imagined the lump getting bigger, taking up more of her body with its invasive mass. When she closed her eyes, she saw tendrils snaking into her body, wrapping around her bones, dissolving them bit by bit. If the cancer had spread and they took her leg, would it be enough to save her life? What if it was too late and it was all useless in the end? Ruby pinched her leg. Typical, she thought, that this would all happen right as she was getting back on her feet. The absurdity of what she'd just thought jolted her back to the garden. Back on her feet! Hah!

She looked over at Eoin. He was leaning back in his chair, tilting his face to the evening sun, and had closed his eyes. His arms supported his head, and his face was relaxed. His T-shirt was clean, but old, and his cargo shorts were smudged with muck at the hem. It always amazed her how relaxed about his body he was. He used it in the Moonlight Garden as if no one was watching him. His strength and agility astounded her; she'd never felt that ease with herself, but he never made her feel like she couldn't do things. Without realising it, he challenged her – passed her heavy wheelbarrows, didn't jump to lift the compost bags she lugged in, told her to dig the holes bigger and to hurry up too.

She hadn't known she was capable of those simple tasks. It made her feel alive, the movement. Crawling in the dirt, scooping soil to make space for seedlings, picking weeds, and starting the chainsaw to cut down dead branches. All those things were living. She'd never be able to do it with a missing leg. All those things she wouldn't be able to do if it had spread.

Ruby looked away. She crossed her ankles and looked down at the offending leg. If only she could reach in and pull the cancer out. As if he could read her mind, Eoin sat up and looked straight at her.

He scratched his chin. 'I've been thinking about how things are going to change for you. What I've come up with is that it'll only change in the direction you want it to go. You have to try to look on the bright side, even when it looks like all the sides are dark, because darkness doesn't last, Ruby, not if you remember where the light switch is.'

'That's very profound,' Ruby said with a fond smile.

'Jürgen's advice, not mine.' Eoin grinned. 'I'm not that deep.'

'You spoke to Jürgen about this.' Ruby lifted her leg.

'God, no,' Eoin said hastily. 'It's something he told me a long time ago. I thought it would do you good to hear it.'

'Somehow, the light switch seems to have blown a fuse,' Ruby said. 'No matter how many times I flick it, it refuses to turn on.'

'So, let's change the fuse,' Eoin said. 'Let's check the bulb, call in the electrician, whatever. All I know is this: that light needs to be turned on and I can't do it for you.'

Ruby clenched her hands together tightly on her lap. 'What if . . . they haven't caught it on time?' Ruby squeezed her hands tighter. She took a breath.

'Oh, Ruby,' Eoin said. He rubbed his face and leaned forward. 'They have. We have to believe that. We have to hope for the best.'

Ruby's face crumpled. 'Okay. I'll try.' She looked down at her hands. 'But what if you don't like me . . . afterwards?'

'Then I'm a shithead and you deserve better,' Eoin said, and she gave a surprised laugh. 'Seriously, Ruby, how could you think that? I'm not into you because of how you look. I'm into you because you make me laugh, you annoy me, you come up with wacky plant combinations, and we like the same movies. Your taste in music is different – you gave me Andrea Bocelli, for God's sake. Now I listen to him all the time.'

Ruby looked at him, her eyes soft. 'You gave me back the Chili Peppers.'

'And they rock, don't they?' Eoin smiled at her. 'You rock, Ruby. You rock my world for all those reasons and for probably a million more. There's not a day that goes by when I don't want to discover another reason to spend time with you. I hope you feel the same?'

The hair on Ruby's scalp tingled. She stared at him for

a minute. His face was so open, so hopeful. She knew she was taking too long to answer him, but she couldn't find the words to tell him that she wanted to spend all her time with him.

'Yes,' she said eventually. 'I do feel the same.' He grasped her chair and pulled it closer to him, and she gasped. She shivered but reached out to touch his face. He closed his eyes briefly, smiling as she stroked the stubble on his cheeks. 'Can I kiss you again, Ruby? Or is it too much too soon?'

'It's . . . not too soon.' Ruby breathed out, unaware that she was holding her breath.

A plate clattered onto the table, making them both jump.

'Sorry!' Josie laughed. 'I didn't mean to do that! I was caught up in all the love playing out in front of me. You two need a room!'

'Ha, ha, funny,' Eoin sat back, blushing. 'We thought you'd forgotten about us.'

'Now who's the comedian?' Josie set the napkins and cutlery down. 'Anyway, enjoy!' She waddled away, waving her hands in the air, stopping at a table to clear it off.

'I wish she'd give Frankie a few shifts,' Ruby said. 'She needs someone to help her out.'

'Well, you could fix it, you know.' Eoin picked up his fork. 'Talk to her, bring her home.'

'Eoin.' Ruby's nostrils flared. 'I can't do that.'

'Why not?' Eoin licked his fork. 'What's stopping you? Pride? Shame?' He shrugged one shoulder and took another mouthful of his cheesecake.

Ruby didn't answer. She watched him eat his dessert,

one mouthful after another. It took him ages. A ringing in her ears started; her jaw ached. Forcing her face to relax, she pushed her plate away.

'I'm not ready for that,' she said. 'I'm not ready to have Frankie and Dillon back in my life.'

'Well, what will it take for that to change?' Eoin licked his fork.

'I don't know. Sheesh, Eoin. Stop asking me these things. I don't want to talk about it.'

'You don't even want to think about it,' he countered. 'Ruby, you need to think about it.'

'I don't need you telling me what to think,' she growled.

'Oh, I know that.' Eoin sat back. 'And I'm not telling you what to think. I'm telling you *to* think. There's a difference.'

'Argh.' Ruby grabbed her fork. Stabbing at her cheesecake, she looked at him. 'You're so annoying. Are we just going to argue all the time?'

'I hope so,' Eoin said. 'That way, I'll know I'm getting to know the real Ruby.' He looked up at her and grinned. 'Besides, you know what comes after an argument, don't you?'

'What?' Ruby grumped.

'Hopefully, you.' Eoin winked at her.

30

Frankie

Later that week, Frankie walked through the holiday home. She was sure she'd packed everything. One last sweep through, from the bedroom she was sharing with Dillon to the kitchen, didn't calm her nerves. The place was spotless. Nothing was out of place. All their things were packed in two cases and a couple of black bags by the front door. Their jackets were hung on the newel post, and their shoes were lined up underneath. Valerie said she'd come up with her car and take the bags and cases in the morning. They'd stay with her for a night or two, until the weekend when John was calling over to talk about selling the house.

Leaning against the hall wall, Frankie nudged the closest black bag with her toe. It was filled with clothes that Dillon had almost grown out of. Was there any point in replacing them this week? They were heavy to lug around and were getting dusty and damp in the black bag. She'd nowhere to wash and dry them properly until she got to

Valerie's. Even then, she had to be careful. John was kicking up a fuss, calling Valerie a fool for turning their family home into a halfway house.

Nudging the bag again, she yawned. There was no point in staying up any later when the alarm was set for stupid o'clock. She reached for the light switch and went to set the house alarm, ready to fall into bed. A soft knock on the door made her jump. Leaning against the wall in the darkness, she held her breath. Who could possibly be at the door at eleven o'clock at night? No one other than Valerie knew she was here – what if it was the homeowner? Frankie crouched further into the shadows as a face peered in the window beside the door. With a strangled cry, Frankie covered her head with her arms, then peeked out to see if the person had spotted her. The woman in the window raised her hand to her eyes, cupping the glass as she peered in. Frankie's mouth dropped open. With small, short steps she walked forward, meeting Ruby's eyes as she did. Ruby waved at her. Frankie walked to the door. She rested her hand on the latch for a moment before opening it.

Ruby stood back on the step, her fleece wrapped tightly around her thin shoulders. Her face was pale and taut.

'Ruby,' Frankie said quietly. 'What are you doing here? It's late.'

'Val told me you were here,' Ruby said. 'I . . .'

Frankie pursed her mouth. Ruby was shaking, her teeth chattering.

'You'd better come in.' Frankie stepped back against the door.

'Are you sure?' Ruby's voice shook.

Frankie nodded. 'Come on, I'll put the kettle on. The kitchen's straight through.'

Ruby was twisting the hem of her fleece, Frankie noticed. It was the biggest giveaway that she was upset. Pouring boiling water into the teapot, Frankie quelled the urge to talk first. While she desperately wanted things to be right between them, Ruby had to be the one to make the first move. After all, she had made the decision to cut ties with her and Dillon. Putting a mug in front of Ruby, she sat down and folded her hands on the table in front of her. Ruby wrapped her hands around the mug, took a sip and raised her eyes to Frankie.

'How are you doing?'

'Okay.' Frankie shrugged. 'Things have been better. How about you?'

Ruby swallowed and nodded. 'Same.'

Frankie scratched the side of her mug with her nail.

'I wanted to make sure Dillon was okay after the other day, you know,' Ruby said.

'He's fine.' Frankie continued scratching. She looked up at Ruby. Her face stony. 'Actually, no. He's not okay at all. He hasn't spoken to me since we left your house. The only words he's uttered were to you when he ran to you. He's walking around in circles and won't look at any of his insect books, or even watch *Deadly Sixty*. I don't know what to do with him, and I'm terrified he's not going to get any better anytime soon.'

Trembling, she looked away from Ruby's stricken face. Why the hell had she blurted all that out? It wasn't any of Ruby's business anyway, not now she'd removed herself from their lives.

312

'Frankie.' Ruby sounded as if she was crying. Frankie shook her head and looked away.

'I'm so sorry. I didn't know it would affect him so much.' Ruby sniffed.

'What did you think, Ruby, huh?' Frankie sighed. 'That he'd just say, "See you around, Auntie Ruby," and skip off into the sunset?'

'I didn't come here for a row,' Ruby said.

Frankie caught the steel in Ruby's voice and met it with some steel of her own. 'What did you come here for, then?'

'I came to apologise.' Ruby put her hands on the table. 'I was scared, and I reacted badly.'

'I'm scared too.' Frankie looked down at the table. 'But I won't apologise for something my mother did. I spent my whole life thinking that she didn't want me. That I was the reason she left the Cove. That I was a mistake. Now I know, I'm *not* a mistake, and I've done nothing wrong. I'm a good person, a kind person, and I won't apologise for that.'

'I hope not.' Ruby stretched her hand across the table. 'I hope you stay exactly the way you are.'

Frankie lifted her head. 'Thank you.'

Rain splattered against the window. Frankie jumped. 'Rain?'

'The forecast said we were in for a few days of it.' Ruby got up and looked out the window. 'It's turned awful out there. The wind has really picked up.'

'Crap.' Frankie put her face in her hands. The laundry wouldn't get done now. 'That's all I need.'

'You're moving out?' Ruby nodded towards the hall where the cases and bags were.

Frankie nodded. 'Back to Val's for a few nights.'

'And then?' Ruby wrapped her arms around her body.

'I don't know.' Frankie rubbed her face. 'I'll figure it out.'

'What about—' Ruby started. Frankie got up and snatched the teapot.

'Fresh cup?' She dumped the tea into the sink and filled the kettle, drowning out Ruby's words. Ruby didn't have to fix her problems. She'd made that clear – they weren't her responsibility. Besides, look what happened the last time Frankie relied on her.

Ruby was sitting at the table, still with her arms wrapped around her body, when Frankie brought the teapot back.

'Can I ask you something?' Frankie stirred the pot, all the time watching Ruby's pale face. Ruby nodded.

'Val said something about . . . amputation.' She shivered. 'Is that what's going to happen?'

Ruby shrugged. She shook her head. 'I don't know. It depends.'

'On what?' Frankie sat down. Outside the wind whipped the trees. The rustling leaves sounded as if the sea was upon them. The rain had stopped as suddenly as it had started.

'On the results next week. On how advanced the cancer is.' Ruby slumped in her chair. 'Pamela says I'm looking only at the worst-case scenario, and she's probably right.'

'Bloody hell, Ruby,' Frankie said. 'That's terrifying.'

Ruby nodded. Shrugging, she tried to smile. 'It's only necessary if the cancer is really bad, like in my nerves or something. To be honest, I can't really remember the things they told me. There was so much information, Frankie, so much.'

Frowning, Frankie poured them fresh tea. 'Please tell me you didn't go to the specialist alone.'

'I didn't want to bother anyone.'

'Ah, Ruby, that's crap.' Frankie snorted. 'It's not bothering someone to ask them to help you. Any one of us would have gone with you – me, Jürgen, Pamela . . . Eoin.'

'I couldn't ask Eoin.' Ruby rubbed her nose. 'I needed to do it alone.'

'Ruby, I get it, I really do, but it's not good to cut people out. You need to lean on us, you know.' Frankie paused, then shook her head. With a half-smile, she continued. 'Take it from someone who learned that the hard way.'

'You're right.' Ruby smiled. 'Eoin's a lovely man. He's taken me completely by surprise.'

Frankie was curious enough to thaw a little. 'Go on . . .'

'I've been so used to James . . .' Ruby winced as she said his name, but Frankie's face remained determinedly blank.

'You should give him a chance,' Frankie said. 'What have you got to lose?'

'Huh,' Ruby said. 'I often wonder about that – what has anyone to lose? When I think of James and Nicole getting together, I think that James probably felt he had nothing to lose – that is, me. I was just there, you know, unlosable. Just something else he owned, something else he controlled.'

Frankie pinched the skin between her finger and her thumb. James sounded awful, like a monster. What chance did she have now she knew she was his, the daughter of a cruel and heartless man and a thoughtless and inconsiderate woman? Did she have the same traits they had?

'He sounds horrible,' she whispered.

Ruby groaned. 'Oh, I didn't mean to say . . . it wasn't all that bad. Honestly. When I met James, he was lovely. He told me he loved me within a week! He brought me gifts and refused to take them when I tried to return them. There wasn't a day that passed when he didn't call me or send postcards from wherever he was. It was so romantic – or it seemed that way at the time.'

Frankie thought back to the love of her own life. Liam had loved her unconditionally, but he'd never bombarded her with gifts or made mad, loud declarations of his love for her. He'd simply been there, sharing his life with her, relishing her ups and hugging her through her downs. There was something quieter and more solid in the love he'd offered when compared to the love Ruby was describing. Even if they'd barely had any time together, Frankie realised she'd been lucky to experience real love. She wouldn't trade a few years of that for a lifetime of luxury with the wrong man.

'Eoin is very different.' Ruby's voice quietened. 'He's more of a listener, you know? Sometimes I don't know what to say or do around him. He never . . . no, it's not him, it's me. I'm not used to my opinions being valid.'

'Sounds like a partnership,' Frankie said quietly. 'Sounds like you could have asked him to go with you to the specialist.'

'I know, but Frankie, I'm really struggling with all of this.' Ruby exhaled.

'You've the best of care behind you, Ruby,' Frankie said. 'You said that yourself. You have health insurance, don't you?'

'It's not just the cancer,' Ruby said, looking at Frankie. 'It's my whole life. My marriage . . .'

'Oh.' Frankie's heart sank. 'Oh, Ruby. I don't know what to say to you about that.'

Ruby smiled sadly. 'I know now that James wasn't the man I thought he was.'

Frankie nodded. The clock on the sitting room mantelpiece chimed midnight. Ruby rolled her eyes and sniffed.

'Well, it looks like tomorrow is already here.' She got up. 'I'd better go. Let you get some rest.'

Taking the mugs to the kitchen sink, Frankie looked out into the wet night. 'Ruby?'

'Yes?' Ruby zipped up her fleece.

'The results next week . . . I'll go with you.' Frankie turned around. 'You shouldn't go alone, just in case . . .'

Ruby gripped the table. 'Really?'

'Of course. We might be at odds, but I still care about you.'

Ruby's eyes glistened. 'I'd like that, Frankie. Thank you.'

'We'll weather whatever storm rolls in.' Frankie spoke, not realising she was saying what Aggie always had said to her. Her voice tightened as the lump in her throat thickened.

'I think you could say . . .' Ruby paused. She looked down at her hands as she wrung her fingers together. 'Well, the truth is, you're all the family I've got.'

Frankie dropped the mug into the sink. 'What?'

'I was reading those letters, from the safe,' Ruby continued. 'It started coming back to me. How close we were to adopting a baby, and now I know that baby was you. Back then, I couldn't believe it, you know. It happened

317

so fast, and then, just like that you were gone. Of course, I didn't know it was Nicole. I thought it was just some poor girl who'd been lucky enough to change her mind and keep her own baby. But my world collapsed. I've never been so heartbroken in all my life.'

Fumbling with the mug, Frankie didn't realise she was crying until she felt the tears scalding her skin. Family. Swiping at her face, she tried to speak, but the words wouldn't come. Ruby stood still, then began to move. Frankie opened her mouth, but something behind Ruby caught her eye. Dillon was standing in the hall, his eyes wide, his Bug clutched to his chest.

'We're family?' he whispered. 'Really?'

Frankie hurried to him. Sinking to her knees she hugged him tightly, then reached back to pull Ruby close.

'Yes, buddy.' She kissed the top of his head and smiled at Ruby. 'We're family.'

31

Ruby

Ruby woke at four on the morning her results were due. After an hour of tossing and turning, she got up and made her way to the Moonlight Garden as the sun rose. She found Eoin there, sweating as he worked as the first light washed over them. Quietly, she sat on their bench and watched him work, her legs curled up beneath her, an old blanket thrown around her shoulders. It was turning cooler already. Autumn would soon be upon them.

He was putting in the base for a sundial and stopped to sit with her only when the concrete was level and the mixer cleaned out. He smelled of clean, hard work, and fresh laundry. Leaning into him, Ruby let her head fall back. The sun was glinting on the waves, yet the moon was still visible.

'Today's the day,' he said, throwing his arm around her and pulling her close. She snuggled down into his embrace, feeling his kiss on the top of her head. 'Do you want me to come?'

'No, thanks. I have Frankie.' Ruby laid her head on his chest. He was warm from his exertions, his heartbeat loud beneath her ear. She let her breath follow his. 'I'm scared.'

He hugged her tighter. 'You didn't sleep, did you?'

She shook her head. 'Neither did you, by the looks of things.'

'Sure, I got a few winks.'

'You're a bad liar, Eoin,' Ruby said softly.

'Maybe I am,' Eoin said. His voice rumbled in his chest. 'Then you'll know I'm telling the truth when I say I love you.'

Ruby sat up and swivelled around to look at him. Her mind rushed like a stormy wind through trees. He loved her! Her heart pounded; he could probably hear it. He smiled at her, his eyes crinkling mischievously.

Nudging her, he winked. 'I'm not looking for a reply. Just saying so that you'll know the truth when I do say it.'

Ruby scrunched her nose. 'I'm a bad liar too, so that makes us even.'

'Exactly how I like it – even.' Eoin tucked a strand of hair behind her ear. 'What time are you hitting the road?'

'Around nine,' Ruby said. 'I'm hoping the traffic will be lighter by then.'

'I'll miss you today.' He pulled her back into his arms. 'I'm getting used to having you around.'

Snuggling against him, Ruby couldn't hold back the smile that enveloped her whole face. His strong arms were around her, and it felt like he'd no intention of letting her go. Raising her face to his, she looked into his eyes.

'The sun is shining; the sky is blue.' She kissed him quickly. 'It's going to be a good day. I promise.'

'It already is,' he said and pulled her in for a deeper kiss.

Drawing apart, Eoin held her face in his hands for a moment. 'Ruby, is this okay, you and me?'

Ruby nodded. He worried more than he let on, she knew. It was there in the fine lines on his forehead, in how he reached for her, in the way she'd turn around and he'd be right there, handing her a mug of tea, somehow just knowing it was what she wanted. Leaning her forehead against his, and breathing in his warm breath, Ruby kissed him gently. He pulled her onto his knee, and wrapped his arms around her. Laughing, Ruby threw her head back.

'This . . . is more than okay with me,' she said, her voice light.

'I just want to make sure; I don't want to move too fast,' Eoin said seriously.

'I appreciate that,' Ruby said. 'It's a new experience for me, this going-slow thing, but I like it.'

Sliding from his knee, she stood up and pulled him up beside her. 'You look famished. Breakfast?'

They left the garden holding hands, his thumb caressing the soft skin of her wrist. Above them, gulls were swooping out to sea, the barely-there clouds were high, and the moon had finally gone to bed. Ruby walked in time with Eoin, realising that he'd changed his stride to match hers. How much more time would they have together? Would they still be able to do this after today? Hopping over the wall, instead of opening the gate, they grinned at each other.

'I'll cook.' He took her hand again. 'I make the best scrambled eggs.'

'That's fine by me.' Ruby smiled. 'But I'll cook next time.'

'Good morning!' Jürgen called. He waved as he walked towards them. 'Looks like you two were up bright and early.'

'Come in for breakfast,' Ruby called. 'This fella says he makes the best scrambled eggs.'

'On my way!' Jürgen grinned.

An hour later, Jürgen departed for the Moonlight Garden, leaving Eoin and Ruby in Ruby's back garden. Ruby sighed and looked around. Her plans for the garden had never materialised, and now the summer was almost over. She turned her back on the garden and walked with Eoin to her car. There was no point in lamenting the garden now, she thought. She probably wouldn't be able to get around it anyway, with one leg. The car boot was filled with boxes of her old designer clothes she wanted to bring to Pamela, who was running a second-hand clothes sale to raise money for Irish Cancer Research.

The Victoria Beckham dress lay on the top of the last box. Ruby looked at it as she closed the boot. It was a relief to see the back of it. It had caused her so much stress, and now, without it, she felt so much lighter. She threw her handbag into the back seat of her car and arranged her jacket on top of it. A bottle of water and a bag of sweets in the centre console completed her travel arrangements. Pulling on her seatbelt, she smiled weakly at Eoin. His face gave his worries away, so she smiled brighter.

'I'll see you later.' Eoin tapped the roof of the car and stood back as Ruby pulled forward and stopped in the gateway and looked back at him through her rear-view mirror. He was standing with his hands on his hips, his mouth pinched shut. He waved at her, and she waved back, then pulled out onto the road towards Valerie's house.

'I'll be fine, I'll be fine. It'll all be okay.' Ruby muttered as she pulled up outside.

Valerie and Sandra were sitting on the garden wall. They both stood up as she wound down her window.

Valerie said, 'Frankie will be down in a minute. Best of luck, Ruby.'

'I'll light a candle for you,' Sandra said. She fiddled with the toggle on her jacket. 'Will you text us as soon as you know?'

'I will, I promise.' Ruby gripped the steering wheel tightly. 'Straight away.'

Frankie raced down the garden path and hopped into the car. 'Sorry for the delay. Dillon had nuts in his socks.'

'Nuts?' Ruby's eyebrows flew up.

'He means knots – you know, those little bobbles in your sock where the seam ties off.'

'Ah.' Ruby nodded. 'Yes, nuts.'

'You know what's nuts?' Frankie said, waving at Valerie and Sandra as Ruby drove off. 'Going down to the Moonlight Garden this morning and seeing you and Eoin in desperate need of a room.'

Ruby blushed. 'We weren't that bad.'

'You guys are adorable.' Frankie scouted through the radio stations. 'No news channels or serious stuff today, *ma chérie*; today, we sing!' She turned up the dial and started singing along with the radio.

'Come on, Ruby!' she called. 'You know this one – it's from your time!'

'My time!' Ruby shouted over the radio.

'Yeah – the Eighties!' Frankie stuck out her tongue, then continued singing.

Laughing, Ruby started singing. All the songs from her teenage years blasted from the speakers, bringing back memories of back-combed hair, lacy tops and ribbons.

'I used to put eyeliner on and wear lace gloves to this,' Ruby shouted over the song.

'You're that close to saying "those were the days",' Frankie shouted back.

'Those *were* the days!' Ruby screamed with laughter. She pulled onto the motorway, and for the first time ever, drove to Dublin without sweating or panicking.

Turning down the radio, she pulled into the car park at the hospital. Frankie was quiet, having stopped singing as soon as they'd started passing signs for the hospital.

'I used to live not far from here.' Ruby broke the silence. 'Funny, now that I think of it. My house wasn't that far from the sea, and yet I never paid any attention to it – the sea, that is. I can show you if you'd like to see it – the house. Not the sea . . .'

Frankie reached for her hand. 'It'll be all right, whatever happens.'

'I hope so.' Ruby looked up at the hospital building. 'It looks so . . .'

'Brilliant.' Frankie leaned forward. 'It looks like they know what they're doing in there.'

'I hope so.' Ruby sat back. 'Right. Let's go.'

*

'I've only been in hospital twice,' Frankie whispered as they walked down the vinyl-floored corridors.

'Really?' Ruby slowed her pace. Cheery artwork hung on the walls, but it did little to unwind the knot in her stomach.

'Having Dillon,' Frankie said. 'He was an emergency caesarean. I was in for a week.'

'Oh,' Ruby said. 'That sounds horrible.'

'It wasn't the most pleasant of experiences.' Frankie snorted. 'I'll tell you another time.'

They passed through another set of double doors into a wide reception area. Ruby handed her hospital appointment card to the receptionist.

'What was the other time?' she asked as the receptionist smiled and told them to take a seat.

'Dillon swallowed a magnet.' Frankie rolled her eyes. 'One of those round ones, like a gobstopper. Don't ask me why – I asked him, and he couldn't answer me. Said he just did it. We were ages in the waiting room before we were sent home for him to poop it out. The funny part was when they ran a metal detector over him to see where the magnet was, and his tummy kept beeping.'

'Kids,' Ruby said. She twisted the strap of her handbag on her lap. Frankie stopped talking and sat back.

It felt like forever, but it was just minutes before her oncologist opened the door and smiled at Ruby.

'Come on through, Ruby. It's good to see you.' He smiled. 'I'll be back with you in one minute.' They watched as he strode over to his receptionist.

Ruby sat on the edge of her chair and nodded to Frankie to sit beside her.

325

'He seems nice,' Frankie whispered. Ruby nodded, tight-lipped. Her knuckles were white where she gripped her handbag.

'Well, Ruby.' Professor Fitzgerald walked around his desk. He leaned forward and shook Ruby's hand, then Frankie's. 'How're you doing? And this is?'

'Frankie.' Ruby smiled for the first time since they'd walked through the hospital doors. 'My daughter.' Even in the cold, bland office, Ruby felt a warmth rush through her as Frankie's hand tightened in hers. She smiled at Frankie, who was wiping her eyes with her other hand. She'd turned a delicate shade of pink, and it dawned on Ruby that maybe Frankie had never been introduced to anybody as 'my daughter' before. She squeezed Frankie's hand again as Professor Fitzgerald noted Frankie in Ruby's file.

'It's lovely to meet you, Frankie,' Professor Fitzgerald said warmly. 'I won't beat around the bush; I know you're eager to hear the results.' He sat back in his chair, his hands resting on the armrests.

Ruby nodded. She grasped Frankie's hand tight. 'Thank you.'

'Your initial tests were concerning, which is why we wanted to be sure before we called you in.' He leaned forward and opened a file. 'But after discussion with the Multi-Disciplinary Team, we've settled on a treatment plan for you.'

Ruby swallowed. 'Okay. Is it . . . will it be soon? What happens first?'

'First we want to go in and try to remove the tumour,' Professor Fitzgerald said. 'We also remove a significant amount of healthy tissue surrounding it, to be sure that there're no cancer cells left.'

Ruby nodded. Leaning forward, she clutched her body tightly. Her stomach cramped as if she'd been stabbed.

'And what about . . . what are the chances of amputation?' Ruby choked.

Professor Fitzgerald leaned back. His smile seemed to fade a little. 'Ah. Well, that we won't know until we operate. The scans indicate that there's a possibility that surgery will remove all of the cancer. All indications point towards your cancer being early, which is good. As you know, it's always good to catch it earlier rather than later, but there has been a not insignificant increase in tumour size since your previous scan, which is a little worrying. Sometimes it's just the tumour that's increased, but I must warn you that there is a possibility of the cancer having spread. Further tests after the operation will clear that up for us.'

Ruby gasped and collapsed back into her seat. 'Oh God.'

'I'm sorry, Ruby. I know you're struggling with the idea of amputation, let alone the thought that the cancer may have spread. I truly wish the news was better,' Professor Fitzgerald said.

Ruby paled, and gripped the arms of her chair tightly.

'What's next?' she said hoarsely. Frankie reached over and slid her arm around Ruby's shoulders. Ruby sniffed and felt a tear roll down her cheek.

Professor Fitzgerald passed her a box of tissues. 'We're going to take care of you, Ruby. We have a fantastic team assembled, and a wonderful counselling unit. Please, don't focus on the amputation. Try to think of getting better.'

'It will be good, Ruby,' Frankie murmured. 'You'll be fine.'

'Let me go through the rest of the treatment plan with you.' The professor leaned forward and outlined the treatment, but Ruby barely heard anything. She nodded while all the time her mind raced and her heart thumped.

'Ruby, I know it's a lot to take in, so I'm going to give this to your daughter.' Professor Fitzgerald turned to Frankie. 'Maureen on the desk will put you in touch with physio, and the other departments you're going to need. And, Frankie, don't let your mother forget we have some wonderful support centres – for both of you. Don't be afraid to use them.' Professor Fitzgerald stood up. 'I'll see you both soon.'

Outside, Ruby hurried to the car, her phone in her hand. 'I have to call Eoin.' She fumbled with her bag, before tossing it to Frankie. 'The keys are in there somewhere.'

Dialling his number, Ruby leaned against the car bonnet, willing him to answer.

'Eoin?' she whispered as he said hello. 'They don't know if they can save my leg. They think they can, but they can't make any promises. And, Eoin, they think it may have spread. I don't know what to do.' Her voice lost power and she went quiet. Pacing outside the car, back and forth, she gripped the phone tight in her hand and listened to Eoin tell her it would be okay. She wished she could believe him but the rushing in her head told her otherwise.

'I'll be home in a few hours,' she said, running her hand through her hair. 'I'll see you then.'

She waved into the car, where Frankie was white and shaking. Poor Frankie, she thought. She pulled a smile on and tried to relax her brow.

'Well?' Frankie asked when she finally sat in the driver's seat. 'Are you . . .'

Ruby rubbed her face, forgetting she had mascara on. 'Oh my God, Frankie. I think I'm in shock. I had convinced myself it was going to be good news . . .'

'We all thought it was going to be better news.' Frankie handed Ruby the car keys. She wiped her eyes.

'Oh don't!' Ruby cried. 'If you start then I'll start, and I don't know if I'll be able to stop.'

'Home so,' Frankie said. 'Let's get you home.'

'I think we need some music.' Ruby started the car.

Frankie found the right radio station and turned up the volume, but neither she nor Ruby sang along on the long journey home.

*

Frankie's phone pinged as they parked outside Ruby's house.

'Eoin said he's at the garden.' She read the text message out, her voice low and quiet.

'Oh,' Ruby said tiredly. 'I thought he'd be here, waiting.'

'Yeah,' Frankie murmured. 'Come on, I'll go down with you.'

'Are you sure?' Ruby swung her handbag up on her shoulder. She tried to smile. 'I wouldn't want to subject you to another scene like this morning . . .'

'Ha ha!' Frankie said dryly. 'I'd rather see you in love

329

more than anything else. Hold on a minute.' Frankie reached out and rubbed a mascara smudge from beneath Ruby's lashes.

Ruby blushed. In love. Is that what Frankie thought about her and Eoin? Maybe they were. It felt good enough to be loved, but would their love survive as she fought this damn cancer? They passed the playground, and the tennis courts, and turned into the Moonlight Garden. It was eerily quiet, and for a moment, she thought no one was there, but there was a golden glow that wasn't coming from the setting sun.

Suddenly she saw them: Josie and May, Jürgen, Valerie, Sandra, Maggie, and Eoin. They stood together in a glow of light. Then she saw that everywhere was sparkling. Dotted amongst the plants and the pathways were tea lights in jars, candles in lanterns, and fairy lights in the trees. A table was spread with a cloth and laden with food.

'We brought gin and tonic cheesecake,' Josie called. 'Thought we might need to celebrate.'

'Celebrate?' Ruby's forehead creased.

'Yeah.' Eoin was at her side. He wrapped his arms around her waist and pulled her close. 'We celebrate the little victories here, you know. I know you think it's all bad but we have a plan and a great doctor on your team, so this feels like the beginning of celebrating a bigger victory.'

'It does?' Ruby frowned, leaning into him.

'Yes,' May said. 'Because no matter what happened today, you're not dead.'

'Oh!' Ruby gasped. 'Right!'

'Sounds harsh,' Josie chimed in. 'But it's the truth. And we won't stand for you thinking and behaving as if you are. You're going to be fine, no matter what.'

Eoin's arms tightened around Ruby's waist. He kissed the side of her head and whispered in her ear. 'I love you.'

Ruby stared at him. 'You're such a bad liar,' she whispered.

'I know,' he said. 'Such a bad liar.' He kissed her deeply, only pulling away from her as the others started to cheer.

Blushing furiously, Ruby dropped her face to her hands. When she looked up May was yanking a cork from a bottle of the supermarket's finest champagne and laughing as the foam sprayed everywhere.

32

Frankie

Dropping her book bag beside the shed, Frankie looked around the Moonlight Garden. They'd left up the fairy lights, and the whole place looked magical in the deepening late September evening. Zipping up her fleece, she wandered around the garden, letting her fingers brush against the sage and rosemary, breathing in their woody, warm perfumes. The moon was high and full, and the sea soft and calm. September had come so quickly and her first night class had been invigorating. Her whole body was buzzing from it, as if she'd been plugged into the mains. A giggle bubbled up inside her, and she let it out into the night sky. Everything was going perfectly, and for once, she wasn't going to think about anything other than how good it felt. She needed to calm herself a little. It didn't feel quite right to be so invigorated after her class while Ruby was going through treatment after treatment instead of taking the class she'd been so looking forward to. Frankie sat down on the bench, which they all now called the Love Bench after Eoin and Ruby, and pinched a dried sprig of white lavender. Holding it to her nose, she took a deep inhalation. Jürgen had a tai chi class lined up for them after the meeting.

One by one, the Moonlight Gardeners arrived. They stood in small groups, chatting and catching up with each other. Frankie looked around. Eoin's sundial was finished, and he'd already started work on the small pond that Dillon had recommended as a great way to bring wildlife into the garden. He'd explained to Eoin that while he loved insects, he understood they could become a pest in some gardens.

'What you need is to introduce a natural predator,' Dillon had told Eoin. Frankie had shaken her head; how did he know such big words? Eoin, hunkered down beside Dillon, got him to talk more.

'The best thing to attract things like hedgehogs – they eat slugs by the way – is to give them a water source. My advice to you is to grow a pond.' Dillon's little face had been solemn, and Eoin had taken him seriously. The pond was now well underway, with a shallow area filled with pebbles for dragonflies and bees to sit and drink water, another tip from Dillon.

'He's a little genius.' Eoin sat beside Frankie on the bench, causing her to jump. 'We filled the pond two days ago, and already we've had a frog and a hedgehog visit.'

'Wow,' Frankie said.

'We're going to plant the far side up with marginal plants and, hopefully, implement a wildflower area,' Eoin said. 'Should make a better hideout for passing hedgehogs. It's exactly what the garden was missing.'

Frankie's heart swelled with pride. Dillon was really

excited about his pond, and was brimming with confidence since he realised Eoin was taking him seriously. Maggie had told her he was more relaxed and happier in school too. Ava and Ben had been down to visit the garden and their parents were becoming regular Moonlight Gardeners because of them.

'If it's all right with you,' Eoin said, 'Dillon was talking about taking photographs of the insects and new garden visitors, and I have an old camera that I'd like to give him.' Eoin nodded to the bag at his feet. 'It's nothing fancy. It uses one of those memory cards, so you'd have to download photos to the computer for him.'

'That's lovely of you, Eoin. Thank you.' Frankie hugged him. 'He'll be over the moon.'

'It's just something small.' Eoin shrugged. 'No point in the camera sitting in the back of a cupboard, is there?'

'It might be a small thing to you, but he'll really feel grown up with that. Is Ruby coming down?'

Leaning forward on his knees, Eoin nodded. 'I think so. She wasn't too keen on trying tai chi, but her team told her it would be fine, and that it would help her relax.'

'They've set a date for the operation then?' Frankie sat up.

Eoin nodded. 'They're waiting for some test results now, so it won't be until the middle of October. She's pretending she's okay, but she's not.'

'Doing her usual of being busy?' Frankie nudged him.

'Yeah.' Eoin nudged her back. 'She's done redecorating the lodge, and now she's at the desk all the time, researching and planning the garden. I can't get her to take enough rest. Remind me to talk to you about that later. I have a plan.' He smiled as Ruby waved from the shed where she was talking to Josie and May. On the days when she'd had the energy, Ruby had gone gung-ho into redecorating Eyrie Lodge after she'd discovered James was Frankie's father, as if she was trying to scrub him out of her future.

'Anything you'd like to tell me now?' Frankie asked as she waved at Ruby.

'No, it's a secret.' Eoin got up. 'Come on, let's get our tai chi on.'

Jürgen clapped his hands and, smiling, gestured to everyone to come closer.

'Good evening, everyone. What a great turnout. It gives me no end of joy to see you all here for tonight's class. Emilio has been teaching tai chi for ten years. Please welcome him to our garden.'

A tall, lean man, who could easily be mistaken for Jürgen's brother, stepped forward. Smiling amiably around the group, he bowed. 'Hello, everyone. My name is Emilio; thank you for your warm welcome.'

Sandra nudged Valerie. 'I think I'll be taking tai chi classes for the foreseeable future.'

Valerie whispered, 'Tai chi is a martial art. Why are we learning to fight?'

Emilio smiled in Valerie's direction. 'You are right,' he said. 'Tai chi is a martial art, but its benefits go beyond that. Many health professionals recommend partaking in tai chi. It's known to reduce stress, calm the body and the mind, and its focus on our core muscles brings us back into balance, physically, mentally and emotionally in a gentle and effective way. People of all ages and fitness levels will find tai chi beneficial and fun. I invite you now to find some space, and to ground yourself, and we will begin.'

Working through the gentle movements, Frankie felt a calmness well up inside her. A shiver ran up her back, over her scalp, and down her arms to her fingers as she smoothly moved as if she was pushing a wave away from her. Her shoulders dropped. There was something mesmerising in the way everyone was simultaneously moving and breathing. The group were one, and when they finished the sequence, she was surprised to find that the air around them seemed to have changed. It was charged with something she could only describe as a luminescence. It had that quietness similar to those glowing deep-sea creatures she'd seen on one of Dillon's nature programmes. She wasn't the only one who picked up on the change in the air. Sandra was glowing, her eyes were wide and bright, blinking rapidly as she came back to herself.

'It was like I was hypnotised,' she said. 'That's magical.'

Emilio nodded. 'You look like you enjoyed it.'

'Oh, she did,' Valerie said. 'I've never seen her so quiet and still. She's normally on the go, buzzing here and there. She can't sit still.'

'It's the kids,' Sandra said. 'And the dogs. They need a lot of attention.'

'Which is why it is vital to carve out some time for yourself.' Emilio gestured around the group. 'You must always put on your oxygen mask first before you can help anyone else.'

'I like that,' Sandra said. 'That makes a lot of sense.'

Frankie shook herself. Tying her hair back off her face, she lifted her face to the stars and stared deep into the night sky. Aggie had believed in God, with her whole being, and was sure there were no such things as ghosts or spirits or watching over anyone once you'd died. Frankie wasn't as convinced, there was too much out there not to believe in something. How else could she explain the sensation of Aggie being around her these days? It was as if she was looking out for her, the way she always had. The feeling was more intense whenever she returned to the cottage to check on the renovations. Frankie sent a kiss to Aggie wherever she was, thanking her for her good fortune. Aggie would be raging; Frankie grinned, after all her adamance about 'When you're gone, you're gone', but how could she explain Frankie's sudden change in fortune?

When Ruby had suggested they renovate the cottage and make it habitable again, she'd said something that reminded her of what Aggie always said: 'You should have your own home, Frankie. Despite all the space here, things grow better when they're not overcrowded. You and Dillon need room to grow.'

Frankie shivered. Ruby was right. They did need their own home, and that was the main reason she'd agreed to let Ruby help her out. Plus, Ruby knew people in construction. The only problem was she insisted on paying for it all, saying that James owed her that.

'You know,' Ruby softly interrupted her musings. 'You're doing that right now.'

Frankie pulled her gaze away from the stars. 'Hey, what do you mean?'

'Putting on your oxygen mask first.' Ruby smiled. 'By doing this night course. It's just the beginning. I feel it in my bones. Not only that, you're also inspiring Dillon. He's started talking about what colleges he can go to, the things that he can learn in schools where everyone likes the same thing.'

'I wish you were coming,' Frankie said. 'Do you regret cancelling the class?'

Ruby shook her head. 'No, not at all. I'm busy all the time planning the garden now I've finished redecorating.'

'Eoin said.' Frankie linked arms with Ruby and led her to the bench.

'It's . . . I'm finding it fascinating,' Ruby continued. 'And dare I say, I think I like it better than the course I was going to do. There's so much to learn and, don't mention this to anyone because it's just a thing I've been thinking about . . . but I've been looking at accessibility in gardens and public spaces.'

Frankie raised her eyebrows. 'It sounds intriguing.'

'It is!' Ruby gushed. 'Intriguing and infuriating – what's infuriating is the lack of it. I've been researching how to include more accessible areas here in the Cove for wheelchair users, and people with all kinds of physical disabilities.'

'This is great.' Frankie leaned towards her. 'What are you suggesting?'

'I don't know yet,' Ruby said. She leaned back on the bench. 'I've a lot more research to do, and I want to talk to a few people about how to go about changing things. The Cove, for example, saw a fifteen per cent increase in tourists this year, and yet there are hardly any facilities for disabled people.'

'It felt like a fifty per cent increase in tourists,' Frankie said, thinking how busy she'd been all summer. 'I agree. We need to do better.'

'I'd like to start here, in the Moonlight Garden,' Ruby said quietly. 'I'm working on a plan to make the garden more accessible. Then there's how the garden helps us emotionally, and, well, there are so many disabilities that I feel as if I've just found the tip of the iceberg. It's become something of great importance to me.'

Frankie smiled. 'Of course, it has. I completely agree with you. It's easy for us to take things for granted and I'm guilty of that too. I'll back you up when the time comes.'

'I don't think there'll be a battle.' Ruby laughed. 'It'll take a lot of work. But I'm ready for it. I've spent my whole life doing little or nothing. It's time I got something done. By the way, how's work at the cottage going?'

'It's flying,' Frankie said. 'Those guys are so fast, and they're so good. They said we'll be in by Christmas if the weather holds. New Year's by the latest.'

'I'm so glad.' Ruby took a breath. 'I know you're anxious to move back in.'

'About that.' Frankie turned to face Ruby. 'The cost . . . I'm not comfortable with you paying for the renovations.'

'We've talked about this,' Ruby said. 'It's the least I could do. James was your father, and he should have made some provision for you.'

'Well, he didn't,' Frankie said. 'Please, Ruby. I need to pay you back. Somehow.'

'I understand, Frankie, I do.' Ruby looked down. 'But I'd rather just pay for it all. I feel guilty that he ignored you for years. Your life could have been so different.'

'Don't go down that path,' Frankie said. 'He didn't bother and there's nothing that can change that. I refuse to think about what should've, could've, would've happened if he'd been halfway decent.'

Ruby cringed, but Frankie carried on. 'You're as much a victim of his as I am. And I need to tell you this: none of this was your fault; you need to stop feeling responsible for his behaviour.'

Ruby nodded.

'And . . . you need to stop telling yourself that you're not good enough.' Frankie tapped her foot up and down. 'It's a terrible habit.'

'I will if you will.' Ruby looked sideways at Frankie.

'Oh, you got me there.' Frankie looked straight ahead. 'Okay. Deal.' She turned and stuck her hand out to Ruby. Ruby took it and shook it hard.

'Deal,' Ruby said. 'You're going to ace this course.'

'I am, I bloody well am.' Frankie punched the air. 'And you, you're going to design an amazing garden. Well, Pinky, next I say we take over the world.'

'I'd say yes, but who on earth is Pinky?' Ruby asked.

'A cartoon character from the Nineties.' Frankie laughed. 'I'll show you later.'

'I think I'm good with maybe not knowing who this Pinky is,' Ruby said. 'Somehow, I feel it might be safer for me.'

'Haha! Go on, Eoin's looking for you.'

Watching Ruby walk towards Eoin, Frankie sat down on the bench. Somehow not thinking about what might have been wasn't as easy as she thought it would be. In another lifetime, she could have been talking with her mother. Ruby would have made a fantastic mother; she knew that without a doubt. She had a warm, simple, strong loving streak that reminded Frankie of a lioness. There was nothing she wouldn't do for her family.

Shaking her shoulders, she shook off the 'could have' moment. Right in front of her was the actual moment, and nothing would change that. The odds of them not being a part of one another's lives were slim to none. Scrunching her nose to hold back the happy tears that fizzed up her nose, Frankie rubbed her arms. Soon they'd be consigned to the indoors. Gardening in the winter on the coast wasn't a pleasant experience, but in the meantime, the Moonlight Garden needed a bit of tidying up. She made a mental list. The hedge could be trimmed in October, and there was a spate of weeds that had popped up in the newest bed that needed pulling. Laughter carried across the garden, and someone called to her. The weeding and planning could wait. She took a mug of tea from Sandra and sipped, wondering what Eoin's secret plan was and who was involved. He looked shifty, leaning against the shed in tight conversation with Jürgen and Valerie. Waving her over, he whispered in her ear. She glanced at Ruby and bit back a huge grin.

'That's genius.' Frankie's eyes sparkled. 'Count me in.'

33

Ruby

The hospital gown was soft but insubstantial against the chill that washed over Ruby. It was late October, but the hospital was stifling warm. Sitting in the hospital bed, she tugged the sheet and blanket up over her arms. Eoin had finally gone to get some coffee and breakfast, and until that moment, she'd been hungry. Now the hunger pangs were gone, replaced by a leaden knot deep in her stomach. The nurse said the anaesthetist would be around soon for a chat, but in the meantime, she was to try to relax and not look so worried.

'It'll all be fine.' The nurse smiled. 'They know what they're doing.'

'I'll take your word for it,' Ruby said in a small voice. But they didn't, she thought as she pleated the blanket between her fingers and willed the nurse to leave her alone. There was still the chance that she'd wake up and find out they'd had to take her leg because they didn't know what they were dealing with until they operated. Smiling, the nurse flicked through her chart, then left the room, her shoes squeaking on the tiles.

The sunny yellow room was comfortable, with an en suite and huge window. The television on the wall was on, but the sound was turned low so that the chat show the nurse had switched on was only a murmur in the background. Outside, there was a bustling noise, the door opened, and an older woman stuck her head in.

'Are you eating, pet?' she asked.

'No, not yet,' Ruby said. She pulled the blanket up a little higher.

'You poor thing, this is the worst part. You'll be grand after when you've had some food.' The woman smiled. 'I'll put you down for a light snack later on so they don't forget you in the kitchen.'

Ruby nodded. 'Thanks.'

'No worries!' The woman was gone, and the sound of the tea trolley trundling away made Ruby's mouth water. Nil by mouth, she rolled her eyes. Such an awful way to prepare for an operation. Her hands twitched and she picked up her phone and googled 'What to expect after a tumour removal' and scrolled through the results.

Tiredness and fatigue, loss of appetite and weight, infection. Ruby deleted the search. Was there nothing more uplifting? Her oncologist and therapist had been brimming with optimism, and she needed to channel some of that. Focus only on the positive was the advice everyone gave her. They all said it'd help with recovery. Sweeping her hand across her forehead, she winced as the cannula in the crook of her elbow pinched. The pillows crinkled as she shifted in the bed, reminding her that everything was wrapped in plastic. Getting out of the bed, she looked out of the window.

Across the road was a massive construction site, mucky and miserable in the cold October weather. The high-vis-clad men scurried about with their heads down against the hard wind. It was the kind of construction site James would've relished working on: city centre, expensive, tight deadline and an even tighter budget. He always came home exhilarated after a site visit, talking about the challenges and the demands he was facing. It kept him alive, that wheeling and dealing; he lived for the drama surrounding those builds.

Ruby leaned her head on the cold glass, her breath steaming up the pane. She'd never felt that kind of excitement about anything. Her whole world had been managed by other people. Interior designers, personal shoppers, gardeners. Every decision she'd made was on the back of someone else's opinion, and always with one person in mind – and that wasn't her. It always went back to James. Tapping the footboard with her slippered foot, Ruby lifted her head from the glass. She'd never expected to feel free after he'd died. For the first month she'd been in shock, dressing only when she had to, eating when Pamela made her. She'd cancelled all her plans and didn't open any mail. No one bothered with her, except for Pamela, who made her wash, put on her face, and get to the solicitors to sort out James's affairs. Affairs. Ruby snorted. What a word.

It turned out that things were relatively simple to sort out. James, being James, had practically everything under control. Every i was dotted, every t crossed. Everything was left to Ruby. He'd left her with plenty, so she'd always be more than comfortable. She'd been shocked by how much he'd had in his personal bank account, which was the one thing he'd not made any plans for, presumably because he hadn't expected anything to happen to him. Back then, she'd thought nothing of the fact that it all belonged to her, but now she realised how twisted it really was. If he'd made a contingency for his money, she knew, deep in her gut, that she wouldn't be as wealthy as she was now.

She was glad that she'd taken his accountant's advice on what to do with her newfound wealth, and not left it sitting in the bank. Yet she'd taken the merest of his advice, done the bare minimum to manage the account, because she'd been afraid. There was so much more she should have done, she realised as she ran her fingertip along the windowsill. She had nothing to be afraid of, other than the outcome of the operation. She pushed that aside. Squaring her shoulders, she nodded. Yes, she was more than capable of . . . anything. She could do anything if she set her mind to it.

Taking charge of the cottage renovations, dealing with contractors and tradesmen, listening to them and learning from their expertise had given her confidence, but it was only the beginning. The more she listened to people, the more she learned, and one thing was for sure: she was very good at listening to people. She'd spent her whole life listening to James and his colleagues at events and parties. The difference now was that she was learning to *really* hear what was being said, and how to say what she really wanted. Now she knew what she wanted to do, and that was to keep Frankie and Dillon in her life, and to work alongside Eoin at the Moonlight Garden, and she had the funds to make it happen.

The thought gave Ruby little solace, all the same. Everything James had left her was tied up to something in her life. The house, the garden, the jewellery, Eyrie Lodge. They all marked moments in her life when he'd made it look as if he was doing something to please her. The house in Dublin had been redecorated because she'd mentioned it was a little dated, and any mistakes then became hers. The jacuzzi bath the designer convinced them was the height of luxury was lauded as Ruby's little extravagance that no one needed. The fire pit was too small. The sofa ridiculously expensive for something so uncomfortable. She'd laughed it all off, been the silly billy, the brunt of his barbed comments that were passed off as little nothings while her upset over being made to look foolish was passed off as drama.

His second anniversary had been a week ago, and she'd marked it by doing nothing. No mass, no candle lit, no tears. She'd been too busy and had forgotten the day, which had been filled with conversations with the plumber, the electrician and the builder, meeting Eoin for lunch, and designing a new kitchen for the daughter, and grandson, he should have provided for.

It had been close to midnight that night, when Pamela messaged her to say she was thinking of her, that she had realised the date. Ruby had read the text with a sense of disbelief. How had it only been two years? It felt much longer. She'd moved house, gained, and lost, and gained back a family, learned how to garden, made new friends, and was managing a building project by herself. It felt like a lot to have done. After a few minutes, she'd gone to the wine storage cellar and taken one of the most expensive bottles of red wine James had bought and poured a large glass. Out on the balcony she'd raised the glass to her nose and breathed in the rich bouquet before taking a huge mouthful.

Far out at sea, lightning had flickered, but the waves that had washed Castletown Cove beach were gentle and soft. Ruby had stayed up late, drinking the whole bottle of wine although she'd been advised to cut back on alcohol prior to the operation. Somehow, she couldn't go to bed until the night turned into day. As the sun had broken over the sea and the lightning faded, she'd drained the last of the wine from her glass and then gone to bed. She'd slept deeply for a few hours before she got up and carried on with her life.

The rattle of the tea trolley dragged her back from that night. Tapping the window, Ruby chewed on her lip. Everything she'd gone through was in the past, she thought as she watched a lorry reverse into the building site. What mattered was what was going to happen later that day. She didn't know what the next step in her recovery would be. It didn't matter how many times she'd gone over it, she simply couldn't imagine a time after the operation. What if the cancer had spread? She felt silly now, worrying about losing her leg all that time when the cancer had been growing and invading her body. She closed her eyes and sent out a wish that they'd save her life, and if possible, her leg too.

'I've never asked for anything,' she whispered. Her breath fogged up the glass. 'Please help me.'

A sharp rap on her door drew her attention back to the room as a man in deep blue scrubs popped his head around her door.

'Is it okay to come in?' he asked smiling. 'I'm Seb, the anaesthetist, and I'll be looking after you today.'

Ruby nodded and returned to the bed where she curled her legs up beneath her to stop them from shaking. Her fingertips found the lump on the top of her calf. She examined it, imagining it had grown larger, as Seb read her charts.

'Ruby, Professor Fitzgerald told me you were quite anxious about today's procedure, is that right?' Seb said, his kind blue eyes on hers. Ruby nodded.

'I sometimes faint when I see blood.' She lowered her eyes and pointed to her cannula. 'Even this thing makes me queasy. I can't bear to think about what's going to happen at all.'

'That's not a problem,' Seb said. 'We've decided that the best course of action will be to place you under a general anaesthetic. Is that something you'd be happy with?'

Ruby nodded, relieved. 'The nurse mentioned that sometimes you gave epidurals for this kind of operation?' Ruby shook her hands as if to shake them dry.

Seb smiled. 'Sometimes. But not this time. Don't worry, Ruby, we're going to look after you.'

Ruby nodded.

'If you're ready to go, we're ready for you.' Seb placed her chart under his arm. 'I can get you a wheelchair . . .'

'I'll walk, thanks,' Ruby said. Her fear that she'd wake up and find they'd amputated her leg washed over her.

Almost unwillingly she got up and followed him down the corridor to a waiting room filled with beds.

'Hop into that one there, and I'll be back in a bit.' Seb tapped the end of one of the beds. He disappeared down a corridor, so Ruby got in and lay back. A smiling nurse took her chart, read it and asked a few questions before she was wheeled into yet another room. Ruby looked around, taking the room in. It was small, a little cramped and filled with equipment and cupboards. Ruby's heart rate on the monitor increased as she realised there were double doors leading into the theatre.

'Hi, Ruby.' Seb was beside her, a mask over his nose and mouth. His eyes were so blue, she thought at the same time she realised he was holding her hand. 'You might have a sore throat after the intubation,' he said warmly. 'But it'll be fine in a day or two. Now, count backwards from ten for me.'

Ruby kept her eyes on his and started counting. Her body felt warm and light, her head heavy.

'. . . seven . . . six . . . I think . . .' Her eyes closed and as she went under, the last thing she thought of was Frankie and Dillon, and how they were going to visit her when she got home.

*

The recovery room was quiet and empty when she came around. Her tongue felt heavy. Her arms and legs didn't seem to exist. She couldn't feel them at all. A cool hand checked her forehead, and she began to shake.

'There you are, Ruby, hello.' A warm voice floated down

349

from somewhere nearby. 'You're doing great. How are you feeling?'

'Cold.' Ruby's teeth chattered. She tried to move her arms, but they were too heavy.

'I'll get you another blanket,' the warm voice said. 'Don't worry, it's a normal reaction to the anaesthetic wearing off.'

Something heavy pressed down on her body. Someone tucked her in snug.

'There you go,' the warm voice said. The owner of the voice came into view, a young woman in scrubs with a hair net and face mask on. 'You'll be right as rain in a few minutes.'

Ruby nodded. Her body began to warm up and the chattering and shaking slowed. She tried to smile but found that all she could do was cry. Tears rolled down the side of her face into her hair.

'Oh, it's okay,' the nurse said, dabbing at her tears. 'You're all done. The operation went brilliantly.'

Ruby nodded. Her throat tightened. 'I can't feel my legs.'

'You won't feel anything for a while,' the nurse said. 'The anaesthetic needs to wear off. Are you warming up yet?'

Ruby nodded, and the nurse smiled again. 'Excellent. We'll bring you back to your room shortly and you can rest. I think there's someone waiting to see if you're all right.'

'Eoin?' Ruby's eyes widened. 'He's here.'

The nurse nodded. 'Don't worry, I'll fix your hair.'

Ruby smiled weakly. 'It's okay, thank you. I'm fine as I am.'

34

Frankie

'Left a bit, more, more . . . stop!' Frankie called from the bottom of a ladder in the centre of the Moonlight Garden where the most flawless evergreen tree was being adorned with lights. It was a bright, but bitterly cold mid-December morning. Her breath billowed in clouds in front of her. 'Perfect! I think it's the most perfect Christmas tree I've ever seen.'

'Are you sure?' Josie looked down from the top of the ladder. Wobbling, she grimaced. 'Please say you are!'

'I am. Come down.' Frankie gripped the legs of the ladder, glad to be wearing her gloves.

Josie slowly climbed down. 'I hate heights. Did you know that?'

'You do not!' Frankie laughed. 'You volunteered!'

'Well, that was before I realised what a slave driver you are,' Josie said, rubbing her backside. 'I've been up and down that ladder at least fifty times today. My butt cheeks are sore.'

'If something is worth doing . . .' Frankie winked as Josie pulled a face.

'I think we've done a pretty good job,' Josie said. She rubbed her hands together.

Frankie looked around the garden. Squinting in the winter sun, she smiled. The sky was pale blue and the air sharp. There'd been a frost last night. It wouldn't last long but for the moment everything glittered like a Christmas card. The grasses and teasels gleamed like gold under a dusting of hoar frost, while the bay trees took on a sage hue. May was standing over at the shed, holding a steaming mug. She waved Josie over as Eoin came around the corner, his phone stuck to his ear. He nodded and waved to the women and made his way to the bench.

Frankie frowned. Eoin looked stressed as he strode back and forth, one hand gripping the phone tightly, the other tapping his thigh as he paced. Following her operation, Ruby had stayed with Pamela in Dublin. It was easier for her to get to and from the hospital for her treatments. Even though she and Dillon missed Ruby hugely, Frankie was glad Ruby had made that decision. Travelling to and from the Cove would have worn Ruby out.

Adjusting her woollen hat, Frankie crossed her fingers. *Please let everything be okay,* she wished. There'd been enough drama this year for one lifetime. Eoin hung up the phone, and strode out of the shed and towards her, a huge smile lighting his face.

'Pamela has convinced her to go out for lunch before they leave Dublin,' he said. 'We'll have a couple of extra hours now to get everything done.'

'Yes!' Frankie punched the air. 'Go Pamela! You don't think Ruby suspects anything – do you?'

'No, she sounded completely normal when I was talking to her earlier,' Eoin said. 'Why? Has she said anything to you?'

Frankie shook her head. 'No, I was just checking. Don't worry, Eoin. We'll finish the garden on time. It'll be perfect.'

'I can't wait to see her.' He grinned as he moved a string of lights higher on the Christmas tree branches. 'It's been a long month.'

'I know. And you've been up and down to Dublin every couple of days,' Frankie said. 'You must be exhausted.'

Eoin smiled. 'I'm okay. It was better for Ruby to stay with Pamela. I think it was better for her mentally to be so close to her consultants.'

'Yes, it absolutely was the right thing for her to do.' Frankie gazed up at the tree. 'It's hard to believe that we didn't even know Ruby last Christmas.'

Eoin stopped adjusting the tree lights. 'That's crazy. I feel as if she's been a part of my life forever.'

'Me too,' Frankie said. 'I don't know what we did without her.'

Together they worked, tidying the lights on the tree, and clearing away buckets, spades, and wheelbarrows into the shed. The annual Moonlight Gardening Club Secret Santa was taking place later, and everyone was excited. It was Ruby's first one with the group, and they couldn't wait to see her face when she saw what she'd gotten.

'They'll get here around five?' Frankie asked, waving at Sandra who was pushing a wheelbarrow laden with compost out of the Moonlight Garden gate.

Eoin nodded. 'They're coming straight here.'

'Oh, Eoin!' Frankie hopped up and down. 'I'm so nervous, aren't you?'

'I might look like I have it all together,' Eoin said. 'But behind this calm, cool and collected exterior I am entirely made of jelly and my stomach feels as if the jelly hasn't quite set.'

Frankie grasped his arm. 'She'll love it.'

Eoin patted her hand. 'I hope so.'

Dillon wandered over to them, his camera gripped tightly in his mitten-clad hand.

'I've run out of space on my camera.' He held it up to Frankie. 'And I want to take pictures tonight when Ruby sees the garden. Can we put these pictures on the computer, Mammy?'

'See what you started?' Frankie said to Eoin with a grin. Turning to Dillon she said, 'So many pictures, buddy, I can't keep up with you.'

'I think I can fix this,' Eoin said, producing a memory card. 'I found this one in the bottom of my desk. It's empty, ready to go. If I give it to you now, you need to save it for later.'

Dillon nodded and took the card. Frankie watched him carefully tuck it into the pocket of his camera bag as he skipped away.

'You're very good,' she said to Eoin.

Eoin shifted his weight from one foot to the other. 'Ah, well, I try. Tea?'

Frankie nodded. She watched him amble over to the sheds. He'd always been a good man, she knew that, and she was glad he'd finally found someone to love. Ruby was just the person he needed in his life.

Frankie tugged her hat down over her ears. The chatter from the shed made her smile. Josie and May had become regular Moonlight Gardeners, and they were planning a kitchen garden space where they could grow produce for the local soup kitchen too. Frankie sighed. She hadn't realised how many other people were in dire financial and living circumstances. She didn't feel like the town pauper anymore. The kitchen garden would be an amazing addition to the Moonlight Garden. Josie and May said they'd give gardening lessons to any newcomers, and already interest was high. It all depended on if they could get the patch of scrubland next to the Moonlight Garden.

Ruby, of course, had taken that project on and was in conversation with the council about it. She'd vowed she'd spend all her time outside of physio working on it. The council didn't stand a chance, Frankie thought. They wouldn't be able to say no once they read Ruby's proposal. It was a brilliant community and economic endeavour that would bring people together and help with the mental health issues poverty brought about. How could they say no?

Ruby had changed, Frankie thought. It was as if she'd come out of the operation a whole new person. Her phone calls and FaceTime videos with Dillon were brimming with life and joy. Her text messages to Frankie made everything sound possible.

But there were times when Ruby would unwittingly reveal how much she was still affected by James. It was clear to Frankie he still held some influence over Ruby, more so now she was studying psychology again. Yet, despite Ruby finally going to therapy and discussing him,

Frankie knew Ruby still didn't understand the extent of his manipulation. Which was normal, Frankie knew. Ruby had lived with and loved the man for over thirty years; she wouldn't change her thoughts and feelings on the entire relationship overnight.

All the same, Eoin was making a huge impact on how Ruby moved forward. Frankie watched him drink his tea. He was good for her, in a million different ways. His easy-going nature, his gentleness and consideration for others complemented Ruby's good nature and her newfound strength. Briskly walking across the newly laid disability-friendly, resin-bound gravel path, Frankie cast an eye over the raised beds. They could do with some mulch. She made a note to get that done as soon as possible.

Reaching the group, she gratefully took a mug of hot chocolate from May. She blew on it before taking a sip. The Moonlight Garden was ready for tonight. It just needed a few tweaks, but it would have to wait until they'd finished Ruby's Secret Santa gift. Jürgen speed-walked through the garden gate, the tip of his nose pink, his hat askew.

'Come on, tea break must be over!' He clapped his hands. Then shook himself. 'What am I doing? It's like the old George has popped up. Never mind me. What's that? Hot chocolate? Yes, please.'

'Jürgen, are you all right?' Frankie asked.

He nodded. 'Under pressure but fine, just fine.'

Frankie laughed. 'We're all done here, for now. We'll be with you after lunch to finish up whatever you need doing.'

'Excellent!' Jürgen said taking a mug of hot chocolate from May. 'I'll see you down there shortly so!' He picked up a spade, and took his chocolate with him. Eoin swallowed down the last of his drink before he followed Jürgen.

'Dillon, come on, buddy,' Frankie called. 'Let's go – we've got work to do.'

May began packing away the flasks and mugs. 'No time like the present!'

Grinning, Frankie winked at her. 'And this will be the best present ever.'

*

It was dark at half-four when Frankie leaned over the sink and washed her face and hands. Ruby was on the way. She'd be in the Cove in fifteen minutes. A frizzle of excitement bubbled up inside Frankie. She couldn't wait to see her, and to see her face when she saw her present. Later she'd find out how Ruby's treatment went, how well it was working and how much more Ruby would need, but for now, she needed to hurry and get back to the Moonlight Garden.

She wrapped a scarf around Dillon's neck, then she kissed his nose.

'Are you ready, buddy? We need to walk fast.'

Dillon bounced on the balls of his feet. 'Let's go! Let's go!'

With the camera bag slung over her arm, Frankie pulled the door behind her. She took his mittened hand. Half jogging, they dashed down the road and through the Moonlight Garden gates just as Pamela parked the car right beside them. Ruby's face peered from the car. Frankie giggled. She squeezed Dillon's hand and hurried away hoping Ruby hadn't seen them.

'She's here!' Frankie called as she flew through the Moonlight Garden gate. The cosy gathering of Moonlight Gardeners around the Christmas tree all looked up. Eoin left the group to go to Ruby.

'Act normal!' he called over his shoulder.

A burble of laughter and chat carried on the frosty air from the group. Frankie and Dillon slipped into the midst of them. Frankie couldn't stop grinning.

'This is going to be a brilliant night, Mammy,' Dillon whispered.

Frankie nodded. She looked up, her eyes widening as Eoin's voice, calm and clear, drifted in above all the chatter.

'. . . and this is the town tree,' he said. He sounded worried, but happy.

Frankie grasped Valerie's hand. Sandra was grinning like a fool, and almost clapped as Ruby came around the corner. Ruby was walking slowly, taking small steps, but smiling brightly. The Moonlight Gardeners all went quiet as she smiled at them.

Frankie's face fell. Ruby looked exhausted. Her eyes were bright, but there were shadows beneath them. Her bright woollen hat looked too big for her head, and her coat seemed to drape on her as if on a hanger. Eoin's arm was around her waist. Pamela was holding her handbag and was standing close to her too.

Ruby's pale face lit up as she saw everyone waiting for her. Her hands flew to her mouth.

'Oh, this is beautiful,' she gasped. 'And the tree isn't

bad either. Let me get in the middle of you lot. I've missed you all.'

Frankie stood back as the group enveloped Ruby. Her hands shook, so she pushed them deep into her pockets. Sandra settled Ruby on her and Eoin's Love Bench, where cushions and blankets were waiting for her. Valerie tucked a hot water bottle onto her lap, while May handed her a mug of her now famous hot chocolate. Dillon pushed forward and squeezed in between the arm of the bench and Ruby. He leaned against her and, closing his eyes, smiled.

'This is the life,' he said, sitting up again. 'Now, I've so much to show you, Ruby. You're going to love what we've done with the pond and the new bug hotel.'

His matter-of-fact, let's-get-down-to-business manner made Frankie grin. The group began to chat again, and someone pushed Eoin into the space next to Ruby. He took her hand and gently kissed it, making Frankie's eyes well up. Liam used to kiss her hand just like that. Jürgen swept into the middle of them all, a huge, beautifully wrapped gift in his arms.

'Excuse me.' He cleared his throat. 'It has been brought to my attention that time is getting on, and we have a pizza delivery arriving at seven, so we'd better crack on.' He peered at the label on the gift. 'Ah here, I think I need glasses,' he groaned, passing the gift to Valerie who laughed and read out Sandra's name.

One by one, as the stars came out and the sea gently lapped the shore, each Moonlight Gardener received and gave a gift. Their joy spiralled into the sky, on clouds of breath and laughter. Frankie held her breath as Jürgen turned to Ruby.

'Now, Ruby, we haven't forgotten about you.' He grinned. 'But your gift isn't here, and it's from all of us. So, if you feel able, we'd like to take you to where your gift is. And we want you to bear in mind that we can change it if you don't like it . . . sort of. So, if you'd please, Eoin, take Ruby home – we'll meet you there.'

Eoin helped Ruby up from the bench. Frankie bit her lip. Ruby's face had gone pink, but she smiled and allowed Eoin to help her walk slowly to the car. Looking back over her shoulder as she hurried towards Ruby's house, Frankie saw Ruby talking to Eoin. Her grip on his arm was tight, but he smiled at her and said something that made Ruby's face relax.

'I hope she likes it,' Frankie said to Valerie, who was practically running alongside her. 'What if she hates it?'

'She won't,' Dillon piped up. 'She'll love it. Trust me.'

Valerie grinned over Dillon's head at Frankie. 'Wise words – listen to him.'

They legged it through Ruby's gate, now wide open, and around the back of her house. Instead of going into the utility room, they continued around the corner and into the garden where Josie and May and Sandra stood on the patio. Jürgen loped over to them.

'She's here!' he whispered. 'God, I hope this goes well.'

Frankie took his hand. 'It will. It's beautiful.'

Ruby's voice drifted around the corner, and the group stood back, holding their breath. Eoin led her, his arm around her waist again.

'Keep them closed!' he said. 'Trust me. I won't let you fall.'

'They're closed!' Ruby laughed. 'And I do trust you.'

'We're almost there,' Eoin said, leading Ruby to the spot they'd all decided was the perfect viewing point. 'Now. Open your eyes.'

Ruby slowly opened her eyes, then gasped. Her hands flew to her mouth, and she began to cry.

'Oh my God.' Leaning into Eoin, she looked around. Her garden, that awful rose garden and expanse of lawn, was now a beautifully landscaped tropical paradise. Even in the midst of winter there was interest. Yew cones added structure to a stunning border softened by evergreen grasses and shrubs. The pathway meandered around beds and trees, begging for exploration. The palm tree Ruby had carefully marked on her plans stood tall and coated with frost. Pointing, Ruby looked up at Eoin. He nodded.

'Yes, that's an arbour and it leads to a proper outdoor sitting area with an outdoor fireplace so you can be warm when you're stargazing. We followed the plans you made. We started the minute you left for Dublin.' Eoin scratched his head and smiled. 'A riot of colour and madness, I believe, is how you described it to me one day.'

'You did all of this in a month?' Ruby asked, touching the soft leaves and plants.

Eoin nodded. 'We all got stuck in,' he said. 'Come, look here.' He took her hand and led her along the path, showing her where he'd incorporated seats to rest, and where spring bulbs were planted. Jürgen stood beside Frankie.

'I think she likes it,' he said.

'She does,' Frankie said. 'It's the best idea Eoin ever had.'

'Thank you,' Eoin said as he and Ruby returned to the

group. 'You've been such a great friend, and your hard work here hasn't gone unnoticed.'

Frankie shrugged. 'Sure, what are friends for?'

'You can try to brush it off all you like.' Valerie joined the conversation. 'You were here, hail, rain or sun, Frankie. You never complained and always had a good word to say to everyone who turned up.'

'What she said.' Sandra nodded. 'This wouldn't be nearly finished if it wasn't for you. You didn't even go to the cottage to check on it all this week because you were *here*.'

Frankie blushed painfully. 'It's nothing, honestly.'

A pair of arms wrapped around her from behind, and a soft kiss landed on her cheek.

'I call bull,' Ruby said. 'It's not nothing. It's everything. Thank you. Now. Hug me already, don't be scared. I won't break.'

Frankie turned around and grabbed Ruby, pulled her tight and buried her face in her shoulder.

'I love you,' she whispered.

'I love you, too.' Ruby kissed her cheek again. Wiping away Frankie's tears, she gave her another tight hug. 'But I heard someone say something about pizza and I'm wondering where it is!'

'It's on the way!' Jürgen called, checking his phone.

'Good!' Ruby called back, wiping tears from her cheeks. 'Let's get this party started!'

'On it!' Pamela popped a bottle of champagne. 'Happy Christmas, everyone!'

Epilogue

In the Moonlight Garden

Turning down the radio, Frankie switched off the car engine and sat back. She'd passed her test a week ago, and still couldn't believe she was driving. This May Bank Holiday weekend last year, she had been washing mould off the walls in her house. Now her house was no longer a mouldy death trap, but a gorgeous contemporary cottage, and she was driving to work and night classes as if she'd been doing it all her life.

Tapping the steering wheel, she grinned. This was just the beginning; she could go anywhere from here. She checked her handbag again for the letter she'd received that day. She needed Ruby to see it, to confirm that it was what she thought it was. Hopping onto the kerb, she spotted Sandra walking towards the garden with Dillon. Frankie waited for them. Dillon waved and grinned. He let go of Sandra's hand and ran down the path to hug her.

Frankie swung him into the air before she kissed his plump cheeks and hugged him tight.

'I've good news, buddy,' she said.

'Me too!' He kissed her back. 'You go first. No! I will!'

'Hold up, buddy!' Frankie laughed. 'Do you want to save it to tell Ruby at the same time?'

'That's a great idea, Mammy!' Dillon slipped from her arms. He took off in the direction of the Moonlight Garden as fast as his little legs would carry him.

Frankie looked after him, her eyes shining. Her boy was growing up so fast. He'd really come out of himself since Christmas. Maggie had sent her a text earlier to tell her how he'd given a presentation to the whole school at assembly that morning, explaining to everyone why bugs were important, even the ones that looked scary, even spiders. By the end of his presentation, there was a group of kids from all the classes across the school who wanted to be his friend, so they'd formed a club. With a swelling heart, Frankie fell in with Sandra and followed Dillon into the garden.

'He's a great boy,' Sandra said as they wandered around the garden looking for Ruby and Eoin. 'He ate all his snacks after school and has his homework done too.'

'Thanks, Sandra,' Frankie said. 'I don't know what I'd do without you.'

'Go away out of that.' Sandra laughed. 'Sure, one more makes no difference in my house. And he's got manners, which is more than I can say for my lot; he's a good influence on them. Himself and my Catherine are thick as thieves, by the way. They've been plotting something.'

'Catherine?' Frankie looked at Sandra, feeling slightly alarmed. Catherine was fifteen, and usually found dancing and perfecting her winged eye-lining technique. What was she doing with Dillon?

'There they are, look!' Sandra pointed to where Dillon was jogging on the spot, beside Eoin who looked hot and sweaty. He lowered a large shrub into the hole he'd dug as the women walked over.

'It's well you're looking.' Sandra winked at him. 'Where's herself?'

'Over there,' Eoin puffed. 'With the master plan.'

Looking around, Frankie spotted Ruby, dressed in her fleece and a pair of grubby overalls, and her signature muddy pink boots, leaning over a table. She looked so much better. There was colour in her cheeks, and she'd put on a little of the weight she'd lost before Christmas. Her hair was beginning to grow back, too. Seeing them, Ruby scratched at the cashmere hat she was wearing and walked towards them with a slight limp.

'You look pleased with yourself,' she said to Frankie. 'I know that gleam in your eyes.'

'You first!' Dillon ran around them in a circle. 'You first! You first!'

'I have news, and so does he,' Frankie said as Dillon zoomed around them.

'I've some news, too. What's going on with you? Have you something to tell me?' Ruby's eyes widened.

'What a day.' Jürgen interrupted them, a pot of narcissus in each hand. He held them up for Ruby's inspection. 'I was thinking of adding these to the Love Bench border. They're almost white.'

'I'd say they're white enough.' Ruby touched the petals. She sniffed the air. 'They're scented!'

Jürgen nodded. 'I think they're perfect.'

'I might add them to the plan,' Ruby said.

Jürgen nodded and ambled away.

'Your news?' Frankie said in a low voice. She took Ruby's hand. 'Have you got your test results . . . ?'

Ruby nodded. She grasped Frankie's hand and squeezed it tightly. Frankie's brown eyes were a muddle of worry. Ruby smiled gently. 'Still not clear,' she said quietly. 'I have to go back for more tests, and then they'll put together another treatment plan for me.'

'Oh, Ruby.' Frankie pulled Ruby into a hug. 'You need to tell Eoin.'

'I will,' Ruby said. 'But the good news is that the council finally came back to us. They've agreed to give us the land. I've been redesigning the plans all morning. Come take a look.'

Dillon raced around the garden, his arms behind him and his tongue sticking out to one side. He zoomed past the two women, laughing as they pretended to jump out of his way.

'I have news! I have news!' He skidded to a halt in front of them. 'Catherine helped me, and we sent an email and a picture, and they liked it and they want to show it on the show.'

'Hold up, buddy, slow down.' Frankie glanced at Ruby who looked just as puzzled as she was. 'What do you mean Catherine helped you?'

'I took some pictures with my camera, and they were really cool. Catherine said they were like tiny dinosaurs or something from *Springwatch*, so we sent them the pictures with the email,' Dillon said slowly. 'Are you with me, Mammy?'

Frankie nodded, not completely with him but eager to try to understand what was going on.

'Okay. So, then the BBC woman sent me an email and said they loved my pictures and want to use them on their show, if that's all right with you.' Dillon sighed. 'So that's my news and you have to say yes, Mammy, cos I told everyone in school, and they think I'm cool now.'

Frankie shook her head. 'Seriously? Is this real? *Springwatch*?'

Dillon nodded his head so hard Frankie had to take it in her hands and stop him.

'Hold on there, buddy. You'll nod your head off.' She kissed his head. 'Of course, it's okay! It's brilliant – congratulations, buddy. I'm so proud.'

'Thanks, Mammy!' Dillon did a happy dance. 'I knew you were a cool mammy.'

Laughing, Frankie turned to Ruby. 'Can you believe this?'

'I can. He's like you, determined and hardworking,' Ruby said. 'Which makes me ask, what's your news?'

Frankie sucked in her bottom lip. Slipping her hand into her handbag, she took out the letter and carefully unfolded it.

'Read this,' she said, handing the letter to Ruby.

Ruby scanned the letter, her heart pounding as she read it. A bubble of motherly pride burst over her. She broke into a huge smile, then looked up at Frankie and then back down at the letter.

'I need to read this again,' she said.

'That's exactly what I did.' Frankie smiled.

'Dear Francesca,' Ruby read aloud. 'Each year, University

College Dublin, in association with The Hazel Harrington-Howard Memorial Scholarship programme, awards scholarships to participants in our Certificate in Psychology course. We are delighted to inform you that you were put forward by your professor, based on your dedication and desire to further your education in this field. Your hard work and determination have been recognised by the board, and we wish to offer you a full scholarship to continue your studies with us. This scholarship . . . Oh my God! FRANKIE! You're going to accept it, aren't you?' Ruby grabbed Frankie and hugged her tight. She handed her back the letter. 'Because you have to! It's amazing!'

'I want to,' Frankie said. 'But I've Dillon . . .'

'Oh, give over!' Ruby nudged her. 'Haven't we managed this far?'

'We have,' Frankie said.

'And what's the problem?' Ruby grinned. Then laughed. 'There's no problem! Nothing we can't handle.'

Frankie started to laugh. 'You're right. What am I waiting for? Oh, Ruby, this is wonderful. I was so worried about accepting it . . . Will it cover more than one year? How will I manage Dillon and study?'

'We'll cross that hurdle when we get to it. That aside, it's going to be tough,' Ruby said. 'But it's completely manageable. And, Frankie, you're forgetting that you're not alone. You have all of us to help you.'

Frankie looked around the Moonlight Garden. Eoin was lifting Dillon up to investigate what was going on at the top of the latest bug hotel extension. Sandra was sorting seed packets in the shed with a group of new gardeners. She waved over and blew a kiss when she saw Frankie watching. Jürgen and Valerie were deep in conversation near the Love Bench; and Josie and May were pottering away at the new raised beds in the kitchen garden.

'Who'd have thought it? This time last year we were both in such a bad place,' she said to Ruby. 'Look where we are now.'

Frankie smiled. She looked up at the sky. 'I know exactly who's looking after us.'

'Well, it's not James, that's for sure,' Ruby said with a significant look. 'And I wouldn't want it to be. Come on, let's go share your news.'

Looking up, Eoin made his way towards them, and took Ruby's hand.

He kissed the tip of her nose. 'Any word from your team?' he asked hopefully.

Ruby lowered her head. 'They called last night. I didn't tell you – I needed to process it first. It's still there, but I'm going in for tests and we'll put together a new plan of action.'

'Oh.' Eoin pulled her to him. He held her tightly and kissed her head. 'Come here, it'll be okay.'

Ruby tightened her arms around Eoin, relishing how alive and strong he was. 'I know. I've got this.'

'We've got this,' he reminded her.

'Yes,' Ruby said. She smiled up at him. '*We* do.'

'I love you, Ruby,' he said. His eyes softened with tears. 'No matter what happens, you remember that.'

'I love you too, Eoin,' Ruby whispered. 'We're going to be okay.'

'Can you guys get some work done? Enough with the lovey-dovey stuff please!' Sandra trundled a wheelbarrow past them. She stopped to fix her gardening gloves and took a long look at them. 'What're you two up to?'

Ruby shared a glance with Eoin, and knew he understood that she didn't want to bring down the mood with her own news. She wanted to enjoy one more uncomplicated night of fun and laughter with her friends. 'Frankie has something to tell you all.'

Everyone turned to Frankie. Clutching the letter, Frankie's stomach tightened. She waved the letter and tried to talk, but found a lump in her throat. Wiping tears away, she cleared her throat and half smiled, half cried. 'I got a scholarship. I'm going back to uni. And I couldn't have done it without you – all of you. I don't know how to thank you all enough.'

Jürgen hugged Valerie again, much to Val's delight.

'I'll get some bubbles,' he cried. 'And pizza maybe – we need pizza too.'

'Excuse me, ahem.' Dillon's little voice piped up. Everyone turned to where he was standing on the Love Bench. 'I have very important news too. My photo is going to be on the telly and everyone will see it. Maybe even David Attenborough.'

'I think we need ice cream too after that news.' Jürgen ruffled Dillon's hair. 'Fair play to you, Dillon. That's some achievement.'

'It is, isn't it?' Dillon said seriously. Behind him Catherine got out her phone and set about direct messaging David Attenborough all about Dillon via Instagram. She crossed her fingers and hoped he'd reply with something nice to say to Dillon.

As the celebration got into full swing, Frankie and Ruby

sat together on the Love Bench. Someone had turned up the radio, and Jürgen's dancing made Frankie giggle.

'I'm so glad I met you,' Ruby said, taking Frankie's hand in hers.

'I'm glad I met you, too,' Frankie said. 'I don't know what we ever did before you – I can't imagine a day without you.'

'It's crazy, isn't it?' Ruby smiled. 'And I wouldn't change a thing. Not one minute.'

'No, not a minute,' Frankie whispered. Dillon ran over to them and squeezed in between them.

'Look, Mammy,' he said. 'We have the best, craziest friends in the world.' He pointed over to the group of Moonlight Gardeners who were in full dance mode.

Frankie laughed. 'That we do,' she said.

As the sun set and the moon began to rise, the Moonlight Gardeners welcomed the newer members as they arrived for their usual spot of moonlight gardening only to find a party in full swing. The garden glowed and shimmered as laughter and music filled the air.

'I never imagined living a life like this,' Frankie said.

'That makes two of us,' Ruby agreed. She looked up as Eoin danced towards her with his hand held out. 'But I like it a lot.'

She took Eoin's hand, then turned back to offer her other hand to Frankie.

'Come on.' She grinned. 'We don't know what the future will bring, but for tonight, let's dance!'

She pulled Frankie up from the bench, and towards their friends. Without hesitation, Frankie went with her. The stars shone down on them, and Frankie knew that

Liam was watching down on her, urging her to get into the middle of it all, as he would have if he'd been there.

Enveloped by the group, Frankie joined Ruby and cheered and danced as the moon climbed higher and higher in the sky. It was after midnight when they finally parted ways and went home knowing that no matter what the future held, they had each other to lean on, and that was the most precious thing of all.

Acknowledgements

Anyone who knows me knows that I've been writing and striving to be a writer for the longest time. This book is only here because of everyone who constantly supported and encouraged me, who fed me food, poetry, stories, love, kindness, and inclusiveness, and who promised me that my perseverance would pay off. You were all right. This is one time I don't mind being wrong! Thank you all; I love you all!

Thank you, Hazel Gaynor, for sending me the tweet that brought this book about. There was certainly something magical in how it all came together – a story in itself!

Thank you, Marian Keyes, for always cheering me on, and for your constant support and kindness xxx.

And thank you to the entire Irish writing community – the Irish writing community is the best ever writing community, and I'll meet you outside should you dare to say otherwise! There are so many writers who've championed me along the way, all of whom I wish I could thank here, but that would be another book.

Thank you to my fellow Dooligans, Olivia, Niall, Annie, Anne, Sam, Lauren, Aisling, Caroline, Cat, Dan, Fiona, Declan, Jane, Honoria, Justine, Ellen, Shane, Pat, and Lucy. You guys keep me writing and pushing through the tough spots. Thank you for telling me that I am good at this. Thank you to Eoin Devereaux, Sarah Moore-Fitzgerald and Donal Ryan for bringing the Dooligans into being!

Thank you to my darlings at The Christmas Collective: Blaithin, Joe, Sarah S, Sarah-Lou, Helen, Jen, Donna, Karl, Marianne, Michelle, Hayley-Jenifer, Emma, Jake, Lucy. You guys are invaluable, and I wouldn't be without ye.

Thank you, Jo Unwin, and Julia Silk, for your time and generosity. I am most grateful.

Without a doubt, a ginormous thank you goes to the marvellous Avon Team. It's been a wide-awake-dream working with you all. You make it look easy, so that tells me how dedicated and hardworking you all are! Thank you, Elisha, Raphaella, Helen, Ella, Becci, and Radhika.

A huge and special thank you to my editor, Thorne Ryan. Working with you on this book has been so wonderful. I feel so lucky to have had you for my debut novel – it's been the best experience, and I wouldn't change any of it!

I have these amazing friends whom I've known forever and who have stuck with me through thick and thin: Caroline, Gillian, and Anne-Marie xxx.

And I found the most genuine, kind and caring friends

through Twitter. Oh, so many! But without whom, I'd never have had the strength to go to UCD or keep writing. I can't thank you all enough. You mean the world to me.

My family are brilliant. Just saying. There has never been a day when they haven't believed in me. Thank you for the coffees, dinners, treats, wine, and cocktails. Thank you for your time, understanding, and peace, and for doing school runs or feeding Cici cat. Thank you for listening to my plot rambling, talking about characters as if they were real, and for your insights and advice. Thank you for everything, Mallory, Ellen, David, Jade, and David D. You are the best.

My mam, Deirdre, taught me how to read when I was barely bigger than a book – thank you. My dad, Michael, always told me I was as good as anyone else – thank you. Ye are the best parents.

To my wonderful in-laws, Pat and Bridget, who gave me my first Writer's & Artist's Yearbook, I want to say I love you, thank you so much.

And Dave, the love of my life. Thank you. There are not enough words or enough ways to express to you how much I appreciate you xxx.